The Perfect Marriage

Also by Elisabeth Leigh
and published by Bantam

GREED
ENVY

The Perfect Marriage

Elisabeth Leigh

BANTAM BOOKS

LONDON · NEW YORK · TORONTO · SYDNEY · AUCKLAND

THE PERFECT MARRIAGE
A BANTAM BOOK : 0 553 40896 8

First publication in Great Britain

PRINTING HISTORY
Bantam edition published 1996

Set in 10/11pt Monotype Plantin by Kestrel Data, Exeter

Bantam Books are published by Transworld Publishers Ltd,
61–63 Uxbridge Road, London W5 5SA,
in Australia by Transworld Publishers (Australia) Pty Ltd,
15–25 Helles Avenue, Moorebank, NSW 2170
and in New Zealand by Transworld Publishers (NZ) Ltd,
3 William Pickering Drive, Albany, Auckland.

Reproduced, printed and bound in Great Britain by
Cox & Wyman Ltd, Reading, Berks.

The Perfect Marriage

1

ANNIE AND TREVOR

'Annie? Are you ready, darling?' Trevor called out.

Annie opened the bedroom door a fraction, and yelled down the stairs.

'Nearly done. Two minutes.'

She hitched the stockings onto the rubber clasps, grabbed hold of the lycra dress and wriggled it up over her hips. Then she breathed in, bent down and picked up the shoes, the stiff patent ones she hardly ever wore. They were the real killers, but she could just about last out the evening. She had no idea what was planned, but it was unlikely he'd want to dance, not now, not in public anyway. If they were off to some restaurant, she could kick them off under the table.

Annie gave a brazen smile towards the mirror and turned sideways pulling in her stomach. After combing through her shoulder-length, fine, dark hair, she surveyed herself critically from head to toe. Despite the padded, underwired bra, her small breasts needed improvement. She lightly pencilled in the cleavage, to make sure it was there and stroked down her dress tightly over her thighs. Why couldn't she manage to lose even half an inch? All those weeks spent charging around on location, and those thighs stubbornly remained the same, too chubby and too short. Oh, for long languorous willowy thighs! Trevor had always said he adored them, that they were perfectly proportioned, perfect for her small stature and petite frame. Still, not bad for forty-one.

Would I give up my job, would I give up everything if I could spread both hands around my thighs and meet thumbs and little fingers without a squeeze? Would wafer-thin thighs make me really happy? Annie wondered. Then she looked away from the mirror and fondly fastened on her wrist the antique, gold-faced watch he had given her that morning. Stuff it, she decided, I am really happy.

She was about to leave, when her automatic pilot sent her hurtling towards the magnum-size perfume bottle on the stripped-pine, marble-topped washstand. The bottle was nearly empty – when had he given it to her? This time, on their wedding anniversary, three years ago. It was Mitsouko, his favourite, though he just said, 'Is there some of that lovely perfume left?' She wouldn't tell him that she had never worn scent, not when it gave him such pleasure. Nor would she ever confess that she felt plain daft in dresses and high heels and scratchy black-net stockings.

'Darling, you look terrific.'

Trevor didn't complain that she'd kept him waiting, even though he looked as though he'd been standing in the hall for some time. He even had her coat over his arm. Annie walked down the stairs, one step at a time, tensing her ankles to accommodate the lethal heels.

'Are we walking anywhere? I can't walk far in these, love.'

The door of the kitchen leading off from the end of the hall was usually kept open but for some reason it was tightly shut. Annie heard a muffled cry.

'Don't open it, don't open it.'

Something was happening in there, but if that was part of Trevor's plan, she'd pretend she'd heard nothing.

'I thought we'd start off at the Langton Arms. As we usually do. Can you manage that far?'

'I think I can make it round the corner,' said Annie, slipping her arm through his.

Still a handsome man, my husband, Annie thought, tottering at his side, even though his softly curling hair had shifted from blond to grey and he was wearing the ancient black velvet jacket and pale blue silk shirt she'd bought him years ago. Armani and Boss and California casual had passed him by, but she didn't care. Whatever he wore, she still enjoyed looking at him, still felt proud when they were out together. There was no man she'd ever met who combined that mixture of sensuality and brainpower and unlike most academics, he had outdoor, masculine features, a well-defined jaw, strong assertive lines round his mouth and lucid bluish eyes.

'I'm hungry, love. I didn't have time for lunch, only a sandwich. Do I get fed somewhere nice tonight?'

'Wait and see,' said Trevor, as he pushed open the etched-glass door of the Langton Arms.

There was no-one in that Annie recognized, except Roger whose wife had run off with an environmental health officer and who was now, it seemed, in permanent residence at the far end of the bar. The Langton Arms only came to life after tea, or supper as the newer arrivals in the neighbourhood called it, but the fire, a real fire, was already spitting and crackling with the junk wood from the nearby builder's yard, thrown on by Eamon, the landlord.

'Here it is, what you asked for. Suitable for the occasion? It's better than warm,' he said, passing across a specially purchased bottle of champagne in a plastic bucket marked Heineken. Trevor poured out the champagne into three glasses and handed one across the bar.

'Happy anniversary, darling,' he said, kissing Annie before putting the glass to his lips.

'To you both.' Eamon took a swig, and leaned over Trevor. 'One or two fellers ask me to remind them, would you believe? How long is it?'

'Don't tell him, Trev!'

'Why not? Go on, you don't look much older than my daughter. Give us a clue.'

Annie held up both hands and spread out her fingers, then repeated the gesture.

'Ten years? Twenty years? I'd never believe, that's shocking. How d'you put up with him that long, Annie?'

'He's not a bad chap.'

'Go on, you're still crazy about him. You tell him.'

Trevor took her hand and held it towards Eamon.

'She said she'd wear a wedding ring if we lasted twenty years.'

'No need, love. I couldn't wear a ring, not now. Anyway, it might be unlucky, it might change things,' Annie replied, smiling at Trevor.

Tactfully, Eamon retired behind the bar to give a cursory wipe to some lustreless glasses. Trevor grasped Annie's hand, and guided her to a corner table.

'Come on, drink up.'

Having drunk the first glass too fast, Annie was attempting to slow down, transfixed by the fizzing bubbles.

'I hope the place we're going to is up to the dress,' Annie

9

said, twisting round to catch a glimpse of herself in the pitted mirror.

'They'll love it,' Trevor replied.

'Go on, tell me. Can I guess?'

'If you like.'

Annie ran through the places where they had been in the last few years. It was unlikely that Trevor would choose somewhere completely new, he preferred the familiar to the unexplored.

'Café des Arts?' said Annie.

'No, not this time. You won't guess, darling.'

'All right, I won't then.'

She could see from his satisfied smile that he had planned the evening for some time, that he would make sure there would be nothing to spoil her pleasure.

'I can't believe it's twenty years,' Annie said.

Trevor took a moment to answer, as though he too was scanning back through the past. 'Does it feel a long time?'

'No, love. Why do you ask?'

'Just to make sure,' Trevor replied.

'And you?' said Annie, brightly. 'You're not fed up with me yet?'

'I knew right from the beginning that our marriage would be good.'

Annie laughed and straightened Trevor's tie, which was too wide and too jazzy, a villain's tie.

'You didn't have to listen to all my friends saying it was almost like marrying my father. Fourteen years difference. How could I bear it? How could I be in love with such an old man? And you were only thirty-five.'

'Thirty-six,' said Trevor, firmly.

It wasn't a snide correction, it was just that Trevor cared about facts, about getting things right, about getting as near to the truth as possible. Annie didn't mind him being pedantic every now and again. Professors were allowed to be.

'Anyway,' continued Annie, 'I told my friends how clever you were, that at least we'd always be able to have wonderful conversations. Then they were jealous. All my friends were going out with either monosyllabic guitar players or bit-part actors. Except Kate. She was seeing some dolt from the City who called himself a photographer and collected vintage cameras. What was his name? Can you remember?'

'I can't, it was too long ago. He was married, I suppose?' said Trevor.

'No, he wasn't,' retorted Annie. 'He was engaged to someone else.'

'Even then. Poor Kate.'

'Not poor Kate. She's done what she wanted to do, she's got a great kid—'

'But having a kid on your own with no money? Come on, darling. That isn't a solution.'

'She wasn't lucky enough to meet someone like you, that's all. Do you realize you're an unbelievably rare example of the male species?'

'I don't see why. I'm quite an ordinary bloke.'

'I must be still besotted, then.'

Trevor's face showed such surprise and pleasure, that Annie giggled. 'Course I'm not, you daft man. I just love you.'

'I love you, too.'

Leaning forward, Annie planted a kiss on Trevor's mouth, and she felt his hand slipping round her waist.

'Shall we forget wherever you're taking me, and go to bed? Then you can tear off my dress, and I'll make you unhook this lunatic corset and then . . .'

Trevor quickly withdrew his hand, and looked towards the bar, meeting Eamon's attentive gaze.

'Keep your voice down, Eamon's listening.'

Annie rose to her feet, and stood up gingerly.

'Are we going to spend all night here? Come on, let's go home. Then we can have fish and chips, I don't care.'

Grabbing Annie's hand, Trevor pulled her back to his side.

'Wait a minute. There's no hurry.'

'My husband – Professor Watson, in case you didn't know – has got the most enormous—'

To Trevor's relief, Annie was silenced by the entry of Maggie, an old lady who lived a couple of doors away in one of the neglected houses still remaining in Langton Villas.

'You're busy tonight,' she remarked to Eamon, settling herself at the end of the bar farthest from Roger. Then she turned towards Trevor and Annie. 'I think I might have a gin this evening.'

When Trevor had bought her what she claimed as her due, he slipped his arm round Annie's waist.

'Come on, darling,' he said, leading her out of the pub, back the way they had come.

Once inside the door of number fourteen, Langton Villas, Trevor slammed it loudly behind him. Having heard the signal, Kate appeared, running down the hall.

'Happy anniversary!' she shouted, coming up to hug Annie. 'Come into the kitchen.'

Annie blinked and gasped. The kitchen was usually a picture of chaos, almost all of its space taken up with a huge pine table cluttered with debris, rickety pine chairs, saucepans hanging from overloaded hooks, grubby Chinese lanterns swinging from the ceiling and objects she and Trevor had picked up over the years from Camden market and neighbouring junk-shops. When they first moved in to Langton Villas, everyone like them who had rejected Hampstead for a more genuine working-class area, knocked through the dividing wall between front room and back room, made an arch and reproduced the Habitat farmhouse kitchen. Annie had never thought of changing it. All their friends met there, their lives focused and unfolded round that great, cumbersome pine table.

Now everything had been transformed, with tall red and white candles gently flickering in the draught from the ill-fitting window, towering bouquets of flowers and leaves disguising the jumble piled up in the darkened corners. The pine table was unrecognizable, its grimy surface disguised in swathes of white lace with a scarlet undercloth, white and scarlet balloons swinging gently above it. There was even a newly polished space on the pine dresser, which was usually hidden under a pile of papers and books but now boasted a display of anniversary cards arranged in order of size. On the white noticeboard, propped up by the sink, Trevor had written in gold letters, 'Closed for Private Function. Annie and Trevor.'

'Kate did it all,' said Bryonie, as she kissed first Annie, then Trevor. 'Isn't she a genius?'

'Oh, Kate, it's so beautiful.' Annie looked down the table at the sparkling antique silver cutlery, silver dishes, the gleaming glasses and the linen napkins. 'Just right for a Georgian banquet! Where did you find it all?'

As she surveyed the table, Annie noticed that there were six places laid, when they were only five, but she knew the reason. She wouldn't have dreamed of making a comment.

'It's not real silver, Annie,' said Kate. 'I borrowed it from one of my old mates from the Beeb days. Remember Martin, in props? He's still there.'

'One of the few who is.'

Leaning against the edge of the cooker was Rick. In the candlelight, he could have passed for a rock-star making a comeback, open shirt, tight jeans and dark, slicked-back hair setting off his large powerful head and strong, commanding face.

'Bryonie's doing her special duck. And I'm doing the basting. I'm particularly good at basting.'

Bryonie, wearing a long red butcher's apron over a plain black dress, opened the newly cleaned oven and rocked back on her heels as a blast of hot, duck-flavoured air hit her face, allowing Rick to manoeuvre his wooden spoon inside the roasting tins.

'Look! Look, Mummy!'

A small child came running into the kitchen with a sparkler, then made circles round and round Annie until it fizzled out.

'Bed-time, Dally.'

'No.'

'Yes, sweetheart. When we go home, you'll get some balloons. Give Annie a kiss good-night.'

Lifting her up, Kate carried her over so that she could press her lips against Annie's cheeks.

'Good-night, darling.'

'Can we open that bottle now?' asked Rick, as he placed himself behind a row of champagne glasses. 'Can I declare this anniversary officially open, me luds and ladies?'

'Wait till Kate's put Dally to bed,' said Bryonie, but Rick went ahead, twisting off the cork in one, swift movement and emptying the foaming liquid into five glasses.

Trevor led Annie to the head of the table, where they both stood, Rick on one side, Bryonie on the other.

'To my darling Annie. Thanks for happy years.' He held up his glass, touched hers, and then put it to her lips. Annie took a swig, then repeated the toast for him.

'More happy years,' she said, her eyes shining in the candle-light.

'Who's been married longer? You or us?'

'We have, Rick.'

'It doesn't show. You and me, we're stayers. Right? The girls are lucky to have us. How about some music?'

Rick went through the arch into the sitting-room, groped

under a shelf, found a dusty turntable and shouted, 'Listen to this. Bet you haven't heard this for a while!'

As Kate came down the stairs, she suddenly stopped. Even after two bars, she recognized it. Then she hurried into the kitchen.

'Hey! Where did you find that?'

'I found it. Annie used to play it all the time,' said Trevor.

'Hippy days, Kate!' Rick pressed a glass into her hand.

Annie's eyes threatened to gloss with tears.

'Christ, my old Santana record, I thought I'd lost it years ago. There's a scratch. Any minute now.'

As the needle began to thump, Trevor rushed over and moved it across. Rick could only take a few minutes of nostalgia, a current affairs man was Rick. He had left the BBC some years ago for the greener fields of Intertel. It had taken Annie more time and more anguish to leave the Beeb for a commercial station. Although they now worked in the same building, Annie had only recently settled in and Rick was tactfully keeping his distance.

'What's happened to this bloody restaurant? I'm sitting down. How about some service?'

Kate tied a white tea-towel over her blue velvet shorts, opened the fridge and brought over a platter of seafood, resting on a bed of seaweed. Trevor served Annie, then waited as she threw back her head, put the shell against her mouth and slowly sucked back an oyster.

'Pure heaven.'

'Aren't they bloody marvellous?' said Rick, biting through the milky, succulent flesh. 'They've Welsh ones, given to me by the Intertel chef. You'll have to make friends with Jean Michel, I'll introduce you. Come and have lunch with me at the Grotto. Everyone goes there, even the department heads. A brief appearance from the Controller of Drama—'

'Who on earth invented that name?' said Annie. 'What's wrong with Head of Drama? Do I look like a controller? I'm running network drama, not Intercity trains.'

'Indeed, ma'am,' replied Rick, gravely. 'You may be running drama, but you control budgets.'

'Pass the plate over, Rick. Trevor hasn't had any oysters yet. There are three each.'

'Promise I won't take four,' said Rick, lifting up the vast platter and presenting it to Trevor. 'My dear mother thinks you die if you eat oysters. Pig-ignorant, the Welsh. Eh, Annie? Lucky we escaped.' Rick picked out a langoustine, and handed it to Bryonie. 'And I bet you're glad you escaped from Roehampton.'

'Yes, I'd rather be in Kentish Town.'

'With *me* in Kentish Town.'

'Yes, with you, Rick.'

'We couldn't be anywhere else. Could you, Trev?'

'Never.'

'Annie's not going to make you move to Highgate, then?'

'I've lived here longer than I ever lived in Wales. Why should I want to move to Highgate?' said Annie.

Rick rubbed his hands together.

'Money. All that money.'

'Not that much.'

'More than me. Why should the Controller of Drama get more than the toughest reporter at Intertel? What about my danger money?'

'You're not in Bosnia now,' said Bryonie. 'What danger?'

'Facing Rufus Tonbridge every morning. That's dangerous. He might choke on a peppermint. With any luck.'

'I've never had anyone choke on a peppermint.'

'Doctors never see the brutal reality, that's why.'

'Just come to my surgery for a day, Rick.'

'Not bloody likely.'

As they devoured the duck, Rick, Trevor and Annie tore the portions apart in their hands, Bryonie used her knife and fork but none of them commented. Neither did they comment when Kate, a vegetarian, brought over a platter of tomatoes and mozzarella cheese. They were all used to the small differences between them, it didn't matter, not with old friends.

'Are you going to tell them, Annie?' said Trevor, collecting the plates after they had demolished a cream-layered *mille feuille*.

'Yes, I can now. I've chosen my new series for Intertel. Alan's just given the go-ahead, the budget's been approved.'

'Great news!' said Rick. 'We were all wondering what the new girl would come up with. Have you got a title yet?'

'It's called *Rough Trade*.'

Annie waited for a reaction.

'Sounds like one of yours, Annie. It couldn't be anyone else's,' said Rick. 'Well, Bry, what's your opinion?'

'I'd certainly watch that.'

'I'll tell you how it happened,' said Annie. 'When I was still at the BBC, I was sent this letter from a girl in Holloway prison. She was doing five years for fraud. This is my life, she wrote. Why don't you make a real film? At first I couldn't be bothered to read it, illegible writing, sentences in one long line, but my script editor thought it had something. When it was typed out, and I could see what it was about, I knew I'd use it some day. Great story. The girl's still in Holloway, but I'll have her as script consultant, if they agree. And Reg will write all the episodes. You'll like it Rick. The lead man is a bent solicitor who bikes around on a Harley.'

'Sounds good. Someone with balls.'

'And the lead girl?' asked Kate.

'A tough cookie who wants to better herself. She takes a job as a secretary . . .'

Kate wrinkled her nose. 'Does she have to? Start off as a secretary?'

'Annie did,' said Bryonie.

'All right then, as long as she doesn't fall for her boss.'

Annie grinned. Kate never missed an opportunity to lay down the feminist line, but the only person round the table who needed reminding was Rick.

'Sorry, Kate. She does fall for her boss. But it's much more than that. Through him, she proves herself, proves that she can do anything she sets her mind to.'

'There's nothing weak or sentimental about it,' added Trevor. He had seen the first treatment, made a few suggestions. Annie often took his advice, but he never pressured her. 'Ben, the solicitor, seems to be a good guy. He does legal aid work, fights for hopeless cases, isn't frightened to challenge the authorities . . .'

He turned towards Annie, so that she could continue. It was her series, her story.

'So when he gets into trouble, she trains herself to use a gun, ride a motor bike – and she becomes his minder.'

'What happens in the end?' said Kate.

'Well, she—'

'Shush, Trev. Don't give away the ending. It's bad luck.'

'Have you cast it yet?' said Bryonie.

'I'll probably use Tony from *Streetcred*. The girl, I'm not sure about yet.'

16

Kate let out an admiring sigh.

'He's gorgeous! Wonderful eyes.'

'If you go for brawny, brainless twits,' said Rick.

'Well, Annie. How's it been this week? Is Intertel living down to your expectations so far?'

'I'll be keeping my head down for a while,' replied Annie.

'You know Annie, once she starts on a series—'

'I'm impossible, aren't I, love?'

They were just settling back, the glasses of champagne replaced by Annie's Greek brandy, when the phone trilled from the sitting-room and Kate jumped to her feet.

'Mind if I answer it? I think it might be for me.'

Annie and Trevor looked at one another.

'Course not,' said Annie. 'If it's for either of us, we're not in.'

Bryonie looked at Rick.

'At least he called,' she said, having heard Kate's delighted greeting. 'But there's precious little left. Only a few vegetables.'

'If he decides to turn up, she'll insist on making him something,' Annie said, with a groan. 'She always does.'

Kate returned to the table, wreathed in smiles.

'It was Gordon. He said he's going to try and come along. Later on.'

'When's later on?' said Rick, but Kate ignored him.

'He's having a drink with a snooker champion,' she said, proudly. 'The Controller of Sport is planning a series about a snooker tour. I do hope it happens. It's so long since Gordon has been out of a studio.'

'That should get them hooked. How did he manage to come up with such a brilliant idea?'

'Gordon's doing very well in the sports department.'

'Goodness! And I hadn't noticed.'

Trevor tried to change the subject, but Bryonie intervened.

'Rick, stop being so unkind.'

'We all know Gordon isn't coming. What's the point of Kate getting all excited? It pisses me off. Any man who dyes his hair—'

'He doesn't dye his hair!' Kate cried. 'That's totally untrue.'

Annie looked at Trevor again.

'Why don't we all go in the other room? We'd be more comfortable there.'

'I'm happy here.'

'So am I,' said Bryonie.

'I'll make some more coffee, then.'

'No, you won't. I will,' said Trevor. 'You're not going to do a thing tonight.'

While Trevor was placing the pot of coffee on the table, Rick came over and whispered in his ear.

'Trev. Got anything else apart from this Greek gut-ripper?'

'Don't think so.'

Rick addressed the others in a loud voice.

'I've forgotten my Havana. Left it at home. Won't be long. Would you like one, Trev?' I've got one for you. Would you mind, Annie?'

'No, Rick,' she said. 'As long as I can have one cigarette.'

'It's a deal. One cigarette.'

Rick stomped out to the hall, slamming the door behind him.

'Idiot! He'll wake up Dally,' said Bryonie.

'No, he won't. She's used to noise. Everyone slams doors in my block.'

'We must find you somewhere else to live,' said Annie.

'I like Holloway. Really.'

Annie dropped the subject. They all felt guilty that Kate, once a successful television designer, was living in a council flat. Voting Labour, which they all did, didn't mean that you weren't behind their plans for more council housing. But that particular block was shoddily built, badly designed, poorly maintained and far too small for Kate and Dally.

It was about an hour before Rick returned. He laid out a cigar in front of Trevor, lit it for him, and returned to his place. Bryonie noticed that a half-empty bottle of Bells had made a miraculous appearance.

'Rick . . .' she began, as he poured from the bottle into a tumbler. Then, she quickly suppressed her objection. Tonight was exceptional enough for Annie to smoke a cigarette, Trevor to puff at a cigar. Why shouldn't Rick have a whisky? As well as a cigar? They had all given up the unhealthy indulgence of younger days, it was only a pleasureable, passing reminder.

'Trev, would you come on *Global Highway*? said Rick, trying to reanimate his cigar. He had forgotten what an effort it was, to smoke and talk at the same time. 'I'm setting up a story on cable TV but I'd like to have a cultural, not a financial slant. You'd be good at that.'

'You know my answer. I haven't changed. How can I write about television, if I'm seen on the screen and get paid by your bosses?'

'Only asking. But you'd be bloody great.'

'I know he would,' said Annie. 'But that's always been Trevor's rule.'

Bryonie reached across Rick for the cream jug. Tonight, she would put a dollop of double cream in her coffee, even after that *mille feuille*.

'Rick, do we have to talk about television?'

'Why is Trevor so stubborn? What's wrong with *Global Highway*? Don't answer, you needn't tell me. You won't do it because you'd only get three minutes.'

'Don't be so daft. Time doesn't come into it,' said Annie. 'You know that.'

'Rick, please,' said Bryonie, as Rick drained the tumbler. His voice was loud, uncontrolled. Any minute now, he would start shouting.

'How about five? Five whole minutes. You can say everything about TV in five minutes. Why do you need more? Isn't that right, Annie?'

'Look, Rick. Apart from the other reasons, you know Trevor and I decided ages ago that we'd keep our careers separate. I don't think we'd have stood a chance otherwise. You've got to have a life outside the studio.'

'Too right,' said Kate. 'That's what Gordon says. You mustn't let it take you over.'

'Fuck what Gordon says,' shouted Rick. 'Where is the bastard, anyhow? Thought he was coming to share my Scotch.'

'He doesn't drink,' replied Kate. 'And if you're going to be such a pig, I'm going home.' Rick leaned across the table.

'Lovely Kate. I'm a tiny, tiny bit drunk. I'll be a good boy, OK?'

'Why do you do it? You're such fun to be with when you're sober.'

'No, I'm not. When I'm sober, I bore myself sick.'

Lurching from his chair, Rick suddenly felt an overwhelming urge to be horizontal.

Nobody said anything as he walked carefully through the

arch, slumped onto the settee and stretched himself out on his back. Bryonie came and sat next to Annie.

'I'm so sorry,' she said, softly. 'Rick's gone and spoiled your evening. I guessed he'd been knocking it back at home. But I couldn't say anything, not tonight. It would have made it worse.'

'He didn't spoil anything. Why don't you let him stay there, and sleep it off?'

'Do you mind? I'm exhausted, Annie. I should get home.'

'Then you can come round to breakfast, if you feel like it.'

'And I must take Dally home,' Kate added.

'I'll order a cab. On my account.' Annie gave her a hug. 'You've made a wonderful, wonderful evening.'

By the time the two women had left, Rick was beginning to snore, belting snores which peaked into a crescendo of growls and grunts. Annie found an old printed zebra-skin blanket and spread it over him. Then she returned to the kitchen, where Trevor was clearing the table. Together they pulled off the cloths and threw them in a corner.

'Fancy some hot chocolate?' asked Trevor.

'After all that?' said Annie. 'All right, I'll make some if you like. Why not?'

'Good evening?'

'Wonderful, wonderful . . . The best idea you could have had.'

Annie slapped some milk into a saucepan, rinsed out a couple of mugs, and opened the economy-size tin of drinking chocolate.

'What are you saying? What am I missing?'

Rick staggered forward into the kitchen, pushing his blanket over one shoulder emperor-style, and lowered himself carefully into a chair.

'Nothing. I thought you were sleeping. We've just been clearing up.'

'I would have helped. I'm good like that. I help Bryonie, you know.' As Annie placed a mug of steaming hot chocolate at his side, he beamed up at her. 'You'd be a marvellous mum. Wouldn't she, Trev? Why don't women have babies any more? Bryonie can't. And Annie won't. All those sperm with nowhere to go.'

'Kate's got Dally.'

'Don't you want your own? Or are you holding back, my old mate? Give her a baby. You can't wait for ever, it'll soon be too late. You can't deny Annie the ultimate experience. Isn't that what they all want?'

'Conditioned to want. A desire created by the mythical biological clock.'

Annie looked wistfully at Trevor. They both knew they wanted to go to bed, but Rick wouldn't let go. When he had drunk too much, he clung to an idea like an angry child clutching a toy.

'Think about it, Trev. You've had your kid. What about hers?'

'Rick, another time. We're tired. This is a complex question.'

'No it isn't,' said Annie. 'It might be for some people, but not for me. Could you see me, pulling out my tits in the Intertel loo, carrying a babysling around on location? Being Dally's godmother suits me fine. Sorry, Rick, but I'm happy as I am.'

'What a pity. Now that you can afford a nanny. And even a car for the nanny.'

'Why does it upset you so much? What difference does it make? Most of it goes in tax, anyway.'

'Get a bent accountant. Everyone else does.'

'Not us.'

'Principles. Glorious old-fashioned socialist principles. Are we the only honest people left? Are we going to be the only ones to clear out the capitalist drains?'

'Rick,' said Trevor, sternly. 'For God's sake, go in there and put your head down. We'll talk about it tomorrow.'

Clutching his mug to his chest, Rick moved back unsteadily towards the settee. 'Tomorrow and tomorrow and tomorrow . . .'

Taking a damp cloth, Annie went round extinguishing the candles until there was only one left, spilling down droplets of wax onto the pine table. The balloons were still gently swaying, as the cold night breeze of January found its way through the kitchen window.

'Rick's getting worse,' Annie said, coming back to finish her mug of chocolate. 'Can't he see that he'll drive Bryonie away?'

'He can't accept that Intertel don't want him to cover war and famine. And he's frightened of losing his job.'

'I'm frightened of having mine. Suppose it's true what they say, that they keep you for a year, then scrap you and bring in someone cheaper once you've delivered the goods? Suppose I don't deliver the goods? I wish I hadn't said yes.'

'Darling, nothing's going to fall apart. You're going to be fantastic and I love you and you did the right thing in leaving the BBC. And nothing will change.'

'You really think that?'

'Yes. Let's get to bed. Tomorrow we can lie in, and I'll even make bacon and eggs.'

'I promise I won't kick up a stink if you burn the pan.'

Annie knew they wouldn't be alone for long, but she liked it that way. Bryonie would come round, Rick would be sober, Kate might appear if Dally was in a good mood and then they'd all sit at the table eating Trevor's overcooked breakfast, pulling the Sunday papers apart, friends bound together through years of familiarity, crises and celebrations.

Their footsteps echoed up the stairs, still uncarpeted because Annie had never found the right colour and besides, there was something comforting about bare wood. Once inside the bedroom, Annie pushed back the door which, having been brutally stripped, was too warped to close properly, while Trevor turned on the brass Victorian lamps with pink glass shades. Earlier, Kate had lit an incense stick and placed a posy of white flowers by the bed.

'It's like a bridal chamber. Doesn't it look beautiful?' said Annie, as she began to unzip her dress.

'Keep that on,' said Trevor, approaching from behind her to kiss her neck.

He liked to undress her beneath the bedclothes, peeling back the soft fabric from her breasts, feeling for the catches of her suspenders which she wore just for him, releasing the stockings without removing them, pushing her pants down just far enough, kissing down her body as though it was some forbidden, furtive pleasure inherited from his dad who had never seen his mum unclothed. Annie felt his probing tongue exploring each crevice, he had always known how to make her wait, how to prolong the tension inch by inch so that by the time he thrust himself inside her, she was almost beyond control. And she never tired of their ritual, even though it was no longer a nightly event. Trevor never made love in a cursory way, he wanted to do it properly or abandon the idea so that every time they came together, however often they had performed the act, it lingered in a sense of wellbeing which stayed with her all day.

'The trouble with getting older,' remarked Trevor, folding Annie into his arms, 'is that I can't do it twice any more. Or only on special occasions. Have you noticed?'

Annie wriggled into a comfortable position. The mattress dipped in the middle like a hammock but she didn't want to change it.

'Oh yes. Didn't you know? I lie awake at nights thinking about it.'

'Why haven't you said anything?'

Annie laughed at Trevor's indignant reply. He couldn't always tell, even now, when she was pulling his leg.

'You must fancy other men sometimes,' he continued.

'Why ask me now?' said Annie. 'Daft bugger. Put the light off. Does it seem as though I'm interested in anyone else?'

The room was now almost dark, the outside streetlight shining through the bamboo blinds. Trevor lay on his back, thinking through the evening.

'You looked so desirable tonight, you're still so sexy—'

'Still? Does it wear off, like lipstick?'

'Familiarity is meant to dull the senses.'

'Not mine, Trev.'

'Weird. Encouraging, really.'

Trevor groaned and rolled over towards the side of the bed.

'What's up?' said Annie. 'You all right?'

'Must have a piss.'

The sluicing of the ancient cistern echoed round the house, and the water gurgled and lingered through the pipes they'd meant to renew but hadn't. When Trevor returned, he sat on the bed, looking down at Annie. She was sprawled across the bed, her face buried in the pillow.

'Listen. You awake, Annie?'

'Mm.'

'I've been thinking. I'm still a boring working-class hubby at heart. It's what I come from. And so do you, come to that.'

Annie grunted, then murmured, 'What are you going on about, love?'

'It's never been an issue between us, being possessive. But you must wonder sometimes—'

'Do you?'

23

'Occasionally, when you're away. All those randy young actors.'

'I don't have to go to bed with big egos. I get them all day. And then I'm always too exhausted. Why should I go hunting elsewhere, Trev, when I'm so happy at home with you?'

'It's good to hear you say that.'

'You'd soon know if I wasn't. I couldn't hide anything, could I?'

'Don't you occasionally get the urge? After all this time?'

'A fleeting moment perhaps. I'll think, he's not bad, could fancy him. But that's all. Before I met you, I used to kid myself that every time it happened, this was it! If you had sex, then it must be love. Everyone loved everyone else in those days, didn't they? One great big love-in.'

'I suppose so. But I was married then, I only read about the love generation or saw it in movies.'

'You're worried you missed out?' said Annie, teasingly.

Trevor smiled, leaned over and gave Annie a slow, sensuous kiss.

'I still adore you.'

'Come into bed.'

Trevor turned off the light, slipped in beside his wife, then wrapped his arms round her waist and held her, half asleep, pressing his lips tenderly against her neck.

2

ANNIE

Annie swung round the backstreets behind the Euston Road, trying to find her way through the one-ways to the back entrance of Intertel. The turbo Saab they had given her still had the unsullied showroom smell, so that she longed to light up a fag, still longed to even though Trevor had nagged at her so long that she pretended she would never touch one again. She wouldn't have chosen this car, but it had the advantage of starting on a cold January morning. When she banged her foot down on the brake, the car halted instantly, jerking her back against the thick padded headrest. She had stopped by a corner, straining to see if it was the right street which led to the Intertel executive car-park, and was assailed by a barrage of hooting. Groping to find a button which would wind down the window, she set off the wipers to a crescendo of anger behind her. Then the window slowly slipped down.

'Shut up. Give me a break,' she shouted, suddenly realizing that the air was sharp outside and that the heating system worked.

Recognizing the yellow posts in front of her, she charged towards them to find a space, then banged her foot on the brake again, checked by the Halt sign on the steel barrier. Luckily her window was still open.

'Can't find the damned ID,' she called towards Bill, the Controller of Security who loped towards her.

'Morning, Miss Griffiths. Cold wind today.'

'Annie by now,' she said, with a grin.

Then she groped amongst the debris stuffed into the glove compartment and found the key to her identity. Bill's blotched, wintry face crinkled with approval as he examined her new plastic smartcard, Intertel's latest innovation. They spent money on stuff like that, even though Annie's computer was over the hill. Memo to self, she thought. Get new gear. Who had last called her Miss Griffiths apart from the hostess at the bank in Kentish Town? Pulling her woolly scarf tighter round her neck, she had second thoughts about correcting Bill. Annie Griffiths, Controller of Drama. It still felt strange.

Bill waved her through towards a row of cars already ranged in their yellow boxes. They came in early at Intertel, but Annie wouldn't change her habits. Annie Griffiths when not on location or mastering a crisis, could not be found before eleven, after the first coffee. Over one space, was written in luminous letters 'Controller Drama'. Next to her space, was the one reserved for Benny Hatton, 'Controller Com. & Ent.' Benny referred to his operation as the Laughs Department, never Comedy and Entertainment and she knew him from way back at the BBC. His white Jaguar, front seat covered in a furry rug, was squashed into his inadequate space like a fat passenger in economy class. Annie didn't think twice, but abandoned her Saab blocking Benny's exit.

'Bill. I'm in a hurry,' she said, fumbling in her sagging holdall. 'Keys for you. You can move it when Benny wants to leave. Couldn't squeeze in.'

'Masses of room down there, Miss Griffiths,' Bill said, craning his neck. 'Don't worry. Allow me.'

On the way to her office, Annie made a mental note to discover whether Bill's drink was whisky or gin. Next time she went abroad, she'd bring him back a bottle. Jean, in reception, gave the welcome smile reserved for Personalities, Stars and Controllers.

'Morning, Annie. Cold outside, is it?'

Annie instantly felt along her nose.

'Bright red?'

'Tiny bit pink, Annie. Not so as you'd notice.'

Annie glanced up at the double-life-sized faces in framed pictures – personalities with a capital P – all caught by the camera with hearty, populist grins except for Gavin Mitchell. Gavin Mitchell, taken from a low angle and staring intently at the lens, looked moody and mean, in that picture anyway. Most of the faces Annie recognized from the BBC, bought by Intertel at vast sums to rake in audiences. This network commercial television station, supposedly gunning for Londoners, had recently been criticized for importing too much American low-grade programming. A few months back, Lord Sherwood, the new Chairman of the Independent Television Commission, had publicly criticized Alan Coker, Intertel's Controller of Programmes, for allowing standards to drop and he had described the service as 'repetitive, predictable and unadventurous'. Coker accepted his difficult position by trying to ignore it, wavering between mass-audience shows which were highly profitable and a few prestigious programmes which looked good in the annual report. He also promised Lord Sherwood that he'd keep an eye on the sex and violence.

This year's schedule was looking good, not a bad line-up. For the young rave generation, Gavin Mitchell covered a random sprinkling of the arts from tattooing and fashion to Booker prize winners in his magazine programme, *Splash!*. Thelma Poole investigated social issues for the Station Which Cares in *Poole Reports*, aimed at caring viewers, those who appreciated her no-holds-barred questioning of rapists, fraudsters and behavioural freaks. *Global Highway* brought all the News which Matters, helped or hindered depending whom you were addressing, by former BBC heavyweight reporter Rick Evans. Benny Hatton, like Rick, was forced to submit to the changing pattern of television. Shortly after Sherwood's tirade against the company, Coker had axed his thirty-minute comedy slot, made him Controller of Comedy and Entertainment and brought in Annie Griffiths, who was known for her fast-moving, edgy thrillers set in the UK. Annie had her finger on the pulse, not even her worst enemy could deny that. Intertel were buying prestige and audiences, with the added bonus that Annie Griffiths was a woman. They had invested in a blue-chip package, as Alan Coker explained to the board when he announced her appointment.

Anita, Annie's secretary, had the coffee ready and bubbling as Annie strode in, flung down her holdall and threw her black leather jacket towards a row of hooks. The bare, yellow-walled office was divided into two sections, as the previous occupant, Sid Forrest, had preferred to keep his secretary as a guard, isolated in a desk-sized box. As yet, Annie had done nothing to make this space her own, except for her usual jumble of scripts and copies of magazines scattered over the blue plastic floor.

Annie was in the middle of casting. A heap of *Spotlight* directories stuffed with paper markers was spread over her desk, although she knew whom she wanted. Anita was fielding the phone, and the faxes were already mounting up in a wire tray with an Urgent tag. Actors absent on location when her appointment was announced, were first congratulating her, then reminding her to look out for their next appearances.

The internal phone rang on Annie's desk. It would either be Benny Hatton, Rick or Alan disguising a polite enquiry with a progress check. For her first two weeks at Intertel, Annie remained in her office, unwilling to acquaint herself with anyone who wasn't immediately concerned with her series. It was Rick.

'Hi, Annie. I'm just back from Manchester. How's it going? Got Anthony Hopkins, have we?'

'Too old. Too expensive. And over there.'

'The States, I assume. Where I should be. Fancy a drink in the bar tonight?'

'I'd love to. But I've too much on.'

'They ought to know you've got two legs, Annie. I've only seen you there a couple of times.'

'They know I'm here.'

'Ten minutes. One drink. See you at six-thirty.'

'All right, one drink. Seven,' replied Annie.

Over a glass of indifferent beer, prelude to something stronger, Rick surveyed the sweeping lines of the Intertel bar, a cheap shiny reproduction derived from a fashionable designer who created champagne bars in the City during the peak of Yuppiedom. He had arrived well before Annie, and no longer cared if he spent more time in the bar than the office. What was the point? He had given up pretending to come up with ideas for stories for *Global Highway*. Once a week was enough for that and Rufus Tonbridge, two years down from Oxford, came up with lukewarm ones every other minute, it seemed, and the producer was addicted to lukewarm ideas more fitted for breakfast shows. Leaning on the bar, in a rough-knit polo-necked sweater hanging over his overtight jeans, Rick adopted an expression which he hoped was a cross between seductive and bored. It worked for Gavin Mitchell, maybe it would work for him.

'Hi, Rick!' said a voice behind him, full of unquenchable enthusiasm.

He slowly gave a half turn, enough to see a mane of hair

glinting silver, inappropriate like an old car resprayed the wrong colour.

'My God, Thelma. What have you done to your hair? Put it in a microwave?'

'I'm glad you like it. I had it done for *The End of the Pier is Nigh*. See it, by any chance?'

'A bit of it.'

'I don't mind, Rick. Eight million people saw it. Alan adored it. Said it was quintessential. The kind of thing only I can do. Jeff's idea, of course. Marvellous review in the *Mail*. Did you catch it?'

'I'm sure someone did. Well done.'

Jeff Walker was both consort and producer, and Thelma Poole paraded him like a diamond engagement ring. Though edging fifty, Thelma thought forty and looked thirty in a long shot. She kept young for her viewers not from personal vanity, but as an insurance policy. If you could still make the covers of *Bella* or *Wow!* how could you be over the hill? How could Intertel fail to renew her contract? Thelma's market position was given added value by a stick-like figure which would soon be augmented to fit in with this year's Real Woman shape. Unlike some less fortunate, Thelma could pile on weight and lose it just as fast. The only thing which bothered her were her ears, far too large for her pretty, doll-like face and incapable of reduction, so her man in Harley Street said. Until the technology for lobe-reduction and aural cavity shrinkage had improved, she would keep her pixie ears covered in a variety of coiffures – long sheets or curls or waves of hair. The birth of Flora and Drusilla had swollen her once shapely legs, which she usually hid under pencil skirts. By now, two generations had grown old with Thelma and she reckoned she would keep going till sixty. Every few months, she surprised everyone – new tits, new hair, new make-up, new dress-style – but never new format or new Jeff.

Thelma, Rick often thought, would have made a perfect First Lady for the yanks. Decent at heart, huge, cornflake smile – but made for tough terrains like his favourite UN boots. He had just brought her over a champagne cocktail (two cherries, don't forget) when they both caught sight of Annie heading for a dangerously high chrome stool next to Benny.

'There's Annie Griffiths. She looks just the same as she did at the BBC,' said Thelma, giving a quick glance at Annie's wide

T-shirt flopping over tight black jeans. 'I used to see her in the bar, knocking it back. You'd have thought she'd have made an effort, now she's here.'

'She looks all right to me.'

'They all say she's quite good, but terrible to work with. I suppose you've got to be a bitch, producing her kind of stuff. Can't say I've ever watched it, wouldn't want to either.'

'Best thing on TV.'

'And she was always interfering on the set, telling directors what to do, making them reshoot for no reason. Terrible temper. They couldn't stand her.'

'So what? Most of them don't have a clue, they need a kick up the bum half the time. Annie is a wonderful, talented woman. I've known her for years. Name one person who gets her results.'

'Of course, if everyone had her budget—'

'They'd still produce the same old crap.'

'Sorry, Rick. I didn't realize she was a friend of yours. I'm only repeating what I've heard, I've nothing against her. Why don't you introduce me?'

'Why? Do you want to move over to drama? You're there already.'

'Well, it's better than kiddies' programmes.'

'*Global Highway*, my dear Thelma, is rated highly by the over forties. Some viewers have even compared me to Tom Jones.'

'You're not that ancient, are you? You're not older than me, surely?'

'No-one's older than you, Thelma. But I like strong beer and strong women.'

'I'm only strong on camera. And I do cry sometimes.'

'Me, too.'

'Only when you're drunk. That doesn't count.'

Thelma looked up at the minimalist clock over the bar and shrieked.

'That isn't the time? Flora's piano lesson, I'm late. I always stay to hear her. Children are so much better today than we were. I only got as far as Chopin *Mazurkas* and she's already on to Liszt. By the way, do try and catch next week's *Reports*. We're doing child prodigies and we've discovered a five year old who lives on a caravan site in Skegness, they're saying he'll be the next Stephen Hawking.'

'Ter-rific. But watch out, you know what they say about

children and animals. Let alone geniuses. Wouldn't touch it myself.'

'You're getting so hard-bitten, Rick. Doesn't suit you.'

Having planted a dry kiss on Rick's cheek, Thelma pulled down her baby-blue bobbled sweater over her breasts, stroked her tights up her calves to pull out the invisible wrinkles, stretched herself upwards like Madame Butterfly about to launch into *Un Bel Di*, and made it clear that she was leaving by tossing a heavy ribbed coat with a faux-leopard collar over her shoulders.

Annie happened to look up, distracted by the redoubtable Thelma, who was making it obvious that she was waiting until someone opened the glass door for her to leave. (She only opened doors for herself when she was working.)

'Glad to see Thelma's still going strong,' remarked Annie, in the middle of her reunion with Benny. 'She and Jeff still together?'

'Still,' said Benny. 'Alan wanted to get rid of him, but Thelma gave an ultimatum: he goes, I go. You have to admire her. Thelma never took time off for babies or nervous break-downs. But I don't think she'll last for much longer.'

'Why not? Doesn't she get whacking great audiences?'

'Lord Sherwood made an insulting reference to *Poole Reports*. Not directly, of course. "Programmes with a peepshow mentality should have no place in responsible broadcasting." The week before, Thelma had gone down into a Soho basement with a hidden camera to follow a stripper, who'd sold her story to *News of the World*, saying the crew paid her to take her clothes off and then implied she was a tart. Sordid stuff.'

Annie shrugged. 'Big deal. What does Sherwood know about responsible broadcasting, and what the hell is it anyway? Why does everyone take that old windbag so seriously? I can't even remember who the last Chairman was.'

'Ah, Annie. You're now feeding in the trough of profit TV. Sherwood is the father confessor. Father, we've sinned, forgive us. Right, my son. Ten adult education programmes, ten programmes for the disabled and one hundred religious broad-casts live from the parish church of Little Wittering.'

'He won't like *Rough Trade*, then. At the moment, there's sex on the back of a motor bike, murder in a virtual reality arcade and a punch-up in the terminal ward of a hospital.'

'Sounds promising, Annie. How's it going?'

'Fine, fine. I'm still working on the scripts. Trying to get the casting finalized.'

'How above something for me? I miss it, Annie. Being in front of camera keeps you young. Just a sit-down part, that's all I want. Not even a walk-on. Too tiring at my age.' Benny enveloped Annie with a fleshy arm, sleeves rolled up halfway, heavy gold signet ring on a bulbous finger, and leaned over her expelling a ginny gust of earlier fill-ups.

'What should I look out for, in the Laughs Department? Any good new shows coming up, Benny?'

'Maybe, maybe, but no-one you'd stay home for. All the young comics do nowadays is nick the worst bits from people I wouldn't have hired in the first place. Name me one who doesn't think describing a check-out at Sainsbury's or pretending to toss himself off on stage, will bring the house down. Cut-price filth, I call it. Well, how about a one-liner for me? I'm serious, Annie.'

'There's nothing right for you yet, but I'm looking for an up-and-coming circuit comedian for *Rough Trade*, cameo but crucial. Someone bright but raw.'

'What's the part? A cop or a robber?'

'A big-mouthed, funny cop who's committed a crime. Minor fraud, so it doesn't count. They want him back, but he refuses.'

'Story of my life.' Benny resisted the urge to stroke Annie's tightly outlined rear. Modern looks, casual gear, she hadn't fallen for the female executive town-house look, everything straight up and down. Look but don't touch, now it was back to the old not-below-the-belt days.

'Still got the hubby at home?'

Annie nodded.

'Thought so. Now my wife, clever lady my wife. Washing-machine breaks down, only the other day she was in the launderette, remember them . . . ?'

He'd lost his audience. Young, virile, brooding Gavin Mitchell had extracted himself from a gaggle of admiring researchers, directors and studio managers, all female, and was accelerating in Annie's direction. Cue clapping. Benny suppressed his joke and gave Annie a wink.

'Well done, Annie love. Get him to buy you a drink. Never gets me one.'

He then leaned away to face in the opposite direction. Gavin came up to Annie and stood with his back turned to Benny.

'Hi, Annie. I've been hearing lots of good things about you. Sorry we haven't got together yet, I've had a killing schedule. Great to have you here. They should have brought you in long ago, everyone was rooting for you. Sid Forrest hung on far too long, hadn't done anything decent for months. Intertel needed a shake-up in the drama department. I told Alan if he didn't bring in a woman, I'd resign. To be honest, I didn't think we'd get you.'

'Why was that, Gavin?'

'If I'd been the Beeb, I'd have doubled your salary. Bet they'd have done it for a bloke.'

The smile stayed on his mouth a fraction too long, his eyes had stopped smiling. She felt he was weighing up every blink of her eyelids or assessing how far she would abandon herself to the power of his attraction. Even his worst enemies were unable to deny that he was compelling on the box. Although thirty-five, he looked younger, with lean energetic looks, fine, smoothly groomed dark hair and a hint of unpredictability irresistible to girls. Gavin was a foreground man who set styles and changed them at exactly the right moment. He was going through a classic phase, Hackett jacket and open-necked shirt with a cravat.

'They should have given Sid another job, there was no need to give him the boot,' said Annie. She had heard from Anita that Sid had been given twenty-four hours to clear his desk. At least in the BBC they gave a few weeks' warning.

'I agree, it was handled badly. But he couldn't face up to it, that his clock had stopped in the Eighties. There are still lots of them around like that. They don't realize television has changed.'

Gavin scanned the bar, eyes flicking past the heads, some turning towards him in case he came over, which was unlikely. He was searching for Alan. *Splash!* would have to break out of its parochial patch. Gavin wanted to take in Europe. If Intertel was veering away from the States, that was no excuse to restrict his programme's remit to Britain's shores. Art, after all, had no boundaries. And it was time he checked out a suite at the Georges V in Paris, said hello to Jean-Paul, and bought in some farm-fresh talent. French accents were in.

'I'm meeting Harold Pinter for a drink in town. He's agreed

to appear in my Genius-Genesis slot. Fancy coming along, Annie?'

'Thanks, Gavin, but I'm working on a script. Must get it finalized this week.'

'*Rough Trade?*'

'That's the one.'

She wouldn't let on that she was pleased he knew what she was working on. The less you let on, the better.

'And I told Trevor I wouldn't be too late.'

'Trevor?'

'My husband, Trevor Watson.'

'Writes in the *Observer*. *The New Statesman*. Occasionally, *Guardian* Media.'

'He does sometimes, yes.'

'I always read him. The only man with the right take on television. We must get together, hope you'll introduce me. Sorry, must rush. They're waiting for me in the edit suite. And I've got two novels to get through by tomorrow. Howard Longley mean anything to you? Great writer. First book at twenty-three, all written in the form of Internet exchanges, computer freaks hunting a global killer. Exciting stuff.'

'Drama potential?'

'I'll let you know.'

Gavin gave Annie a brief eye-crinkle of regret as though he wanted to stay with her all night, said an abrupt 'ciao' and strode through the drinking crowd craning his head upwards. Two minutes later he reappeared at the far end of the bar with Alan. Benny swivelled round.

'You know what, Annie? I'd like to book that git as number one in a Rotherham club. And watch him die.'

'Don't, Benny.'

'Why not? Something I missed? Are you part of his late-night line-up?'

'I'm married. Remember?'

'And I'm not. Not for the moment. So you won't come back and share a pizza with me? Shame. Mind if I say it? I lust after you, Annie Griffiths. Always have, right from the time when you were rushing around with a clipboard in a miniskirt. Remember when you asked me what a POV was?'

Annie giggled.

'No. Too long ago.'

'Always asking questions, you were. I knew you'd go far. Was I better looking then?'

'You always said hello, asked me how I was doing. I remember that. And you saying there was nothing too tragic for comedy.'

'Some girls like ugly buggers. A few anyway.'

'I don't think it matters.'

'Annie, darling. You do a man good. Even though you don't mean it.'

'You know I do. Couldn't lie to you, Benny.'

'Lie with me then.'

It wasn't what he said, but his timing, his rubbery face, the face of a comedian, always on display, always truffling for laughs. In television, they weeded out the ugly ones. You got used to machine-tooled faces turned out like supermarket carrots, steam-cleaned, no bumps and no irregularities. The only ugly specimens they allowed had to be on-screen funny. And even that was changing. Benny's fourth wife had just left him, and he was reconnoitring for the fifth. Although she felt physically repulsed, Annie liked him. Benny Hatton, chat show host, stand-up comic, occasional crooner, a household name for at least two generations, now sitting at a computer in the office down from hers, all white leather and gold-framed pics from shows long-gone, offering seduction over a pizza to the Controller of Drama. That took guts.

Rick threw himself into the chair next to Annie, pushed forward the heavy watch on his wrist and tapped its face.

'Five minutes. I've been timing him. Gavin Mitchell has just spent five minutes with Alan. Five whole minutes. Must be serious. I get two if there's a crisis, five if I've asked a controversial question. The most controversial thing that twit has done is to interview some phoney about milk bottles filled with urine in the Hayward. As though anyone cares a shit. Six minutes now. He's probably blackmailing him for more shares. Did you know he's got five per cent? What have you got, Annie?'

'How can you ask me that, Rick? I'd get rid of the whole system.'

'Just checking.'

'And how about you, Benny? Have you got some shares stashed away?'

'Wife number three has most of 'em. What they call a

marriage settlement. But I've still got my premium bonds.'

Rick slurped from a whisky tumbler and made a face.

'They've watered it down, the bastards. How's the drama, Annie?'

'Raunchy, red and raw.'

'Great. That'll wake 'em up.'

At around half-past nine, Annie left Benny with a full glass of gin, Rick with an empty glass of whisky and made her way to reception. Anita, who was used to working late, the old devoted school who'd followed Annie from the Beeb, wouldn't have it any other way. She was weighing up bargain offers with the security boys. Bulbs in plastic tubs, going cheap, variegated, look a treat in window boxes.

'Annie? I've just bought two hundred. Bit much for a patio. Do you want some?'

'No thanks. Not tonight.'

Annie gave a wave, and ran towards the executive car-park. Once she was out of the Intertel orbit, she could point her thoughts towards the place which kept her sane. Home. Home and Trevor.

She drove in frustrated circles round Langton Crescent, Langton Avenue, Langton Close, too narrow for one car, let alone a double rank on either side, until she found an inadequate space in Langton Villas and parked her grime-spattered turbo Saab at an angle under a streetlight. Then, with her bulging bag packed under her arm, she walked hurriedly towards number fourteen. There was smashed glass on the pavement, another video gone. No-one could get insurance in her Kentish Town street, but they had stopped worrying. Cracked paint and weeds were not the markers of poverty in Langton Villas, but self-esteem. Its inhabitants, semi-Bohemians with jobs, disdained cosmetic concerns, whether on houses or faces.

Annie was just reaching for a can of lager, the only sustenance in the fridge, when she heard Trevor's step, heavy even though he was wearing light shoes.

'Hi, darling.'

He planted a kiss on her cheek and looked ruefully at the empty shelves.

'I didn't get anything in. So you'll have to have frozen

ghastlies. Kate ate the last of the cheese when she came round yesterday. And the salad. Vegetarians always finish everything up. I wonder why they're always hungry? I've eaten, darling. If you call pork pies eating. Got held up in a committee meeting which extended to the pub. Have they given you some cheap red carpet yet?'

Annie made a face. Trevor, who made telling pronouncements in learned journals about commercial television, and occasionally wrote dense arguments for the broadsheet media sections, could never grasp the practical details.

'I left the Beeb, remember? They don't have red carpets at Intertel. Tonight, I had a drink with Benny, saw Rick, his usual self, oh yes and I met Gavin Mitchell, who produces and fronts that late-show magazine for kids called *Splash!*. Anyway, he seems well disposed. Or maybe he's itching to move over to the Real Life department. Not much around at the moment, though. I've spent all day pissing about with actors, Jerry Finch can't make up his mind. There's a girl I can't decide on who'll be either fantastic or totally wrong. Clary Hunt, she's called, hardly any experience. Awful voice, great face and body. And I should have been working on the script. I'll have to do some tonight.'

'Darling, you don't have to do anything. If Intertel have given you an impossible schedule, you'll have to get more time. You're the boss now. It's up to you.'

'I know. I keep forgetting. It doesn't seem any different. I'm still doing the same things, just a different title.'

'A different place, Annie.'

'I try not to think about it, that the buck stops with me. If *Rough Trade* bombs . . .'

'It won't.'

'How do you know?'

'Because every time you start a new series, you see visions of hell and damnation.'

'I hate this job.'

'You don't.'

'Tonight I do. I need a decent assistant. The Controller of Personnel is "looking into it". Looking into what? Just find me someone who loves actors and watches drama, I said. Not some creep who knows Shakespeare backwards and talks like Noel Coward, like the one she came up with last week.'

'Finished?'

37

'You bet.'

Annie pulled a drawer halfway out from the ice-clogged freezer, and extracted a hoar-frosted pizza.

'Fancy this?'

'You have it. I've eaten, I told you.'

There was something Trevor had to watch, for his seminar on *The Documentary*, but Annie's eyes wanted blankness.

'Annie? Darling? You asleep?'

She had abandoned her soggy Quattro Stagioni and was lying across his legs on the settee, clutching at the zebra rug, her face nestling against his thighs.

'Almost. Bed soon?'

'I'll fast forward. I get the drift. What's the opposite of fly-on-the-wall documentary?'

'Fly off the wall. Director would rather use actors but has to have human beings instead. And he, occasionally she, writes the script first. OK, Prof? Do I pass?

'Every time.'

'Fast forward me to the bedroom. I won't make trouble. Not tonight.'

Trevor blanked the screen, and lifted up the small slender body lying on his. As he went up the stairs, he kicked aside a toy left the day before by Dally. Annie was almost asleep when Trevor undressed her, she could cut off with ease, and then fizz unexpectedly into life like a Catherine wheel on a damp night. He scrawled some notes, turned off the light, drew her hair back to kiss her neck.

'Gavin Mitchell wants to meet you,' said Annie, suddenly stirring.

'Really? How flattering. No harm in clapping eyes on the man who makes all you women go weak at the knees.'

'Not *my* knees,' replied Annie. 'But I need him as a friend, not an enemy. With Gavin it's either or. Everyone says to watch out. He'd be quite capable of persuading Alan to give me the elbow, like he did to Sid Forrest. I don't trust him.'

'By everyone, do you mean Rick? You know he's always throwing mud at Gavin Mitchell. I don't understand why. I sometimes watch *Splash!*. Mitchell is bright, has an eye for the swinging arts, but he's nothing special.'

'He is to girls, Trev. There were five or six of them around him in the bar, all adoring soppy looks. Rick hates that kind of competition. Anyway, he didn't warn me. Benny did.'

'Benny Hatton? God, is he still hanging on? I'd forgotten he'd landed up at Intertel.'

'What do you think I should do about Gavin? Give him your phone number at college?'

'Ask him round to dinner?'

'Why on earth should I? He's not a friend of ours.'

Annie was relieved that Trevor had decided not to pursue the subject. She was also annoyed at herself and her brain was racing, in spite of fatigue. It was all so trivial. She didn't want Trevor to meet Gavin. She didn't want him to be sucked into the politics of Intertel and she had no intention of entering that arena herself. Annie had firm ideas about whom she allowed to enter her private life, and refused to make the dinner table a place for political alliances. Trevor had always respected her desire to keep the division clear between work and home. Her idea of politics, like his, was working for the local Labour party whenever she had the time, not buttering up people who might do her some good.

Trevor let it drop a few days later that Gavin had phoned, and had invited him to have drinks at some newly opened club received with rapture in *The Face*. Annie immediately suspected that Gavin wanted something from him, but Trevor disagreed. He just wanted to talk, exchange ideas. Was it surprising that he was curious to meet Gavin Mitchell? It would do no harm to his university career, making an occasional appearance on Gavin's late-night youth programme. *Splash!* was watched by most of his students. Where else was there a platform for significant young artists, musicians, writers? Where else would Nobel prize winners discuss their work with kids young enough to be their grandchildren? Gavin was breaking down the barriers of age, class and culture, which Trevor admired. There was no need to make personal judgements about the man. He couldn't understand why Annie wanted to keep him at arm's length.

A few days later, Gavin collared Annie in the bar at Intertel. She was talking to Rick.

'Hi, Annie. Hoped I'd find you here. Can I get you some more château-bottled Euro-trash from the bar?'

'Thanks.'

39

Gavin's jacket was open and Rick immediately noted his firm waistline emphasized by a perfectly tailored shirt (evidently not see-through Hong-Kong silk, but proper, creamy thick stuff), and his neat stomach which didn't protrude even a fraction over the hand stitched, slender belt. Rick tried to disguise his beer-sagging gut by standing Grenadier-Guard upright, not his usual position.

'I'll have a Scotch,' said Rick. Now the bastard would have to buy him a drink.

'Rick, I caught your report on child poverty last night. Good stuff. We need more like that around here.'

'Thanks for the tribute, Gavin.'

He sounded as though he meant it, so Rick attempted a friendly grin. That was the trouble, it was hard to maintain dislike for someone who liked what you'd done. He'd ask Bryonie to record the goddawful *Splash!* one night so he could watch it and return the compliment.

'Could we have a word?' Gavin said to Annie.

'Now?' she answered.

Rick knew when he was beaten and anyway, Gavin hadn't taken up his order.

'Don't worry, Annie. I'm just off. I'll get a cab. Cheers, Gav.'

Gavin wanted Annie's opinion, just half an hour in his office, he'd appreciate her judgement. As they took the lift to the fourteenth floor, Annie was aware that he was looking at her, not staring at the floor indicator. She could sense the strength of his presence. No wonder Rick was jealous. At the same time, it felt as though he was giving her some kind of test.

'I had a really good meeting with Trevor. Your husband's a great guy. I'd expected him to be the cliché prof, banging on about people you've never heard of. But he wasn't, not at all. We had a drink at Tim Sherwood's new club, I expect he told you. Not a bad place,' Gavin said, as the lift doors closed behind them.

'Which Sherwood might that be? Son? Grandson?'

'Second marriage, I think. Now he's on to number three.'

'Is that why he's so keen on keeping sex and violence off the screen? Maybe he gets enough of it at home.'

'I'd go for that. *Entre nous*,' said Gavin.

He was walking close beside her, then stopped, leaning across her to unlock his office. It was the first time Annie had seen this spacious room (larger than hers, she noted) with its walls covered in framed awards, photographs of Gavin on location with a battery of famous faces. At one end of the room was an L-shaped scarlet upholstered seating area to which Gavin directed her.

'Alan's trying to keep the building dry,' said Gavin, going to a small refrigerator hidden inside a black lacquered cupboard. 'Glass of bubbly? It's nothing special, just a plebby sparkler.'

'Sure.'

Annie made a note to herself that her office should better reflect her standing. Gavin, after all, was not her equal in rank but his voice was loud at Intertel. The young audience, his audience, that's what they were all after, hooking the new generation. Now she had met him a few times, she could begin to assess him. He gave the effortless impression of being superior, made even Alan look like a minion. There was just a slight hint of condescension, as though he knew best but would listen to other views. She couldn't quite place his accent, but thought she detected one or two flattened vowels which, to her experienced ear, stuck out strangely from his educated, well-modulated London tones. Not northern vowels, though. She could tell Yorkshire from Lancashire, Highland from Lowland, Brixton from Stepney.

Gavin eased the cork off out of the bottle and poured out two glasses of champagne.

'Look at that. Steady as a rock.' For a moment, he appeared like a ten year old, showing off to his mates. Spontaneous. Annie hadn't thought he could be.

'Trevor's a good guy. It's so rare to be with someone who talks sense,' Gavin began. 'We've got a lot in common, actually. Two working-class lads made good. He comes from a bit farther up the M1 than I do, that's all.'

Annie gave an astonished laugh.

'What's south of Nottingham? Oh yes, Leicester. I always forget about Leicester.'

'No, not Leicester. Birmingham. My dad's still there in the council house where I was born. So's my mum. You didn't know I was a Brummie, did you?'

'Why hide it? I like the sound of an accent.'

Gavin seemed unwilling to sit down, as though his nervous energy had been stockpiled like a night storage heater and was now timed to blast off its heat. Trevor did that, too, pacing

41

round the room, picking up objects, putting them somewhere else.

'Surprisingly enough, audience research has proved that the kids associate regional accents with people who make them laugh. But if someone's got something important to say, they prefer the Establishment voice. A turn up for the books that was. Even the agency was surprised. Isn't that amazing, that my viewers actually appreciate the kind of accent they can associate with authority? They'd never admit it, of course. Did you ever see Sir Kenneth Clarke's *Civilisation* series?'

'Oh yes.'

Annie smiled. How shocked they'd all been, she and her college friends, when Trevor tore the series apart in the lecture hall. 'Ruling Values – a Critique of *Civilisation*', she could still remember the title.

'Sir Kenneth was a genius, in spite of his politics.'

Annie tried not to sound surprised.

'So you think it matters?'

'Tory politics always make a difference,' replied Gavin. 'Though I can understand it when people try and pretend that politics are dead. Disillusionment, opiate of the people. We're living in apolitical times. Why pretend otherwise?'

'I don't think that,' retorted Annie. 'Politics are never dead, they just change their hue slightly. Blue and red still say something people understand. They still mean a lot. Green hasn't had the same impact.'

Then she realized it must sound as though she was giving a pep talk to actors.

'Sorry, Gavin. I can't hide it. I'm still proud to be a socialist. Unfashionable, I know.'

Gavin collected his glass and sat down, swinging one leg high over the other. Soft, new, polished shoes.

'Anyone who sincerely sticks to the right, has to be insane. Or a deluded, talentless, brain-damaged idiot. We should get rid of all the right-wing farts hanging around here. I'm on your side. How couldn't I be?' said Gavin.

'Honestly?'

He couldn't help smiling at Annie's joyful expression, and then she giggled. It was like discovering someone had been at your school.

'You've got a super laugh. Did you know that? I bet the actors love you. Don't they do anything you say? I would.'

42

'Sometimes they do. When I'm not in a rage.'

Annie got up and stood in front of the giant screen suspended from the ceiling. 'Shall we have a look at your programme now?'

'The tape's ready to go,' replied Gavin, without moving.

Annie examined the buttons and pressed one. The programme ident blasted into the room, and there he was, Gavin Mitchell, closet socialist, in his designer tie and tailored jacket dropping off his broad shoulders at exactly the right point. Annie forgot she was meant to be making constructive comments as she watched the assembled shots of actors rehearsing in a warehouse. She found herself looking from Gavin's watching face to his giant close-up on the screen, then back again, unable to decide which was real. Rick had told her that he was married. She ought not to care if he was or not. Just curiosity. What was he like at home? His wife was some kind of a writer, dabbled in poetry, Rick thought, devoted to their two children, motherly type.

'Great footage,' remarked Annie, as the screen went blank and she tried to recall what she had seen.

'I'm not sure about the order,' said Gavin. 'What do you think?'

'I'd cut your main interview in half and put the first bit up front,' replied Annie. The working part of her brain rarely let her down.

'Excellent idea. Thanks a lot, Annie. You're right. It'll make all the difference.'

'Any time. But I must be getting back.'

'Yes, me too. I'll go down with you to the car-park.'

Gavin picked up Annie's leather jacket, and held it out for her. It seemed more of a sexy gesture than a polite one, and it made Annie feel uneasy, as though he wanted her to give some sign in return that she found him attractive.

'We've got some appointments coming up soon,' remarked Gavin, as they walked down the corridor. 'You'll be taking your first board. It's fun. We have tremendous arguments. I looked down the CVs and there's an ex-student of Trevor's. Ask him if he remembers someone called Lucinda Sherwood.'

'Not another one,' said Annie. 'How many are there, for God's sake?'

'She's the sister of Tim. Second marriage again.'

'How on earth do you keep up, Gavin?'

43

'I don't. But I have good researchers. Did Trevor ever mention her?'

'No,' said Annie. 'But that doesn't mean anything. He only tends to talk about the bright ones, the ones who interest him.'

'They all want to get into television, the children of our brainless aristocrats.'

As she removed the pile of scripts from the front seat of her Saab, Annie wondered what it was about him which made her feel uneasy. Lips a little too thin? Perhaps, but it wasn't physical. Then she decided he was altogether too polished, too polished for a socialist, too polished for someone who would have to believe in the rights of men, the rights of women. More Jeffrey Archer than Michael Foot, that was it. She couldn't imagine him really believing in anything. It was nagging her, that Trevor had been taken in by him.

She teased Trevor about his budding friendship, when they met up with Rick and Bryonie in the Langton Arms, a Friday ritual which ended in a Chinese takeaway and, usually, a barnstorming argument which cleared the air for the next week.

'He's bright and informed, that's all. And he isn't afraid to come out with provocative statements. Really, Annie, we only had a drink together. He's not about to become a bosom friend. But he's a good person to have on our side. The left needs some media muscle from time to time.'

'Isn't it obvious why Gavin's all over you?' said Rick. 'He's a prat who wants to get in with all the other prats. And nick some ideas from you so he doesn't look as dumb as he undoubtedly is. You wait, he'll be trotting out Professor Watson's views and pretending they're his own.'

Bryonie tried to halt the rise of bile, without success.

'I thought we weren't talking about television tonight, Rick.'

'We're not, only passing by the subject. But why should Trevor be taken in by the biggest arsehole at Intertel?'

'Rick, calm down.'

'Anyone who never buys me a drink is an arsehole. Well, Trev, I suppose he said he'd get your face on the box. That's his usual line. Don't be fooled. You'll be giving your all for fifty quid and a taxi home.'

'He'd be right for my students. He's agreed to come and talk to them, no fee.'

'That is generous. I mean, think of it, what a great

44

opportunity to chat up your long-legged lovelies without paying a penny for hospitality. Inviting the good-looking ones to be part of the studio audience. And what do you get out of it?'

'A chance to get a word in about what's happening to television.'

'Ah, now we're getting there. Trev, my old mate, are you planning a new career? Trevor Watson, TV celeb, wheeled out for any occasion, spout off on anything? Quick-quotes Watson?'

Annie made a rueful face at Bryonie.

'Rick, you know Trevor better than that. He'd much rather put his views in print. Wouldn't you, love?'

Trevor shrugged, smiling at Annie.

'It's about time someone broke through all the hypocrisy. If he gets me on *Splash!* I don't imagine I'll get asked a second time. But someone needs to be blunt, now that Dennis Potter's gone. And *Splash!* seems as good a place as anywhere. I'd hardly get on *Global Highway* dishing the dirt on right-wing bias in current affairs.'

'He's right,' said Annie.

3

TREVOR

They had paused halfway through the Sunday walk, Annie, Trevor, Rick, Bryonie, Kate and Dally. This was when they took the country air of Hampstead Heath, dressed for the occasion, muffled up, jeans and wellies, striding over the unkempt grass, treading the hallowed ground where, in early morning, legend had it that Michael Foot, great old mouthpiece of socialism, could be heard hollering for his dog over the unpeopled space as though he was rounding up sheep in the Welsh valleys. Bryonie had seen him once, in her jogging phase before she decided that the balance of medical evidence proclaimed it more harmful than beneficial. This Sunday, Kate had made a kite for Dally, which Rick, through dint of racing along the ground, had managed to make airborne. They were all laughing, breathless, cheeks red with exertion. Trevor and Annie were sitting on the bank of a secluded hillock which led down to an open space which Rick referred to as 'the glen'. They had all been coming here for so long, that it was as though it belonged to them.

Kate, thoughtful Kate, had brought along a large Thermos of coffee, which, since it was a cold March day, Trevor had decided to open prematurely.

'Why don't you leave some for the others?' Annie suggested, as he proceeded to fill two giant plastic cups. He immediately tipped some of hers into his. Being an only child, he had never had to watch his parents divide a cake into equal portions for his siblings, like Annie had. He knew by now that she found his unconcern appealing, so different from that desperate fairness you had to display at all times if you were a mother, or standing in a British bus queue. Trevor was blessed with a wife who didn't want to change him and accepted all the male

46

foibles which drove Kate and Bryonie to screaming pitch. Nothing would disturb his good mood today, his feeling of happy comfort as the wind tousled his hair, gloved hands clutched round the warm cup, leaning against Annie, looking up at the clean sunlit sky, scraps of white clouds dotted like melting ice-flows. If he missed his Sunday walk, it would be a bad week.

He could tell that Annie was thinking about work, because she had stopped observing what was around her, staring into space with a frown, even though she was meant to cut off, just to enjoy the open air and forget about that great glass building.

'Trev? Do you remember a student called Lucinda Sherwood?'

'Vaguely,' he said.

The coffee had gone sour in his mouth and he tipped out the remains onto the grass.

'Too strong for me. Why does Kate have to make it so strong?'

'I'm on an appointments board in April sometime, and I was going through the applicants. It was on her CV.'

'I could check for you,' he said. 'Must have been a few years ago.'

'Not that long ago,' replied Annie. 'About four or five years.'

After a moment's reflection, Trevor continued.

'Oh yes. She was the one who sent that script I showed you last year. Or it might have been the year before. I think you flicked through it. Thought it wasn't bad.'

At that moment, Kate's bright yellow kite hurtled to the ground like a stricken helicopter, straight down and crash. They could hear Dally's screams. Rick picked up the shattered frame, and came running towards Annie and Trevor.

'Did you see that? This kite has lived, folks. It flew, it bloody flew.'

'Don't worry, darling. I'll mend it,' said Bryonie, depositing Dally next to Annie. Kate collected the pieces from Rick.

'I'll make another one. There's lots of paper left over.'

'Look, look, Dally. Over there. I can see the tail.'

Annie picked up Dally, and ran off down the incline to hunt down the bundle of coloured fringes which were rolling over along the grass, pushed and nudged by the wind. The screaming continued, and Trevor could see the contorted little face over Annie's shoulder, like a wretched monkey. He walked away, towards the thick-trunked trees on the edge of the copse, staring up at the windtorn sky, clutching his arms close to his body with the cold.

Trevor shivered, and suddenly the fresh breeze seemed bitter and piercing, causing his eyes to water. In the distance, he saw the blurred form of a young woman striding in his direction, with fine light hair struggling to escape from a headscarf and a loosely belted camel coat. She was walking towards him, as though about to greet him, clutching something in her hand, coming nearer and nearer. The way she moved seemed disturbingly familiar, those long, loose strides with her face turned upwards to catch the wind. A black dog came bounding up to her and leaped high in the air, waiting to sink his teeth into the stick she was holding. With relief, he observed that it wasn't anyone he knew, after all. He watched them both veer away towards the other side of the dip and then he realized that Rick was trying to attract his attention, waving his arms, shouting, his hands cupped round his mouth, so that his voice dominated the wind.

'Come on, Trevor. Pub time.'

Running down the hill, Trevor arrived panting by the group who were all on their feet, Dally grizzling in Kate's arms.

'We've had enough of the cold,' said Annie. 'And so has Dally. Hasn't she been good, though? Why don't we all go to the pub?'

By now, Rick had had enough of surrogate fatherhood.

'Bloody hell, woman. I thought you two were cooking dinner. Can't a bloke have a decent pint in a smoky, noisy, kid-free zone?'

'We'll have a quick one. Do you mind?' said Trevor, giving a guilty glance at Bryonie.

'I'm quite happy to miss out,' she said, with a grin. 'But I'm not spoiling my beef.'

Trevor slipped his arm through Annie's.

'You coming, darling?'

'No, I'll help Bryonie.'

'You don't have to, Annie. Kate's coming back with me,' said Bryonie.

Annie planted a kiss on Trevor's nose.

'Off you go, Trev. Make sure Rick sticks to beer.'

The two men hurried off over the tufted mounds of grass, leaving the women with Dally tottering at their side. In half an hour, they could reach the Langton Arms, mid-way between Langton Crescent and Langton Villas. Annie's and Trevor's house in Langton Villas was larger than Rick and Bryonie's in Langton Crescent, having an extra floor added on, but in Langton Crescent the gardens were bigger. The terrace architecture was almost identical, flat-fronted artisan dwellings prettily stuccoed with arched first floor windows. Some had lapsed into decay, others had been lovingly restored by appreciative owners. Fiercely protective of their neighbourhood, neither couple would have dreamed of living anywhere else.

While Bryonie, Kate and Annie were preparing lunch, Trevor and Rick were talking of higher things in the Langton Arms. This was their place, the scruffy local where the regulars looked up with a grunted greeting as you came in, no-one noticed muddy boots or grubby shirts and no-one cared about television. On Sunday, the pub had an influx of customers who came from the rented rooms of Kentish Town and never appeared at other times – young girls whose legs were thinly covered by black nylon as opposed to opaque, unarousing polyamide, their faces like carnival masks, thick eyeshadow and scarlet lips.

'There's a pleasant sight,' declared Rick, as two girls attempted to worm their way through the Sunday crowd to approach the bar. 'I'll get them a shandy. Bet they drink shandy.'

Trevor caught his arm.

'I'm sure you're right. But they came in with those two young lads playing darts.'

'And they're buying. Even better. Big tits and they're buying. I wish I'd spent the night with them. Maybe they'll get bored with those louts and come over in our direction.' Just then, one of the lads caught his blatant stare, aimed his dart away from the board in the rough direction of Rick's eyes, then turned on his heel and prepared for a savage shot.

'What do you think, Trev?'

'About what?'

'Those two girls. Don't they make you want to miss lunch?'

'Not particularly. I wouldn't know what to say to them.'

'Yes, you would. "I bet you come from Islington." That'll get them going.'

'Why do you do it, Rick? You wouldn't talk like that to Bryonie or Kate.'

'It reminds me of what I was like, hanging out in Cardiff pubs, chatting up the birds, before I got levelled out by the fucking bourgeois education system. It made me into something I'm not, Trev.'

'Like it or not, you've moved on. Why pretend?'

'Sometimes, Trev, my old mate, you behave like a prick. I haven't moved on. And I haven't changed. Ask Bryonie.'

Trevor sipped his beer and cast his eyes round the pub, alighting on a girl who was glancing over her shoulder as she, too, sipped her beer, clearly assessing him.

'She's not bad,' said Rick, following his gaze. 'You're in with a chance, I'd say.'

'It doesn't interest me. Really. I prefer my girls on the screen.'

'Come on, Trev. She meets you on the corner of Langton Villas, pulls you into a doorway, heavy breaths, lifts up her skirt, black stockings, rubbery suspenders . . . Did I tell you about Gemma? She's a production assistant at Intertel? What a girl! Makes the bed shake like a white-knuckle ride.'

Trevor looked disapprovingly at Rick, unable to hide his distaste.

'Suppose you fell in love with one of the girls you play around with? What then? How would you cope? Would you tell Bryonie?'

'Bryonie knows, of course she knows. How can I hide it, Trev? That's the man she married, I've never lied to Bry. It's just a hobby, better than darts. And who's talking about falling in love? It's all good fun. But you don't agree. If a beautiful naked girl appeared out of nowhere, you'd tell her to get dressed, I bet.'

'I might have the thought, the desire even. For a minute or so.'

'And you'd have a hard-on.'

Trevor waved a hand to lower the volume, then sipped the foam from his beer and carefully wiped his mouth.

'Possibly. Yes, all right.'

Rick moved closer for more intimate revelations, even though Trevor would never return his disclosures however much he egged him on.

'Then what? Would you touch her? Or would you wait for her to lie on the bed?'

'If she was a prostitute, which she probably would be,

I'd ask her to leave. I've never been one for the transitory experience. I always want to repeat things. Basically, Rick, I'm boring. I like the same bedtime stories. Besides, my wife wouldn't be too keen.'

Rick was uncomfortably reminded of Bryonie's penetrating investigation after every foreign trip. Who, when, where?

'And if she never found out? What then?'

'I don't think, of course one can never be sure, but I don't think it would mean the end of our marriage if she did. Annie's much more tolerant than I am about infidelity. Different generation. Annie's never been jealous, thank God.'

'Lucky sod.'

Rick's glass was almost empty, but Trevor made no attempt to order another.

'Come on. We'd better get moving.'

As they strolled round the corner to Langton Crescent, Trevor found himself wondering how his closest mate coped with lust and marriage, and why Bryonie stayed with him. Only Annie had an instinctive grasp of those kind of intricacies. He found a suitable moment to question her about Rick's behaviour later that evening, when they were alone. The fire was well stoked, and the intense red glow brought out the colour in Annie's cheeks as she lay on the matted sheepskin rug in front of it reading the *News of the World* with professional attention, scouring for slants on stories, or the seeds of some future plot.

'I do worry about Rick sometimes,' he said reflectively.

Annie leaned up on her elbows. If he had been able to paint, Trevor would have rushed to find some paper and a brush. Woman reading by the fire, her rounded buttocks and legs sprawled comfortably behind her, looking towards the artist impatiently.

'If Bryonie can't make him cut back, nobody can. How much did he drink at lunch-time?'

'Couple of pints. But I wasn't thinking about his alcohol consumption. More his constant preoccupation with his cock. He said, quite blithely, that he's having an affair with Gemma, an Intertel PA I believe.'

Annie laughed.

'Boasting, Trev. He doesn't stand a chance. Rick goes for well-endowed ladies. You must know that. Anything which comes to hand.'

'It's tough on Bryonie. I don't know how she puts up with it. Would you?'

'How would I know? I'm not married to Rick, thank God.'

'If she wasn't so keen to have a child, I suppose she'd have booted him out.'

'Oh, love, you don't understand, do you? Rick goes home every evening whenever he can. He likes being a wicked rampager during the day, so he can tell Bryonie how dreadful he's been. Or, in my opinion, how dreadful he'd like to have been. If Bryonie isn't around, he can tell Kate. All talk.'

'Are you sure? How do you know? That's not the impression I get.'

'I can tell.'

Women were supposed to be the mysterious ones. Trevor found men far more difficult to figure out.

'Why does he do it?'

'Chase women? He's working with technology all day. Things work, don't work. Someone important refuses to come on the programme or gets grabbed by the Beeb. A camera goes down. Another person doesn't make it, stuck in traffic. So he goes to the bar and they're all wingeing away. What do you do? Be as provoking as you can. That's Rick. And that's television. Even if Rick does lust after one of the PAs when he's away, or gets his end away on the odd occasion, that doesn't alter his feelings for Bryonie. He'd go to pieces if she left.'

'But there must be an element of guilt. Are you saying it depends on duration? Is a quick affair less significant than a long one?'

'You've missed the point. Calling Rick's lunges affairs is a huge exaggeration. If any girl got serious about him, he'd run a thousand miles.'

'Women always say that. Suppose he met someone he was serious about? What then?'

Annie tore out a page from the paper and sat cross-legged like a child listening to a story, looking up at him.

'How could he cope with that? And how could it happen? In all the years we've known him, there's never been anyone he could bear to go home to, apart from Bryonie. Surely you realize that, love?'

'I never quite know, with Rick. He might be struggling in secret, he might have met someone who could rip his life apart. How do we know? It could explain his drinking. Or his chasing other women to try and forget. A conflict he can't resolve.'

'Honestly, Trev. You're so wide of the mark. Rick drinks because he works to deadlines and the rules keep changing. And he can't get Bryonie pregnant. If Rick was a dad, he'd be completely different.'

'I hope you're right,' said Trevor. 'I'd like to understand him better, but he refuses to be drawn. Do you think he's frigntened of women, under all that bravado?'

Annie looked mystified.

'Frightened? Of course not. Now he's stopped roaming round the world, he just wants constant reassurance that he's the sexiest man at Intertel, leader of the pack, even if he hasn't just come back from the hills of Bosnia. Rick's the easiest person to understand.'

'And me? Am I easy, too?'

'Most of the time.'

About ten days later, Trevor was in his study when Annie came in and handed him a script.

'I found this. I knew I had it somewhere.'

'Don't ask me to read anything at the moment, darling. I've something to finish.'

'It's Lucinda Sherwood's outline, *Grains of Evil*. I thought I'd better take another look at it, since she's been short-listed for a job at Intertel.'

'Good. I hope they don't give her a hard time,' said Trevor, without looking up. 'When's the board?'

'In a couple of weeks, I believe. Her idea's got a lot going for it. It may not be Intertel material, more Channel 4 perhaps, but I think she ought to develop it. Have another look, see what you think.'

'I will, when I've a moment.'

'Do you think she'd be good to work with? Could you imagine her fitting in at Intertel?'

'Difficult to say. It really isn't fair for me to make a judgement. Wouldn't it be better if you put out of your mind that she happened to be a former student? Often the ones I thought were hopeless, end up with the best jobs. And vice versa. She might be all right, she might not.'

'You don't sound very enthusiastic.'

'People change. It's a long time since she was a student. I don't know what she's done in the meantime.'

'Stop being so bloody diplomatic. Would you employ her, if you were me?'

'Darling, that's an impossible question.'

Annie was growing impatient. Trevor was always so protective of his students.

'You didn't like her. Because she's the daughter of Lord Sherwood. Is that it?'

'Why on earth should that matter? We don't select our students because of their parents. Unlike television.'

Annie ignored his jibe. If a handful in television had succeeded bearing the names of political dynasties, landed families or literary giants, it was because they had talent. She sympathized with his contempt for inheritance, his hatred of anyone getting advancement for the wrong reasons. But since he wrote about television and didn't work there, he exaggerated their importance.

'You liked Lucinda's script when you first read it, didn't you?'

'Yes, yes. It showed promise.'

'I thought so, too.'

'Did you read it all?'

'You know I did.'

Trevor placed the script on a shelf above his desk. Annie was still standing beside him, as though waiting for further comments. He placed a marker in the book he was reading, and turned towards her.

'She was very lively, bright, quick off the mark, always rushing around, full of enthusiasm. Absolutely determined to make it in drama, nothing else would do even though I told her it might be easier, if she wanted a job in television, to make a start in education. That didn't interest her. I remember, she always got people to do things for her. I suppose it helped, she was a good-looking girl.'

Annie grinned.

'And I bet the boys loved her.'

'She was quite a hit with my young men. But she hated criticism. Still, I expect she's changed by now.'

'Do you think we'd get on?'

Trevor looked at her doubtfully and smiled.

'There'd be no problem about that. But do think about it, Annie. You could be in a difficult position. Intertel will want

54

her for the sake of her father, not for her ability. As Chairman of the ITC, he could wipe Intertel off the map, if he chose. How could they turn down one of Lord Sherwood's children?'

'Lucinda isn't a child. She's a woman in her mid-twenties.'

'Anyway, even if you think she's suitable, everyone will think you're hired her for the wrong reason, to curry favour with the board.'

'I can deal with that, love. If she's any good, I'll give her a chance. I don't care where she comes from or who she is, we need good women around. And I need a good assistant.'

'Fine.'

Annie was taken aback, beginning to wonder if he had lost confidence in her ability to make decisions. Or was it simply that he was over-tired? Had she chosen the wrong moment to bring up what must be for him a trivial concern?

'You're cross, Trev.'

'No, I'm not. But I wish you'd be more aware of the politics of television. You can't just pretend they don't exist.'

'I'm concerned with giving women opportunities. I thought you were, too,' said Annie, heatedly.

'Of course I am.'

'But only the right women. The ones who fit into your idea of the underprivileged victims of oppression. The ones who struggle and fight. There are others, Trev. You can care without living on a Nottingham council estate. You can have talent and live in a stately mansion. The suffragettes wore good clothes and had upper-class accents. Do you condemn them for that?'

'Really, Annie, I am aware that society has changed. You're being simplistic.'

'What's wrong with being simplistic?'

A few days later, Trevor found an envelope marked Private and Confidential waiting in his pigeon hole at college. Instantly recognizing the fine, handwritten script, he ripped it open.

Dear Trevor,
* I thought I'd better tell you that I applied for a researcher's job at Intertel. They've just written to say that I've got an interview and that Annie will be on the board. If she asks about me, I hope you'll say good things about your former student.*
                                    Love, Lucinda.

All morning, he thought about her letter and wondered if he should reply. Annie could so easily have found out. It made it worse, that as far as he knew she had never suspected. If she had asked, he would not have been able to hide what had happened. Hadn't Lucinda told him that she was thinking of living in the States? New York? Los Angeles? Why had she come back? He had just finished giving a lecture and was preparing to leave, when his secretary asked him if he would take a call from Lucinda Sherwood. Of course, he would have to. If she did end up working for Annie, he would have to remind her that if she once mentioned . . . Trevor prayed that her respect for Annie would extend to his marriage.

Slowly he picked up the phone.

'Trevor Watson.'

'It's me. Lucinda. I had to speak to you. Listen, I'm on the short-list for an interview at Intertel. Isn't it brilliant?' she said, breathlessly.

'Wonderful. I did get your letter.'

Trevor tried to calm his racing pulse, to stifle his delight at hearing her voice.

'How's Annie getting on at Intertel? I've read loads about her. You must be so pleased.'

'Thrilled. She seems to be settling in faster than I'd hoped. How about you? I thought you were determined to make it in Hollywood.'

'Oh, I did stay a few weeks, met loads of people. I showed my script around, and they kept saying how fantastic it was, then nothing happened. I couldn't wait to come home, honestly. You're not annoyed that I rang?'

'Why should I be? It's good to hear you again.'

'Could I come and see you? I know it's stupid, but I'm awfully nervous.'

He longed to say yes, but the fear returned. Hadn't it all been decided, after the letter, that they would never meet again? How could he trust himself? Why did he feel the same rush of pleasure now as he did then?

'Do you really need to? I've got a lot on at the moment.'

'Please, Trevor, I must see you. Just for a coffee. It won't take long. Could you help me go through what they might ask me? I'm absolutely dreading it. You can't imagine.' She sounded as though she needed his help, almost imploring. He had told her, You know I'll always help you. How could he let her down?

'I really don't have a clue what questions they'll ask you,' he answered. 'But we can talk about it, if it would be any good.'

'Fantastic, thanks so much. I'm hopeless at interviews. With people I don't know, my mind goes a blank. But it never does with you, Trevor. Can you make it tomorrow sometime?'

'Tomorrow's difficult. I'll have to consult with Annie. I believe we're meant to be somewhere tomorrow.'

'I'm meeting Mummy the day after. She'll be in England and I haven't seen her for ages.'

'I might be able to make an hour or so around tea-time. Could you manage that?'

'Oh yes, of course.'

'I'll see you in the Russell Hotel. About four.'

Before, he had called her darling but now he was unable to betray his affection. After the letter he wrote six months ago, as vivid in his mind now as though he had just written it, they would be to one another what they always should have been: mentor and student. They would both know, that it had been different but that was no reason to prevent them from keeping in touch, from seeing one another from time to time as friends. If the suggestion had been his, if Trevor had planned his meeting with Lucinda as the rekindling of a *liaison dangereuse*, he would have thought about it differently. It was not as though he had made a deliberate decision. Having a quick afternoon tea in the unromantic, functional foyer of the Russell Hotel would make it clear that he intended nothing more than to help a former student. There was no harm in going over a few points which might be raised in her interview. She had seemed tense on the phone. What had she felt, hearing him again? It must have been hard for her, knowing that once their conversation would have been easy, intimate, teasing, suffused with the confidence of mutual love.

4

TREVOR

It was always difficult to tell beginnings, but there was a date underlined in a diary from two years ago which Trevor had hidden at the back of a filing cabinet. He no longer thought of it as an affair, because affairs had no history, passing indistinctly into memory like rare heatwaves in April. Love was a history of development and discovery, ripening with the passage of time, each moment savoured and recalled. He wished he had written down thoughts, conversations, reflections, instead of brief jottings under dates but the details of his meetings came flooding back, like starting a book you had last read as a child and remembering how you felt then.

At that time, Annie was still assistant head of drama at the BBC. It was late in September when Lucinda sent the letter, three years or so after she had graduated with a good degree, but not as good as he had hoped. Too many balls and parties, she said, when he conveyed his disappointment. Why have Finals in the summer? Unfair. He told her that she underrated her talent, that if only she could knuckle down, but he gave the same pep talk to so many. She was not one of the students he thought about afterwards. Lucinda Sherwood, he assumed, would soon be married, once she had completed her brief flirtation with study.

The letter she sent was handwritten from an address in Chelsea, a formal letter on thick deckled paper. She'd be so pleased to have his opinion, she knew he'd be honest and helpful. Something she'd written, a script outline. Could he spare half an hour to talk to her? He wished he had kept the letter, but he destroyed it soon after their meeting. Usually he hoarded notes, cards and letters in neat folders, ready for reference if need be, but he had grown used to hiding the evidence, tearing up her notes in tiny pieces, never signing his name not even on the books he gave her, never leaving a permanent mark.

Lucinda arranged an appointment to see him at an inconvenient time, in the first chaotic week of the autumn term, with newly enrolled students clamouring for attention. Late September was either winter or summer and this particular one was hazy and warm. Lucinda had come to ask him a favour, although she made it seem part of his job. Trevor was never sure about where to draw the line, but he always tried to be friendly and accessible, the kind of lecturer whom former students would write to later, or drop in on when passing by. Yet he didn't want to help Lucinda Sherwood, he only wanted to help those who needed it.

Directed to his cramped college office, Lucinda described what she had done since she left his course. Three months learning how to make filo parcels (whatever they were, Trevor had no idea) and creating a pretty table at some cordon bleu cookery school with a French name. Two years working for a public relations company in Knightsbridge, six months answering one telephone and twiddling her thumbs in a film company which was waiting for a Channel 4 budget to come through, and a spell as a waitress in Harvey Nichols' brasserie.

Everything about her said: the enemy. She had discarded the classless student uniform of jeans and casual sweaters, now there was no need for disguise. A pale V-necked grey tunic skimmed her hips, and a black linen jacket hung from her shoulders. He noticed the shoes, which had thick high heels and slim straps pulled tightly across her slim, ballerina ankles. She had pulled her light brown hair behind her ears, showing off her smooth unblemished skin covered with a light dusting of powder, and she was wearing a pair of tiny drop-pearl ear-rings with three rows of matching pearls slung casually around her long neck. The pearls looked expensive and real, although Trevor couldn't tell if they were fake, neither did he care. Most of all, he resented her leaning loose-limbed against his desk as though it was some worthless piece of nursery furniture.

Now it came back to him. He remembered her appearing occasionally at lectures, accompanied by loudly tittering girls. He wasn't aware that there was a type of girl he went for, but she certainly wasn't it. There's no doubt she would have been perfect for the screen, but he preferred loveable flaws, like the gap in Annie's front teeth, the scar on her knee. There was nothing loveable about Lucinda, but then she wasn't trying to be loveable.

'I can't bear it, Professor Watson. Can you imagine, working all day long with stupid people? Everyone assumes I'm some idiot from the Shires, reading *Tatler* and going crazy over a broken nail. Who are you seeing tonight? How many parties this week? Dinner, how absolutely super. Do tell me where . . . No-one talks about anything important, it's so awful. They all expect me to fill in time till I get engaged, just because I happen to be one of Lord Sherwood's daughters.'

She didn't have to remind him. Every time she walked into a room, a bar, a club, she would never be anonymous. Lucinda Sherwood, daughter of Lord Sherwood, chairman of the Independent Television Commission. As long as he was chairman, she could have any job she wanted and even when he eventually retired, the Sherwood name would guarantee her success.

'I'd have thought in this case, since you're obviously serious, you could take advantage of your connections. Lord Sherwood has far better contacts than I do.'

'Sure. If I want to be assistant to the assistant of some boring MD, read *Tatler* and go crazy over a broken nail. I want to work in drama. And I mean work.'

'Doesn't your father understand that?'

'He's useless. He's not the slightest bit interested in what I do. Anyway, why should I rely on my father? Why does everyone think just because he's got an important job in television that he can hand me out a job? His friends all sit on the boards of TV companies, they don't make films. Anyhow, I want to make it on my own.'

'It's always tough, making it on your own,' Trevor said, forcing a smile. 'But you mustn't give up.'

'I know it would be easier if I was ordinary, I mean ordinary kind of background, or had a whacky Liverpool accent or something like that.'

'Would it? It's hard for everyone, at the beginning.'

'Was it for you?'

'I wasn't competing in a multi-million industry, Lucinda.'

'And you were brilliant, everyone at college thought you were fantastic. I'm not sure if I'm brilliant, but I know I'm good.'

Trevor got up from behind his desk, and collected some papers together.

'I'm sorry. I'd really like to suggest something positive, but I don't see how I can help at the moment.'

'Wait, I've got something to show you.'

Lucinda opened the catch of her soft, capacious bag, and withdrew a beautifully bound folder which she placed on the desk.

'I've written an outline script for television. Would you show it to your wife? Just an opinion, that's all I want. I'm not asking for a job. Well, yes, I am. I'd give anything to work with Annie Griffiths. Anyone would.'

Trevor scribbled a note on his pad.

'I can't promise anything. I'll have a go. I'm afraid Annie gets hundreds of people asking the same thing. They're cutting back at the BBC.'

'I know. I do read.'

'Of course. You were taught by me.'

He thought she was going to say something more, but she didn't. Merely stared at him for a few seconds, her widely spaced, blue-grey eyes challenging his. Then she softened into a smile, which spread languidly across her face.

'How did your wife start off?'

'Annie was a secretary once.'

'That must have been a long time ago.'

Trevor gave a non-committal nod. For students, five years was a long time ago.

Anything over ten was a lifetime.

'I have to go in a moment. I'll take your script.'

Before he could pick it up, Lucinda snatched the folder from the desk and held it tightly against her chest.

'It's called *Grains of Evil*, don't forget. If it's not back in a month, I'll ring you. Annie can read it quickly, it's only a twenty-page outline. I don't want to begin a proper script if she thinks it's a hopeless idea. Can I call you at home? It's impossible to make calls where I am during the day.'

Reluctantly, he gave her his phone number. Then she handed him the script.

He missed lunch, read it through, turning the pages quickly at first, then lingering in fascination. After rereading it, he wondered if he had misjudged her. Then, recalling past experience, and the scanty volume of work she had produced at college, he began to suspect it had been written by another. It was too assured, too elegantly written. Within her circle, getting away with plagiarism would be considered amusing and clever. In the past, he had detected several essays containing paragraphs which seemed vaguely familiar, and which he had tracked down laboriously to establish their provenance. These days, he brought up the subject in tutorials, just to keep the cocky ones on their guard. Whose soul had she stolen? Which writer had she plundered? Or was it the plot of some steamy French novel plucked from Daddy's library?

It was a couple of days before he mentioned it to Annie.

'Some ex-student of mine has sent me yet another script. I had a quick flick through, it's just an outline. Could be interesting. See what you think. Parts of it aren't bad.'

Annie had a pile of manuscripts on the kitchen table and was used to scanning text while life went on around her. If the page took over, she'd leave the table and lie on the settee in the living room.

'I'll take a look.'

Half an hour later, she came back to the kitchen.

'Did you read it all, Trev?'

'Only skimmed, didn't really take it in. What's it about?'

'A young country vicar who's seduced by a harem of wild fourteen year olds in a neighbouring village. They're a gang from school, daughters of local farm labourers. Set in Fen country, East Anglia somewhere. They destroy him. Not my kind of thing, but it's got originality. Depends if she can write dialogue.'

Annie threw the script towards Trevor.

'Ken Russell would love it – precocious little girls, writhing sex in the cornfields. Was she any good?'

'Brighter than average, I suppose.'

'I'll think about it. It's certainly an interesting idea . . . different.'

A month later, almost to the day, Lucinda rang. He was in his study, some book review he had to write, but he couldn't remember which one. He did recall that voice. On the phone, she sounded older, warm but imperious, like the wife of an ambassador or an army commander.

'I was waiting for you to call me about *Grains of Evil*. I suppose you thought it was awful.'

Some girls from her background softened down the emphatic diction of the public school and affected a sloppy mid-cockney intonation like comedians adopting mid-Atlantic, but she didn't bother. And she didn't ask if it was a convenient moment, which it wasn't, but continued before he had time to interrupt.

'I showed the outline to a friend of mine whose father has a big agency in Hollywood. He said if I changed the location to somewhere like Wyoming, and rejigged the characters into mid-West, there'd be a chance. A chance of a feature, that is. Actually, he said it was a great idea, that I ought to write a proper script.'

'Good. Why don't you? So he thought it was commercial.'

'I was terribly excited at first. Then I realized it just had to be shot in England. And it's not really a big-screen movie, I conceived it for TV. Did you give it to your wife to read?'

'Yes.'

'Honestly?'

At last, she sounded fractionally unsure.

'I said I would.'

Trevor tried to recall what he had said, what Annie had said or even where he had put the script.

'And did she read it? Is she there? Can I talk to her, just for a few minutes?'

'Busy at the moment. I had a look at it, and was impressed, you've certainly a talent for describing atmosphere. Annie thought it showed originality.'

Trevor heard her gasp, and suddenly she became the young girl he remembered.

'Wow! Great! Did she discuss it with the Head of Drama? I know nothing goes ahead if just one person likes the idea. And that it takes time. But this is important to me, Professor Watson.'

There was an interruption. Annie must have been yelling that supper was getting cold. He never liked strangers to be party to his domestic arrangements so he put his hand over the receiver.

'Look, Lucinda, it's difficult to talk now.'

'Could you meet me next week then? I'll take you to lunch somewhere. A friend of mine has opened a super place in

63

Charlotte Street, not far from you. Proper Greek food, not boring old cabbage salad and kebabs.'

'The week after would be better. But it'll have to be brief. I don't go in for long lunches.'

She was sitting at the corner table, everything around was blue, azure blue and yellow, white cloths, beaming dark-skinned waitresses, handwoven abstract tapestries on the walls, modern design, unrelated to the scruffy Cypriot tavernas Trevor frequented with his mates. He'd arrived late, and knew from the loudly enunciated conversation bouncing off the glow-white walls and the white-scrolled metal chairs that it wasn't his kind of place. It had nothing to do with the Greece he knew and loved, the scraggy, hospitable islands he had visited with Annie over the years.

'I'm really pleased you could come, Professor Watson.'

He found himself shaking her hand, the firm academic handshake.

'Former students rarely take me to lunch.'

He allowed her to choose from the menu, he and Annie never fussed about food.

'I have to leave at two-thirty. Sorry about that, but as it's term time . . .'

'Lucky we don't have to clinch a deal,' she said.

This time her hair was pushed forward, soft waves like a tide on the turn rippling round her face in the warm conducted air. She was either beautiful or pretty, though Trevor could never define the difference. Annie said that pretty made you want to kiss, beautiful made you want to look. Now he was looking. Her movements were too studied, as though she had taken deportment and ballet classes. When she picked up her knife and fork he noticed how lightly her fingers rested on them.

'You must have thought I was frightfully pushy. It's inherited, Mummy's pushy too. But only for silly things like raising money for charity. She'll do anything to stop me making films. Her plans for me are quite different. I expect you can guess.'

'To find you a suitable husband, I assume.'

Trevor edged his chair in her direction, they had been sitting opposite one another at a round table, but he was unaware that he had done so.

'Dead right. And I've absolutely no intention of getting married. However it starts off, girls always end up taking

64

their husbands' names, even when they work. Can you imagine? Here's my script, courtesy of the copyrightholder, owner of the matrimonial property. I say, Mr Bloggs's wife has written something, what a clever girl! Why not read it if you've got a moment? Isn't it ghastly? Could you imagine me doing that?'

Trevor was manhandling a piece of hard-crusted roll, and replaced it on the plate.

'Lady Bloggs, surely?'

'No-one uses titles now,' said Lucinda. 'Except politicians.' Her look of contempt was transferred to the roll. 'The bread lets this place down.'

Her comment stopped him in his tracks, he was about to confirm his approval of her independence, his approval of all confident, determined women. But then he realized she was probably picking from the feminist menu what suited her at the time. In a few years, she would be married to some upper-class twit who made pop promotion videos, called himself a 'movie-maker' and talked to his estate manager at weekends. At this point, Lucinda began to remove her jacket and he had to check his impulse to slip the sleeves from her arms, and drape the beautifully tailored object carefully over the back of her chair. Unlike the members of Lucinda's family, he'd had to learn how to behave graciously with girls by observing Cary Grant and later Gérard Philipe at the University Film Society. Then, with the advent of feminism, he'd had to unlearn it all.

'You've been married for ages, haven't you?'

The waitress leaned forward, and carefully positioned a plate of marinated vegetables in the centre of the table.

'Shall we talk about the script? Don't you want to know what I thought?'

He wasn't expecting such a girlish laugh, though he must have heard it at tutorials.

'I bet you were embarrassed. Gratuitous eroticism. Five out of ten.'

'Not at all. It was essential . . . to the idea behind it. I did wonder, where the idea came from. There didn't seem to be any obvious influences.'

'It's a true story. It happened to my brother Tim. He's not a vicar, of course, I changed that. Now you'll be thinking, What a frightfully decadent family. I suppose we are.'

'The same could be said of Buñuel. And Proust. I don't see

65

that decadence precludes making an interesting statement.'

'I loved your lectures, Professor Watson. Everyone did. I wish I could be a student again.'

'Thanks for the compliment.'

'I never minded you being slightly left wing,' Lucinda said, crunching a sliver of cucumber. 'Is it true what they say, that you're still a Marxist?'

'You can make up your own mind about that. What do you think?'

She looked at him fearlessly, it no longer seemed like arrogance.

'I don't think labels matter any more. We're all in the same boat, aren't we?'

'You think so? I wouldn't say that.'

Lucinda ate her way delicately through the first course, but then her appetite appeared to return. As she compared her opinions with his – had he seen this, had he seen that? – she managed to devour a whole grilled fish, stripping it neatly from the bones. He knew that she was waiting for him to bring back the topic which was the reason for lunch, but he had no intention of making it easy. After she had half demolished the blueberry tart, she put down her fork although she had been consuming it with enthusiasm.

'Please tell me, Professor Watson. What did Annie really think? Will she be getting in touch? Has it got a chance? I'd rather know.'

He cleared his throat.

'Let's see. Well, she told me that the next eighteen months are pretty jam packed with ideas for development. But she was interested, Annie can recognize talent.'

'I know,' Lucinda said, as a blush crept up her cheek. 'I watch everything she does.'

'It might be an idea to show it to someone else. She did say it's not quite her kind of thing. Doesn't quite fit in with current plans. But she did think it was impressive.'

Lucinda looked down at her plate, and Trevor knew that she would leave the rest of the tart untouched. It often happened, with a student who failed to deliver. He knew what it was like. Expecting an A, hovering between B and C. There were only so many ways of couching a rejection. Like saying no to someone who fancied you but left you cold, it was hard choosing between brutal honesty and comforting banality. He watched her push her plate away and smile. A brave smile, a resigned smile, he couldn't tell.

'Never mind. I tried. I'll try someone else. I'm glad you liked it.'

'I did.'

He was mistaken, the rejection didn't seem to have affected her, or she wasn't showing it. Without warning, she started to elaborate her ideas, how she would transfer it to the screen.

'It's like an erotic *Lord of the Flies*. But I'm not interested in realism, I hated the film version of that. We saw it at school.'

'If there's anything else you'd like to show me, I'll be happy to see it,' Trevor said. Lucinda gave an embarrassed laugh.

'That's sweet of you, Professor Watson. There is something I'm working on, but it's not nearly ready yet. I know some people can turn out a play in six weeks, but I take ages. I couldn't bear you to read anything I wasn't satisfied with.'

'You're a perfectionist, I understand.'

'I suppose I am. Once I've started, I do finish things in the end. I couldn't imagine having a drawer full of uncompleted work, that would be dreadful.'

'Do you have to be so hard on yourself?'

'It's probably my father's influence,' she said, with a laugh. 'Daddy never wants to see anything unless it's finished. Once I heard him saying to my stepmother, "The trouble with Lucinda, she has no staying power." '

'So you haven't shown him your script, I assume?'

'Heavens, no.'

When the bill for lunch arrived, Lucinda insisted on paying. Trevor was faintly embarrassed. Was it because of his masculine pride, or because it emphasized the fact that she was used to the constant availability of money, and he wasn't? He wasn't sure, but he felt ill at ease. Outside the restaurant, a cab slowed down and stopped in front of them. He hadn't noticed her hailing it.

'Sorry I have to go, Lucinda. I did enjoy lunch,' he said, with a formality he didn't intend.

'As soon as I've finished the dialogue script, you'll be the first to know.'

He watched as she leaped happily into the taxi, settled into the back seat and smiled at him through the window as it drove away. Afterwards, he kept remembering fleeting images – the split second when the expression on her face swiftly changed, so that at one moment she was a very young girl, at another a mature woman, the relaxed grace as she got up from the lunch table, how she leaned forward intently, as though she was determined to discover what lay beneath his polite replies. It was as though he had suddenly viewed flash frames of a film he had seen before, whose images were familiar even though the plot was forgotten.

Unexpectedly, Annie brought up the subject of Lucinda a week or so later.

'I had a letter from that ex-student of yours. Wasn't that her outline script you showed me? *Grains of Evil*, interesting idea.'

'Oh yes. Lucinda.'

'She's after a job at the BBC, in television drama. Would I consider her. I hope that doesn't mean all your bloody ex-students think they're going to use me as a short-cut. Still, she does have some talent. Do you think I should see her?'

Trevor found it strange that Lucinda hadn't mentioned it at lunch, but she must have feared another rejection.

'Why not?'

'Was she one of the Sloaney girls who subsidized the others?'

The paragraph Trevor was reading began to dissolve into a blur.

'Quite pleasant, in spite of her disadvantages. Good when she made an effort, which was rare, if I remember rightly.'

'What does she look like?'

'Quite pretty, I suppose. In that upper-class conventional way.'

'Helen Bonham-Carterish?'

'Mm.'

There were other occasions when Annie said, 'What happened to that ex-student of yours, the Sherwood girl? You know, the one who wrote that rather good outline? Wasn't I meant to see her sometime?' but Trevor said she hadn't contacted him again.

5

TREVOR

Lucinda did contact him again, but not for several months. When he heard her voice on the phone for the second time, he was surprised that he could instantly summon up every detail of their lunch together, what she was wearing, the changing moods reflected in her eyes, her long, expressive fingers, even the place where they had been.

'The restaurant where we had lunch has been sold,' she remarked casually, as though they had regularly kept in touch. 'It's gone Californian.'

'That's a shame,' said Trevor.

'Next time, we'll go somewhere else. When you've had a chance to say what you think of my dialogue script. It's ready, and you'll be the first to read it! I haven't shown it to anyone, not yet. I'm so excited, I think *Grains of Evil* is really good, really strong. I can't wait for your reaction.'

'Send it to me at college, and I'll read it immediately. Then, if you like, I could phone you.'

'Would you? Great!'

'Where should I call you? At work or at home?'

'At home, then we can talk. Did I give you my number?'

'I don't think so.'

As Trevor hastily scribbled down her number, he felt as though he was receiving illicit information and pushed the scrap of paper under a book. Later, he would copy the number not in an obvious place like his diary or address book, but on the back page of his chequebook.

'Of course, you have to know the place where the story's set,' continued Lucinda. 'Do you know East Anglia?'

'I know Cambridge,' said Trevor.

'That's not East Anglia. Haven't you been to the fen country, all those dykes and great stretches of flat fields and shrieking birds?'

'I don't think so.'

'You must come, you absolutely must. You'd love it, I know you would. It's bleak and wild, incredibly atmospheric. And the skies are fabulous. Why don't we drive out there?'

'I really haven't a moment,' replied Trevor, quickly. 'It's impossible in term time.'

'It won't take long. We can go there and back in an afternoon. I can take time off from work, they won't even notice. Just say when you can manage. But you have to see the landscape, you have to sense what inspired me. I can't explain, but I know it's important for you to see it. Do you understand?'

'Not altogether. Let me think about it. I'll have to consult my diary,' said Trevor, fearing that he had been too abrupt.

'How about next week sometime? I'll send you the script today, you'll have read it by then.'

Lucinda sounded so cheerfully determined, that it was churlish to refuse. When they had fixed a day and time, Trevor added, 'As long as I'm back by seven.'

'I promise. I do know how busy you are. Thank you, Professor Watson. I can't tell you what this means.'

'You're script had better be good,' he said, teasingly. When he had put down the phone, he had to reassure himself that it was not the first time he had gone on location with students. There was nothing wrong, he decided, in looking forward to getting out of London for a few hours.

Trevor had deliberately chosen to meet Lucinda in the follow-ing week at a time when Annie would be away on location, but it wouldn't have made any difference if she had been at her office in White City. As she was in the middle of shooting *Streetcred*, her latest series for the BBC, he saw no reason to tell her of his plans. When Annie was filming, she would scarcely have noticed if London had been hit by an earthquake. But the moment she had finished, he would come back into her life again. He was used to it by now, the weeks when they only kept briefly in touch, because it didn't seem like absence.

The evening before he was due to go to East Anglia, Annie developed a sudden, streaming cold. She was huddled up in bed, nose in a box of tissues, and a battery of remedies which had not the slightest effect.

'Are you sure I can't get you anything? Need more aspirin?'

Annie was propped up against a pile of crumpled pillows, trying to plan out a script through tearful eyes, a wodge of tissues held against her mouth, nose rough and red like a new brick wall.

'Nope.' She turned on her side. 'Could you sleep in the spare room tonight?'

'I don't mind, darling.'

'I do. This is meant to be spring. I haven't had a thing all winter. Why do I get a cold in April? I'm hot, sweaty, foul and ugly. And the sheets are wringing wet. I hope you don't get the bloody thing.'

'I rarely do,' Trevor said, feeling a slight prickling in his nose, the result of empathy. 'I've opened a tin of soup.'

'All right, love. I'll have some.'

Trevor hurried down to the kitchen, where a small blackened saucepan was bubbling on the stove. While attempting to tip some of its contents into a bowl, Trevor misjudged, and some scalding liquid poured over his hand. Holding it under the cold tap, he stared at the angry red flesh and wondered whether burns should be bandaged or not. Deciding that Annie's need for hot soup took precedence, he quickly wrapped his smarting hand in a tea-towel and returned to the bedroom, clutching a tray. Annie noticed immediately.

'What have you done?'

'It's nothing, a slight burn. I should have used a larger saucepan.'

'There's some ointment in the bathroom cabinet. God, Trevor, why do you have to be so incredibly clumsy?'

'Self-flagellation. So I can feel bad too.'

'One's enough,' replied Annie. 'And I'd like a spoon. And some bread.'

Patients were never saintly. Downstairs to the kitchen again. Then upstairs to the bedroom. She demanded butter, hard in the fridge, had to be melted. Down, then up again. No wonder women were always going backwards and forwards, or making boomerang circles, ending up in the same place.

'Can I sit down now?' asked Trevor, pulling a stool from under Annie's pine dressing table. 'I think you should stay in bed tomorrow.'

'Can't,' sniffed Annie. 'Got to be in Calais.'

'Must you, darling? Is it essential?'

71

There was a tricky scene in Calais with some violent football supporters. One of the most powerful scenes in the series.

'I must be there. If I'm not, there'll be a disaster. The director can't handle crowd scenes. Two days with an overnight should do it. Then I'll be back.'

His heart missed a beat. Two whole days. Two whole days, donated by Annie. Two days when he would be alone to . . . the shame of it. Why was he thinking like this?

'I don't think you should go.'

'Why?' she said crossly.

'No point, when you're feeling like death.'

'I won't tomorrow. Christ, it's only a cold. What's come over you?'

'You'll pass on your bug to the whole cast. Think about that.'

'I don't give a damn. Besides, it's all exteriors. Healthy outdoors. I don't have a budget for colds, bad periods or lovers' quarrels, let alone "I can't get into it today". Stuff it. I pay for professionals. And if that bitch Susie turns up late again, I'm sending her home. If this episode isn't in the can by Thursday . . .'

Annie refused to finish the soup and settled back onto the pile of pillows, red-lidded, red-nosed, hair in sticky strands straggling over her forehead, swollen cheeks flushed with fever. Trevor felt her brow, and was relieved. It was still hot. So sorry, Lucinda. I'll have to stay at home. Annie's got a cold, no, flu. Awful virus going around. Annie's sick, I'm calling the doctor. Hardly ever ill. Just one of those things. You could take some stills, send them to me, then we could talk again. Difficult to make another time this term, exams coming up, always some student takes it badly. Remember?

Having checked that Annie was asleep, Trevor hovered around the phone, picked it up and, began to punch out Lucinda's number. The answering voice sounded just like hers.

'Lucinda?'

'Who's that?'

'A friend.'

'Lucy's out. Actually she's hardly ever in. Best thing is to call early tomorrow. She might be here then. Bye.'

How old would she have been? Twenty-five, twenty-six, Trevor guessed. The best age, according to Rick. By then, he said, they knew what it was about, and didn't mistake the cramp heralding orgasm for a desire to piss, could let go like the River

Spey in autumn's rush, rolling over you, rolling under you, dogs in hay, couldn't get enough of it. At her age, there'd be someone she liked doing it with, long, lanky and exuding youthful sexuality, and maybe a couple more. If he betrayed by a smallest gesture what was tormenting him, she'd laugh. Or worse still, dismiss him with the weapon they all possessed and used like a scalpel, scorn. Come on, Trevor. I'm not that desperate for a lay. Not that he would dream of using the word (in his youth, only Henry Miller had lays) but young people were more brutal with language.

Lucinda hadn't replied to the message he left on her answerphone, and Trevor assumed that he would have the day to himself. Early that morning, Annie had insisted on leaving. Having checked that her overnight bag had gone, Trevor decided to remain in his study, instead of going into college. Suppose Lucinda had failed to get his message? He took down one book after another from his shelves, unable to concentrate. At last, hearing an insistent series of toots in the street below, he opened his window. There she was, double-parked brazenly just outside his front gate in an open-topped car, waving at him, wearing a large straw hat fastened across her chin with a chiffon scarf. Trevor tore down the stairs, then halted suddenly by the front door, and walked slowly down the path towards her.

'Hi. Didn't you get my message?'

'No, I didn't.'

'I said it was unlikely I'd have time to—'

'But you are coming? I've been away. Sorry about that.'

'I really should stay. I'm supposed to be finishing some work.'

'If you hadn't liked my script, I'd have cancelled. But you did, you did! You can't imagine what it was like, waiting till you rang. God, I was going crazy. I almost called you several times. You did mean what you said?'

'Of course I did.'

'We can take my car, it's fast, it'll only take an hour and a half to get there.'

Lucinda jumped out of her black convertible BMW and walked round to open the passenger door. Trevor glanced back at the house, still undecided, then turned to observe her. She was wearing skin-tight jeans and a cropped T-shirt which revealed a thin band of creamy flesh marking her slim waist.

'We'll go in your car, Professor Watson. If you'd rather, that is.'

'I don't have a car.'

'Really? How on earth do you manage?'

'Just a moment, I've forgotten my briefcase.'

Trevor ran into the house, checked that the windows were locked, collected the briefcase and climbed into the passenger seat. He could work later, when the unusually warm sun had disappeared. Annie was always saying he spent too much time indoors.

'I hadn't a clue how to get here, that's why I was late. Where exactly are we? Anywhere near Brixton?' asked Lucinda, as she revved the engine.

'Brixton is south-east. This is north-west. Kentish town, suburb of Hampstead, not to be confused with Hampstead Garden Suburb. Do all your friends live in Chelsea?'

'Mostly. How does one get to the A1? There's a road atlas in the back somewhere.'

Trevor was insensitive to the way people handled cars, but he was aware that Lucinda drove differently, unlike Annie's spurts and lunges, and she didn't utter comments like 'What the fuck does he think he's doing?' or peer round in a traffic jam. Years of sitting next to Annie at the wheel had made him impervious to the rights and wrongs of propelling a machine from A to B, but it was obvious that Lucinda would never have owned a car that failed to start in the morning.

'Turn right, then left.'

'I said I'd drop in on some friends for lunch, it's on the way.'

'Fine.'

Navigating was an activity like late-night shopping in Oxford Street or doing crossword puzzles, one of the many antidotes to lechery, and Trevor found himself checking his watch, timing his return. He began to have second thoughts about the opening of his latest piece for the *Guardian*. Perhaps it was too ponderous. Annie would read it over, she was good at making his style more approachable, less academic.

'You can drive if you want,' said Lucinda, as they drew into a petrol station.

'It's not something I particularly enjoy. But if you're fed up.'

'Not at all.'

It was in the middle of deciding whether they should take a B road to avoid traffic congestion, that he found himself studying her profile. There was a tiny bump on her nose which he hadn't noticed before, even though he knew every feature, every angle of his favourite actresses. His screen heroine, conjured up in the study of movie stills and stop-frame images, was a soft-edged Antonioni girl, Monica Vitti rather than the chiselled features of Catherine Deneuve. If Deneuve had been born in the Shires, she would have resembled Lucinda.

'How old do you think Manfred is?' Lucinda asked.

'Manfred?'

'My hero.'

'Yes, your hero.'

It was why they had come, after all, to discover his landscape. Then he added, 'It's set in the present. Why have a name like that?'

'Because it means hero in old English. I looked it up.'

'I wouldn't call him Manfred, myself, not if it's for television.'

'You think it sounds pretentious?'

'A little.'

'Then I'll change it. What should I call him?'

'Depends how old he is.'

'I didn't say in the script. But he should be quite old. About forty.'

Trevor winced.

'Why not make him fifty? Very old. Almost as old as me.'

'I don't think of you as old, Professor Watson. Are you worried about it?'

'I'm worried about not having original ideas any more. Becoming a repetitious old bore.'

'What's wrong with repetition? We say a lot of the same things every day. And think how many times people have sex in a lifetime. That's not boring, is it?'

'Sometimes.'

Trevor kept his eyes on the map. He hoped she was not about to embark on an amorous retrospective, like Kate after one glass too many. He didn't want her to have times to remember, not while he was sitting next to her. They might possibly meet again, have significant meetings, without the burden of expressing their significance. He might even change her life, become her guru, but he would remain detached. The reason he was with her at this moment, was straightforward. He admired her talent. There was no limit to the generosity of

75

a teacher when confronted by evidence of superior ability. It was what had first drawn him to Annie, her eager intelligence.

The crunch of gravel under the tyres halted Trevor's reflections and he looked up as they turned into a narrow drive, bounded by wired fences, with fields on either side.

'We won't stay long, but they'll give us lunch,' said Lucinda, as she drove towards a large red-brick farmhouse surrounded by sharp-edged modern barns, with neatly ranged tractors in the yard. Jersey cows with muddy rumps and glassy eyes turned their necks to observe their arrival, pressing against red-painted pens. A tall woman stood by the porch and waved.

'That's Jemima. She's frightfully rich, but you'd never guess. Her father was John Huntley.'

'And what did he do?' asked Trevor.

'Huntley car tyres,' replied Lucinda, as though he ought to have known.

From the moment they were introduced, Jemima carried on the kind of non-stop chatter which Trevor usually managed to avoid. He supposed that this bony woman with long wiry grey hair, and a sleeveless padded jacket incongruously worn over a tailored woollen dress, had been imprisoned in the country as a punishment for being rich. Within a few minutes, she was reminiscing about her golden days in Chelsea, what super fun they'd all had. She said it was a long time since anyone clever had visited them, but was disappointed to hear that Trevor was a professor of media and not history. She adored history and wished she had studied archeology. They drank sherry in the drawing room, whilst Jemima described the restoration of the local church, shouted at the various children to take off their wellingtons, but tolerated the two golden retrievers sprawled across the only unbroken sofa.

Over lunch, served in the kitchen, her husband Henry carved a side of cold beef into steak-sized cuts. After they had eaten, he left the children to eat a sticky pudding, and dragged Trevor off so that he could give his opinion of a Tudor oil painting in the hall, a stiff portrait of an unpleasant fat-jowled squire in a ruff. Through the open door of a downstairs room, Trevor couldn't help overhearing a conversation between Jemima and Lucinda. 'Is he your latest, dear?'

'Honestly. You must be joking. I told you, he was my professor at college.'

'I didn't really imagine he was . . . that you were . . . well, one has to ask, doesn't one?'

Trevor tried to maintain an appreciative gaze, as Henry ran through a list of possible artists who might have painted his ancestor. It was as though Jemima had given his face a hard, well-aimed slap. Did she assume that he was the kind of man to seduce young girls? Then he felt an irrational pang of regret that Lucinda was able to dismiss him so lightly.

As they were leaving, Jemima said goodbye to Trevor as though she meant it, wishing him no ill-will but making it clear that she had no desire to see him again. Lucinda had mentioned over coffee that he lectured about film and television, and Jemima was horrified to discover that you could get a college degree in something she had banned from the house. She never did know precisely what Lucinda had been studying, didn't have a clue about that kind of thing, one never thought to ask.

'We must drop in on you when we're in town. The Chelsea Flower Show, Henry's promised to take me even though he hates crowds. He's such a darling. Why don't you come along with us?'

'Love to.'

Since Trevor was not included in the invitation, he began to stroll round the side of the house, towards Lucinda's car which was parked in the yard.

'Sweet people,' she remarked, as they drove away. Trevor began to long for Annie's bitchy, pointed assessments of intrusive meetings she wished to avoid.

'How far now?' he remarked.

'Oh, it's quite near. That's why I dropped in on Henry and Jemima.'

'I thought you were dying to see them.'

'Hardly. They're Mummy's friends not mine. Didn't you like them?'

'Perfectly pleasant.'

'When he was fifteen, my brother Tim had Jemima in the school holidays. They had great fun, did it all over the house, every day a different room. She told Henry she was helping him with his O level geography.'

'She must have been desperate,' said Trevor.

'Henry considered fucking more than once a month was unnatural even when he was young. Quite a lot of men do. Does that surprise you?'

He was surprised that she had used 'fuck' so casually, but that was another indication of generation. Sex had lost its mystery for them. Then he became aware of her thighs, rising as she changed gear. She was leaning back in her seat, her legs stretched apart, the tight jeans etching the divide of her crotch.

'Where I come from, we don't talk about sex. Or rather we didn't. It was quite different then, another world. So I wouldn't know.'

'You always see differences, don't you, Professor Watson? Whereas I see similarities.'

He felt rebuked, then relieved, as though she was mapping out a correct distance between them. Soon they stopped at the end of a row of ochre-washed cottages, and Lucinda leaped out of the car and ran swiftly down the road with long, graceful, rhythmic strides as though she might take off, like a heron winging its way towards a surfacing fish. He followed her, refusing to run, strolling along the curb until the road swung round and he found himself in front of a hedge which Lucinda identified as hazel.

'Jaspar's house. That's what I've decided to call him. Isn't it perfect? Isn't it just how you imagined it? I found it when I was driving past. It used to be a rectory and I didn't even know. The owners left a year ago, couldn't sell it. Come on, let's go in. I've kept a copy of the key.'

Trevor could appreciate its filmic quality, the squat yellow-brick rectangle set on a slight hillock, with bushes set in two half moons to either side. Stray crimson-edged trumpets with wind-flattened, creamy petals were pushing their heads above the long grass and weeds of the overgrown beds, the only splashes of colour.

'Are those flowers wild?' he asked.

'The narcissi?'

'Ah. That's what they are. I think we've got some of those in our garden.'

Lucinda picked one and began to thread it through the lapel of his tweed jacket.

'What did you say it was?'

'A narcissus. You must know that.'

'I can't tell one flower from another. It's a kind of botanical dyslexia. I suppose if Annie was interested in gardening, I might have—'

78

'Something you don't know about. Now I can teach you something.'

They smiled at one another, and Lucinda stood in front of him, fingering the trumpet. 'People don't pick flowers any more. Remember where Jaspar picks some flowers for one of the girls in the cottages and she laughs at him? She's going to say, "If you want to give me a present, I like scent. Proper scent. Flowers die. That don't." '

As they went inside, Trevor shivered, enveloped by damp and the fungal odour of an uninhabited house. He could see nothing extraordinary, except for a few unvalued possessions which had been left behind for a future occupant, broken chairs, a stained print of Gainsborough's *Blue Boy* in a plastic frame and mud-stained newspapers scattered over a threadbare carpet. Lucinda was gazing round the living room, moving over to different corners of the room, tilting and turning her head like a roving camera. Then she took out a small notebook from her pocket.

'What kind of furniture would he have? I think it would be Edwardian, rather ugly. Do you agree?'

Beginning to resent this tedious character whom he had never met, and who was effectively protecting Lucinda like an unseen minder, Trevor showed his irritation.

'Don't you think this is the kind of thing to do later, if you get something upfront to start shooting?'

'Hold this, please.'

She passed him the end of a metal tape-measure and criss-crossed the room, noting down the measurements she needed.

'I'll have to be getting back before long,' he said, listening to a sudden shower flattening itself against the locked windows. 'If it's like this in Calais, Annie will be cursing.'

He stayed where he was and heard her hurriedly ascending the uncarpeted stairs.

'Do come up,' she shouted. 'You must see this view.'

A featureless field stretched behind the house, edged by a straggling windbreak. Observing it from above merely allowed him the view of a narrow road in the distance. Lucinda came behind him, while he was looking out, then reached across to push up the window.

'This one should open, the sash isn't too rotten,' she said, grunting as she strained against the frame. Her brief top had sprung up to just below her breasts, revealing a wide band of inviting, taut skin above the tight belt of her jeans. Trevor instinctively slipped his hands around the exposed flesh, then regretted it, expecting her to flinch away.

'Let me try.'

But she didn't move. If she had, it might never have happened. He turned her head towards him and pulled her body against his. As she returned his first, unplanned passionate kiss, he could feel her trembling, unexpectedly limp and warm, yielding as he stroked down her back, pressing her buttocks. Then she tossed her head, so that her fine hair fell across her face, her veiled bright eyes fixed on his. Gently pushing back the silken strands, he kissed her brow, blood racing, panic taking over, seeing the future in a flash like a drowning man. No, it was impossible, he didn't want it, but he wanted her.

'This isn't sensible,' he said with a sigh, resting his hands on her shoulders. 'But you make me forget everything.'

'I've noticed,' Lucinda replied gaily, her eyes sparkling. 'But don't go away and say I seduced you. It didn't happen like that. I didn't think you were interested.'

'Christ, Lucinda. How could I not be?'

He squeezed her so tightly, that she gasped. Releasing his grip, Trevor slipped one hand between her legs, and held it there in the heat of her crotch.

'You're far too desirable. What have you done to me?'

Tilting back her head, Lucinda drew her lips into a pout, then she extracted his hand from between her thighs.

'I don't try to be.'

'But you can't help it.'

Her hands were round his neck, she was almost the same height, it was a strange sensation having a woman looking directly at him in flat heels.

'Do I call you Trevor?'

'Why not?'

'Is that what Annie calls you?'

'Trevor is fine.'

Trevor released himself from their embrace, and wandered over to the half-open window. Sticking his head through the opening, he breathed in the muggy spring air and was overcome with melancholy. Lucinda did it so gracefully, reminding him of his wife without implying that there was anything sordid in what they had just done, that he should have been grateful. But he wasn't. He assumed it was her way of conveying that she found him attractive (otherwise she wouldn't have allowed him to kiss her) but didn't want to go any further. After all, he would be about the same age as her father. Trevor planted his hands firmly in his pocket, and was surprised when Lucinda came up to him, and slipped her fingers round his, still in his pocket.

'You've got to see the rest of the house, Trevor. One more room. When you've given your opinion, which I'm at liberty to ignore, we'll go.'

She sounded efficient, insistent, determined to fulfil the schedule she had set herself as she pulled him after her and opened a thin wooden door. Trevor found himself staring at a narrow, painted metal bed abandoned in a room with fading pink elephants bounding across the tattered wallpaper.

'I'm going to keep this room just as it is,' she said, sweeping her hand across a loosened patch. 'There's always one room in a house which the owner leaves, meaning to redecorate one day, and never does. And it represents Jaspar's lost childhood.'

Although she seemed to be seeking a sign from Trevor that he agreed, or approved, he gave a brief glance at the ceiling, festooned with blackened cobwebs, then sat on the bed, which gave a metallic croak beneath him.

'I might keep that, too,' she continued. 'The sound of broken springs, I think it's appropriate. Don't you?'

'I think we should talk,' replied Trevor. 'We can't just pretend nothing has happened. Come and sit beside me.'

Lucinda leaned against the cracked paint of the bedhead, and stroked his head.

'It was just a kiss. A breathtaking kiss.'

'Come closer, Lucinda. I can't say what I have to say without touching you.'

She came and sat on his lap and he cradled her in his arms, hoping that the affection he felt would drive out the urgency of lust, he would think of her as a child, a child who had to be refused.

'I'd rather say this, however painful. Do you mind? I am married, happily married. I can't pretend I'm not.'

'Oh, Trevor! I know Annie's wonderful. I'm sure your marriage is great. There's no way I'd want to take you away from her. But I do so want to be friends. Can't you accept friendship? That's all I want. I'm not a kid, you know. And I don't dream of a white wedding in Brompton Oratory followed

81

by a two-up two-down in Fulham, thank you very much.'

The thoughts rushing in Trevor's head resolved themselves into platitude.

'It's so bloody hard.'

Lucinda giggled and Trevor felt himself blushing. Rick would have had her by now, the afternoon shaft, feelings denied and translated into physical tactics, quick relief from taunting desires, he didn't want that, she wasn't like that.

'Listen, Lucinda. I don't want to make you unhappy. Or to make you hate me. It would be so unfair. What could I offer you? An occasional afternoon, a guilty evening out somewhere discreet when Annie's away. I couldn't ask you to accept that.' Trevor paused, he didn't really want her to answer. 'Besides. I can't allow myself to fall in love with you.'

Lucinda disengaged herself and tugged down her T-shirt.

'I wouldn't let you. Isn't it against the rules? Your rules.'

'What are yours?'

'Why don't you find out if I have any?'

He noticed her shivering, even though an orangey, late-afternoon sun, glowing through the rain clouds, was attempting to penetrate the grimy windowpanes.

'I'm going to kiss you again. Just once.'

She lay back on the bed and dropped her head back, and it seemed that the best way to fulfil his mission was to lie on top of her. And then he needed to stroke down her thighs, to feel inside her legs, slightly parted now. She arched her back, and he unzipped her jeans, pulled them down just far enough. Knowing she wanted him, made him forget reason. Afterwards he would try to think which mad moment impelled him to go against his better judgement, to give her what he had tried to keep for the woman he loved. It wasn't as though it was a life-time commitment, that was obvious.

As they drove away from the house, Trevor sat in the car with folded arms, leaning against the passenger window, trying not to steal a glance at the rise and fall of Lucinda's thighs when she pressed the brakes. They said little, but she asked if he minded some music. He smiled and nodded. The sound of a flute, Debussy he guessed, lulled his thoughts for a while until he forced himself to turn them back to his article. When he arrived home, he would write the final paragraph.

'What are you thinking, Trevor?' she asked.

'How lovely you are,' he answered, with a laugh. He was glad she didn't ask him when they would meet again. As they neared Kentish Town, he asked her to drop him in the high street, so that he could walk back home through the rain, allowing it to wash away her kisses.

When he pushed open the front door, he half expected to see Annie there. Already, he was imagining the confrontation. 'Where have you been? I thought you were working at home.' He even called her name, but there was no answer. The kitchen was deserted, dirty plates piled up haphazardly, and an old message was still scrawled on the board – *Bread in fridge, no milk, we need eggs. Luv Annie.* He couldn't understand why he had done it. He rubbed off the message and wrote, *Darling Annie – love you – miss you,* then wiped it clean again.

Trevor ran a hot bath, soaked away the smell of his betrayal, washed his hair and suddenly had an irrepressible urge for a cigarette, although he had given up ten years ago. He retrieved an old packet which Rick had left behind once in his smoking days, and which he had kept at the back of a drawer in his desk, extracted an untipped cigarette and realized there was nothing to light it with. Forced to ignite his stale weed from the cooker, he panicked. Annie would smell it, even a day later. He rushed out through the french windows then dragged violently at the cigarette, standing in the darkness, amongst the broken bricks and nettles in the garden, a raincoat pulled around him, reeling with disgust at the dry, brackish taste yet trying to keep it alight in the stinging rain. When he came back in, he cleaned his teeth for the second time. The following morning he rang Lucinda, his brain addled from sleeplessness but he knew he had to do it.

'Lucinda, it was the most wonderful day. You're a beautiful girl. If I was twenty years younger, I'd have run away with you, done anything you wanted. But I don't want to spoil things, it's not right. Why should you have to go through a sordid affair with a happily married man? You deserve far better than that.'

'You don't want to see me again?'

'It's better that way, better to decide now than to be miserable later.'

'Not at all? Never? Not even as friends?' Lucinda said.

Trevor swallowed, trying to push away his guilt.

'No. I don't think we should.'

In the silence which followed, he could imagine her

83

stiffening, pulling herself back from any display of emotion. Her eyes would be dry, she might even be angry with him, but Lucinda wouldn't make a fuss. No-one did, not from her background. The differences between them were too great. After the physical attraction had passed, what would remain? He tried to soften the blow.

'It's better for both of us not to meet. Not for the time being, anyway.'

'It's a shame. We had a great time. It wasn't just having sex. I thought it was more than that, I thought you liked being with me. We don't have to have to go to bed. But can't we be friends? Can't we go to the cinema or something? You must have girlfriends like that, don't you?'

'Not really.'

'Why not try it? I promise I won't ask anything more. I'd just be glad to see you. Is that wrong?'

'Of course it isn't. I don't want to muck up your life, I don't want you to resent me, Lucinda. It's not fair on you. You should be going out with ardent young men, one day you'll want to get married, have children—'

'I don't think like that. You're making me into something I'm not. Just because we've seen each other naked, why does that change everything? I don't understand you, Trevor. I never guessed you'd be like this, really. After all you said about women being free now, about not having the restrictions that your generation had, about how we should take our freedom and make new relationships, and here you are sounding like Mummy wittering on about family obligations.'

'I know, I know.'

'You should be ashamed. What about your radical views? Were they all a cover so you'd get our sympathy? So we'd think you were one of us? I can't bear it. If you only knew how we all admired you, wanted to be like you. We thought you were so different from all those other bores. I wish I'd never gone to University. I wish I'd gone to work for some cruddy film company in Soho.'

There was a catch in her voice, and then he heard her give a sigh.

'Lucinda, please.'

'Sorry. I can't help it. I shouldn't have said that.'

'No, you're right. You're right. But you're asking me to be Superman. Didn't Marx cheat on his wife? And Freud?

84

And don't you think they felt ashamed, hated themselves?'

'So there's no point.'

'I didn't say that. I'm just trying to explain, that it's not easy for me. I love Annie and I don't have the advantage of a liberated family.'

'Fuck that.'

He knew he had hurt her, but Lucinda put down the phone on him, and he was unable to reach her until several days later. This time, he would take her to lunch and they could talk more calmly. He would gently suggest that the gap between them was too wide. Sooner or later, they would have bitter disagreements, throw up insults, hurt one another, say what they would later regret. The barrier of class and language couldn't be ignored, let alone the chasm of years between them. He could see no future, and Lucinda needed a future.

At the last minute, Lucinda called to say she couldn't make lunch. Could they meet later for a drink? As they sat outside in the garden of a Chelsea pub, there was only one moment when she left to find him a beer, that he stopped looking at her. On a neighbouring bench, Trevor observed a man around his own age, older perhaps, clasping the hand of a young girl. They looked easy in one another's company, no-one was staring as though they were freaks. Then she gave him a playful kiss. Suddenly reasured, Trevor lost his desire to make this their final meeting. They were quite near Lucinda's house, and she might invite him back.

What was the point in denying it? She took him straight to the bedroom, and within seconds they were naked, sprawling across her high double bed, rolling onto the carpeted floor, laughing, kissing, breathless . . . When they were finally exhausted, Lucinda whispered that what she felt for him was more powerful, more intense than anything she had ever known.

'It's hard for me to admit, but I feel the same,' Trevor said. 'I can't imagine being without you now.'

They met again in April, more often in May and June, and almost every day in July when Annie was away, catching up on good weather to reshoot some scenes for *Streetcred*. Trevor visited Lucinda's house in Chelsea, grew used to seeing the chintzy furniture, the velvet green curtains, the family portraits on the walls and no longer cared when he put a hot cup of chocolate, which she made specially for him, on the antique bedside table. Then, towards the end of August, he was dreading having to tell her, but he knew he had to.

Lucinda was in the kitchen, unpacking the food they'd hastily picked up from Safeway's in the King's Road, which she had chosen. Baby avocados and Gravadlax, which he'd never had before. It was the only time she ate properly at home, she said, after they'd had sex. Made love, but she wouldn't say that.

'Darling, I'm going away in a couple of weeks.'

'Why? Where?'

'I'm going to Greece, we always do.'

'You and Annie?'

'Me and Annie, Rick and Bryonie, Kate and Dally, her child. It'll only be for a couple of weeks.'

'Oh.'

'I don't want to go, darling. But it happens every year, I'm afraid.'

'I wish I could go. Just with you.'

'You wouldn't like it. It's always far too hot, very unsexy. We don't do anything, except go to the same tavernas, walk along the beach, swim, just a basic holiday. Rick will drink too much. Kate will insist on her child keeping the same hours as we do. Annie will spend most of the day swimming or flopped out on the beach. But she likes Greece, I can't persuade her to go anywhere else.'

'Why do you go, if you don't want to?'

'Habit, I suppose.'

'God, I hope I'm not becoming a habit.'

Trevor pushed his hand down her shirt, while she was fanning out slices of avocado on a Wedgwood plate.

'I feel so different with you, I want to be with you, to share everything with you. We can't continue like this.'

'Do you mean it?'

He pressed her lips to his, then pushed his tongue down into her mouth, the wide mouth which opened to his touch, and kissed her until he felt her heaving for breath. Only then did he slowly withdraw his tongue, clasping her tightly to him.

'Just give me time, my sweet. But I know I can't keep going back to that house, pretending that nothing has changed.'

She made no reply, but started tearing the salmon into thin strips, which she inserted prettily around the avocado slices. He loved watching her.

'When I come back . . .'

'When, Trevor?'

'When I come back, we'll decide what to do. I know I have to tell Annie.'

'What if she can't cope? What if she tries to kill herself? Mummy tried to, when Daddy told her he wanted to marry Imogen, she tried to drown herself in the lake. Tim saw her when he was walking the dogs, and pulled her out. It was so awful.'

'Why didn't you tell me before?'

'It's not something we talk about. Mummy was in a terrible state. Please, Trevor. Let's stay as we are.'

'Nothing awful will happen. I promise. I think Annie will understand.'

Early in October, a letter arrived for Lucinda at her house in Danvers Street.

> *My darling, darling Lucinda.*
> *How can I tell you this? I thought of you every day, every night, all I wanted to do was to kill time, longing to return to England, longing to see you again. I know in my heart we should be together without having to conceal our love – but, oh God, I hate writing this – it just can't be. Annie has heard that they'd like her to be the Controller of Drama at Intertel. She can't decide whether she should take the job, desperately needs my support. Frankly, she's in rather a state, and I know I couldn't tell her now. I'll always love you. T.*

Trevor didn't expect her to reply, not immediately. When she had recovered, she would probably give him a call. He just wanted to hear her say that she understood, that she wouldn't hate him for what he had done. But there was silence. For several weeks afterwards, every time Trevor went into college, he would ask if she had left a message, scour the letters in his tray. He knew he couldn't contact her, however strong his desire to hear her voice. He had done the right thing, but he never realized it would be so painful, never realized the power she had to invade his thoughts. Then, when Annie finally decided to begin a new phase in her career, full of high spirits and excitement for her future at Intertel, Lucinda's image gradually faded away.

87

6

TREVOR

Trevor had already placed the order for tea when Lucinda walked through the doors of the Russell Hotel. He tried not to stare at her, but he had instantly registered the small changes which had happened since they last met. It came as a shock that Lucinda's face was now framed by a straight curtain of fine blond hair. Before, it had been soft brown. Her eyes looked bluer, too, but it could have been the effect of the colour thrown upwards by the short, powder-blue scoop-necked dress hugging her thighs. The suede boots she wore were exactly the same tone of blue. They were both trying to act as though they were some kind of business associates, like the men around them shuffling through papers, opening and shutting briefcases.

'You do realize, you could be working for Annie?'

'Of course. That's why I applied.'

'You're not worried?'

'Why should I be? You and me, that was ages ago. It just happened. It must have happened before with other girls.'

'You know it didn't.'

'I don't mind either way. You're a very attractive man.'

He couldn't say it. I don't want Annie to know. Whatever you do, make sure you never tell her. It would sound despicable.

'Mind you, I'm not sure if Intertel is the right place for you.'

'Why do you say that?'

'Television usually ends by destroying creativity. In the old days, it was different. People were allowed to grow, to find their feet. Now, if you don't produce the goods, they throw you out.'

'If I get the job and don't like it, I'll be the one to leave,' Lucinda replied. 'But at least they won't be able to say I got in because of my father. He thinks working in TV is a last-ditch option.'

'Is that why he's Chairman of the ITC?' said Trevor, more sharply than he intended. She hadn't reminded him until now of her connection, and he had appreciated her tact.

'At least he tries. And anyway, he only says that in private.'

'Sorry if I offended you, Lucinda. I've never met him. I'm sure he's a perfectly decent man.'

'Maybe one day you will,' she said, brightly. 'Daddy always likes to know what the opposition's thinking.'

They both laughed, as though they were sharing a private joke. Lucinda had a way of dismissing prickly subjects with cheerful abandon.

'These sandwiches are dry. Horrid sliced bread. Bet it was frozen.'

'You don't have to eat them.'

'That's not the point, Trevor.'

He smiled, remembering how she studied everything, everything she took into her mouth. She replaced the half-bitten sandwich on the plate, and took up a wodge of chocolate cake.

'This looks better. At least it's moist. Have some.'

'No thanks.'

'Of course. You only like chocolate in mugs. Preferably in bed. Or have you changed?'

'I work harder than I used to.'

Lucinda leaned forward, forcing him to look into the grey-blue eyes he was trying to avoid.

'Few more tiny wrinkles.'

'I was thinking, perhaps you might talk about your script. In the interview.'

'Yes, yes. I'll do that. But I must ask you something first. There's no point in pretending I don't want to know.'

She hesitated, biting her lip.

'Know what?'

'If there's anyone else. You don't have to answer. Silly, but I'd like to know.'

Trevor resisted the impulse to take her hand, to place it between her legs like he used to.

'Yes it is silly. Why should there be anyone? Didn't you believe what I said? That I'd always been faithful to Annie?'

'Men always say that,' Lucinda replied, with a rueful smile.

89

Who was *she* seeing? Trevor dismissed the thought, it was not his business to know.

'What's happened to *Grains of Evil*? Did you take up my suggestions, about developing the character of Jaspar?'

'Oh yes, it works much better. I finished it ages ago. Damn, I meant to bring it. I've left it at home. You've got to see it, now it would really work on TV.'

'Have you sent a copy to anyone?'

Lucinda flushed and glanced away.

'I couldn't bear to. Not when I thought I'd never see you again.'

'It's your script,' said Trevor, gently. 'After all, I only made a few tiny suggestions.'

'Do you mind going back by my place, so I can give it to you? Have you time?'

There was no way in which he could have construed her suggestion as an invitation to go to bed. Most girls today were mercifully frank about what they wanted, another bonus of the Movement, and Lucinda had taken her cue from her contemporaries. She was open in the modern manner. There was a way of saying 'Why don't we go back to my place?' whereby it was perfectly obvious that the intention was sex. Lucinda hadn't said it like that.

'Are you still living in your mother's house? Still in Chelsea?'

She nodded, nibbling at the chocolate cake, evoking wonder from Trevor at how she managed not to drop a single crumb. Trevor's thoughts had lunged into lust but he immediately stopped himself in his tracks.

'I don't know if I've time to go over there.'

'I could send it to you, but I've only got one copy and it might get lost.'

Trevor scrutinized his watch, and calculated his movements.

'I'm sorry, but I've got to see Gavin Mitchell tonight. He wants me to get a few items together for *Splash!* Have you ever seen it, a late-night magazine, goes out on Mondays?'

'Oh yes, I watch that sometimes before I go out. It's OK. I don't know why the girls go on about him, though.'

'I might have to appear on screen, but I'm more used to projecting in a lecture hall. I'm just as nervous as you.'

'You, Trevor? How can you be nervous? That's stupid.'

'I am, a little.'

'You must let me know when you're on. Promise?'

'All right. I'll try and remember.'

'God, you're so cool about it. I wouldn't be. Oh, now I'm getting all panicky again. Gavin Mitchell is going to be on my board. Could you say something to him tonight? Say you think I'd be good in drama? Say you know I've written a super script?'

'I'll say that not everyone thinks he's God's gift to women.'

'You wouldn't dare!'

Trevor was about to take away the teaspoon she was fiddling with, turning it over and over, but instead he clasped his hands on his lap.

'You *must* tell Gavin how much I want to work in drama.' She was looking at him with an intensity he found disturbing. 'It's all I care about. I never wanted to do anything else.'

'Just like Annie,' said Trevor, then he added quickly, 'You'll never guess where I'm meeting Gavin.'

'Where? Where?'

'Your brother's club. Tiger Tim's, isn't that the name?'

Lucinda tossed back her hair.

'Oh, he would go there, wouldn't he? Tim hates having celebs from telly at his place.'

Trevor smiled.

'I don't think Gavin will let the place down. He's quite civilized really.'

In the taxi from Bloomsbury to the King's Road, a sudden jolt threw her against him, and in an instinctive gesture, he had sought her lips, now only a few inches away, and then pushed his tongue inside her mouth, gripping her thighs to his. She stopped him as he began to run his hands up her legs, or he would have taken her there and then, shielded from observation by the darkened glass.

'We shouldn't be doing this,' he whispered, his chest heaving. 'Shall I get out now?'

'I love the way you kiss,' she replied. 'I tried to remember how it was when we first did it. Ages ago, weeks and weeks. Why is it that physical impressions slip away? I thought about it for days afterwards, then after a while, I couldn't recall the exact sensation. Now I can, though.'

She edged her way close to him, and he felt her butterfly lips alighting on his, an enveloping perfume released by her warmth. And then they were outside her house in Danvers Street.

'You can wait here, Trevor. I'll get the script and you can take the taxi back if you like.'

'No, I won't do that,' he said. 'I'm sorry I lunged at you.'

'Did you?' Lucinda replied with a vague smile, as she skipped up the steps. He watched as the door closed behind her, then all he knew was that he had to follow her inside. He barely remembered paying off the taxi, or pressing frenziedly on the doorbell, but suddenly he was leaning against the swirls of dark wallpaper in the hall, pulling her towards him. She wriggled out of his grasp.

'Come and see what I've done upstairs.'

She led him into the living room on the first-floor room which he always remembered as being spacious although it was half the size of the one at Langton Villas. He wondered if he was still trapped inside a blinding dream, inside a place which was familiar, yet strange. The light was dazzling, falling on a shiny white floor dotted with an odd, strangely shaped assortment of white metal and black wooden chairs and tables. A large white canvas with jagged arcs of red and black was suspended over a low calico-covered sofa, where a patchwork material of multi-textured scarlet fragments had been tossed across the back. A bulbous cactus-like structure stood in one corner, hung with metal chains like a parody of a Christmas tree. In another corner, was a sprinting figure who was carrying a clock under his arm. White, ribbed curtains billowed down from a heavy black pole.

'What have you done?' said Trevor. 'I hardly recognize it.'

'Do you like it?'

'Very much. Most unusual, having a floor painted white. I wouldn't know where to start, to create something like this.'

'Remember all that Sanderson chintz, great heavy armchairs everywhere, fitted brown carpet, nasty Victorian furniture? I always hated it, so I threw everything out. Mummy had a fit when she came over to London. Actually a designer friend did most of it. Super Japanese guy called Koike. Have you heard of him?'

'Can't say I have.'

Trevor paced round the room, and ended up by the window, facing Lucinda, now splayed out like a loose-limbed puppy, one leg hanging down from a bowl-shaped, black shiny chair.

'Sit down for a moment, Trevor. It's so nice having you here, being in my room.' His lucidity began to return. They would talk, and then he would go.

'Why don't you find your script? I could have a quick look.'

Lucinda stared at Trevor, her eyes now more grey than blue. He was about to say that she was more beautiful than he remembered, but he had lost the knack of the light compliment.

'You do know Koike, Trevor. He did the sets for Joey Le Ray's *Dead Mission*. You showed it to us in the first term. Anyway, he's branched out into fashion. Laundry-bag things, not my style. Why don't you get him to do your place? He's brilliant.'

'It says something about you, but I dread to think what it would say about me. Old professor trying to keep up with the times, perhaps?'

'That's so silly. You do say ridiculous things sometimes.'

'Thank God you said that.'

'Why?'

'Never mind. It makes me happy.'

It was at this moment, Trevor realized later, that he accepted their intimacy. From now on, what difference would it make whether they talked or acted as lovers? He had tried so hard to deny his feelings, but now he was prepared to use all his strength and accept the consequences. It was impossible to resist what they had both known from the first moment, and impossible to deny such an enduring attraction. Lucinda ran out of the room and reappeared with a cool glass of something excellent, judging by the way it slipped down his throat. He sat on the edge of the calico couch, drained his glass, bent over and lifted Lucinda up in his arms.

Carrying her to the floor above, he headed for her bedroom. Through an open door, he observed a wide, low bed with light drapes hanging down from the ceiling like fluttering Olympic flags, which had replaced the old four-poster he remembered. He placed her carefully on it, and stroked the outline of her body through the feather-soft wool of her dress. There was no need to speed up the moment when he would slip it from her shoulders, lift up her lacy camisole and gaze at her full breasts, the nipples which would become like hard berries under the first, tentative pressure of his lips. Her eyes were closed, and the sun filtering through the blinds gave her pale skin an opal bloom. There was no way he could deny what he had tried to push aside. Trevor trembled with awe, with the realization that he would be unable to root her from his life.

'I love you. I don't know what I'm going to do, but I love you.'

Kissing down her belly, Trevor stretched off the black covering of her lacy pants and gazed at the perfection of her body before slowly parting her legs. Then he hurled himself inside her and they both rushed into orgasm, crying out in unison. Holding her tightly to his chest, Trevor felt his eyes moist with tears.

'No-one has ever made me come like that,' she murmured. 'And no-one ever will. You make love like an angel. I missed you so much when we parted, if you only knew.'

After they had rested, he took her again, slowly savouring each moment, allowing each movement a gradual rise and fall. Soon he heard her deep rhythmic breaths, but he stopped himself from falling into sensuous sleep. He had to pull himself back. Somehow he would have to dilute the power she had over him. If he abandoned himself totally to her, it would only be for minutes, not hours, not days. There was something unreal about this violent release of passion. What he had with Annie was different, a love woven into the fabric of his life. There was no way he would allow Lucinda to tear it into shreds. He stared at his watch, then gently pushed back her hair.

'Darling, wake up. It's half-past seven. I'm going to have to go. I feel awful leaving you.'

Lucinda sat up with a start, eyes wide open.

'Gosh! I've got to be at a dinner party in Clapham in an hour.'

'And I must make a couple of calls.'

She retrieved a small phone from under the bed and Trevor left a message with Tiger Tim's husky-voiced receptionist to tell Gavin that he would be late.

Lucinda jumped off the bed, rushed to the bathroom and turned on the shower. There was no time to soap her body but he stood at the open door, watching her step into the deep, old-fashioned bath with brass taps pitted with age like the ones his dad threw out. Then he stepped forward to give her a tender kiss on her neck, drawing back as the water splashed onto his hair and face. Never mind, it would dry by the time he reached the club.

'Lucinda, my sweet. I really must be off now.'

The water was still cascading. He turned off the shower, and swathed her in a towel.

'I'll have some time free in about a month. We could go away for a day or two if you like.'

'Not before then?'

'No, darling.'

'Can we go to Paris for the weekend? April in Paris?'

'I'll see. Perhaps.'

He was glad she hadn't asked for more details, but she rarely did. Lucinda accepted what he gave, but he knew she had the right to be more demanding. He had treated her unfairly, he knew that. Knowing it, did nothing to lessen his guilt. Nearer the time, so it wouldn't sound calculating, he would mention the exact date. 18–21 April. Annie at Southwick Manor. Lucinda's interview was on 28 April. Both dates were in his diary, but the 28th was marked 'Annie's Board'. It was usual for him to make a note of what Annie was doing, she knew that was his habit. With two busy lives, you sometimes needed a prompt.

'I don't know about Paris. But I promise I'll call you.'

'You've still got my number?'

'Of course I have.'

Lucinda shouted 'Bye', that was all. It wasn't until he was in the taxi that he realized he had forgotten to ask for her script. All he felt was joy, exhilaration, still enveloped in the sweet smell of her body. How could he be so meanhearted, conventional and careful? For the moment, it would have to be that way. One day, perhaps, he would make it up to her.

That evening, when Trevor was sitting under one of the pencil spotlights at Tiger Tim's, he found himself peering at the menu and choosing for Lucinda. Her kind of food, rustic Anglo-Italian she said it was called, and they were mostly girls like her, occasionally sweeping their eyes round the strange interior, half country house, half bric-à-brac showroom, to see if there was anyone they knew. Gavin came rushing in half an hour later, and Trevor wondered if it was intentional. He apologized profusely as though he had struggled across an arctic ice-flow to be with Trevor. There was no preliminary small talk.

'But I don't need to tell you all this,' Trevor said, after he had dished out to Gavin a mixed platter of his views on contemporary culture, and new directions for *Splash!*. 'You're much closer to the young generation than I am.'

'I'm thirty-five. Old for telly.'

Gavin grinned, and glanced away. Trevor noticed several faces staring with interest. Gavin Mitchell. Who was with him? Then Gavin extracted a tiny pad from a perfectly tailored pocket which, Trevor observed, showed no signs of gaping or sagging, unlike his own.

'Don't mind if I make a few notes?' Gavin asked, wielding his pen and apparently in no hurry to savour Tiger Tim's Rosy Risotto with pink peppercorns. 'Only I liked what you were saying.'

Trevor watched as he covered several sheets in a spidery scrawl. Only now did it strike him that if Gavin took to Lucinda, she might end up working for him instead of Annie. And if that were to happen, it would make it easier . . . but no, he couldn't allow himself to think like this.

'By the way, an ex-student of mine is coming for a board at Intertel. She dropped me a note, said you'd be one of the poeple interviewing her.'

'Of course, I meant to ask you. Lucinda Sherwood, one of Sherwood's brood. Short-listed for a research job. I saw your name on her CV. The most impressive thing on it, I have to say. What's she like? Any good?'

'She is, surprisingly.'

'You mean, she actually completed your communications course? Lots of those kind of girls don't,' Gavin remarked, as he pulled down another wafer-thin sheet of paper and began to cover it in small, almost invisible letters.

'Yes, she got her degree. Quite a good one, considering.'

'Considering what?'

'That she's got stunning looks and has a hectic social life.'

'So she's a bright girl, then?'

'I'd say so. Not over-academic, but extremely intelligent.'

'Then she sounds just about right for *Splash!*.' Gavin gave a broad smile. His teeth were slightly discoloured, which endeared him to Trevor. 'Come to think of it, it'll be good for the show to have an upper-class voice for a change. We need to make a dent in the *Tatler* set and she could be the answer. Nothing to do with her father, naturally.'

'Naturally,' said Trevor, echoing his irony.

'I look forward to seeing her.'

Trevor felt a prickle of jealousy at the thought of her in constant contact with Gavin, but he knew that she would be unlikely to succumb to his charm. *Splash!* may have been the last place he would have wanted her to be, but it had certain advantages. He should be able to persuade her. If they were going to meet from time to time, they would both have to make certain compromises, certain arrangements. Obviously, they would both take the utmost care, making sure that nobody knew. Lucinda would understand that he couldn't have gossip reaching Annie's ears, that would be intolerable.

It was barely a week later, when Trevor was leaving a colleague's house in Fulham one evening, that a black car drew up beside him.

'Trevor! I thought it was you. What are you doing here?'

He almost didn't recognize her. Lucinda's hair was piled up on her head, long sparkling ear-rings dangling from her ears, lips given a new, opulent shape by dark lipstick and she appeared to be naked. Coming closer, he could see a black sequinned strapless dress clinging low onto her breasts. Then, leaning through the window, he kissed her neck.

'You look gorgeous. Going to a party?'

'I was . . . Why don't you come with me?'

'Darling, I can't. Unfortunately, I've got to be back.'

'Talk to me for a minute. Then I'll go.'

Lucinda opened the car door. Trevor glanced down the street, and then sat beside her.

'Can you drive round the corner?'

'Sure. Who have you been seeing? Someone else?'

'Paul, a colleague.'

'Honestly?'

Trevor kissed her neck again as she stopped the car in a side-street.

'You've no reason to be jealous. None.'

'Neither have you. I'm not interested in anyone else now. I don't care if I don't go to this party, either.'

'You'll enjoy it.'

'I wish you'd come. Remember Terry from college? He's just got the finance for a low-budget movie. All the actors are doing it for free. He'd love to see you again.'

'No, darling. But you can drop me off somewhere, if you like.'

'Kiss me first. Just one kiss, then I'll take you wherever you want.'

'I'll spoil your make-up.'

Lucinda laughed, and threw her arms round his neck. Clutching her waist, he pressed his face in the divide of her breast, breathing in the sweet smell of her body. Then she pushed his head down on her lap, leaning back against the driver's seat.

'Kiss me there,' she whispered.

Crouching down, angling himself to avoid the gear-stick, Trevor pulled up the brief skirt.

'Go on, do it, do it, no-one's around. I want to feel your tongue. I want you to make your mark on me.'

When she moved her legs slightly apart, Trevor realized that she was wearing nothing underneath apart from a brief suspender belt and thin, glittering stockings. He closed his eyes, and thought of nothing but her pleasure, sucking gently while she panted until her thighs shivered and she shook with delight.

'You bad girl,' he said, sliding back into his seat and pulling her hand onto his swollen cock.

'Let's do it in the back of the car.'

'I don't think so.'

'Then we'll go to Chelsea.'

'I must get back.'

'Can't you be late sometimes? Just a little late?'

Trevor thought a moment. Sometimes he worked with Paul, didn't come home until one in the morning. He would have been working late tonight, but Paul was too exhausted.

'I'll come to your house. But I can't stay long.'

Later, after he had taken a shower, Trevor arrived home in a taxi. Although he had rehearsed a plausible explanation, it wasn't necessary. There was a message from Annie on the answerphone. *Tonight I'm having a few drinks with Benny and some mates. No idea when I'll be back, don't wait up. Lots and lots of love.*

Lying in bed, his body still vibrant with energy, Trevor found that he had no regret for what had happened. There was another way. If they both saw one another more often, their passion would burn itself out. When he stopped seeing her the year before, it had been an arbitrary decision. Far more sensible to give themselves another few months to allow the affair to run its allotted course and then it would be over, properly over.

Two days later, he phoned Lucinda and they met again.

During the long passionate hours he spent at her house, mostly in bed, he found himself repeating his declaration. This time he meant it.

'I'm in love with you. I don't know what I'm going to do about it, but I'm in love.'

'We're both mad enough,' she answered this time, as she fluffed up the pillow he had placed under her hips to raise her towards him.

'Are you happy? I want you to be happy, sweetheart.'

'I am, I am. Why shouldn't I be?'

'Because I give you so little.'

'You give me everything I want.'

'Really?'

'Really. You're still the most fantastic man I've ever met.'

Lucinda told him about a married girlfriend of hers who had fallen in love with a man she could only see once a year. For one week, they expressed a whole year of yearning and love, booking a hotel room and never going out.

'How can you say that's love?' said Trevor, as Lucinda lay sprawled over him, tweaking out a grey hair. 'Just because she had good sex with a man she could only see once a year.'

'It wasn't just the sex. If they'd liked golf, they could have played golf together for a week. It wouldn't have made any difference.'

'You're saying it doesn't matter, that nothing develops.'

'Why assume that it has to? What's wrong with everything staying the same?'

'Then she must have an awful marriage. Poor girl, her one, brief escape.'

'Not at all. She likes her husband.'

'I'm sorry. It's beyond me,' said Trevor. 'Strange friends you have.'

Lucinda rolled onto her back, and flung out her arms, gazing at the heavily spiked Mexican candelabra which Trevor tried to avoid noticing. Then she began to stroke slowly down his body but he took her hand away and pressed it to his lips.

'I can't, darling. Look at the time! I hate to leave you, but I must be getting back. It won't always be like this, I promise you.'

99

'How do you know? If we saw each other every single day and did everything together, you'd get frightfully bored.'

'Never. Why do you say that?'

Her remark, he realized, betrayed the legacy of other men, young men, shallow men who had failed to see the glorious woman hiding behind the girlish sheet of hair, the unsuspected intelligence imprinted on that conventionally beautiful, perhaps pretty, face.

'There are lots of girls like me, Trevor.'

'I never meet them. Where are they hiding?'

Then they both laughed. It didn't seem to occur to Lucinda that she could be loved for her own particular qualities.

'I only think of you, my darling. I hear your laugh, see your face on the pillow, as though you're constantly beside me. I even wrote a poem about you.'

'Show me.'

'No.'

'Go on. I want to see it.'

'You'll have to wait.'

'When? When?'

'When it's finished.'

'It'll never be finished. Is my name on it?'

'It will be, when I give it to you.'

Trevor knew that the period of wild happiness would be measured in months not years, but as long as they both imagined that there was a future, talked of the future, convinced themselves in one another's company that their love would never be cut short, it was bearable. Lucinda assured him that the few hours spent with him were more precious than he could imagine. She never hinted at what he feared most, that he should leave Annie for her, that he would have to make a choice.

7

ANNIE

Annie arrived late at Southwick Manor, when the cocktail party for the Women in Management course in the Thomas Hardy bar was drawing to a close. She had gone because Alan had suggested it, persuading her to find a date in her diary. Television is a business, like any other, he had told her, rather unconvincingly Annie thought. When she remonstrated, no time, impossible schedule, he gave her a mild rebuke.

'We've all done them, at one time or another. You might even find it useful.'

She agreed, once she had persuaded herself that she might get a series out of it. *Women at the Top.* Something like that. Why hadn't she put her foot down? Refused to go? I'm still the new girl only four months into the job, she thought, and new girls are always afraid of being caught out.

No-one would expect students to attend twelve lectures in a day but this was intensive, information culled from years of experience, force-fed to the busy. By the time the third speaker had walked up to the perspex-sheeted lectern to embark on a golden half-hour, ten minutes for questions, Annie had forgotten the first, scheduled precisely at 9.30 a.m. In the D'Urberville room, there were rows of polished shoes side by side on the Wilton carpet, neat newly coiffeured heads bent downwards as they recorded the four-day event for which their companies had paid over a thousand pounds, some on pads, some on notepad computers. Annie had drawn rings round the 'Subjects for Debate', summarized in the expensively laminated brochure which was too large to fit into her briefcase. Profit and Innovation. Path-seeking. Motivation. Structured Promotion. Incentive. The Assertive Message. Positive Leadership. Woman in a Man's World. Fast Track to Success. Performance

Appraisal. Stress Management. Prioritization. Quality Management. Exploring New Horizons. If this was how they talked, the capitalist jungle was less exciting than a suburban lawn.

They were all in varying interpretations of suit, the kind which regularly appeared every spring in varied shades of navy. At the first coffee-break, Annie could see them all giving her cursory glances, taking in her black jeans and leather jacket. She wasn't used to meeting 'women of status' as they were termed in the brochure. Like women anywhere, they were sizing one another up, in the pleasantest way, taking in details of coiffure, fabric, shoes and handbags, whilst making friendly enquiries about one another's jobs, or rather 'the workplace'. Annie had to choose between denying herself coffee or welcoming an eager participant with a smile. She walked towards the enticing aroma and stood in the queue, where a red-aproned waitress was pouring three-quarter portions of Kenco coffee into thick, stunted cups.

Marjorie introduced herself. Downside Technics, a small company in Surrey, making mini-speakers with maxi volume.

'And where are you from? I bet it's somewhere creative.'

'A television company.'

'How absolutely marvellous,' said Marjorie. 'My daughter wants to go into television.'

'Don't they all?' replied Annie.

'Chérie has four A levels. My husband and I think she stands a good chance.'

Having delivered her rebuke with a toothsome smile, Marjorie strode towards a woman with taut, highly coloured cheeks whose neck was hidden by a Cleopatra welter of gold chains weighed down by bright, multicoloured glass appendages. A fashion buyer or someone in Selfridges who bought costumes never suits, Annie guessed. A minute later, she heard a jangle of bracelets, and a sample bottle appeared from a crocodile attaché case.

'I'm the executive in charge of the perfumerie department,' Annie heard her say. Distancing herself in case she needed to engineer a hasty exit, Annie settled herself in a chair at the end of a row, stretched out her legs out into the aisle and attempted to aim her concentration towards the earnest woman who stood at the lectern on the platform. She was apologizing profusely for mislaying her slides. It was unfortunate that she was about to give her all on The Assertive Message.

*　　　*　　　*

At the end of six lectures, six portion-controlled question times, one help-yourself lunch-break (cold gelatinized checken with a vegetarian option, a stiff sculpted *mille feuille* of reheated onion lasagne) they were all comparing experiences after forging alliances, networking, some would call it making friends, knitting themselves together, group sessions on leatherette settees in the D'Urberville room, sweet sherry, nuts and shrivelled gherkins on the house.

On the second day (two more days of sessions, group interaction, role-playing, quizzes, questionnaires and events yet to come) Annie had decided to wear her Ralph Lauren jacket with a T-shirt underneath but kept the black jeans. The perfume executive was flattered that Annie Griffiths, who had been profiled in *Vanity Fair* and *Cosmopolitan* but not yet in *Hello!*, had found time to attend. Annie now knew that she was called Sidonie.

'Isn't that Calvin Klein or am I mistaken?' asked Sidonie, who had passed on from conversing with some of the other ladies – not all fitting into her concept of executive status but she wouldn't let on that she knew. Senior secretaries should be encouraged towards management. Sidonie brushed a delicate finger over the pile of Annie's sleeve.

'I think it is,' replied Annie. 'I bought it because it was black and it fitted me.'

'Calvin always gets it right,' said Sidonie, admiring Annie's throwaway style and hoping they would maintain a rewarding contact. 'What do you think so far?'

'You mean, has it changed my life?' Annie laughed. 'I'll have to wait and see.'

'There really should have been some men here. Don't you think, Annie? I mean, at times, one needs to be confrontational, not merely supportive. One can't be nice about things all the time. Women do so want to be nice, don't they? I think I must be an absolute bitch to work for, I'm so demanding. As my husband constantly reminds me.'

Annie was admiring the way the largest glass pendant kept to its place on her broad breast-bone without shifting to one side when she moved.

'The Stress Management talk was quite the best. That's what we all need, don't you think? Tell me, do you have little tricks of the trade in television? I'm sure you do, Annie. How do you stay sane?'

103

Annie reached forward, it was now her turn to accept her ration of caffeine.

'Going home at night.'

'Marvellous. What a simply marvellous answer.'

The Marketing Director of Natural Aura Beauty Products, a small company unknown to Sidonie, more Body Shop than Selfridges, settled into her front seat, displacing an illegal occupant with a tap on the shoulder pads. Annie began to doodle on the Women in Management file with an unwieldy Biro, present from the organizers.

Jane was the only one who looked promising, plainly unsuitable in layers of clashing fabrics, with growing-out roots betraying the blond frizz, and undisguised black shadows under the eyes. She was from local radio. Annie went up to her at the bar, another cocktail intermission before dinner.

'In the last month I've lost my boyfriend and my job,' she said, in a cheerful, cracked voice. 'I don't know what the fuck I'm doing here. Except the arseholes paid for it six months ago before the annual report came out, and no-one else would come. What's your game?'

'Drama. I produce for TV.'

'I saw your name on the delegates list and wondered. Annie Griffiths. Haven't you got some superpower job now?'

'Controller of Drama at Intertel.'

'I knew I'd read it. Will you buy me a drink?'

'What'll it be?' asked Annie.

'Gin. Double. I'm skint. OK?'

'Don't worry, Jane. They've given me a budget for research.'

Annie spent the evening listening, as Jane consumed one gin after another. She had a confidence in her own ability which had survived a series of jobs, but they never lasted long. Then she told Annie about Rod, who'd left after she'd had an abortion, wanted a child, she didn't, wanted her to be faithful, she didn't. The last lecture of the day, Sexual Harassment in the Workplace, Mountain or Molehill, had created most controversy but Jane wasn't impressed. Self-defence for women would sort that out. Quick chop in the balls. This lot wouldn't even know what they were. Jane's bravado wouldn't keep her in work, not that kind of work. On the set of *Rough Trade*, she'd be a winner.

'Have you ever acted?' asked Annie.

'All the time.' Then she flashed a gap-toothed smile. 'If there was anything decent on telly, I'd be up for it. I'd be no good. I'd boss the director around. Too late now. I'm going to get out of the business, find a decent living.'

'Like?'

'Being a child-minder. There's always kids around. I like kids, they speak my language.'

Then she laughed, a smoke-raddled laugh, a market trader's laugh. Annie could never have employed her, yet she hoped she would hear of her again.

That night, Annie ordered supper in her room. It took an hour before the operator managed to connect her to London.

'Hello, love. Was that Rick on the line? Or was the phone out of order? I've spent ages trying to get through.'

'I must have knocked the phone off the hook. I was just going to ring you. How's it all going?'

'Horrid. Waste of time. I want to be home. Why on earth did they send me? There's only one person I can talk to, at least she feels the same as I do. Jane's a wild anarchist, they don't know what to make of her. If she wasn't so plastered all the time, I'd have hired her like a shot. Still, she might be able to write. We've both decided to leave early. There's no point in spending another day in this dump. Don't you agree?'

'Maybe.'

'Have I interrupted you? Are you working?'

His tone sounded brusque, as though he was in the middle of a tutorial.

'I was thinking it might not be such a good idea to skive off. Seeing that Intertel has spent a fortune sending you out there. Can't you last out just one more day?'

'I don't need it, Trev. If I can't do things my own way, they can stuff the job. If the Controller of Drama can't decide what's valuable and what's not—'

'You never know, when you come back you might find it wasn't such a waste of time after all.'

'Are you saying you don't trust my judgement?'

'Of course not. But if you go back to the office—'

'I thought I might spend a couple of days at home. We haven't spent much time together recently.'

'It's a pretty bad week for me, I'm afraid.'

'Oh?'

'Committee meetings, which I have to go to. And a couple

of visiting academics from Moscow who need to be entertained.'

'If they're not too stuffy, why not ask them round? Rick speaks a few words of Russian, Bryonie went on that medical trip. And Kate likes vodka.'

'It's an idea. I suppose we could invite them all to dinner,' said Trevor.

Annie could sense that he was tired. But his voice sounded flat, as though something had happened which he couldn't say over the phone.

'Are you all right? Or has it just been an awful day? I do so want to be with you, love. You'd hate it here. The bed's so hard it must have come from a casualty ward.'

'I must get on. Let me know what you decide,' Trevor said, after a pause. 'But it's not a bad idea to stick to the rules for a while. Until you're settled in. That's what I'd do.'

'You mean, start wearing suits and talking about cost-efficient drama? You know I'm hopeless at that. They hired me for what I am.'

'We'll talk about it when you get back.'

By morning, Annie had repressed her impulse to invent an urgent phone-call which would have meant her instant departure. He didn't have to spell it out. In any case, it was only an act, adopting the exterior they expected. In the final self-assessment session, where they were all handed out a many-paged questionnaire, she knew the answers she should give, even if they were blatantly untrue. She was learning the ploys of the management game, putting down what they wanted to hear. Annie found to her surprise that she could play it well. It was no different from being at school, she decided, discovering the right tactics to pass the exams with only a few weeks' work. She left an hour early, before the farewell luncheon in the Oak room, so she would be spared the 'must meet again' from Sidonie and Cynthia and Marjorie and Jacky.

Annie would work on the idea. *Women at the Top*, provisional title. Women who didn't play by the rules but knew how they worked. Breaking the code. Making millions the wrong way. Beating the system. Exposing the management fraud. It hadn't been a waste of time.

When she returned to Langton Villas, there was a note from

Trevor on the kitchen table, which he must have written before he left for college that morning.

> *Darling. I'll be late tonight. Have to take Russians to*
> Macbeth *at the National. Don't wait up if you're*
> *shattered. Bottle of wine in fridge. Love T.*

He had really made an effort. The mugs were hanging on hooks all facing the same way, saucepans arrayed on the shelf in order of size, clean tea-towels neatly stacked, the old enamel sink was as spotless as it would ever be, and on the gleaming table, it almost looked as though he'd polished it, there was a vase stuffed full of tight-budded apricot roses and branches of spring leaves. Annie decided not to go into the office. There was still the pang of guilt, then she told herself that the Controller of Drama was entitled to quiet moments on her own. It would take some time not to be fiercely conscientious. Hadn't they all groaned with agreement when some dreary speaker had pointed out that women were conditioned to work twice as hard as men? Alan, she had heard, spent at least one day a week playing golf.

When Trevor came home, it was after midnight but, he explained, he couldn't avoid treating his visitors to supper after the show. Annie had recovered her energy. Trevor, too, seemed to be recharged. *Macbeth*, which they had seen together a month ago, was even better, he said. The Russians loved it, and wanted to take off for Scotland immediately.

'But you won't go?' said Annie.

'I'll do my best to put them off. But we're trying to set up an academic exchange, so one has to pull all the stops out.'

'Not this weekend, darling.'

'All right. Not this weekend, then.'

They did manage to spend most of the next weekend together except for Sunday afternoon, when Trevor had to meet one of his colleagues who was helping with The Book, Professor Watson's definitive *History of World Television* with an ever-expanding synopsis. When he started writing Chapter One, Trevor would say, the work would be done. It was the research and preparation which took the time. Seeing Trevor's drawn face, Annie rejected her earlier idea of taking off to the country, as he was getting increasingly impatient with long drives out of London. What was wrong with Hampstead Heath? Did they have to suffer crowded roads to see the same sky and grass and trees somewhere else? Annie decided to turn her attention to the house. It was, after all, time they renewed the kitchen, made a few attempts at modernization.

When she returned from a solo shopping recce, laden with brochures, magazines and swatches of fabric, Trevor showed an interest she had never observed before, and strong likes and dislikes about design she had never suspected. That was typical Trevor. Often he would ignore something until it was under his nose, and then, once the something had caught his interest and attention, he would throw himself into it with painstaking zeal. Now he had pushed aside the periodical he was reading, and was studying *Interiors* inch by careful inch.

Annie leaned over his shoulder and stopped him turning the page. Her attention was caught by a bare, grainily photographed room, with an emphasis on space, white light and black surfaces, punctuated by a red pot, a scrawly red light fitting.

'This looks interesting. How about trying something like this, something totally different that we'd never have thought of? Get rid of everything and start again.' Annie looked round the kitchen and through the arch into the chaos beyond. 'We could see the shape of our rooms again, I think it could work in here. Then it would be like having a new house, a new identity. I'd love it, wouldn't you? And if we decided we didn't like it, we could always put it back like it was. You get used to the idea that houses never change, but why not?'

'Let's think about it, Annie.'

'Don't you love that white floor?'

'Fine for a drama set, but not for Rick's boots or Dally's toys. It would look like grey sludge in days.'

Trevor leafed through the magazine and stopped to contemplate a renovated barn in Berkshire.

'That looks more liveable, to my mind. But we don't have that kind of space. Not that we need it, of course.'

Annie moved away, confident that after a while he would come to a conclusion. He didn't like to be hurried, understandably. Then they would reach a compromise, some of her ideas, some of his. She left him bent over the designer images and went out for a couple of hours to see Kate. Kate, of course, wanted to start straight away and change the house from top to bottom. When Annie got back, the magazines were once more in a neat pile and Trevor was in his study.

'Mind if I interrupt?' she asked.

He looked more cheerful now.

'Sure. I've finished marking for today.'

'So,' said Annie, resting her hands on his shoulders. 'What are we going to do?'

'About what?'

'The house. Have you decided? There's so much we could do. I've just been talking to Kate, she's full of wild ideas. I'd still love a white floor.'

Trevor swivelled round in his chair and smiled.

'Go for that idea if you like, but I'm rather fond of that brown. It's practical. Don't you think a black-and-white décor is the kind of thing my students would go for?'

'How do we know till we try? We might find we like it.'

'I can't help it, I'd be content with something corny and comfortable.'

'Three-piece suite with a pouf, chintzy curtains, a sideboard and a chiming clock?'

'We don't have to get the pouf.'

'Or the three-piece suite.'

Never mind, he had made the effort, he had considered the options. With Kate's help, Annie would find a compromise. A grey floor, perhaps. There was no hurry, and in any case it was impossible for a while, not until the next show was on the road. Then she found him pulling on some boots, wearing one of her old sweaters which had stretched to man size.

'I thought I'd make a contribution, do something to the garden. There might even be something of interest for the Department of Archeology, hidden under the nettles.'

She stood watching him for a while through the window, hacking at the towering nettles with a rusty spade. He still had surprising attack and energy for a man of fifty-four, and he looked as though he was enjoying himself, throwing his feet onto the spade, leaning over it to penetrate the rock-hard soil, flinging out rusty cans that the former occupants had dumped heedlessly in the garden. It didn't matter that he was too exhausted to make love that night, he still took her in his arms, his arms clasped round her waist until she went peacefully to sleep lying on his chest.

8

ANNIE

Alan hovered by the open door of Annie's office, evidently ill at ease with the open management policy embraced by Intertel.

'Mind if I come in?'

Annie straightened her back and reminded herself that she was the Controller of Drama, and not Annie Griffiths who hadn't done her homework. She wished he hadn't tied his tie with such venom. He reminded her of a senior tax inspector who had done a life swap and forgotten to dress for his new job.

'Well, how did the course go, Annie?' he began.

'It gave me some ideas,' she replied, with a grimace, wondering if he was expecting a full report.

'You probably thought it was a waste of time. I'm sure some of it was. But we all have to take these kind of things seriously nowadays. Don't dismiss it out of court.'

Annie began to shuffle papers around her desk, trying to make neat piles.

'Do feel free to alter your office, Annie. We don't mind the Hollywood gloss.'

He walked round the room, peering at some production stills pinned onto a board.

'Those would look nice framed, don't you think? A few more plants? Comfortable seating perhaps? I know your predecessor shunned such things, but . . .'

Then he smiled and his face seemed unwilling to accommodate the gesture.

'A smarter interface,' said Annie, displaying one of her newly acquired phrases. 'I have been thinking about it.'

'When you're ready, Annie. I know you've other things on your mind.'

No, not a tax inspector. Annie revised her opinion. He was more like a police superintendent, harassed by some government report.

'Just one more thing. This afternoon's board . . .'

'Is it this afternoon? Damn. I made a note in my other diary. I'd completely forgotten.'

'Do you have something in your wardrobe, a little more formal? Usually, we don't make strictures, but this is the public face of Intertel.'

'A suit?'

'I was thinking, perhaps a suit. Or a jacket and skirt would do. At executive level, that's all. I'm not laying down the law for other occasions. I know it's a bore, but it's what's expected here at Intertel. You'd be surprised, but we're probably more formal than the BBC. Do understand, I'm not being critical. If I had my way, everyone would wear whatever they liked.'

Annie grinned. He would have passed with a top grade at the management course. How to Get Your Way Without Letting On.

'Will you have some coffee, Alan? It's not hot but it's real.'

Not even a flicker. Benny would have taken a feed line like that in half a second.

'That's very kind, but I'm forbidden caffeine. Thank you for being so understanding, Annie. See you this afternoon.'

Although Annie's office door was always open, she closed it after Alan had departed and made a call to Kate. She could hear the rumble of the washing-machine.

'Kate. Where for a suit? I need one fast . . . No, I know . . . Of course I won't wear it afterwards.'

Kate, who rarely had more than a couple of pounds in her purse, could locate every stylish clothes shop in London. Once, when she was a BBC set designer, she had been a fashion junkie. Now she merely gazed in front of the windows where she had once bought, and created an approximation of what she had seen from a random collection of charity shop oddments. Even with a bawling brat and no money, she still managed to look stunning.

'Let me come. I must come with you. I don't have to collect Dally till three.'

Annie cancelled a business lunch, and together they swanned down South Molton Street where Kate took over in the forbidding shop in which she used to spend half her salary.

They still knew her. Kate put together an ensemble in half an hour flat, subtle greys and pinks, a foulard, a fine linen skirt, and a heavy jacket whose severe tailoring was belied by frivolous details. Kate gasped with pleasure as Annie stood hesitantly in front of the mirror. The salesgirl had retreated, sensing the hand of a master.

'Trevor would go crazy. Over a thousand pounds!'

'Go for it. You look like a star, Annie. Now we've got to find the ear-rings, and the shoes and the bag.'

'No we haven't,' replied Annie, firmly.

'I know just the place. Just you wait and see.'

Kate had her way. Annie couldn't resist the delight on her face as she hunted for the right colours, the right shapes. She was behaving like a kid who'd been given a bundle of cheques for her twenty-first, and was intent on spending the money all at once. Even in her days of didactic feminism, Kate had always believed in the French ideal of fashion as an expression of personality. It was just unfortunate that Kate's personality was an expensive one.

'I daren't tell Trevor what all this has cost. He'd have a fit,' remarked Annie, as they piled into a taxi. Then, from a gold bag containing her carefully folded jeans and jacket, she pulled out a silk scarf Kate had admired.

'This is for you. Commission.'

'Annie, you're a darling.'

'I'm taking this all off after the board.'

'Why? Why look gorgeous just for them?'

'No wonder men hate suits.'

Annie wriggled against the tight shoulders, then pulled down her skirt so that it stretched tight over her bottom.

'Right now, I'm back in South Wales with Mum telling me she could live for a month on what I've spent. And Dad telling me to throw away my tart costume and brandishing a paraffin can when I wouldn't.'

'And did he burn it? Annie, what a monster!'

'Poor Dad, couldn't do anything right. He poured over the paraffin, shouted and screamed and then couldn't find any matches. That's why he stuck in a penpushing job in Cardiff Town Hall till they gave him a gold watch. Even though he was a mean bastard, I miss him. He wouldn't change his mind for anyone.'

*   *   *

When Annie pushed open the door of the Senior Board Room they were all sitting there – Alan Coker, Gavin Mitchell, Tony Sheldon, Controller of Personnel, and Tania Hobson, a representative of the Fair Deal Committee which attempted to monitor cases of discrimination, without necessarily changing their course. Tony and Tania had compiled the short-list, which was now down to eight. Two candidates for two junior posts would have to be chosen, one to work on *Splash!*, one as an assistant to Annie. Someone had placed Lucinda Sherwood last. Annie wondered whose manipulative hand had arranged the order. At interviews, especially after a long day, it was the last person who usually made the most vivid impression. Six men, two women.

By mid-afternoon, Annie had almost made up her mind whom she would select. Howard Morgan was Welsh, a graduate from Cardiff University, had acted in minor roles at the National Theatre and was now organizing a theatre group for the Arts Council. Gavin was rooting for a graduate who had a second-class degree from his former college at Cambridge. Suitable *Splash!* material, didn't seem worried about the salary, pleasant looking and clearly a hard worker who had no ambition to be a producer.

'I'm unhappy about this,' said Tania. 'Do bear in mind that hiring two men for these key posts would block female advancement for at least another year. I hope you'll give Mary Cornish and Lucinda Sherwood serious consideration. And I'd like to suggest that we allow an overrun in her case as we're running late already.'

'I'd support giving women more time,' remarked Gavin. 'I know I have the tendency to cut them short. But I do recognize my failure. I'm afraid it's an inherited defect, us working-class lads.'

As he smiled in Tania's direction, everyone nodded.

'Then I'll bring in Miz Sherwood.'

'Is it still company policy not to use titles?' asked Tony Sheldon. 'Isn't she the daughter of Lord Sherwood?'

'I think Prince Edward has the right idea. Titles should be kept for foreign TV festivals and bookings at the Savoy, in my opinion. Does anyone object to calling her Lucinda?' Gavin's faint trace of irony, betrayed by whirling doodles on his pad, was undetected by Tony. He found Gavin far too arrogant, even for television.

Annie straightened her jacket, pulled down her skirt which was clinging uncomfortably round her thighs in the over-heated boardroom and tore off another page from her pad. Interviewing was like auditioning actors, you had to project people into a variety of situations and imagine their behaviour. And you had to stand by your mistakes. She was pouring herself some tea from a tray in front of her when Lucinda Sherwood walked in. Annie liked her appearance, it was fresh and unobtrusive, cool tans and cream, well-cut, slim-fitting trousers, a loose jacket and a polka-dot open-necked shirt. She hadn't tried to make an impression in something clingingly fashionable. Trevor hadn't told her she was beautiful, but he rarely registered how people looked. Students nowadays all look the same to me, he said once.

After the introductions had been made, the smiles were becoming wearier now, Lucinda moved calmly to a chair at the head of the table. She answered the first question, about equal opportunities, with hesitant diplomacy.

'If you're an artist, it doesn't matter who you are . . . People don't discriminate in art . . . I can't think of anyone who does,' she concluded. Gavin raised his eyebrows and leaned forward.

'Really? Are you quite sure? Have you ever thought about the ratio of male to female artists in, say, the National Gallery?'

'We're getting off the point,' remarked Tania. 'I'm concerned with women being overlooked in the employment situation. Would you agree that we all have to make special efforts to ensure that women are encouraged to reach their potential? And take their rightful place as the equals of men?'

'Absolutely,' Lucinda replied.

Tony Sheldon instantly seized the opportunity to put the question he considered crucial to any appointment.

'Your experience, Lucinda. Would you say it would make a valuable contribution to the television playing-field?'

'I worked as an assistant for Nebula Films, they make documentaries for Channel 4. That was good, because I did most things, it's a small company.'

'What did you like best about it?'

'Making things visual and exciting. Changing things at the last minute, rethinking ideas quickly, persuading people to do things for very little money. And making a dull subject come alive for an audience, at least I thought it was dull at first. It was about urban regeneration. They used quite a lot of my ideas, and I was pleased with that.'

'Could you give other examples?'

'Oh yes. I spent some time in New York and Los Angeles. I went to screenings, had meetings with agents, met a lot of film and TV people there. I was trying to find some backers for a script I'd written. Then I decided it wasn't right for the States, and I'd do better here. In any case, I think television's got more style here, the style I like anyhow. They wouldn't run *Splash!* over there, for example.'

'Why not?' said Gavin, stroking a stray hair off his cuff.

Lucinda's mind went blank and she took a deep breath. Then she suddenly recalled the discussion she'd had with Trevor, trying to argue her corner. It was not to her benefit, he suggested, to argue from a corner. Tell them what they expect to hear.

'They're far too reverential about art. If you take the view that there are minority subjects and majority subjects, that's what you get.'

'And do you agree with this view?'

'Certainly not.' She softened and gave an undirected smile.

'Lucinda, would you put on difficult drama, which some people would find hard to grasp, or even alienating?' said Annie. She turned deliberately to take in the faintly flushed face, the grey-blue eyes looking straight into hers. There was a steadiness in Lucinda'a gaze which could indicate either toughness and ambition or an honest directness. Annie decided it was the latter.

'It depends what you call difficult,' replied Lucinda, stalling for time. She waited a moment, and could hear the clunk of the boardroom clock as it shifted the seconds.

'I'd try and find ways of appealing to different audiences at the same time. The complexities would be hidden, perhaps, but there for those who wanted to seek them out. And I'd make sure the actors were compelling enough to keep people glued to the screen. Even with the best script, the best locations, a drama can fail. But you could have Marlon Brando in close-up for half an hour, and even if he was saying rubbish, barely audible, you couldn't take your eyes away.'

'And if Marlon Brando wasn't available?' said Annie, with a smile.

'I'd look for an actor with an unconventional face, Gérard

115

Depardieu type maybe, who understood about the tension of silence.'

Gavin glanced at Annie, but without knowing why she was grinning to herself. The tension of silence, Trevor had used that phrase in a recent article. Lucinda would have picked it up from the *Guardian* Arts page. Annie was pleasantly surprised.

Her interrogators looked at one another, and Alan nodded to indicate that his question was about to be aired.

'How would you say, Lucinda, that your experience might be used in the context of Intertel? Practically speaking, that is.'

Lucinda clasped her hands together tightly as he waited for her reply. Lord Sherwood had little time for Alan. Boring little wet, no balls, was how Daddy described him in private.

'I'm good at getting things done, I know about deadlines, organizing, working under pressure. And I'm good at working in a team.'

It was useful to slip in the clichés of job description, Trevor had said. Alan nodded without replying, which probably meant that Trevor's assessment was correct. A second later, Gavin raised his Mont Blanc pen to shoulder level, kept it there and leaned back in his chair, as though about to direct a chamber ensemble from a sitting position.

'There's something I'd like to ask. Are you good with difficult people? Let me give you an example. I'd like to have Terry O'Mara on my programme. Have you heard of him?'

'No. I'm afraid I haven't.'

'He's a young Irish primitive painter, living in Guatemala. Commands huge prices in the States, enormously talented, enormously reclusive. How would you go about persuading him to appear? Well? Any ideas?'

'I . . . I'd have to research his work first, then go out there and talk to him. And if he's a recluse, it might take some time but if he was good enough, it would be worth it.'

Gavin smiled, rolling his elegant pen between finger and thumb.

'That's my job. But you'd have to look after him when we'd planned his appearance in Britain, organize his travel, find exactly the right place for him to stay, bone up on his work. And at the same time, we might be having problems with a band who were throwing tantrums, and you would have to sort that out, too. Do you think you could cope?'

'You mean, sometimes I'd have to be a nanny. That wouldn't bother me at all.'

Annie repressed a smile. Gavin leaned back and waited, keeping a set expression on his face.

'Could you tell us, Lucinda, what major changes you'd like to see on my programme?'

Lucinda wrinkled her brow, and looked towards Annie. Even though she had no desire to begin a discussion about Gavin's programme, Trevor had advised her to hide where her real ambitions lay. They never liked specialists, he said, not at the beginning, and preferred those who could turn their hand to anything on offer. Luckily, they had rehearsed what she would say about *Splash!*.

'I think it's a great programme, I really do.' Lucinda paused and looked straight at Gavin. Instinctively, she had begun to talk more quickly. 'It's built up a loyal audience. If it was me, I'd probably try a few heavier items, short, presented in the same way, but sometimes dealing with serious issues head on.'

Gavin replaced his pen carefully on the leather folder in front of him, and turned away. He could have said something, she thought. She longed to shout at them, 'Do you want me or don't you? Do I get the job or don't I?' Then she thought again of Trevor. Keep calm, darling. You look gorgeous, imagine I'm just sitting here, admiring you. But in spite of his encouragement, she was beginning to lose her nerve. Did they expect her to continue talking, or to end the interview? Her eyes suddenly met Annie's, but she wasn't betraying either sympathy or interest. She doesn't like me, she thought. Then Annie turned to address Alan.

'I happened to have seen Lucinda's script which she tried to sell in the States. Perhaps we ought to talk about that. I was rather impressed.'

'You read it? I showed it to Professor Watson, he thought there were too many characters. I don't think he liked it very much, but he's rather academic sometimes. We didn't always see eye to eye. Well, you know. I don't mean to criticize. He's a wonderful teacher.'

Lucinda looked confused, and her pale cheeks turned candyfloss pink. Annie remembered what it was like, preparing for an interview and then being taken offguard, saying something you hadn't prepared, knowing you might have offended someone.

'Don't worry. You are allowed to criticize my husband. Lots of people do. He probably wanted to keep you on the studious straight and narrow, before you saw how dreadful television can be.'

Suddenly, Lucinda found herself addressing the whole board, without knowing precisely what she would say. It was now or never.

'I know I'm being interviewed for two jobs. But I hope you don't mind me saying that what really excited me was the thought of being chosen to work in the drama department. I know that's where I'd be good, and that's where I'd be happy. I don't think anyone can touch Annie Griffiths, I've always thought that. *Streetcred* was the best series I've ever seen.'

She paused, took a breath, stopped looking round the table and talked directly to Annie. 'I'm not saying all this just because I want to work with you. Which I do, of course. But what's the point of working on something if your heart isn't in it?'

Annie gathered her notes together and rose from her chair,

'If we agreed to take you, when could you start?' asked Annie.

'I've got family commitments for a couple of weeks. I could start after that.'

Gavin slipped his narrow leather notepad into his pocket, and began to button up his jacket.

'Thank you for coming to see us, Lucinda. We enjoyed meeting you.'

As soon as Lucinda had left, Gavin turned towards Alan.

'Just the girl we need. I think she'll fit in marvellously. And a good mind, I imagine. Wouldn't you say? I can put her on the teenage talent slot, see how she gets on. Just the right personality. Firm but not pushy.'

'And that will bring our female to male ratio up to thirty-five per cent,' added Tania. 'We might reach our target next year.'

'I don't think we should underline the fact that she's the daughter of Lord Sherwood,' murmured Tony Sheldon. 'It might not go down well with the other staff. Nil publicity would be a wise move, in my view.'

'Surely Lucinda has enough going for her, I can't see it mattering,' said Annie. 'In any case, she's hardly going to run down the corridors shouting out his name.'

She looked round at Alan, Tony and Tania. 'It looks as though Gavin and I are going to fight over her.'

In the Hospitality Suite, where they retired for a drink, Annie continued the argument. Although she tried not to let it show, she resented Gavin's assumption that he was entitled to every attractive woman who walked through Intertel and she hoped Lucinda wouldn't be taken in by him, admittedly a vain hope. If she hadn't instantly warmed to Lucinda, it might have been different. This was always how she had selected people. Once she had absorbed a look, a voice, she knew. And she was going to take Lucinda.

'Annie, why are we arguing over this?' said Gavin, after putting a forceful case for his entitlement to Lucinda's presence. 'I really don't mind. If you want to have her in the drama department, go ahead. Anyone would think we were fighting over an issue of principle. It's not as though either of us depends on having Lord Sherwood's good opinion.'

'I didn't even think of that for one moment,' Annie replied, indignantly.

'He was very pleased at your appointment, if it matters to you. He thought you were the right man for the job.'

'I don't care what anyone thinks, Gavin.'

Suddenly he put his arm on her shoulder.

'We are friends, aren't we? I don't give a toss either. And I'm really glad you're at Intertel. We really needed someone gutsy in drama.'

'Thanks, Gavin.'

'You're still cross, I can see. Can you blame me for preferring Lucinda to Howard whatever his name was, the one we selected? I'm just a bloke, like any other, prone to predictable reactions. By the way, Annie, I think Trevor's smashing. Did I tell you?'

'I think you did.'

'Lucinda was lucky to have been taught by him. I wish he'd been my tutor. There was no-one like him at Cambridge.'

They didn't mention Lucinda again. Gavin invited Annie to a book launch, but she found herself declining with slight regret. She had told Kate she'd pick her up later, Dally was staying with a neighbour, so they could have an evening together. Trevor didn't know whether he'd be back in time for supper, but these days he was taking on so much work, she wondered how he managed to eat at all.

★   ★   ★

'Shall I do extra for Trevor?' asked Kate, as she chopped away at the onions, thumping down the great old rusty Sabatier knife they'd bought in France somewhere.

'You needn't bother. He probably won't be hungry even if he does get back in time. He says it's easier to get a quick bite in a nearby café, and then carry on working. I wish he'd ease off. And that Gavin wasn't getting him so involved with his programme. Some weeks I hardly see him.'

Kate threw the onions into a black-encrusted frying pan, black from the time when Trevor tried his hand at cooking.

'But I always try and be back at weekends,' Annie continued. 'Trevor says weekends are the only time he can get on with his book. Oh well, once it's out of the way . . .'

There was a sound of the door being pushed open and Annie ran into the hall.

'You're in luck, darling,' she said, winding her arms round Trevor's neck. 'Kate's doing supper.'

'I'm exhausted. Mind if I take a shower? I'll help later.'

'Too late,' said Annie. 'The girls are at it, Trev.'

'Be down in ten minutes.'

Kate looked up as he rushed out of the room.

'He didn't notice. Typical. Funny how men don't notice things, but I bet he sees a comma in the wrong place at twenty yards.'

'Thinking about his bloody book,' said Annie. 'I wish he'd get down and write it. He says he's already planned out ten chapters. That's the stage he likes. Planning. I can't stand it. I like to walk on a set and think there and then what I'd like the director to do. Fat chance. Can't I take this gear off?'

'No,' replied Kate. 'I want to see when it registers.'

Trevor thought he would wait until he had taken a second helping of Kate's vegetarian chilli, for which he had discovered an unusual appetitie.

'Annie? Didn't you have your appointments board today?'

'You're so good, Trev. Fancy you remembering. I forgot all about it till Alan reminded me.'

'I put it in my diary.'

'Well, it was in mine too. Not that it made any difference. I'd scribbled it down in the wrong one.'

Kate was unable to contain herself.

'Come on, Trev. What do you think?'

'Of what?'

'Annie's transformation.'

'Oh, the new clothes. Absolutely right for the part.'

'But not to Professor Watson's taste. He prefers high heels and short skirts.'

Annie winked at Kate.

'Come on, be honest. You think I look like Edwina Currie.'

'Heaven forbid! I can't help it, I just like you in jeans. Tight ones—'

'Implying that Annie's giving in to male expectations?' cut in Kate.

'Wrong. Quite wrong. I wasn't thinking that.'

Trevor gave his oh-what-a-foolish-man smile to placate the women.

'You can't get round it, we're still dictated to by men,' said Kate.

Annie took the floor before Kate had time to spring to the attack.

'Well, Trev. Today, I've just given employment to one of your protégées.'

'So Lucinda's made it?'

'I know it won't surprise you. But we were very careful to consider her on merit, so you can't accuse me of giving in to pressure to curry favour with her dad. Not yet, anyway. Actually, she came across very well. I'm going to give her a chance. Even though she did have a little dig at you.'

'Oh? What did she say?'

'She said you were rather academic, then the poor girl was embarrassed as hell. Putting down Annie Griffiths' husband, what not to do in an interview. I didn't mind. She did go on to say you were a wonderful teacher, and I think she meant it.'

'How about Gavin? Was he as impressed as you were?'

Trevor put down his fork, overcome with the bitter realization that his strategy for Lucinda had been both a failure and a success. It had worked too well, she had performed to his blueprint, but it was as though he had been playing into Annie's hands. Well done, my darling Lucinda. Faultless performance. Then he reproached himself for being only concerned for himself. It was what she wanted more than anything, to work with Annie. But would she accept that the price of her ambition was that they could no longer meet? Or could they? Strictly a working relationship. There was no need to be intimate with your boss, though many girls were. An image flashed through his mind, Lucinda bending over Annie, seated at her Intertel desk. Erotic, and impossible. The wife and mistress together, both adoring the same man, one in ignorance of the other's passion. Christ, this is the plotline for a film, he thought with horror. What am I doing? How did I get myself into this?

'To be honest, I didn't think you'd take to Lucinda,' he said.

Annie surveyed Trevor's face, which showed irritation rather than pleasure.

'Because in your view she's upper-crust confident, stunningly beautiful, which you didn't mention of course—'

'I did say she was good looking.'

'—right-wing spoiled and thinks the world will donate her a living?'

Trevor piled another heap of rice onto his plate, spilling some grains over the table.

'Well, Professor Watson, you might be surprised. Would you have guessed that she reads the *Guardian*?'

'Does she?' replied Trevor. 'Did she mention it?'

'No, but she quoted from a piece of yours. All right, she might have just swotted up on the *Guardian* Arts page for the interview, it doesn't mean she doesn't have goddawful Establishment views. I'll soon see, won't I? Maybe she'll change. Who knows, once she's been grubbing around for grotty locations, she might even find there's life beyond Chelsea.'

Trevor frowned, trying to conjure up an anonymous figure, a statistic in the class profile of Britain, instead of the beautiful, soft-skinned naked girl lying sprawled across the bed with the fluttering flags.

'They don't all live in Chelsea. I thought it was Brixton nowadays.'

'No. Her address is SW3. Probably around the King's Road. Anyway, I don't care where she lives. Lucinda's coming in two weeks. If she starts trotting out your ideas, at least I'll know all the answers.'

'Good. I hope it works out. I'm glad you've found someone you like.'

'You don't sound it.'

Kate began to clear the plates, while Trevor opened another bottle of wine.

'Trev, why don't you trust Annie's judgement? Why shouldn't it all work out perfectly well? What do you think will happen?'

'Nothing will happen,' said Annie, firmly. 'And I want Lucinda to do well. Trevor doesn't realize that I sometimes think of the next generation. It's no good being up at the top and looking down and seeing no-one. That's what screws up the bloody Brits. Why be afraid of who's coming behind you? I want other people to succeeed, I really do.'

'Women to succeed,' added Kate.

After supper, Kate showed no inclination to go home. It was thoughtless, when she must have known that they saw so little of one another. But then Kate had never been in a marriage, never appreciated the checks and balances of saying what needed to be said, instead of hoarding up the uncertainties, or the discussions which needed some kind of conclusion. At times, Annie found her insensitive, and then she chided herself for denying Kate the warmth of a pleasant home which she lacked. She watched her washing up, as though she was fulfilling a much-loved ritual, sweeping the cloth round Annie's dishes, putting the bowls in the right places, arranging the bottles and jars in ordered rows on the pine shelves. Trevor had put on a video and was reading a book lying on the settee, one eye on the screen.

By the time Kate had left, Trevor was fast asleep, the book resting face down on his chest. Annie switched off the video, and was unable to decide whether to wake him up. She had noticed that he was sleeping more than he used to, going to bed earlier, as though he was unable to throw off his exhaustion. It had never crossed her mind before, that you began to slow down after fifty. Then she thought of him attacking the garden, throwing the spade into the earth, piling into the hard ground. This was not the moment to voice her concern that he was pushing himself too hard. She would ask Bryonie's advice, he trusted her, and she might suggest sending him for a medical examination. Men died before their time. She would never forgive herself.

Annie wrote 'Ring Bryonie' in her ragged notebook, and then, on impulse, she ripped out a spare page. 'I love you. Come to bed!' she wrote. Having removed the book, she placed the paper on Trevor's chest, lightly swept back the stray grey curls from his ear, then studied his face, the closed lids, the lips which seemed to have a half-smile as though he had sensed her presence, turned off the lights and crept quietly upstairs.

9

ANNIE

Annie pushed open the door of the office which Lucinda had closed, not yet being familiar with the ways of Intertel. It would take more than two weeks to make the transition from Chelsea flower boutique to a high-pressure media factory.

'Bloody chaos in here,' Annie muttered, more to herself than to Lucinda. Then she threw her hands up and shrieked, 'Where's my shooting script? It was here before lunch.'

Lucinda shuffled around the papers on her desk, and pulled out a red folder.

'I put it in here. So you wouldn't lose it.'

'No need,' snapped Annie. 'I can find my way around muddle. Why waste time just moving things from one place to another? Utter waste of time.'

'Let's have one corner in order.'

'All right. If you must. The boss's corner. The Alan Coker Chapel of Rest.'

The office bore little resemblance to the official residence of the Controller of Drama, but Annie didn't care. Then she relented. When she had a moment, it might be wise to make a gesture towards convention, bring in a designer with time on his hands. Rick had dropped in one evening and said her space looked like a newsroom on full twenty-four-hour alert. Annie told him to get lost, but Rick persisted. Spend their fucking money, Annie. It wasn't as though it would go on programmes, and Benny had just spent twenty grand on his, even if it did resemble the waiting-room of a Harley Street abortionist.

Lucinda began to make a valiant effort to clear the papers, scripts, odd bits of shopping, pages ripped out from magazines, piles of tapes and retouched photographs sent by agents to display the available talent which were piled up on the couch.

'Don't bother with that,' said Annie, as Lucinda began to load a pile of papers onto some empty shelves. 'That's enough order for one day.'

She walked round to Lucinda's desk, screened off from Annie's larger section of the room by an anti-graffiti melamine slab popular in government offices.

'We can get rid of this, though. Intertel took down the walls in this place and put up daft screens everywhere.'

'Don't you want privacy sometimes?'

'Not that kind. Everything here happens in the open, screens don't make any difference.'

Annie tossed over an Internal directory.

'Call someone in maintenance. They'll take it away.'

Reading through her correspondence, Annie could hear Lucinda carrying out her wishes. Tentatively, she was explaining why the screen needed to be removed, could someone possibly attend to it. Without thinking, Annie rushed over to Lucinda's phone, and took it out of her hand.

'Annie Griffiths here. I want someone to remove that damn thing this afternoon. Right?'

Then she put down the phone.

'There's no time to pussyfoot around in this place, Lucinda. You'll get used to it. Everyone has to act bullying and tough, otherwise nothing'll happen.'

'Oh, I can when I have to. But when I get cross, no-one takes me seriously. They don't realize I'm trying to do my job like everyone else.'

'You're doing fine. And in any case, most of them aren't trying.'

Annie wondered if she was being too hard on her, but she couldn't be anything else.

'I hope you understand I can't say nice things to you, not when I'm hurtling towards the final fence. It doesn't mean I don't appreciate what you do.'

'Lucinda sat on the edge of her desk. Even near the end of the day, her make-up was subtle and fresh, her shirt uncrumpled.

'I knew it might be difficult when I came here.'

'You still want to stay?'

'Annie, what a stupid thing to say. It is what I expected, you know. Professor Watson used to tell us what we were in for.'

'So Trevor prepared you for this shitty place? He knows

126

nothing about it. You can't know, not secondhand. The Controller of Budgets has told me to shave off a week from my schedule. Way over, he said.'

'We'll need that week. As it is, we'll be going flat out. And what about contingency?'

'Quite. You tell him.'

'I will, if you like.'

Annie laughed.

'You can buy him a drink. Soften him up. Tell him how marvellous I am.'

'It's outrageous, having that loony telling you what to do. Why doesn't someone fire him? Why do you put up with it, Annie?'

'Because I'm making programmes in a system. I'm not batting off with a student film crew and taking all day on one shot.'

'Trevor used to talk a lot about it, what television was really like, how it had changed. His lectures were great. He used to warn us, he said commercial television was a wild-west industry.'

Annie chuckled and put down her script.

'My line. Dear Trev, he never misses a trick. You know something? Now, I think what he says is often obvious. Maybe I've lived with him too long.'

'You don't mean that.'

'He always reads to me everything he writes. If I don't like something, he argues, then scrubs it out. When I'm not there. All right, I'm being unfair. Or it's a reaction, so people won't think I'm the adoring wife. I can't stand women who drool over their husbands' achievements.'

'Neither can I. The girls in my year were unbearable. They were all madly in love with him and used to ask stupid questions, just to have him look in their direction.'

'Were you like that?'

'Gosh, no. I thought it was a schoolgirly thing to do, to have a crush on a professor. I did admire him though, because he never said what you expected. Once he told us that the ideas and ideals of television came originally from the upper classes, not from the jumped-up entrepreneurs who came into the industry for a fast buck. I was quite surprised he mentioned that.'

'Why should you be?'

'It didn't fit into his political perspective. The other students sneered and said it was a bourgeois analysis. They saw everything in terms of politics, but I didn't. Why should politics come into art? You do what you want to do. Otherwise you're being manipulated by someone else.'

'I'm being manipulated by Alan's business plan for Intertel. Don't kid yourself. I wanted twice the budget for *Rough Trade*, and I sat there raging, watching it whittled away.'

Annie grinned. It was a bond between them, Lucinda's admiration for Trevor. It had been so long since she had been his student, now it came back to her, groping for ideas, wondering what you thought, struggling to put your half-baked ideas into a shape – and then, once you'd left his tutorials, you didn't need to question any more. He made everything fall into place. Only when they'd left as graduates did his former students start to wonder whether there was another point of view which was equally strong, equally irrefutable. Some of them never did wonder.

'I hope you didn't take on board everything Trevor said. He often goes too far, to make a point, or to be controversial.'

'Well, you do take it all frightfully seriously at first. When someone's older than you, and a professor and very brilliant. But I wanted to be doing drama with you, I've wanted to for ages. When I was meant to be doing my homework, I used to watch your series. *Laughing in the Dark*.'

Laughing in the Dark was Annie's first full-length series, the one which resulted in bigger budgets, an office of her own, but most of all several statuettes and framed awards. That was ten years ago, when Lucinda had barely reached the age of consent.

'What attracted you so much?'

'I wanted to see how things really are. Without pretending. What it's like to have nothing that I've had. I could live with nothing, you know.'

'Could you? I couldn't. When you've had nothing, you want something. Living with nothing is bloody tedious, scrimping and saving and telling yourself how virtuous you are. No thanks. That's why I liked the villains in *Streetcred*, no pretence, no faffing about morality. Raw humans, no messing.'

Lucinda still hesitated a fraction before she said Trevor's name, as though she was avoiding being thought over-familiar. Annie was beginning to recognize the delicacy of the rooted good manners which would have come naturally to her. And she still had to remind herself how powerful Trevor's influence could be. What he achieved was lasting and, if pressed, Annie would have conceded that his work was more important than her own. What had she created? A few series which might be remembered for ten years at most. In only three short years of a student's life, he was able to overthrow years of uninspiring teaching, to open windows and reveal undreamed-of vistas. They had told her this, at graduation parties, how you only needed one good teacher in your life, and how lucky they were to have found Trevor. They would always remember Professor Watson, would only see him as he was then, the long-legged, handsome man with the mop of thick, fair, curling hair, gesturing in the air, rocking on his feet as he expounded his enthusiasms.

After a couple of weeks had gone by, Annie brought Lucinda along to the first meeting with Hugh, the director, Clary Hunt and Tony O'Mara, the two principal actors. Following this meeting, Annie would know instantly whether she possessed the instinctive sympathy to gain the actors' confidence, whether she would be an asset on location.

'Trevor won't be seen dead in here,' said Annie, as she signed in her guests at the Groucho Club.

'Why ever not?' asked Lucinda.

'No decent beer, that's his excuse. He's made a few suggestions for the script of episode one, but we'll get feedback from the actors first.'

'What were his comments?'

'I'll tell you later. Make a note of what everyone says, then we'll discuss it together afterwards.'

'Anything else I should do?'

'Make the actors feel good. Listen to them. Tony's quite experienced, but Clary will be scared. Her nerviness will be good for the part, so I want to keep her just a little on edge.'

'Isn't that the director's job?'

'I chose Hugh because he's brilliant technically. Actors, I can look after – so if he wants to spend all day setting up something spectacular, they won't get in the way.'

Annie walked swiftly round the armchairs and settees to establish a working corner at a back table. Clary arrived first, sauntering across towards them in a tight black leather jacket, shiny black skin-tight trousers and a scarlet baseball cap. She sat down like a model, carefully positioning one leg across her thigh. Then Hugh came hurrying in, a sandy-haired young man in John Lennon glasses, with a vast shoulder-bag weighting down his bony shoulder, accompanied by Tony O'Mara, who was going through his blonded, *Baywatch* phase, the result of a commercials shoot in Hawaii. Annie made the introductions and ordered champagne.

'Thank God we're not meeting in some ghastly rehearsal room,' said Tony, sweeping back a blond lock. 'Still, Annie's one of the old school.'

'What's the new school, then?' asked Clary.

'Treating actors like shit.'

'No-one treats me like shit. Just try it, mate.'

'Wonderful to have confidence. Wish I had.'

'You sendin' me up?'

'Course not, love.'

Annie spread the scripts over the table.

'So what's the story, folks?' began Tony. 'I only came off location last night, Ricky worked my balls off, only had time to whip through the script.'

Clary sniffed, and pushed her cap, which was obscuring her eyes, to the back of her head. She had worked with Tony once on a commercial, but while she was background bargirl, he was foreground action. Following his upbeat reception as the lead male of *Streetcred*, and his fashionably androgynous but tough and versatile looks, he was now able to choose his parts. Even if he had been to drama school and played *Macbeth* in rep, and Clary, until Annie picked her out, had only come as far as one-liners in soaps, now they would have equal billing. She'd make sure he didn't forget.

'I love the character of Ben,' continued Tony. 'Yet again, brilliant casting, Annie. Even better than Roy in *Streetcred*. I'll be changing my hair colour, don't worry about that. Ben would have it black. Shall I dye it black? Or would brown be better? Dark brown?'

Lucinda looked from Clary to Tony, and then caught Annie's eye. She gave a hint of a wink and picked up a script, just as a tray of champagne glasses was set before them.

'Right. The story first. It's not always obvious,' began Annie tactfully, well aware that at first most actors only read the parts which concerned them.

'I hope we'll have decent rehearsal time. My part needs a lot of development, Annie. I see it as . . .'

Hugh gave a despairing glance at Lucinda and folded his arms. He was one of those directors who preferred to communicate with lighting cameramen. You either had patience with actors or you didn't.

'We'll talk about that,' said Annie.

'Can't we 'ave the story?' muttered Clary.

'Trish, that's Clary, is a girl who temps, loves her freedom, loves a challenge. She answers an ad for a secretary and is employed by Ben Oakes, a successful criminal lawyer with a passion for motor bikes.'

'Shame it wasn't horses, I'm good with them,' said Tony. 'I fall off motor bikes, Hugh, but I do it with bravado. Keep it in close up and I'm all right. Do I take it I'll be insured? Or do we have a stuntman, Annie?'

'Morley hasn't got back on his availability. Check that, would you?'

Lucinda made a hurried note, and Annie continued.

'Trish becomes indispensable and stays full time with Ben. Then, she starts to fall in love with him. She learns that he's receiving threats from an anonymous client. His life is in danger. Trish takes on the role of protecting him. She learns to handle a gun, ride his bike.'

'Well!' said Tony, directing his comment at Clary. 'We both get to ride a bike. Hope it's a Harley.'

Clary nudged him in the ribs.

'Shut up. Let 'er finish.'

'Now Trish is determined to hunt down the man who's after Ben. His name is Perry Barnes, a financial dealer holed up in a Scottish castle.'

'Who's playing him?' asked Tony. 'Anyone I know?

'Not finalized yet. Anyway, Trish tracks down Perry and meets him in a Virtual Reality arcade in Blackpool. She is forced to use her gun, and fatally wounds him.'

'I never done stuff with a gun,' said Clary.

Annie gave a reassuring smile.

'You'll get the idea in no time. We'll take you to a shooting club. Now, before Perry dies, he tells Trish that he was in on a fifty-fifty money-laundering operation with Ben. Together, they were planning to open a casino but at the crucial moment, Ben failed to come across with his share of the cash and Perry lost everything. Refusing to believe it at first, Trish starts to investigate. To her horror, she discovers that Ben, too, is a crook who's been syphoning off millions of clients' funds. Although she still loves him, she gives key evidence to the Fraud Office to get him arrested.'

Tony leaned forward, pondering the percentage of his on-screen appearance compared with Clary's.

'It's wonderful, really really exciting,' he began. Then he threw himself back against the chair. 'Of course, the whole series depends on my relationship with Clary. That is key, absolutely key. You can't possibly do it without intensive rehearsal, not one of your walk-on-the-mark-and-spout jobs.'

Lucinda broke in.

'We are allowing time for rehearsal, don't worry.'

'Thank God for professionals,' said Tony.

At Annie's suggestion, Lucinda walked over to the bar with Hugh. He had directed one episode of *Streetcred* for Annie, but he knew he could do better.

'I want this to be more *Chinatown* than *Chinatown*,' he said to Lucinda, once he realized she shared his passion for film. 'But honed down for the small screen. Every shot must count.'

While they were going through the locations for the first episode, Lucinda brought out a file of pictures and descriptions with approximate measurements.

'You've done an amazing job, Lucinda. Really grateful. I hope you're coming on location.'

'Depends on Annie and how much she needs me in the office. I'm sure she'll get you a good production assistant.'

'In any case, I'd like your opinion on a location I'm keen on. It's a derelict house I noticed on the riverbank near Chelsea Harbour, owned by some retired admiral. See if we could rent it, then we could use it for Ben's house interior and exterior. That river view would be magic.'

'Sounds great. And it might be an idea if I set up my office there. There's no point in going backwards and forwards to Intertel all the time.'

Lucinda smiled happily. To have the principal location of *Rough Trade* but a short walk from her home would be ideal. And if Annie was happy with Hugh, she wouldn't be spending all her time checking on his progress. Once they started shooting, there would be breaks, occasions when she could escape for a couple of hours. They could meet during the day. Hadn't he confessed that at college he always took on more than he needed to, that he knew he worked too hard? She would persuade him to cut down his obligation for the summer term. Hadn't she always told him that they would find a way to be together more often?

Annie began to look forward to coming into her office and finding Lucinda seated at her desk. She had an instinctive way of understanding when they could chat, when she should just get on with the essential tasks which Annie needed to be accomplished. Soon Annie found out where she could be most effective. Agents and actors were won over by her ability to see their point of view, and to allay their anxieties. She checked and double-checked, and was always fair. She told Annie what she had done, what she had not been able to do and why. It was not long before Annie began to depend on her. Even if she was unable to do something, she explained why, always asked what was important, what wasn't. In a short time, she had made Annie value her judgement. She didn't mind when she made suggestions – small changes to dialogue, an extra scene which might make the story flow better – and she had a good eye for casting, knowing how to fit the pieces together like Kate throwing together a set. Lucinda had taken instinct-ively to the small screen, accepting its limitations without yearning for Hollywood production values, like the usual young newcomers to Intertel. Annie would be proud of her one day.

Annie's office had undergone a transformation – tiny spotlights beaming down like distant stars on light, grainy desks, un-dulating Italian chairs and a taffeta-covered pink casting couch in the shape of a grin. So far, half the locations had been found and there were six scripts of *Rough Trade* still being worked on. Shooting would begin in a month's time. May had been shiny and hot, but Annie wanted murky and cold. She hoped the forecasters would slip up, that June would revert to a showery normality instead of aping a Mediterranean climate.

One evening in early June, after Lucinda had been out all day with the designer, finding props for the admiral's house in Chelsea, Annie decided the moment was right. She hadn't wanted to probe, but she had wondered if she was pushing Lucinda too hard. Sometimes she felt that Lucinda was terrified of making a mistake, that she was setting herself impossible standards. The strain was showing on her face, hollow cheeks and over-bright eyes.

'Would you like to take Friday off?' Annie asked. 'We're doing well at the moment, things seem under control. You could take off, visit some friends, forget about all this. Is that friend of yours around, the one who's been calling all week?'

'Jeremy, you mean?'

She looked accusingly at Annie, as though she had no right to ask the question.

'He rang today, while you were out, that's all. Is he your special boyfriend?'

'No, no. I mean yes. I suppose he is special. I've known him a long time.'

Annie came over and leaned against Lucinda's desk.

'Do you get on well?'

'Yes.'

'Good, I'm glad. You need someone. We all do. Look, we usually have a few mates round on Fridays. Would you like to come round, when we've started shooting? Once the show's on the road, it'll be easier. You're welcome to bring Jeremy along.'

'I know it sounds awful, but I usually go home at weekends. It's super of you to ask me, Annie.'

Lucinda picked up her bag and smoothed back her hair.

'Mind if I go now?'

'Sure. Get some rest. We'll make it another evening then. Yes?'

'I'd like to very much.'

Annie was aware that Lucinda'a diary was crammed with social events, family dinners, parties, country weekends, invitations from boyfriends whose names were constantly changing. They all sounded so young, unworn voices. They sometimes rang the office when Annie answered, requesting to speak to Lucinda in exactly the same manner, 'I say, could I . . . ?' Annie smiled. She had to remind herself that at their age the difference between twenties and forties was dramatic. They were the colour generation who would never have seen black-and-white television. Sometimes she forgot how old she must seem to someone like Lucinda. Not having children, she hadn't needed to be reminded of passing years, or what was appropriate for her age. If Lucinda had seemed embarrassed in refusing her invitation, it could have been her way of signalling the divide between them. Another girl in her place would have agreed instantly to Annie's hospitality, seeing it as a way of developing a closer relationship which might lead to swift promotion. But Lucinda wasn't like that. Annie respected her for it.

When Annie asked Lucinda once again to come over to Langton Villas, she said there was a party she had to go to that night, she'd promised her friends. On her way home, Annie wondered if she was being aloof, she sometimes gave that impression when she was asked about her life outside the office. Occasionally, she referred to her family. It must be difficult for her, adjusting to her two different lives. Her mother, she told her, disapproved of television. Absolutely ghastly job. Why did she want to go into those horrible places full of horrible people? Daddy, too, would have been much keener on her starting at the bottom with something like picture restoration or garden design; there were plenty of opportunities for well-educated girls to have an interesting career. She admired her father, Annie could see that. She tried not to hold it against him that he was now on to his fourth marriage, even though her mother had been so devastated when he asked for a divorce that she tried to kill herself. 'I don't believe anyone should be married to Daddy,' Lucinda said once. Not surprisingly, she often announced that she had no intention of getting married herself. One day, Annie thought, she would be an ideal producer.

Annie was unaware that Lucinda was the subject of gossip in the Grotto, as she had carefully resisted Rick's lunch invitations. She was building her team, determined not to be distracted, but he caught up with her one day, while they were both waiting by the ground-floor lift.

'Why haven't we seen you, Annie?' Rick said. 'Or doesn't your gorgeous assistant take lunch?'

'Too busy. But we might be in the bar this evening, if everything goes well.'

'Can't do tonight. I promised Bry I'd be home early to cook dinner.'

'Another time, then,' said Annie, feeling a pang of resentment. Why couldn't Trevor do the same, just occasionally? Then she added, quickly, 'I'm not trying to avoid you, Rick, but we're going flat out, aiming to get the whole of *Rough Trade* in the can by the end of August. And I'm not going to miss out on our annual hols in Greece.'

'You'd better not. Bry's booked the villa. I'd better mention it to Alan. "Look now, Alan, I want no big stories in September, else I quit." Will I like *Rough Trade*? Plenty of clothes-off rolling-on-the-bed scenes?'

'Lots of action.'

'I'll look and despair. Things are quiet at the moment. And I mean arctic bloody desolately quiet. I ask you.'

Rick punched the lift-button as he spoke, punctuating his dialogue with boxer-thrusts of impatience.

'Your Lucinda doesn't waste any time. Benny saw her getting out of Gavin's car, guess where?'

'Some working men's club?'

Gavin's penchant for taking his chauffeur-driven car to 'real places with real people' was well known at Intertel, though he did so less often than they supposed.

'Dead right, Annie. You could describe Langan's as that, though I wouldn't. I don't suppose she happened to mention it? Just in passing?'

'Why should she?'

'She might have said, "Gavin took me out to dinner last night. What a boring stuck-up little prick he is. I don't understand what anyone sees in him." But I suspect she has little between the ears.'

Annie laughed.

'You mean, she hasn't agreed to have tea with you yet.'

The lift came to a slow halt at the ground floor, disgorging a crowd of youths in Doc Martens, tapered, drainpipe slacks and bright red and blue T-shirts with graffiti lettering scattered over the chest: 'Dive in with *Splash!*' Rick ignored them and pushed past, holding open the doors for Annie.

'Am I that obvious?' he said. 'Does my technique need a little refining?'

'Your technique needs putting on hold. How's the housing report coming along?'

'It's been shelved. Too much foreign news. More on the Torrington murder. The usual excuse. Christ, I hate this place.'

As the lift stopped at his floor, Rick braced himself and set off like a wild boar.

That evening, Annie and Lucinda managed to put in an appearance at the bar. Usually, Annie was surrounded by a crowd of people, but when she was with Lucinda, she noticed that everyone kept their distance as though they thought her far too superior to giggle in a corner or exchange company gossip.

'It's difficult to make friends here,' Annie began. 'But once they get used to you being around, it'll get easier.'

'It doesn't worry me,' replied Lucinda. 'I haven't done anything yet that they can talk about. One day I will. But I really don't care whether Thelma has had her tits done or how often Gavin cheats on his wife. Why is everyone so interested?'

'Lucinda, don't take this the wrong way, but you haven't been here long. It's a game they all play, creating their own little world to protect them from the thought of all those viewers out there. The great love-hate relationship with the public.'

'Gavin doesn't seem worried.' Lucinda smiled, and placed her glass delicately back on the bar. 'Am I the only person here who doesn't fancy him?'

'Just as well.'

'What do you mean, Annie?'

'Gavin would like nothing more than to see Lucinda Sherwood flashing up on the credits. Did you have a good dinner at Langan's?'

'What did Gavin tell you?' said Lucinda, indignantly. 'All he did was to give me a lift. I didn't have my car and he was going to Langan's. I was meeting a friend there, so I accepted. That's all.'

Annie laughed.

'There's no need to be defensive. I was curious, that's all.'

'Gavin's been trying it on ever since I came here. Why wouldn't I come to his department? I'd have a much better chance with him. It's the last thing I want, interviewing other people all the time, it's not me, Annie. I said I was happy in drama and wouldn't leave unless you kicked me out.'

'And what did Gavin say to that?'

'Oh, nothing much.'

'Come on. I won't be offended.'

'Actually he said that I wouldn't last long, that you had a reputation for firing people at the Beeb if they did just one thing wrong. Ruthless, he called you. I just laughed. If men are jealous, they always say you're ruthless, don't they?'

'I suppose so.'

'So what's Gavin ever done? What's he so proud of?'

'Gavin takes himself seriously as a poet.'

'Really? Does anyone else?'

Every now and again her voice changed. Now Annie could imagine her batting comments to and fro, across some formal dining table where reputations were shredded or repaired according to the whim of the guests.

'What makes me really angry is that he asked to see a copy of my script, then pretended he'd read it. I knew he hadn't. When I said you were impressed, all he said was that Intertel never went for untried writers, not in drama.'

'Silly fool. What does he know? Don't be upset about it, I'm sure he's like that with everyone.'

'You were impressed, weren't you, Annie? You do think it works?'

'Yes, I do.'

'When *Rough Trade* is finished, you are going to consider producing it? I don't want anyone else to touch *Grains of Evil*.'

'Don't worry. We'll discuss it seriously when I get back from holiday.'

Observing the tension in Lucinda's face, Annie wished she could give a firmer commitment. But how could she explain that some of the best scripts were never produced?

'It's got to be done, Annie,' Lucinda said emphatically. 'The first thing you write, the first thing that's good enough to show, even if you don't know it at the time, it's always the most important. Like *Citizen Kane* for Orson Welles. He had to make that film. He would probably have killed to make it. I understand that. I'd give up everything, work for nothing, just to see *Grains of Evil* on the screen.'

'You think you'll be an Orson Welles?' said Annie, with a smile. She had met many writers who thought that they would open the eyes of the world. But Lucinda had an intensity about what she wanted, an unnerving passion which almost appeared as ruthlessness. She wasn't sure whether she could work with her.

'I'll settle for Buñuel. I won't be Spielberg, I promise you that,' Lucinda said lightly, as though aware that she had betrayed more than she intended.

'Spielberg has done some marvellous things,' said Annie. 'Though Trevor would agree with you, he doesn't rate him either. Buñuel's his hero, too.'

'Can I get you another glass of wine?'

Annie looked over at the clock by the bar. It was just possible that Trevor would be back home, as he'd promised not to be too late.

'I'd love to stay and talk. But I can't, not tonight.'

As Annie left, she turned round quickly to see if Lucinda would remain in the bar. She was still there, sitting on a high stool with her back to the drinkers, legs crossed, staring distractedly into space holding a glass. Although others were clearly noticing her, she appeared to ignore them. As she walked to the back entrance, Annie was trying to decide whether Lucinda took her beauty for granted or even despised it. She never betrayed by a slight gesture, a lowering of her gaze or a flirtatious turn of the head that she was proud of arousing male desire. But she could hardly be unaware of it. Annie sensed that there was some wound, some cruelty in her family history which she would never reveal.

During the momentum of work which was leading up to the first shooting day of *Rough Trade*, Annie was besieged by demands. If she wasn't careful, Hugh would escalate the budget out of control, but she knew that to achieve the look they both wanted, it would need endless care – and constant compromise. She was trying to fight back her feelings of dread. All those weeks when anything could go wrong, when one sick actor, one row, could rock the whole production. Alan, she had heard, was quite capable of knocking a programme on the head if the figures were racing ahead of calculations made by the Controller of Accounts. If something were to go wrong, Annie prayed it would happen at the beginning of the shoot, when there was time to recover.

The night before day one of the shoot, Annie was unable to keep still, pacing round the office, pestering Lucinda to find out what they had forgotten. At last, she persuaded her to leave. Everything was set for a glorious shoot. The late June weather was showery with sunny intervals, perfect for the first set-up. Lucinda waved a cheerful goodbye as she went towards the multi-storey car-park to collect her BMW, leaving Annie piling her bags into the boot of her Saab. While she was putting the key in the ignition, the thought struck her that she had not checked her car for weeks. She knew it. Tonight she almost wanted something to go wrong. She had to pay her dues so that the following day would pass without a hitch. The engine refused to ignite, rasping fruitlessly like a retching child who is unable to be sick. Annie swore, then jumped out of the car in time to see the black blur of Lucinda's BMW halting at the security gate. Bill, who was just starting his evening shift, must have heard the wheezing of her Saab, because he was walking towards her.

'Motor trouble, Annie?'

'Hell!'

'Open up the bonnet. I'll give it a once over.'

While she was fumbling for the bonnet catch, Lucinda caught up with her and knocked on the half-open car window.

'Annie! What's up?'

'Christ knows,' said Annie, wishing she could give one mighty kick, like she used to with her old Renault, which did the trick on most occasions. 'Why can't they give me a bloody car that works?' Seeing Bill with his nose close to the engine, like a sniffer dog hunting out drugs, made her even more livid.

'Leave it, Bill. Don't waste your time. I must be off.'

'Up to you.' He raised his head, and stood back scratching his head, as the bonnet dropped back again.

'Do you want a lift?' asked Lucinda. 'I can go your way quite easily.'

'You'll regret it. I live way out in the sticks. Take you ages.'

'Come on. Kentish Town's not that far.'

'How did you know that was my patch?'

Lucinda gave Annie a startled look, as she helped her to decant her bags from the boot. 'I think I read it somewhere.'

'Oh?'

When they had piled everything up in Lucinda's car, she suddenly turned with a smile to Annie.

'I know, it was that interview in *The Times*. You said you preferred Kentish Town to Hampstead.'

'So I did,' said Annie. 'Do you always remember silly things like that?'

'You're training me to pick up on detail.'

'Good girl!'

As Annie settled back in the passenger seat, Lucinda took out a comb from the glove compartment and ran it quickly through her hair. She did this automatically, something which would never have occurred to Annie. Then she took her almond silk scarf with the pink roses, twisted it expertly around her brow, then tied it at the back.

'It's beautiful, that scarf,' remarked Annie, having noticed that she wore it constantly, like a talisman, and that somehow it always toned with whatever she was wearing.

'A boyfriend gave it to me for Christmas. He always gives

me lovely things. It would suit you, Annie. Here.' She pulled off the scarf, and draped it over Annie's shoulder. 'Your colours more than mine. Would you like it?'

'It's sweet of you. But I'd only lose it. I'm hopeless with scarves and umbrellas. Besides, it looks good on you.'

Having retied the scarf, Lucinda took out a small black compact from the glove compartment, quickly dusted her face and glanced in the driving mirror.

'Are you seeing Jeremy tonight?' Annie asked, as she directed Lucinda through the maze of one-way streets which eventually allowed them to approach Langton Villas.

'I might. But he wanted to go to see some ghastly rock band he thinks is marvellous. The trouble is, he's not that keen on seeing movies. Not real movies, that is.' Lucinda slowly applied the brakes, by coincidence near number fourteen.

'Just stop here. Trevor should be back. Would you like to say hello?'

Lucinda declined, and said that another time she'd love to.

'I really appreciate the lift,' said Annie. 'Do you know your way back?'

'As long as I head south,' Lucinda replied confidently. 'Tell me if you need a good garage, Annie. Mine's super. They'll sort out your Saab in a day. Shall I pick you up tomorrow?'

'I'll have to take a cab into Intertel, I've left some things behind I need. Could you meet me there? Six a.m.?'

Lucinda grinned.

'Fine.'

'I hate early starts,' said Annie. 'Maybe I should get a driver.'

'No point. I don't mind, really.'

Annie's natural inclination would have been to give her a friendly kiss, not a showbiz kiss but a token of physical affection which she felt for Lucinda. When you worked with someone all day, it seemed natural to express the closeness of having someone a few feet away from you. But she sensed that such a gesture would be alien to Lucinda. Annie wanted to show her that it was not unnatural to show emotion, to break down the steely barrier of class. One day she hoped Lucinda would express the passion which occasionally flashed from her grey-blue eyes, ridding herself of the harsh censor who seemed to be holding her back, the legacy of Lord Sherwood. Annie knew, if she ever met him, she would hate him on sight.

As she came through the front gate, Annie looked up and

saw Trevor at the window of his study, his face pressed close to the glass. When she burst into the hall, throwing down her bags with a thud, he came running down the stairs. Annie rushed into his arms, and he held her tight.

'Has anything happened? I thought you'd be back earlier tonight.'

'You'll never guess, love. My car went phut. So much for the Saab. Lucinda gave me a lift. Are you starving?'

'I'll cook. Let me cook.'

'That would be great, I was really hoping you'd offer,' said Annie. The resentment she had felt earlier melted away. She followed Trevor into the kitchen and slumped into a chair. 'Lucinda insisted she'd pick me up at six tomorrow morning. Isn't that sweet of her?'

'Darling, why not take my car?'

'Wouldn't dream of it, Trev. If Intertel have given me a clapped-out wreck, that's their look-out. When I get back, I'll order a chauffeur.'

'Annie Griffiths reclining in the back seat of a limo? You're not going to sit in the back reading the *Financial Times* with a portable phone pressed to your lips?'

'Only if I'm making a sexy call to you. Otherwise, I'll be in the front, driving the poor driver crazy. Do you think they'll give me one?'

'A what, darling?'

'A chauffeur with a cap. I can't wait to drive up to Swindon and tell him to park outside the dole office.'

Trevor looked blank.

'What are you doing in Swindon? I thought you were using that house in Chelsea?'

'I'm shooting there. Christ, Trev. What's come over you? I told you several times, you must know the script by now, there's that great scene in episode one where Ben crashes through the bulletproof glass and—'

'Of course. I'd forgotten it was Swindon.'

'The weather forecast's foul. Isn't that wonderful? I need rain for the exterior.'

'But you're not overnighting, I hope.'

'I wanted to get back. But I've booked in to a hotel. We've got the next morning for reshoots. Bound to need it. In any case, I'll need to crash out and get some sleep with that schedule.'

142

'I hope Lucinda's a good driver.'

'Better than me. Which wouldn't be difficult. She's one of those people who drives as though she's making love to the gearbox. Smooth as silk.'

Trevor ripped open the shrink-wrapped meat with such energy that it flew from his hands and landed on the floor. He picked it up, and held it under a gush of running water. Annie made no comment.

'I wish you'd take my car, though,' said Trevor.

'I thought you said you were going to be away this weekend?'

'I can go by train, Annie. It doesn't matter.'

'Don't be ridiculous. You know you'll need it.'

With her first Intertel salary cheque, Annie had insisted on putting a hefty down payment on a lusty, bright red Japanese convertible for Trevor. Initially he had objected, saying it would not be appropriate for a puritanical left-wing professor to own such a growling, showy beast. And besides, he disapproved of the Japanese patriarchy-based economy. But Annie had teased him, saying she knew he really wanted it and he wasn't ready for the pipe and carpet slippers yet, not for a few years. And she did know, after all this time, how much he hated sitting in the passenger seat, clenching his teeth whenever she went over sixty. In any case, what was wrong with having the dream of the working classes? They'd respect him for it, and if one of his mates from Nottingham had won the lottery, wouldn't he have bought one just like it?

Drying the meat with a paper towel, Trevor's movements became calmer.

'How's it going with Lucinda? I hope she's not driving you mad.'

Annie grinned. 'Only sometimes. I suspect she'd rather be working with Buñuel instead of Annie Griffiths. But we get along fine. And she does what she's told, I didn't think she would. Not one of the bolshie crowd you're always complaining about.'

'Glad to hear it.'

'She doesn't spend much time hanging round at Intertel. I don't blame her, she's got lots of boyfriends from what I can gather.'

'Oh? Lots of personal calls? You don't put up with that, surely?'

'She never talks for long so I don't mind. Don't you

remember, how we used to spend hours on the phone? When I used to ring you at the end of every day at the BBC?'

'That was different. We were madly in love.'

'Were? Aren't we still?'

'Of course we are. But we don't have to spend hours on the phone any more.'

'I wouldn't mind, if you called me at the office sometimes. I like being reminded that I don't live there.'

Trevor insisted on making over-elaborate preparations for supper, constantly checking the steak, taking what seemed hours in making a simple dressing for the salad, making the simple task of boiling potatoes seem like an exercise in *haute cuisine*. Fearing that she would burst out in irritation, Annie left the kitchen until he called out that the meal was ready. By then, her appetite had gone and she'd have to pretend she was hungry. Why did he have to go to all that trouble? Couldn't he see she was tired, and just wanted a quick meal? She was being impossible, she decided. He had every reason to call her an ungrateful bitch. What man, apart from Trevor, could put up with such a woman?

10

ANNIE AND LUCINDA

For weeks to come, Annie would be immersed in *Rough Trade*. When she was not on location, she was working late in the office, her window one of the few illuminated specks in the great glass building. During a shoot, you had to work late, you thought of nothing else.

Whatever difficulties arose, Annie's goodwill never faltered. She may have stormed when Lucinda, after days of negotiation, eventually obtained the use of a former admiral's house by the river in Chelsea. It was far too expensive to hire. Couldn't she have found a warehouse further down river? Lucinda insisted that she had seen no other place which so fitted Ben's character, nowhere else so perfect. The tiresome retired naval captain living in Hampshire who had inherited the derelict house, had struck a hard bargain, but if the central location wasn't right, it would affect the whole series. Annie relented.

Now the admiral's house had been transformed into the *bijou* residence of a successful lawyer. The designer had constructed balconies on the front, with trailing plants, and showy lamps which reflected in the water. One floor of the interior was redressed with striped wallpaper and highly buffed reproduction antiques, the other would be used for the interior of Ben's chambers. Everything was ready for the first love scene, when the camera would pull back from a passing barge on the river, and slowly track inwards to the bedroom. Clary arrived late, just as Hugh was preparing to abandon the shoot. Tony was learning his lines when she ran into the room.

'Are you moonlighting? Another little modelling job for *Elle*?' Tony remarked, as Clary threw herself into a chair and fumbled for her script. 'Sorry, darling. But I've been ready for hours.'

Hugh was outside standing on the muddy bank with the

production assistant, trying to communicate with the captain of the barge, who was being swept into the wrong position by a strong tide.

'Where's Annie?' asked Clary, trying not to seem rattled. 'She comin' then?'

'Not today,' said Lucinda, crouching down beside Clary. 'What happened?'

'Had a row with me boyfriend. I feel awful. I got up early, specially. Can't do this scene, not today.'

'We'll run it through. You'll get into it. You're going to be absolutely fantastic. Just ignore everybody, think of what it's like, when you first fall for someone, when nothing can keep you apart—'

'Does Hugh want us to thrash about?' asked Tony, ignoring Clary. 'I'm keeping my pants on, if you don't mind. I'm not being paid to reveal my all, not on this show.'

'Be quiet, Tony,' said Lucinda. 'This is the most difficult scene in the series. And Clary needs your help.'

'I'm being very thoughtless,' Tony replied. 'I do apoplogize.'

The movements were set out on the floor. First kiss against the window. He pulls off her dress as she moves back to position two. Dialogue. Slow walk to edge of bed . . . Lucinda began to take them through the moves.

'Can't do it,' said Clary.

'Yes, you can,' replied Tony. 'You've been lusting wildly after me for weeks. Now's your chance. I've succumbed to your charms. My wife's left me, I'm hurt and wounded and now you're going to make my eyes round with wonder and desire.'

'I'm off men today. I'll be dreadful. I can't do it if I don't feel it.'

She covered her face with her hands and sat with her shoulders hunched. Lucinda hesitated. Today she was glowing with Trevor's love, nothing could go wrong and the director would soon be ready.

'I'll go through the scene with you both. If it'll help,' she said, quietly.

'Wonderful idea, darling.' Tony put his hand on Clary's shoulder. 'Men never understand how to do it.'

Clary brightened.

'I'll 'ave a go then.'

As she began to coax them both into a performance, Lucinda

didn't consider that no-one expected her to do this, nor was it in her job description. All she knew was that it had to be right, and she would make it so. She cut some of the dialogue, and invented gestures which would make the scene come to life.

'You'd make a good director,' said Tony, as Lucinda tidied the bed.

'Maybe one day I'll direct a script I've written.'

'I didn't know you'd written a script? What's it called? Why don't you send it to my agent? I'm always looking for new writers. Is there something in it for me?'

'The main character's a vicar.'

Tony looked hurt.

'Shame. I don't do vicars.'

'Can we go ahead now?'

Lucinda could see that Clary was tensed up to start shooting, so she ran down to where Hugh and the cameraman were lining up the shot.

'They're ready,' she shouted.

'We're not,' Hugh shouted back. 'Another half-hour.'

'You'll be lucky,' Lucinda heard the cameraman say. 'There's a cloud coming up.'

When she came back into the house, the make-up girl was devoting herself to bringing out the freshness of Clary's face, touches here and there, using a light foundation to make it appear as though she was wearing none. Everything changed when viewed through the lens. Tony was preserving his strength, bent over *The Times* crossword.

'You were marvellous with Clary, darling. Girls always throw tantrums before the big moment. But it doesn't bother me, I'm used to it. Do you have someone, someone gorgeous, may I ask?'

Lucinda gave an evasive smile. How could she possibly explain?

'Sort of.'

'I've had plenty of sort-ofs.'

They both laughed.

When they looked at the scene in rushes, Annie said she knew Clary had it in her, knew all along that she projected that sensual quality on film you could never predict with certainty. And Hugh was thrilled that the light was perfect.

'We had a few problems that day,' Lucinda said, casually. 'I hope you don't mind, but they wanted to cut a few lines, and I said if you thought it worked, you wouldn't mind.'

'It works,' said Annie, grinning broadly at Lucinda.

Lucinda had set up a corner of the Chelsea house for her office and Annie was able to trust her more and more, often leaving her on her own to cope with Hugh and the actors. Lucinda loved every moment, the total concentration, the exhilarating knowledge that nothing else mattered except what you were doing, the rush of energy which appeared from nowhere when a crisis suddenly erupted. Annie was confident that before long she would make her up to associate producer.

It was now the end of June. Lucinda had come straight from the Chelsea location to be with Annie, even though it was late. There was a problem to sort out, and Annie wanted her opinion. They were standing by a tape deck placed next to the monitors and playback machines in a corner of the office.

'I'm still not happy with the title music. It keeps bugging me. Let's hear it again.'

Lucinda listened attentively, coming near to the speakers.

'It is good,' she said, after a few bars.

'But what you'd expect,' replied Annie. 'Sometimes you need what people expect. Sometimes you don't. This won't just be a conventional thriller series. At least, it'd better not be.' She grinned, doubtfully. 'That music doesn't hit me between the eyes. There needs to be a hint of mood. Darkness. What shall I do? Junk it and start again?'

'I suppose the composer got a vast fee?'

'Vast enough. They don't come cheap, those guys.'

'Can the budget take it?'

'No,' said Annie, with a grimace. 'But neither can I. Every time I hear that damned tune, it gets worse. If I could find something on an obscure label, I don't mind if the recording's raw, perhaps that's what it needs.'

She stopped the tape.

'What, though? Any ideas? I've used up my supply for today. Ideas, zilch. Come on, Lucinda. Get me out of this hole. You're good on music.'

'Most of the stuff I've got is a bit . . .'

'Way out?'

Lucinda laughed.

'No. A bit rappy. But I have got some discs my brother bought for me. You might like them, they're kind of

148

techno-classical. Makes me feel edgy when I hear them, as though I want to be somewhere else.'

'Right. You've whetted my appetiite. Let's hear them. Where are they?'

'At home.'

'Then I'll get a messenger over.'

'Why don't you come over to my place?'

'Damn. I've too much to do here.'

Lucinda caught Annie's look of disappointment. She was getting used to how things happened. Often what turned out to be the best ideas happened on the spur of moment. And spur-of-the-moment ideas had to be acted on quickly. *I want it yesterday.* It's what kept the adrenalin going, why she never wanted to work anywhere else.

'If you're not exhausted, Annie, you could listen to them tonight, after we've finished.'

'You're on.' Then Annie relented. 'You aren't cancelling some club date, are you? Don't do that, if you've something planned.'

'Oh, it was nothing special.'

A moment later, Annie was at her desk again, her mind fixed on another problem to resolve. Lucinda liked working when everyone had gone, watching Annie undistracted, observing how each part of the production was knitted together, how the shape began to emerge. She now identified with what Annie was doing. *Rough Trade* would be as important to her as it would to Annie – until they started work on the next series.

The phone rang, shattering their concentration. There were always people who tried to contact Annie after hours, no matter how late.

'You take it,' Annie called out. 'I'm not available unless it's Trevor which is unlikely. He never likes talking to me in the office. But don't say I'm not here. I don't want some weirdo to think you're on your own.'

Lucinda continued typing with one hand, and picked up the receiver in the other.

'Annie Griffith's office. I'm afraid she's not available at the moment. Can I help? . . . I can't talk now. I'm frightfully busy . . . No, I couldn't. It's difficult at the moment . . . I can't talk now. I've got loads to get through before tomorrow . . . No. I don't think so.' Lucinda began to be flustered, Annie listened, she could hear her voice rising. Some insistent caller.

'I can't make any plans . . . Not until I know what's happening . . . Things might change . . . No, I mean yes. Annie's here. We're working late.'

Annie looked up from her desk across the room.

'Who is it? Someone giving you a hard time?' she called out. 'I'll take it if you like.'

As her hand grasped the receiver of her phone, Lucinda pressed down the button to cut off the caller.

'It's Jeremy. I keep telling him not to phone me at the office. He just doesn't realize, what it's like. I wish he'd leave me alone.'

She was upset, but Annie knew why, suddenly remembering what it was like when the wrong person answered – the boy you weren't keen on who phoned you up all the time when the boy you were keen on maintained an aloof distance. She had gone through all that, of course, before Trevor, but Lucinda was older.

'Jeremy can't know what it's like,' said Annie, giving a sympathetic smile. 'No-one ever does, really. They think you can just switch off. But you can't. Maybe he'll come to understand.'

'Doubt it.'

'Do you like him?'

'He's all right,' said Lucinda, with a shrug.

'But he's not special enough.'

Lucinda stretched out her legs to the side of her desk.

'Sometimes we have a giggle, but that's about it. Trouble is, we've known one another too long. If I'd met him now, I'd have thought, God, what a bore. He seems so young, always going on about his friends I never see any more and where we're going on holiday. I told him I don't care about holidays. I've changed and he hasn't, I suppose.'

'Yes, you've changed,' said Annie. 'You're much more confident now. He might find that hard to take.'

Annie shuffled some papers together and stuffed them into her briefcase.

'We've done enough for tonight. Thanks for working so late,' she said, slinging her jacket over her shoulder. Lucinda seemed reluctant to leave, she was in no rush to leave her desk. Suddenly Annie had the impression that she was lonely, that all the young men coming and going in her life were failing to give Lucinda what she needed: someone who would support her, appreciate that she had chosen a tough life, and accept her for what she was.

'Lucinda, there's no need to hear your music now, if you don't feel up to it. We can do it another time.'

'No, no. I want you to hear it, honestly.'

'I'll need your address then,' said Annie.

Trevor was still up, working in his study when Annie came in, books in neat piles on his desk.

'I must get this finished by tomorrow. I'm late for the deadline as it is. Where have you been, darling? Anywhere interesting?' he said.

'I was working late with Lucinda.'

Annie sat down, pulled a straw hat from a carrier bag and placed it on her head.

'Does it suit me, Trev?'

'What's that? You don't usually go in for hats.'

'You needn't look so shocked,' said Annie. 'It's not for me. It's for one of my actresses.'

'Where did you find it?'

'Christ! Does it matter? Lucinda gave it to me.'

'Her hat, then.'

'Yes, yes, she wore it once. I went back to her house, and I saw it in the hall. Perfect for scene forty-six.'

'That was nice of her. To invite you to her place. Where is it?'

'Chelsea, in a spectacular house, period but all done out by a Japanese designer. She knew exactly what she wanted – I wouldn't have a clue, not for a house.'

'I hope you're not about to be sucked into the Sherwood menagerie. I wouldn't get too friendly, Annie. They're the kind who pick people up and drop them when the mood suits them. And she is, after all, your assistant. I know you hate it, but sometimes it's as well to keep a little distance.'

'You think I shouldn't have gone?' said Annie, crossly. 'There was a perfectly good reason, as it happens. She wanted me to listen to some discs she had, for the title sequence. Why should there be an ulterior motive? Why are you so suspicious?'

'Darling, I'm only being cautious. Trying to protect you. Did you find anything suitable?'

'There's a track which will be either fantastic or quite wrong. I can't decide. I'd like you to listen to it. Would you mind?'

'Do I have to? I'm sure it's fine.'

'You look tired, love. Anything up?'

'I've got a few problems with this piece.'

'Anything I can help with?'

'Not really. But I must get it over to Paul tonight. There are a few things which need checking before tomorrow.'

'Can't it wait till morning? Don't go now, let's go to bed.'

'Unfortunately, he's catching an early flight to Brussels. I'll be as quick as I can.'

'Where does he live? Somewhere miles away, I bet. If you really have to go, put your bloody foot down just for once. You look tired, love. Are you sure you're not taking too much on?'

'I'll slow down once term is over. Don't worry, darling.'

While Annie was undressing in the bedroom, she heard the front door bang, and shortly afterwards, the sound of a key turning in the lock.

'I forgot my briefcase,' Trevor shouted up the stairs. 'Don't wait up. Paul will probably have a few things to discuss. But I'll be as quick as I can.'

When he came back, Annie was still awake, lying in bed waiting for him. Trevor's love-making was brief, as though he wanted to please, but Annie knew his heart wasn't in it. It was difficult for him to penetrate her, and it annoyed her that he kept apologizing.

'Look, love, you don't have to, if you don't feel like it.'

'I don't know what's come over me. Of course I feel like it.'

'You're tired. We both are. You know what I was thinking today, driving back? Why don't we have somewhere out of London, away from work, where we can both relax? We really need it. Somewhere in the country.'

'Oh, Annie. You're not falling for the country cottage, are you? How could we? What do we tell our Labour Party friends? How can we own a second home, in this day and age?'

'I want somewhere, Trev. I need it, really I do.'

'Darling, you must understand, I want nothing to do with it. You go ahead if you want to. You get a place.'

'But would you come?'

Trevor kissed her neck, nuzzling against her chin.

'I'm sure you'd persuade me.'

He was holding his cock, trying to encourage it, but Annie delicately pulled his fingers away, and pressed herself against him, folding her arms round his neck.

152

'Sometimes it's just enough, feeling your body against mine. Know something? I can never sleep properly when I'm away and you're not there. When I wake up with you, I feel as though I've been floating on top of a bed of feathers.'

He kissed the top of her head, then slowly disengaged himself and turned over, spreading himself over the other side of the bed.

'I don't seem to be able to sleep in my usual position any more. Good-night, darling. I'll be up early tomorrow, I'll try not to disturb you.'

For a while, Annie stayed awake, unused to the space between them. Trevor was getting older, his habits were changing. She hoped the day would never come when, like her parents, he would decide that he needed a separate bed, that the days of physical intimacy had come to an end. She couldn't imagine waking up without the warmth of his body, seeing his curling hair straggled over the pillow, watching for the moment when his eyes opened and met hers. In the country, it would be different – waking up to the sound of the birds, looking up at an open sky, logs piled on the fire, long walks in the country, long hours in bed . . . Annie edged close to Trevor, put her arms round his waist and lulled by his warmth, drifted into sleep.

11

TREVOR

As the weeks went by, Trevor made several attempts to consider his marriage, to try and clarify the confusion by applying the tools of analysis. Above all, he needed to find reasons for his behaviour which had so far eluded him but although he could formulate the questions, he was unable to find answers which satisfied him.

Was it in his nature to keep faithfully to the side of one woman? Could he expect one woman, even someone like Annie, to fulfil all the expectations of a complex partner? Had he blotted out the craving, which might have always been there, to explore a relationship with someone else? Had he been denying the existence of a hidden dissatisfaction? Was it really all he wanted, long tranquil years stretching ahead, doing the same things, seeing the same people, declining comfortably towards old age?

Had he blindly obeyed the rules, the shalt nots of his class? If she was constantly in his thoughts, why pretend that she wasn't? If he felt a rush of joy in her company, why deny it? And why deprive himself of an experience which would never come again? Being with Lucinda, Trevor concluded, was part of his voyage of self-discovery. That could be the explanation. For all these years, he had given to Annie, given to students. What had he given to himself?

But was that a reason to walk out of a marriage, which, though incomplete (perhaps like all marriages) had given them both joy and comfort all these years? 'We're growing apart.' Isn't that what they said, the couples who were tiring of one another and didn't dare say so? He and Annie were not growing apart, their affection was unwavering. How could he admit to her that he was compelled to share his feelings – not the ones he shared with her – with someone else? How could he expect her to understand?

He had to protect her from discovering what was, after all, his own private dilemma. If she only knew the cost, how it pained him having to invent half-truths, evasions to cover his tracks. If only there had been a small sign that she suspected, if only she had dragged it out of him so that he could break down and confess and say – no, of course I've been mad. I promise not to see her again. And then? Would he tell her everything? Everything that happened last year? This year? No, he couldn't do that. We only met a few times, he could say, she was always off somewhere. She knew my marriage came first. And if she asked about sex? Would he admit that it was good? Better? Different. Perhaps that's all it was. Perhaps he could dismiss the whole affair by saying that. Just sex. Needing a new experience. Getting older, proving myself. Annie might accept it then.

If he could convince himself that this was so, perhaps there would be no need to tell her. Did telling make it better or worse? It was impossible to predict whether Annie would go screaming into the attack, saying she'd never believe him again, telling him to get out of the house – or whether she would laugh, say she'd known all along, what an idiot he'd been. He couldn't take the risk. He was facing too many uncertainties.

Was it true, as Lucinda insisted, that no-one suspected at Intertel? There were times when Trevor wondered whether to confide in Gavin, to see if he could detect a knowing look, an indirect reference which would confirm or allay his fears. Was there the slightest rumour linking his name with Lucinda's? Then he decided against it. How petty it would seem. Gavin was helping to make him into a television performer, encouraging him in a new direction. He would hardly appreciate being drawn into his private affairs. Academic making a fool of himself with some girl. Why should he care?

Desperately, Trevor tried to keep the compartments of his life under control. Annie thought he was doing too much, and constantly reminded him.

'When are you going to start writing your book? It's much more important than doing newspaper articles or appearances for Gavin. I don't know why you say yes to everything. And why *Splash!*? You're too good for that programme.'

'It keeps my hand on the pulse.'

'What?' Annie snorted. 'Whose bloody pulse? Gavin's, I suppose. When I've finished *Rough Trade*, why don't we start writing your book together?'

'We could try,' said Trevor, doubtfully.

'At least it would mean I'd see you.'

How could she understand? He was stretching himself to the limit. What was wrong in that? But however hard he tried to keep the balance between Lucinda and Annie, he was aware, only too aware, that he was giving too little attention to his wife. He was determined to make it up to her.

The one day Trevor had planned to be alone with Annie, Gavin invited them both to lunch. Without consulting Annie, he accepted immediately. If he had refused, Gavin would have been offended – he had a reputation for being insulted if his invitations were rejected. He tried to persuade Annie that they needn't stay long, they would have a late breakfast in bed, go for a stroll over Primrose Hill, a quick meal at Gavin's house and the rest of the day to do whatever she wanted. He tried to calm her anger.

'Annie, we'd both made a special effort to have one day together. Is it so awful to spend a few hours eating someone else's lunch?'

'I don't want to.'

'Why are you being so awkward? You're always complaining you don't see me.'

'I'm sick of you making all the plans. Do you ever think about what I want to do?'

'Constantly, darling.'

'Sorry, I hadn't noticed. It's obviously more important for you to have lunch with Gavin. Why are you being so bloody selfish?'

'I can always cancel—'

'Don't do it for my sake. Kate and I are driving out into the country. She thinks I should buy a country cottage.'

'That's a crazy idea.'

'Not to me.'

'Shouldn't we talk about it?'

'If you can spare some time.'

'Annie, you're not being fair. It's you who's working all hours—'

'So you're blaming me now? It's my fault that we never have

156

a decent conversation any more. When did we last go out for a meal together?'

'You seem to prefer being with Kate.'

'That's pathetic, Trev. Why take it out on Kate? When you are at home, you're so bloody moody, you make me glad to go out.'

'I get tired, that's all. It's quite a strain, you know, becoming a TV pundit.'

It was meant to be a lighthearted comment, but Annie took it the wrong way.

'You don't have to do it. It's certainly having a bad effect on you. Why didn't you keep to your resolution? That's what I want to know! You're making things difficult for yourself, and for me. And did you really think I'd jump at the chance of being stuck with Gavin, banging on yet again about the current state of television?'

'I said I'll cancel the lunch.'

'Do what you like.'

He was glad when she left.

Now Trevor was sitting in front of a white-starched cloth laid out with silver cutlery and posies of flowers. He hadn't expected such formality at Gavin's house, but neither had he expected that he would be married to a woman like Celia. She appeared older than him, without a trace of make-up on her pale, academic face, her long dress an unflattering floral mix of sludgy pink and green. It was an antidote to conversation, Trevor thought, all the passing round of dishes of greens, carrots, Yorkshire pudding, potatoes, the large platter of sliced-up beef, the fiddly gravy-boats, do have more of this, more of that. Annie would have hated it, she was right to stay away. He had no desire to talk, even though Gavin was trying to draw him out. However, as the red wine oozed comfortably through his pores, he couldn't resist bringing up the dominant subject of his thoughts.

'I gather Lord Sherwood's daughter is having a difficult time settling in at Intertel. Or so Annie says. To be expected, I suppose.'

'Interesting girl,' said Gavin.

'You think so?'

'Though she doesn't exactly muck in with the lads. Not like our Annie.'

Gavin looked towards Connie, a young black lecturer in media studies sitting next to Trevor.

'Let me explain, Connie. Annie Griffiths is Controller of Drama, Trevor's wife as it happens. She's made an enormous impact at Intertel. When Annie's around, she seems to give women confidence. Even Gemma, my PA, who's never shown the slightest interest in women's issues, has started telling me off for not representing them enough on *Splash!*. And she's quite right. We need to be reminded. They are over fifty per cent of our audience.'

'We've made a study of women's issue programmes,' said Connie. 'Ninety per cent are ghettoed into the afternoon slots.'

Trevor immediately broke in, he had no intention of hearing yet again the arguments he would expound better himself.

'If the younger generation starts making their mark, and girls like Lucinda do well, attitudes might change.'

'It shouldn't matter even if she doesn't do well. And I would guess that she must be over sixteen. Is it so difficult to refer to her as a woman?' said Connie, throwing Trevor a withering glance.

'She's quite talented, you know. Quite capable of becoming a producer eventually.'

'I'm sure,' replied Gavin. 'But I'm willing to bet she'll be in front of camera within a year or so. You needn't tell Annie, but I intend to give her a chance.'

'Don't be too sure,' said Trevor, ignoring the arrival of a hefty apple pie which the other guests were admiring.

'Name me one good-looking girl who'd turn down the offer. How well did you know her?'

Relieved that Gavin obviously had no knowledge of their meetings – that fear was constantly in his mind however hard he tried to banish it – Trevor had an irresistible urge to say her name out loud.

'Did I ever mention the script Lucinda wrote?' said Trevor, looking towards Gavin.

'You've read it? She gave me a copy but I haven't got round to it yet. What's it about?'

Then Trevor took flight. He talked about the characters, the landscape, all the time hearing Lucinda's breathy voice, full of excitement as she brought to life the story which had obsessed her.

'Sounds great,' remarked Gavin. 'It's the kind of thing

Intertel should be doing. Original one-off drama. As long as it's low budget and late-night, there's an important minority audience out there.'

'It's fairly erotic,' said Trevor.

'All the better,' replied Gavin, under his breath.

'But I don't think she'd be happy with a skimped production.'

'If her head's screwed on, she'll be happy with *any* production,' Gavin retorted.

Celia continued passing round the cups, unwilling to participate in the conversation, keeping a wan, unconvincing smile on her pallid lips.

'Lucinda spent two years writing it,' Trevor added.

'Really.'

Under the table, he clenched his fingers together and felt a trickle of sweat running down his back and his mind wandered. Lucinda sitting on her bed, naked, her hands linked together over her knees, a half-curtain of hair trailing over one cheek, looking at his cock resting across his thigh, with a smile of satiation. He knew he would always want her.

When lunch had ended, and the guests were gathering in the hall, Gavin brought out some books from a glass-fronted case, signed them, and handed out copies to his guests.

'I'd like you to have something of mine, Trevor,' said Celia, as he was putting on his raincoat. 'It won't take up much space, my latest collection of poetry.'

'I didn't know you were a poet, too.'

'Few people do.'

'I look forward to reading it,' Trevor said. He felt sorry for Celia, another unsatisfied woman taking refuge in verse.

By the time he arrived home, it was later than he realized. Annie was back from the country, accompanied by Kate and Dally.

'Hi, everyone.'

'We've seen some marvellous places,' said Annie. 'And had a fantastic time.'

'I'm glad. I'm really sorry I couldn't go,' Trevor replied.

'How was the TV lunch? What did I miss?'

'The conversation was quite stimulating.'

'Better than you'd get at home, no doubt. Never mind, as long as you don't bring Gavin back here. Where have you been? You're dripping wet.'

'I walked home from Primrose Hill, got caught in a shower.

Here, darling. I've brought you something. Take a look in there. I'll just go and get myself dry.'

Having pushed a dripping Sainsbury's bag into her hand, he went upstairs to towel his hair. In the mirror, he noted with satisfaction that the walk had given him a healthy shine, his eyes were bright despite the wine. Sometimes, he knew that he was beginning to look his age, but now he could be taken for someone ten years younger.

In the kitchen, Annie was poring over a heavy, lavishly photographed book entitled *These Ancient Shores – a collection of Words for Our Time by Gavin Mitchell*. There was a portrait of Gavin on the front cover, staring moodily towards a sea of white pebbles on some windswept, deserted beach. In the mid distance, was an aesthetically arranged driftwood branch, on which was perched a menacing gull. Annie opened the heavy cover, while Kate peered over her shoulder and read out the dedication.

'For my dear friends Trevor and Annie. And it's signed, illegibly, Gavin.'

Annie snorted, it was too soon for the 'dear friends', then she leafed through the large printed text.

'He takes a good picture,' commented Kate, pushing her face forwards to examine the contours of Gavin's face. 'Shame about the words. His wife Celia writes about real things, but her books are much smaller. Apparently she's a very fine poet.'

'Celia Mitchell? I've never heard of her,' said Annie.

'Oh, she doesn't use his name. One of her children goes to Dally's nursery school. She doesn't say much. You wouldn't expect her to be Mrs Mitchell.'

Annie closed the book and put it on a pile of Trevor's review copies, about to overbalance on the pine dresser.

'Did you know Celia wrote poetry?' said Annie as Trevor came into the kitchen.

'I think I did,' Trevor replied.

He'd take her volume, which was still in his raincoat pocket, as a present for Lucinda. Annie never read poetry.

'Why don't you stay, Kate? I can make Dally something to eat, and then she can sleep upstairs.'

Typical Annie, complaining they had no time together, then asking Kate to stay. Trevor could feel another row brewing, and retreated to the sitting room. It was a while before he heard Kate answer.

'I think I really ought to go soon, Annie. Gordon said he might drop round with a bottle of wine, I've made his favourite soup.'

'It wouldn't hurt if you were out once in a while.'

Kate chose not to listen, leaned Gavin's book against the back of the dresser, then went to the table and gathered up the evidence of Dally's creativity. Annie called through the arch to Trevor.

'I'm just dropping Kate home.'

'Can't you get her a taxi?'

Once Annie had left, Trevor tried to quell his irritation by calling Lucinda, before he remembered that this weekend she would be at Sherwood Hall. Three more days.

The following week, he could only see Lucinda once and he complained about her schedule, he hadn't meant to complain.

'I'm sorry, darling,' he said, as he sat beside her. She was stroking his hair, caressing his cheek, waiting for him to make the move towards the bedroom.

'Sometimes it's difficult. I spent the whole weekend being resentful that I couldn't spend it with you.'

'What happened?'

'Gavin asked us both to lunch, and Annie refused to go. She drove off in a huff, went to the country with Kate and Dally. I spent all the time thinking that you should have been beside me. Annie was being intolerable.'

It just slipped out, he had broken his rule. Until now, he had promised himself that he would be loyal to Annie. How he hated the men who tore their wives to pieces behind their backs.

'I'm glad I'm not married,' Lucinda said, nibbling his ear.

He was not being disloyal, Trevor decided. Lucinda was not only his lover, she was a friend. Why should he hide anything from her?

'She doesn't understand that I'm under pressure, too. If we can't enjoy weekends, what's the point? Still, I didn't mean to grumble about Annie. It's not fair on you. She is your boss, after all.'

'Why not? If that's how you feel. I don't mind.'

Trevor kissed her in reply, warmed by the strength of her desire.

'I want us to have more time together. To be able to meet sometimes at the weekend. What's the point of my staying at home, being bad-tempered and restless? I was mean to Annie. And I should have been more sympathetic. She wants to get a place in the country. The last thing she should do, having something else to worry about.'

'It could be a good idea,' said Lucinda. 'Then you could stay on your own in London sometimes.'

'That's a wicked thought, and I couldn't allow it.'

'We'll have lots of time together next week, the cast's in London. Annie's quite happy for me to work on my own in the admiral's house. She said she wouldn't bother to come, not unless there was a crisis. She's beginning to trust Hugh, at last. If everything goes well, she might even let me direct a scene.'

'Marvellous, darling.'

Trevor put his hands under her shirt rested them on her taut nipples and kissed her once more, deeply and urgently.

One late Sunday afternoon in July, Annie came bounding in, grass in her hair, as though all his energy, all his passion, had passed into her. She had been on a picnic with Rick and Bryonie, Dally and Kate.

'Trev, you should have come, the Heath was gorgeous, it was hot enough to swim. A day of perfect sun, and you stay indoors. Rick's asked you to go the pub later. Why don't you go? You haven't seen him for ages.'

'I'm not feeling too good. Stomach pains. It's probably something I ate.'

Annie looked at him with alarm.

'But you had those a few days ago. Shouldn't you see a doctor?'

'It'll go.'

She came and sat beside him, displacing the pile of papers he had been attempting to read.

'Is anything wrong?'

'No. I expect I need a holiday. I'll recover once we get to Greece.'

'Are you sure it isn't anything else?'

'I've had a letter from Edward. He's getting married.'

'Wonderful, Trev. At last! Aren't you pleased?'

'He doesn't say much, just that he'd like us to meet.'

'Does that mean we'll be going out to Australia? Let me know when. It's about time for the great reconciliation.'

'I don't even know what my son looks like. He's marring a girl called Janine. All these years and all I've received is the occasional postcard. I suppose he wants to be set up by his dad.'

'You might be surprised. You might find he's a smashing young man.'

'I'm not going to Australia, that's for sure.'

'Don't you care about him?'

'Of course I do,' Trevor snapped. 'He's my son, in spite of everything.'

'Shouldn't we talk about it?'

'I've said everything there is to say.'

'That was ages ago. Have you been in touch with Margaret?'

'Annie, I really don't want to go over all that again.'

Later that evening, he found her studying the details of some property, crouched over the kitchen table, attempting to draw a plan. She gave a mischievous smile.

'I've done it, Trev. I've bought a cottage, for us. I know you're going to give me a furious lecture, but just listen.'

Trevor looked up and smiled back at Annie.

'I am listening, darling.'

'The cottage we saw, it's fantastic. Lucinda found it, she really is marvellous at tracking down places. Look, I've made a rough sketch. It has three bedrooms, a front parlour with a proper fire, an overgrown garden which we can make into something gorgeous, and the most amazing view at the back, over a valley. And it'll only take two and a half hours to get there. Two hours if I'm driving. Even if we could get away only once or twice a month, you could write your book, we'd have peace and quiet, no social obligations, fresh air. All right, I know you hate the country but you could just look at it out of the window.'

Trevor tried to hide his pleasure.

'I prefer reading about it.'

'It's not a luxury, Trev. I've thought about it. If I'm going to continue at the pace I am, I need somewhere to unwind. And you're beginning to look as though you've just come out of the nick. What you need is a good fresh-air tan and some healthy living. Wouldn't it be marvellous, to take off into fields instead of walking round Hampstead Heath and saying how unspoilt it is? Imagine, smelling woodsmoke curling up into the sky, looking out onto shiny, rain-drenched trees, watching the seasons instead of looking at your diary to find out when it's the first day of spring?'

'Is this Annie Griffiths talking? I thought you only liked the country in tiny doses.'

'Just for weekends. Not all the time. And we can afford it now,' said Annie defensively.

'True.'

'You're not keen.'

'Give me time to get used to the idea. Still, as long as you don't start making jam and inviting the vicar for tea.'

Trevor wondered if the words he'd rehearsed sounded natural, but Annie's enthusiasm didn't falter. He was unable to look at her, to see the joy on her face.

'How much did it cost you?' he added, suddenly remembering that he should have asked the obvious question.

'Not telling. Is it so awful, to spend some of our money? We don't have to save up everything for our old age. Why not enjoy it now? What's wrong with that?'

'Nothing wrong, it's your money. I wouldn't dream of telling you what to do with it.'

'My money? Don't be ridiculous. It's in our building society, it's our money. Wouldn't it be a good idea to have an escape? Then the weekends won't get eaten away, people ringing me up, Gavin pestering you to come up with ideas . . . '

'Don't worry, I won't allow my television work to take up too much time.'

'And then we could have a couple of days together, shutting out everything, just being with each other. Like we used to! How long is it since we had late breakfast on our own, stayed in bed and talked about silly things, or us, instead of work?'

'You're right,' admitted Trevor. 'But I might not be able to be free every time you wanted to escape. Or the same might be true of you.'

'I'd make an effort,' said Annie.

'So would I. I really would.'

Trevor gave a dubious smile, trying to look as though he was being slowly convinced by her argument.

'Don't you want to know where it is?'

'Wales, I suppose. The Black Mountains?'

'No, no. You're way off the mark.'

'Where then?'

'It's a mile outside a little village in Wiltshire and it's called

164

Honeysuckle Cottage. But don't get the wrong idea. There's no honeysuckle and it isn't a cottage. Just a simple farm labourer's house, not far from Sherwood Hall. It's beautiful round there, apparently. Lucinda's going to show me the area. I've promised we'll take off some time as soon as I can manage. Here, have a look.'

Annie handed over a sheet of paper with a murky polaroid picture glued at the top.

'The photograph's awful, I took it. But it's perfect, it really is. Where's the road atlas? Then I can show you where it is.'

Annie scoured the pile of books and telephone directories piled on the kitchen dresser.

'Damn. Where's the atlas gone? Have you had it?'

Trevor shook his head. It was in Lucinda's car, he had lent it to her when she had lost hers. He must remember to get it back. Lucinda said he worried too much, but she didn't appreciate – how could she? – his efforts to avoid unnecessary pain.

'We'll have to do some modernizing, but the structure's sound,' Annie said, placing the sheets of paper into a folder. 'Will you come and have a look at it next weekend? I'll need to take some proper pictures of the rooms, measurements, that kind of thing, then we can get the builders in.'

'I can't promise, but I'll try. Tell you what, I'll put off that meeting with Paul.'

Annie grinned. 'You're coming round to the idea, aren't you? I know you, you'll be thinking out all the pros and cons, and whether we should or whether we shouldn't and what could go wrong and suppose it becomes a millstone round our necks, look what happened when Bryonie found that place in Suffolk and Rick refused to go down there—'

'I wasn't thinking that at all,' said Trevor. 'Am I becoming that old and predictable?'

'Can't I still tease you?'

'Raw nerve,' replied Trevor.

The following weekend, when Annie had arranged to view the cottage with Trevor, she had a crisis at Intertel. Having viewed the rough assembly of episode one, Alan had decided that in the light of Lord Sherwood's recent statement about curtailing scenes showing the detailed mechanics of sex, that section would have to be pruned. In vain did Annie argue that the first love scene with Ben and Trish made sense of Trish's motivation later in the series, that it was not a cold-hearted exploitation of naked bodies. Alan stood firm, though he did congratulate Annie on the power of the acting. It was just too provocative to go out only weeks after the wide coverage of Sherwood's remarks. Cursing, Annie told Trevor that their visit to Wiltshire was off. She would need to complete the edit and be available all weekend.

'If it would help, I could go down on my own,' he suggested, hesitantly.

'Great! Would you mind?'

'If you trust me. You can tell me what you need.'

Annie gave a delighted smile.

'Tape measure and camera, that's all. Then we'll get my designer to draw up some plans. It's going to be simple. This time, I won't let Kate loose on it. She'd probably want to change it into some kitsch fantasy.'

Trevor couldn't wait to tell Lucinda but this week she'd be away in Scotland shooting in some remote castle – by now he knew her schedule by heart. She said she'd be back on Thursday. Annie would be coming up for a day, then flying home. That was Tuesday. Tuesday he'd get in something special for Annie, they'd have an evening together. Thursday, he'd be out. (Now that term had finished, he was catching up on seeing his friends.) Friday, he'd be out too, most likely. Each week he went through his diary with Annie, so that she would know he was making an effort, and each week he filled the gaps with likely people to see, no-one Annie knew, dreary academic people, people who'd help on the book or even some journalists who'd give him ideas for *Splash!*.

It was already late on Thursday by the time Trevor reached Danvers Street, and he started to run when he saw the white glow on the upper floor of Lucinda's house. He rang her bell, almost choking with anticipation and fear. Six days without being in contact, it was unbearable. How would he be able to hold himself back, when all he wanted was to tear off her clothes and lunge inside her?

'Hi.'

Trevor stepped back. A young girl with a towel swathed around her hair, shining skin and a T-shirt knotted round her hips, surveyed him with a puzzled expression.

'Is Lucinda at home?'

The girl turned towards the staircase and screamed.

'Lucy. Someone for you.'

Then she leaped up the stairs, two at a time. Trevor waited for a moment, nauseous, clasping his hands together in case they betrayed him, listening for Lucinda's footsteps. But all he could hear was the thumping beat coming from a distant speaker, not the kind of music he associated with Lucinda. Could she be with someone else? Left alone in the hall, he found himself staring at an oil painting of huntsmen leaping a ditch, out of keeping with the optic wallpaper on the corniced wall. He was about to ring the bell again, when the girl reappeared, surprised to find he was still there.

'She was in earlier, she's not in her room. Probably gone to Tim's club,' she said.

'Want to leave a message or something?'

'Are you staying here?'

'Just for a couple of days. I'm Amanda, friend of Lucy's.'

'I see.'

Trevor shifted his weight from one foot to another.

'When she comes in, could you tell Lucinda, I need to see her on Saturday. Will you tell her that?'

'OK.'

'You won't forget?'

Amanda glanced at him with amusement, and pulled the towel off her hair, so that a tumble of damp black curls fell about her face.

'Who shall I say?'

'Perhaps I might leave a note.'

'Go ahead,' she said, making her way back upstairs.

Extracting some paper from his briefcase, Trevor scribbled a message, folded it carefully and placed it on the hall table, propped up against a black, wooden African head. Why hadn't she rung him at home? She knew the code. Two rings, stop. Then three rings, and if he didn't answer by then, that would mean they couldn't talk. For the whole of Friday, he stayed by the phone. Where was she? The silence was intolerable.

Early on Saturday morning with the sun already beating down, Trevor was just about to leave when Annie came rushing out of the house in her dressing-gown.

'Here, love, I thought you might need some refreshment,'

she said, as she placed a cool-bag on the back seat. 'There's some cans of beer, French bread and deli stuff. There probably won't be anything to eat round there. Wish I could go with you.'

'So do I. Next time, yes?'

She kissed him joyfully and ran back into the house. As Trevor started the engine, he found himself wishing that Annie was less concerned for his well-being. If she had taken him for granted or if, like so many couples, they had rubbed along, each going their separate ways except when it suited them, it would have been possible to tell her. There would have been a row, then a reconciliation, the usual compromise. What she did take for granted was the certainty that nothing threatened their being together. Why did she make that assumption? Then he hated himself for wanting her as she was not, for his convenience. As soon as he had overcome the clogged part of the M4, he put his foot down and welcomed the miles which would separate him from Langton Villas.

The heat was singeing the hedgerows, sending out waves of ripe sappy leaves, when Trevor stopped the engine of his Toyota, to which he had become unaccountably attached. He left the hood down, since he had known it was one of those days when no grey cloud would besmirch the clear sky. The house in front of him looked a good solid dwelling, with a porch. In case he omitted to retain a detail, he noted down the defects. One. Needs a paint. Two. Windows tatty. Some trees at the back. He checked with the specifications: to one side, a mature orchard. Apples or pears, how did you tell the difference? Three. Old fruit trees, probably apples and pears. Annie had told him to look at the roof. He looked up and could see nothing remarkable like a gaping hole or gaps in the slates. Four. Roof seems in good nick. Then he walked round the back. Five. Lots of weeds. Anything which grew tall and prolific, he assumed were weeds. It was just possible to see the bare shape of a small room through the grimy windows. Fingering the house-keys which Annie had handed to him, he put aside his notepad and remained outside, straining to catch the distant growl of a car.

Trevor removed his jacket, and placed it on the grass. Around him he could hear the twittering of birds, otherwise it was silent. In the distance, he could see trees shrouding what appeared to be a substantial building. That must be the farm, which had housed its workers in this cottage at one time. He leaned against some white flowers ranged in a row against the front. Then he ran over to his car and from the boot, he extracted a bottle of champagne, carefully shrouded in an old jacket and often replaced, which was kept for late-night refreshment when Lucinda's supply had been exhausted. Would she come? His gaze was fixed at the end of the track which led to the cottage. Had she changed her mind? Was she beginning to tire of him?

Trevor had almost given up. Taking Annie's camera out of his pocket, he walked backwards trying to find a position which would allow him to include the cottage and surroundings in one shot. Then he heard a low reverberation and swung round to catch sight of Lucinda's black BMW bumping along the rutted track. Hurriedly stuffing the camera back into his jacket pocket, he leaped to his feet and waved.

She was dressed all in white, like an expectant bride, no, more like a colonial queen – white, ribbed cotton jodhpurs and a fine cotton white shirt, hair tied back in a red scarf. 'I made it in fifteen minutes. Isn't that amazing?' Lucinda said, as she slammed shut the car door. Then she flung herself into his arms, and he clutched her to him, eyes closed, breathing in her perfume, stroking her hair, when all he wanted was to throw her to the ground. After he had slowly extracted himself from the long, lingering kiss he had imagined for days, he drew back, gazing at her as though he had just awoken to the day from a hundred years' sleep.

'Did you get my messages?'

'Of course I did. I always get them.'

'You've got your camera?'

'In my bag.'

'What happened? Weren't you able to call?'

'You knew I'd come.'

'I wasn't sure. I thought you might not be able to make it.'

'Lucinda smiled. 'What made you think that? I didn't have to ford rivers and crawl along rope bridges.'

He pulled off her scarf, and ran his fingers through the silky strands of her hair, then traced them lightly over her lips. She smiled, a glorious welcoming smile, crinkling her eyes against the strength of the sun.

'You look stunning. Do you realize I've never really seen you in the country? You seem different. Even more beautiful.'

Again, he thrust his tongue into her mouth then kissed her neck, down her breasts, until she stepped back.

'Hadn't we better look over the cottage?'

He kissed her fingers and turned her round to face the grubby grey exterior, brightened by a tangled spray of roses hanging from an indifferent porch.

'Well? What should I say about it?' Trevor asked.

'Simple and unpretentious,' Lucinda said. 'You think it's an ideal choice. Right?'

'Ideal – not sensible?'

'Country places aren't ever sensible.'

'Particularly not in this case. But you understood perfectly what Annie wanted.'

'We did talk about it. Annie always knows exactly what she has in mind.'

'Only too well.' Trevor sighed. 'I won't always be here on my own.'

'Of course not.'

'But sometimes I could stay over on Sunday night, travel up to London early on Monday morning. It would mean taking two cars.'

'You don't have to think everything out, Trevor. It will just happen. Doesn't it always with us? We don't have to plan things.'

'It's a fine little house.'

'I knew Annie would like it.'

'I like it. You haven't told anyone, have you? Not Tim, for example.'

'Why would I tell Tim? Trevor, honestly, there's no need to worry. This is Annie's secret hideaway.'

'What about the people who live near by? Won't they wonder who's taken the cottage?'

'It isn't as though it's in a village. People round here are used to weekenders appearing and disappearing, there's nothing unusual in that. And they respect privacy. Why should they care, anyway? Come on, don't you want to look inside?'

Lucinda took the keys from Trevor and angled them precisely into the locks. As the door swung open, he could see a surprisingly light and spacious living room, with a kitchen at the back.

'It's all a bit basic, but you won't have to do much to it. Nothing major.'

They looked at one another, and smiled complicitly. It didn't matter what it was like inside, they both knew that. Trevor's apprehension melted away in her presence.

'You can take the pictures later. Let's lie in the sun while it's still hot,' he said.

They walked across the unkempt lawn, and then he stopped. He began to unbutton her shirt, she was unresisting, then he felt round her waist and grasped hold of the zip of her jodhpurs.

'I want to do it here. Now,' he whispered.

She was still unresisting as he bent towards the ground and pulled her down with him. She wanted him with all the glorious urgency that he wanted her. The sun blinded his eyes, he wondered why her bare skin appeared a shade darker than when they last met, only days ago. In London, everything seemed pale. Her eyes were now more blue than grey, and her soft hair shone in the sun, like the girls in *Smiles of a Summer Night*, scented with the heat. As he stroked down her thighs, the sun beating on his closed lids pulsed red, and his breath was suspended in rapture.

'I love you. I think of nothing but you. It's becoming unbearable, Lucinda.'

Lucinda opened her eyes, and met his gaze, a slow smile reaching across her face. 'No, not unbearable. It's beautiful,' she answered. 'Nothing can take away what we feel.'

'I can't imagine life without you. Does that sound nonsensical?'

'No,' she answered, staring up at the sky, losing herself in the blue expanse.

'I don't know if I can stay with Annie for much longer,' Trevor said, in a low voice.

Suddenly Lucinda sat up and reached for her shirt. 'Don't get dressed, darling, not yet.'

Lucinda continued pulling on her jodhpurs, inching them up her long, narrow thighs, and then she began to fasten a few buttons on her shirt.

'Whatever you do, you can't walk out on Annie. She'd never get over it. You can't, Trevor. I don't mean that as a moral judgement. Why should people be glued together all their lives? But Annie's different. She needs you.'

'And you?'

Lucinda said nothing, she was thinking of *Grains of Evil*.

Would Annie still produce her screenplay if Trevor left and moved into Danvers Street? It was too much to ask.

'Darling, I know you're trying to save my marriage. But it's too late. I'll have to find the strength, I know I will. How can I exist like this, going home and thinking only of you for hours on end?'

Taking hold of his hands, Lucinda pulled Trevor to his feet, and linked her hands behind his newly razored neck.

'Why not love us both?'

'What are you saying?' he said, flinching under her touch.

'Why destroy one thing to have another? We don't have the kind of love which ripens over the kitchen sink, Trevor. If I started worrying about whether you had a clean shirt for the morning, I'd run away. I know I would.'

Her eyes were clear and wide, her brow untouched by the wrinkles of sorrow or experience.

'That's impossible. With us, it wouldn't be like that. I need you, I want the whole of you. You do love me?' Trevor announced in a determined voice.

'Everything changes when I see you. Is that love?'

'We will be together one day. I promise you that.'

The way she looked at him, he knew she wanted to believe him, but couldn't allow herself to, not yet. He could understand why she wasn't abandoning herself to him. How could she? When he was still going home each night to Langton Villas? Yet she had given him an unspoken challenge.

'I'll get my camera.'

Lucinda knew exactly what would be required and had brought a battery of lenses to photograph the rooms and encompass small details like damp patches. Annie wasn't practical, not with equipment, but in television there was always someone around to do it for her. Following her round, Trevor was lost in admiration, the way she stood perfectly balanced on one heel, the way she knew exactly what needed to be done. When she had finished, she removed the film from the camera and slotted it back deftly into the black tube.

'Here. It'll be easier if you have it processed.'

Trevor hesitated, reluctant to take it from her.

'Darling, I've just thought of something. I couldn't have taken your pictures, not with my camera. It's only got one lens.'

'Say you asked the estate agent to come, and he took them for you.'

'I could, I suppose. Isn't it ridiculous, the stupid things we have to invent? I'm afraid I'm none too good at it,' said Trevor, stuffing the tube into his inside pocket.

'It's no different from little fibs you tell children. And you don't have to say anything unless Annie asks. I don't know why you're so bothered.'

'It looks as though there'll be a lot of work to do here. How long will it take to be ready?'

'Not long. Paint the walls white, stick some wicker furniture in, maybe some Greek rugs, a few earthenware pots, it'll be super. Ideal for a holiday home.'

'Do you like it? That's what matters.'

'I wouldn't care if it was a caravan.'

He wanted to touch her again, cover her in kisses, back-row-in-the-Rex kisses, but she had to drive back to Sherwood Hall, they were expecting her for lunch. Trevor bent over her, giving her one final kiss before she drove off. He couldn't bring himself to leave, not immediately. Lying on the grass, he waited until the sun's rays weakened and a slight chill reminded him that he ought to head back to London.

By Monday evening, Trevor had the photographs in his hand. Lucinda had taken one automatic shot of them both together, throwing their heads back with joy, with their arms round one another's necks. This he removed, and placed in a sealed envelope at the back of his filing cabinet. Although Annie was exhausted when she came in, well past midnight, she insisted on seeing the pictures. If only she had been less enthusiastic.

'Maybe I could meet you there this Saturday. I could get there by the afternoon. If all goes well, I should be finished by lunch-time.'

The photographs were spread over the kitchen table, he had sorted them in order so that he could give Annie a guided tour through the cottage, having noted the damp patches, and the rotting window frames.

'Good pictures,' remarked Annie. 'Especially for an estate agent.' She tipped back on the stool, screwing up her face with pleasure. 'I'll leave early anyway. Why not? Then we can meet down there. Shall I ask Kate and Dally?'

The relief that Annie had suspected nothing gave way to a loving generosity.

'And we might persuade Rick and Bryonie to come. And take a picnic. Great idea.'

Annie was in the middle of a tough week, but her face was alive with happiness. More than once she asked, 'You do really like it?' Trevor really did and was even prepared to slap some white paint on the walls. They could take a few things down from the house, no need to buy lots of furniture. That bright rug they had brought back from Greece and put in his study, for example. She wanted to go there at once, she was so thrilled that Honeysuckle Cottage would soon be theirs. Or, as Trevor thought to himself, in the end it would be hers. When he eventually moved in with Lucinda, Annie would want to keep the place. She loved it, it would be a haven for her. How relieved he was that Lucinda hadn't found some twee thatched place with tiny windows and beams which hit his head. That was his fault, having preconceptions about the country. But he had taken to it, too, he really had. Of course he would go down there. Whenever he could manage it.

By all the laws of coincidence, Annie should have found out by now, but Trevor was certain that she suspected nothing. Lucinda listened carefully to the location gossip, but it was clear that no-one at Intertel suspected either. Trevor's life was taking a turn he had never anticipated, subtly altering its course. Annie no longer seemed interested in discussing anything other than *Rough Trade*, and was either too tired to talk or buzzing with what had happened that day. If he tried to start a conversation, she often apologized, said she couldn't concentrate, so he gave up trying. He had made the effort, it wasn't as though he was withdrawing from her but it seemed more natural to discuss with Lucinda day-to-day events, books, films they had seen or would see, where they would have supper. And he described his friends so well that she almost knew them. Annie was becoming more and more distant.

Then it began to trouble him that he still had to keep Lucinda hidden away. He wanted everyone to know. But that was impossible. Lucinda was putting no pressure on him, she insisted that what she had predicted had come to pass. She was happy, Annie was happy, they were seeing one another often. What more did he want? Trevor put aside his doubts and admitted that he, too, was happier than he had ever been, that it was the most perfect July he could ever remember.

*　　*　　*

In early August, Trevor met Gavin to discuss plans for the autumn. They had recently been out of London together, recording an interview. As Lucinda had been shooting with Annie only an hour's drive away, she had been able to come to his hotel late at night. No-one would know, she assured him as she slipped away at dawn. Even so, Trevor decided that now was a good time to take Gavin into his confidence. He had seen them together fleetingly several times, but had never questioned him. He was a friend, he was entitled to know.

Trevor invited Gavin to meet him at his Chelsea health club, to which Lucinda had introduced him, and they were examining one another through clouds of steam in the sauna.

'Good place for an interview,' said Gavin. 'The naked truth. How about that?' He grinned, his smile was like the sudden fissure in a pastry crust, uneven and uncontrolled. Trevor was determined not to smile on camera. Each presenter had a trademark, and that sprawling smile was Gavin's.

'Am I fit for the South of France?'

Gavin patted his stomach, and leaned against the wooden planks, assessing its firmness.

'You'll do,' replied Trevor. 'Not quite man in *Vogue*, but nearly there.'

'You're not so bad yourself. Where are you off to for the hols?'

'Greece again. Annie and I always go there in September.'

'Ugh. Family holidays. At least you don't have children. Why do we do it?'

'It's not like that with Annie. We always have a good time.'

'Do you still make out in bed?'

Trevor nodded. He was growing used to Gavin's direct line of questioning. If you spent your time doing it on screen, the habit spilled over.

'Lucky sod. How are you fixed this week, Trevor? Only I'd like you to see a few people before you go away so we can round up a few ideas. There's a club date on Wednesday, and I've arranged a meeting with the poetry event group on Tuesday—'

'There are problems. I'd promised myself I'd finish chapter two.'

'Can't you knock that out while you're away?'

'Sounds fine in theory, but you know how it is. Wife and

friends on holiday, they wouldn't take it too well if I shut myself away.'

Trevor leaned across and opened the wooden door of the sauna, hoping he wouldn't pass out.

'We'll take a shower,' said Gavin, sensing his discomfort.

As they were towelling themselves down in the shower-room, Gavin appeared to be unaware of the other lean, muscular bodies in the proximity of his, and continued to talk whilst checking himself in the mirror.

'Alan is trying to push my programme into a later slot. I know what that means. In a few months' time, he'll suddenly announce it's to go out fortnightly. Then, who knows? Alan has never learned to fight. Too much compromise, not enough toughness. I need your support, Trevor. You carry weight with Alan. In fact, I said we'd all meet up on Friday. The more we have planned, the better.'

Trevor glanced nervously at the other occupants, but it was as though they were invisible. He supposed there was some unwritten rule that you could say anything in such surroundings, but he took the precaution of lowering his voice.

'It's not just the book, Gavin. I have other . . . other problems at the moment.'

'Anything I can help with?'

'Not really.'

'Are you sure?'

Trevor grunted.

'There's something I can't resolve, that's all.'

It was easier to talk when they were both sitting in the café Trevor frequented with Lucinda, conveniently near to Danvers Street.

'Doesn't Lucinda live near here?' remarked Gavin.

'Round the corner. How did you know?' asked Trevor, suspiciously.

'I think I dropped her home once.'

'I've wanted to tell you several times, but I'm seeing a lot of Lucinda.'

'I guessed that,' Gavin said, with a knowing grin. 'But I haven't said a word to anyone, don't worry.'

'It's no longer a casual affair. In some ways I wish it was.'

'Difficult one, that.'

Gavin narrowed his eyes and frowned sympathetically, as he did when interviewees broached a delicate subject which had

176

not been discussed before, providing an unexpected bonus to compensate for boring yards of video. Within a few seconds he had made a swift summary of the situation which, in his mind, had developed as quickly as the time-laspe opening of a flower. Blow-up of marriage. Scandal at Intertel. Annie's assistant, Lord Sherwood's daughter, having it off with a married man, and a leftie to boot. Husband of the woman who produces that foul-mouthed series. Daddy goes berserk. Annie takes time off to recover. Extended leave. What could be better? It only needed a few weeks, a few well-timed meetings, to suggest to the members of the board that Annie Griffiths was an embarrassment, and an extravagance Intertel could well do without. And by culling from the drama budget, he could put his own plans in motion.

'I shouldn't have said anything,' said Trevor. 'But I thought it would make sense if you knew.'

'Poor Trevor, you're deep in it, aren't you? I don't blame you, but do look out. She's an ambitious girl, but I bet she'd rather someone else paid for her little numbers from Chanel.'

'I thought that, at first. But none of that matters, strangely enough. I'm wondering whether we should live together, when I get back. This summer's been fantastic, seeing her all the time. I can't bear the thought of her not being there.'

For a moment, Gavin envied the depth of Trevor's passion. It must be the first time, the first body-blow to his marriage. Otherwise he wouldn't have taken it so seriously.

'Do you really want to be with her, rather than Annie?'

'I don't know, Gavin. I really don't know. I can't hide it any more. I love that girl. I love Lucinda. What the hell am I going to do? Two dragging weeks without seeing her, I can't bear the thought of it. And yet I want to be with Annie, I really do. I love her, I love her too. Does this sound insane? I do wonder, if I'm of sound mind at the moment, if I'm capable of delivering a judgement about anything. Sorry, Gavin. Let's talk about the programme.'

'For God's sake, Trevor, do you think it hasn't happened to all of us?'

'Not like this. I wouldn't wish it on anyone.'

'I've fallen for several girls since I married Celia. The first one I fell for, I almost left her but I didn't, thank God. Then there were others. In the end I thought, Why hide it? You can't go on pretending to be a dog on a lead. I said "If you want to walk out, I won't go running to lawyers, but I'm not going to change." She knew what I was like, when she married me. If she'd preferred it, I'd have gone. And I promised there'd be no sleazy disputes about who got what, we'd stay friends. Either she was going to accept me as I was or we'd have to part. There's no agony-aunt solution, believe me.'

'And did she ever leave?'

'She decided not to. But she goes away with the children, to friends, whenever she wants to. Why should I restrict her freedom?'

'And you're decent to one another?'

Gavin laughed.

'Why on earth not? We have rows, like anyone else, but now we're independent, it works far better. Celia writes her poems, meets her friends, does some work for Amnesty International. Sometimes she even watches my programme.'

'Do you love Celia?'

Gavin pushed his hand through his hair, a noncommittal gesture he used to play for time in the studio.

'I do when I write poetry. Remember the one near the middle of my book, "Celia Picking Up Pebbles"? I think that's my best so far. It has a Hardyesque feel about it, don't you think?'

Trevor nodded, and tried to remember where Annie had hidden his book.

'People don't realize,' continued Gavin, 'but Celia's an extra-ordinary girl. Doesn't do herself justice. She should be in some top Civil Service job, she'd be a marvellous administrator. And she's great with the children. But all she really cares about is writing poetry. The things she's really good at, don't interest her.'

'Would you tell Annie, in my place?'

'She won't say anything, but she's bound to know. They always do but they don't let on. If it's been going on for weeks—'

'It's not like that, Gavin. We don't hide things. But what I dread most is that some stranger with a grudge will call her up, drop a note, make the whole thing into a sordid drama.'

'At Intertel, everything gets out in the end, you have to face it. Annie's the kind of person they all like to talk about.'

'You haven't heard anything, have you?'

'Can't say I have. Gemma wouldn't be on my show if she wasn't discreet. And if Annie did know, do you think Lucinda would be sitting in Annie's office? If I were her, and I knew,

I'd say, look my girl, you take extended leave. Then I'd arrange for her to be transferred to another department. Simple, end of story.'

'You don't think she'd fire Lucinda? I'd hate to be responsible for that. And yet, of course, it would make life easier. Terrible, thinking like that.'

'That's not how we work at Intertel. And besides, I can't see Annie being vindictive, can you? Keep cool, Trevor. I'm sure you can work it out.'

'So you're saying I should tell her?'

'I'd wait till you're on holiday, have it out while you're both relaxed. She wouldn't thank you if the grand confession came in the middle of her schedule. Whatever you do, don't make my mistake, don't take her out to a swanky dinner or you'll have a full-scale drama over the coffee-cups. It'll be easier than you think. I'm sure she'll understand. At least Annie isn't twenty.'

'At the moment I can't see any other way out. I just don't want to live at Langton Villas. That'll be the hardest part, making her believe me.'

Gavin waved at the waitress, and adjusted his cravat.

'It'll sort itself out, I know it will. What can I say? You've gone along with it for years, but marriage doesn't work any more, not for people like us. We have to face up to it. The problem of the couple. Why pretend we're happy in the strait-jacket of bourgeois marriage.'

Gavin, a television man through and through, was used to making quick assessments and quick decisions. How could he dismiss the complexities of marriage so glibly, as though it was an inconvenient, unprofitable business partnership? Finishing his *cappuccino*, Trevor pondered whether an instant solution to a vexed question was any less valid than the lengthy debate he was having with himself, combing through all the possible outcomes, all the subtle variants of what was acceptable in his situation. Then he stopped pondering and paid the bill. He would continue to see Lucinda and tell Annie. Towards the end of the holiday would be better. The Movement had never insisted on monogamy as a fundamental right, after all. It was the hypocrisy which Trevor found increasingly hard to bear. He had almost told Annie on one occasion, but was unable to bring out the words. I'm in love with two women. Isn't it better for all of us to have it out in the open?

12

ANNIE

It was mid-August, with only two more weeks of shooting to go, and Annie had a newly born, trembling intimation that *Rough Trade* was heading for success. They were keeping to schedule, cast and crew were working well, the characters now formed so precisely that they could have been in a bus queue, and maintained their identity. The leads were strong, but without the tiny details built up by the minor characters, they would have been acting in a vacuum. There were no empty patches in *Rough Trade*, the canvas was filling out and Annie knew it would come together with the impact which was expected of her. At Intertel, there was a buzz of excitement when the actors came in to the Grotto or hung round the bar. Confidence was high, even the cameraman had congratulated Annie.

'Good young chap, that director. Gets it right,' he said, checking his shots with Annie at the end of a non-stop week. 'You've got a winner, Annie.'

'You never know,' replied Annie, pleased yet fearing to show her pleasure.

She would encourage the actors, but would never be rid of the sickness in the gut, not until *Rough Trade* had passed in front of the eyes of the critics. After *Streetcred*, they had stood up and clapped, but you could never tell if it would happen again. A change of fashion, one critic deciding that this was yet more of the same, that the flare of originality was dying down to a flicker, and all that work could be reduced to obscurity.

When she was viewing rushes in the airless theatre in Soho, sprawled over the faded once-plush seats, bent over the low light scribbing notes, she would occasionally glance at Hugh. As the lights went up, he looked towards her anxiously.

'What do you think, Annie?'

'It's going to work. The action scenes are great. Clary's performance gets better and better. Maybe, if we have time, we'll reshoot some of the early scenes. Now the part is so much in focus, we want the same quality right at the beginning.'

'Are you coming on location next week?'

Annie grinned.

'Don't think I need to. But I will if you want me.'

'Thanks, Annie.'

There was no need to say more. Hugh, although inexperienced, had justified Annie's initial confidence. The trust within the team was one of the lifelines of production. Annie decided to take a couple of days off.

Trevor was not at home that weekend. He was spending more and more time working on the cottage, helped by a couple of local builders, determined to get it finished before they went to Greece. Trevor said he liked the new experience of working at something physical, taking a break by charging off over the fields. By now, he had stripped the doors, and painted the outside. He didn't want her to go down there until it was civilized, he said, not until every room was completed. It was his contribution to her place. She didn't understand why he kept referring to it as 'her place' or, in the presence of Rick, Kate and Bryonie, as 'Annie's cottage'. Because it was her idea? Probably because it still rankled, having a second home. When he had become used to it, she hoped he would say 'our cottage'. But his good spirits had returned, and Annie realized that she had almost forgotten how he could be. There was nothing like it, he enthused, the complete exhaustion after a day's work, which freed the mind. Stifling her impatience, Annie admired his new-found pleasure in physical tasks, his hardened muscles, his sun-tanned limbs. Their closeness would revive in Greece, on the island they refused to name, their yearly refuge. In September, they would have two weeks to pull their lives together, to enjoy their friends, to sit on the terrace of the villa they rented each year, stuffing down grapes and stretching out in the warm aftermath of the fierce summer sun.

It was Sunday morning and Annie was lying in her bath, wondering whether the yellow stains trailing down from the overflow could be removed or whether she should renew all the fittings in one fell swoop. Still bubbling with energy, charged from the shoot, she began to make herself a schedule. The builders were already at Langton Villas, tearing up the kitchen floor, scraping down the dark blotched walls of the sitting room. Soon the pine would vanish, the kitchen would be shining white, and the sitting room would be a riot of colour, the donkey brown, a daring choice in the Seventies, replaced by clear, warm African colours of brick red and sky blue, Kate's choice.

Annie began to think back over the weeks. It was tough on Trevor, that great chunk of shooting time when she would only talk of *Rough Trade*. How he must be sick of it. Yet he rarely complained. They had only been out together a couple of times, once to the theatre, once to see a film. He was resigned to her life, resigned as he never used to be. Annie was puzzled. The pattern of the years had undergone a subtle change. It was hard to pinpoint what had happened, but something had changed. Was it that he rarely asked her how things had gone? Or if he did, he seemed unconcerned about the reply. Forgetting her birthday, that was understandable, she was away on location. But he never rang that day. And he hadn't asked her along to that film preview, a director she admired, when he knew she was free. Afterwards, he said, 'But why didn't you say? Why didn't you remind me? You can't expect me to learn your schedule off by heart. Anyway, I thought it would have been the last thing you wanted to do, to see a film. Weren't you off having a drink with the cast? That's what you usually do.' It wasn't that he was resentful when she complained, just surprised that she had minded. She was still upset, thinking about it.

Had anything changed, or had her disquiet resulted from the distortion of weeks living submerged in another world created shot by shot, scene by scene, the sealed world of *Rough Trade*? Had he changed, or had she imagined it? He had cut his hair short, said it made him look younger, and exchanged his old jacket for something she would not have chosen. But no-one made regular appearances on television without changing their appearance, and he had appeared on *Splash!* – three times or was it four?

Perhaps what bothered her, Annie thought, was that when he was at home, he seemed either a little distant or excessively attentive. No, darling, I'll do the shopping. No, darling, you're tired, I will . . . let me, let me. When he had come back from filming with Gavin, yes it was then, he was so elated, that she had said, jokingly, 'Trev? Are you on something? Does Gavin go in for extras? I wouldn't be surprised.'

'God, no. But I enjoyed it. Never thought I would. They all loved the haircut, by the way.'

'All who?'

'Oh, the crew. Gavin. The PA. Smashing, she said it was.'

'Which PA?'

'You might know her. Gemma, I think she's called.'

'The one Rick fancies with huge tits?'

'I didn't expect to hear that from you.' Trevor laughed slightly, to soften the rebuke. 'Or are you allowed to be sexist on *Rough Trade* nowadays?'

'I'm allowed to be how I want, Trevor.'

'Don't let's argue about it. Gemma's excellent, she keeps Gavin's team together.'

'During the day or after hours?'

'I don't find her attractive, if that's what you're getting at.'

When she asked how it had gone, all he said was, 'Fine, fine. Gavin was pleased.' But he didn't relay the details she would have expected, he didn't elaborate or invite her to share in his experience.

Then there was the time he had come back late from a private view, when they had arranged to have a meal with Bryonie and Rick. He didn't seem concerned that she could have gone with him, or that she had expressed a desire to meet the artist, someone she used to know. Said it was a last-minute arrangement, he couldn't contact her. Not long ago, she asked him to take Kate to a friend's wedding, miles away, and he forgot. He was forgetting too much. It was as though his life at home was a routine interlude to something else. And when did they last have sex? Her last period had been three weeks ago. They hadn't made love since just before then. Hadn't he said something about having pulled a muscle in his back, painting the ceiling? Was that before or after?

For the first time, it crossed her mind, like it crossed her mind when the boiler was about to burst, that Trevor was hiding something from her. Now that she had admitted it to herself, the feeling of unease grew stronger. She recalled a recent conversation which she had blotted from her mind. It took place over breakfast coffee, while Trevor was skimming the morning papers.

183

'Trev?'

'Mm?'

'I wanted to make love last night. I feel awful now. Were you really asleep?'

'Darling, what are you talking about?'

'We haven't done it for days.'

Trevor leaned towards her.

'Really, Annie. You're imagining it. Don't tell me you count every time we have sex? We've been together too long for that, surely? Haven't we always had times when we just want to go to bed to be with one another? We're not in our twenties any more.'

'I kissed you and you turned over. Immediately. As though to say, Don't touch me. It hurt, Trevor. I couldn't understand why. It's not as though you were exhausted, or in a bad mood. You weren't.'

'Annie, don't be upset. When men get older, they sometimes go through, well, times when the libido is low. You've been very stressed. And I'm very aware that I mustn't force things. I do notice, you know. Believe it or not, I was trying to be thoughtful.'

'But you knew I wanted to make love?'

'Perhaps I misunderstood the signals. We men do, darling. Last night, I thought you were just going through the motions, as though you didn't really want me to do anything about it.'

'I did, Trev.'

'Don't take it to heart, darling. It was my fault. I find it harder now, to switch off, and, well, it's more of an effort than it used to be. To be honest, I did want to sleep in my own space.'

Annie looked startled.

'Is it me, Trev?'

'Of course not. How can you think that? Once we're away on holiday, I'm sure I'll feel different.'

'But you've been so full of everything, Trev, better than you've been for ages. Earlier this year, before I started shooting, I was worried, I even wondered if you were getting ill. What is it, love? Something you haven't told me?'

'I'm absolutely fine. You'd be the first to know if anything was wrong.'

Annie had no idea how the question sprung into her mind, just at that moment.

'Trev, there isn't anyone else, is there?'

'What a crazy question. Of course not. Do you think I wouldn't tell you if there was? This isn't like you, Annie. I'm sorry, I didn't realize you were so upset.'

Trevor raised his paper again, so that she could no longer see his face, and the swiftness of his movement surprised her.

'Are you telling the truth?'

She had never, in all the years of their marriage, asked him that.

'I love you, Annie. Nothing has changed.'

At the time, Annie had believed him. But now she began to wonder whether there was some secret fault running through the bedrock of their marriage which had lain undetected, and which might crack open when she least suspected it. For the first time, she asked herself, what if? Had it happened between him and another girl, just once? Gemma perhaps? Creeping into his room when everyone had gone to bed? No, he would have said something. Or would he? How would he have begun? Annie, I've a small confession, but I think you ought to know. I've been so stupid, so terribly stupid. Please forgive me. Trevor as a Thirties matinée idol, on his knees to his wife, hatted and tailor-suited as she set off for her Job as Reporter. She admitted it, she was frightened. Wasn't it inevitable that Trevor would take to the adulation of television, so different from the adulation of students, and would reach out for the prizes of fame? Suddenly she saw him getting his own show, drifting away in a rainbow bubble of importance, surrounded by adoring researchers, buoyed up by expense accounts, with an entrée to anywhere in the country, anywhere in the world. The machinery of Intertel would suck him in, despite himself. Before long, she wouldn't recognize him – Trevor Watson, ego-bound, champagne-quaffing, girl-chasing, pontificating television personality. Then embarrassment took over. Embarrassment at creating a character who had nothing to do with the man she knew so well. It could happen so quickly, so irrationally, like Desdemona's handkerchief she'd tittered over at school. Othello picks up a handkerchief and murders his wife? A handkerchief? she shrieked in class. How can we write an essay on that? Annie Griffiths had seen it all on the page, passion and betrayal going on for yards. That was fiction, other people's lives. Her own existence was rooted in a small microclimate which, until now, had been warm and safe from the gusts outside. Was it the fear of thinking you knew someone and suddenly realizing that there were hidden parts you would never see? No, that wasn't the reason. They had both agreed, years ago, that marriage blossomed from respect for individual freedom and had never cross-questioned one another. Obsessive jealousy, ugly emotion, undignified emotion, was merely a symptom of the bourgeois preoccupation with property, or of the pre-Movement tendency to regard women as possessions. Who, amongst their circle, would have asked, 'Are you faithful to your wife?' Not one. They had stood side by side, marching for the miners, marching for the dockers, marching for women's control over their bodies. You didn't march to proclaim that your partner was going elsewhere for sex.

When she and Trevor first met, Annie had two boyfriends. She went out with either, according to her mood. Tony was a good dancer, so they went to parties together, spent hours listening to his favourite sounds. With John, she went to films and stayed up all night talking. She went to bed with both of them and thought nothing of it. At first she continued seeing them, she wouldn't tell anyone she was going out with a married man. It took her a while to realize that what had happened with Trevor was 'serious'. She had fallen in love. You didn't keep your former boyfriends then.

After their second date, after their first passionate kiss, she remembered Trevor asking, 'You don't have to tell me. But is there anyone else?' She told him about Tony and John. Which one did she go to bed with? When Annie replied, 'Both. Why not?' Trevor was shocked. How could she possibly? He couldn't hide his childhood reaction, even though of course he realized that women were entitled to the same freedoms as men. They laughed about it afterwards. Why was it easier then?

Trevor told Annie she had taught him the meaning of freedom and pleasure and keeping the light on in bed, and he never asked her again about Tony and John. It didn't matter now that they would be together for ever and ever, sharing confessions of love in the rented room lit by guttering candles and scented with joss sticks as they lay on her lumpy bed with the creased Indian bedspread.

Is there anyone else? How could she ask that question now? If she did exist, the secret girlfriend, Annie didn't want to know her name, she didn't want that certainty. She, the other, was someone, an anonymous someone. But she needed to ask. 'If you are going to bed with someone else . . .' No, she would put it differently. 'Trev, if you're screwing another girl, another woman, I'd rather know. You needn't tell me who it is, but I need to know.' And then what? Promise never to see her again? That wasn't Annie's culture, she had rebelled against the sad, marital taunts of her childhood. It wasn't the way they used to talk, she and her mates, and you never quite grew away from how it was then, not if you'd lived through it. Child of the Sixties, girl of the Seventies, she couldn't conceive of being so . . . uncool. In the days when you hopped into bed and out again, you never got heavy. Sex was natural, free and easy. Heavy was out, heavy was parents. Heavy was how they talked in Victorian novels, in the old black-and-white movies you laughed at in dope-filled cellars where the strobe lights fought in competition and the bands sweated their guts out with blasting long-held chords which reverberated in your stomach.

She would say nothing to Trevor. Let it lie. Wait until she had some proof. What if the others found out, if there was anything to find out, before she did? Whispers in the corridors, muttered confidences on location, rumours running round the internal phones? No, I have to find out, she thought. But only if everyone else knows. She despised herself for such mean-mindedness. Does secrecy make it better? Or worse? Would I mind? Would it make a difference? If it had only happened once? Or even a few times? How many times, over how long? A night, a month, a year? All in a matter of weeks? Starting with passion and ending with what? Having lunch together?

It put you in a weak position, interrogating your husband like a police suspect. Back home in Wales, the menfolk called it nagging. Nag, nag, nag. Shut up, woman. Ugly word. Better to ignore it. What if she did give in to her desire to know? Then, surely, he was entitled to ask her. I'll tell you if you tell me. All right, let's talk about it, if you insist. Come on, Annie, are you saying there's never been anyone else *who meant something* in all these years? No-one? After all that freedom? Expect me to believe that? A girl who enjoys sex like you, all those opportunities, never even once? Not last year, the year before or the year before?

What was the point in confessing, in going back all those years, when she could barely remember his face? Annie squirmed at the memory although once she wouldn't have given it a second thought. It was years ago, she would have been what? Twenty-eight? Twenty-nine? Before her thirtieth birth-day, anyway, the year they made her up from associate to full drama producer.

She was on location, a deserted beach in Spain, one small scene to go. Most of the crew had left, it was the last quick exterior, the breaking-sunrise shot they hadn't had time for. Mel, the cameraman, one of the best, could be trusted even without a director. She needn't have stayed but she insisted. On this occasion it was not duty which called. Mel moved like a cat, but he had the strength of a rock-face climber. Cameramen grew tough like explorers, they knew about the way light fell on distant hills, when shadows lengthened, when winds would clear obscuring clouds and they knew the meaning of every creak and squeak of their temperamental cameras. In drama, they always looked the part. Men's men, and it was the ultimate turn-on when they were working for a woman.

Mel made sangria in her room and they stayed up together. He was perched upright on one twin bed, she opposite him with crossed legs on the other, no point in sleeping when there was a dawn shot to get in the can. On location, bedrooms weren't private, they were often an extension of the bar, a retreat to discuss plans, to review the day's work away from curious faces. If he hadn't come and sat next to her, Annie wondered whether she would have made the first move. He kissed her suddenly, pushing her back on the bed, and then she was startled at the familiar face so close to hers.

'I'd like to make love to you, Annie. Not you as my boss. Just you as Annie.'

'Don't be ridiculous. Let's stay as friends. I want to work with you again, Mel.' His hands slipped down her shoulders, and he pushed her up the bed, so that she was resting on the bolster. She told him no, she couldn't bear doing it on the bed, it was too much like home. So they rolled onto the carpet, she slipped down her jeans and he came into her as though he had wanted to for weeks. After that dawn shot was in the can, they kissed for minutes on end, warmth rising up through her body as the sky turned from cold aquamarine to soft pink.

Two months later, the doctor confirmed that she was pregnant.

Annie was having meze with Trevor in the local Camden Town taverna, where Micky gave you five-star Metaxa on the house from pure joy, joy of having you sitting there eating his dad's food, though he pretended the elderly man was a proper chef. Stavros, in a stained white jacket a size too small, was making a hairy-armed appearance with a Humpty Dumpty smile as he handed across the plate of tarama, hummus and tsatziki through the wooden hatch. Annie had just conveyed the news.

'Are you pleased?' asked Trevor, scalding his fingers as he tore the hot pitta bread in half.

'I don't know. It doesn't seem real, having a baby inside me.'

She couldn't tell whether he was excited or holding back.

'Our baby.'

'Yes,' Annie replied. 'Except it feels more like the day after one of Rick's curries. Baby Vindaloo.'

'It can be like that at the beginning. Then suddenly you'll be rushing out to buy a pram, looking out for bargain offers on Pampers—'

'Perish the thought!' Annie giggled nervously.

'I bet I catch you wearing great full dresses when there's nothing to show, walking on flat feet and practising a waddle. Then, after you've shoved out the messy bundle, you'll say it's the biggest orgasm you've ever had.'

'That's Kate's line,' said Annie.

'Then what happens? The little tyrant takes over. I escape to the pub and you devote yourself to Mummyhood. No, Annie. Why should we go through that?'

'Is that what happened with Margaret?'

'I'm sure you'd be quite, quite different.'

'Sure?'

'Margaret became middle-aged overnight and refused to admit that she'd changed. She thought I was inventing it all, as an excuse to get out. I used to wonder, why did we make such an ugly baby? Edward looked like a fat-cheeked bull-frog, and he used to crawl like one. I tried to love him, but he spent most of the time screaming at me. Mumma, mumma, mumma. That's how it seems, looking back.'

'I'm not like Margaret, am I?'

'No, darling.'

'And I can tell you, I feel nothing at the moment except I'd like to take a pill and wake up in the morning without it being there.'

'Margaret told me once that she never remembered not wanting to be a mother.'

'Mummies stayed indoors, I always wanted to be outside, somewhere else. When I was taken to my first panto, I wanted to be Cinderella's fairy godmother, standing on stage with a wand which blinked on and off and wearing bright pink lipstick and rouge on my cheeks.'

'And Cinderella who gets the prince?'

'No, I didn't want to be her. She was soppy. Cinderella never got to fly on a wire. Who did you want to be, Trev?'

'First, a rag and bone man with a pony and cart, then George Orwell, then Che Guevera. Then your husband.'

'Don't believe you. What about Gérard Philipe?'

'I had the wrong build.'

After the second Metaxa, Trevor realized that they had not reached a conclusion. He knew Annie well, so well. She would leave it all to the last minute.

'We've got another month to decide. It's up to you, now, darling. You know how I feel.'

'You think everything would change, that I'd grow like your ex-wife, give up my job, end up as a house-frau ekeing out the day with cooking and cleaning, nose buried in Dr Spock, drooling over the first baby words.'

'It's only a fear, Annie.'

'I wouldn't, Trev. Never. Our kid would fit into our lives, do what we did. You know I wouldn't make a fuss over motherhood. And I'd carry on working. Why not?'

'Don't get me wrong. You'd be a fantastic mother, I don't doubt it.'

'But you do doubt it.'

'Not that part.'

'Afraid my mind would go into bottom gear and stick there?'

'Good God, no. I wouldn't allow it!'

They smiled at one another, and all Annie could think of was – whose baby was she carrying? And whether it was the first and last time, and whether Trevor would change his mind one day.

'If you want to have the baby, I'll be right behind you, Annie. I want you to be happy.'

She was longing to say, I don't want it, I don't want it, I don't want the risk of seeing a creature emerging from my womb who's the spitting image of Mel. But she knew she couldn't.

'Do you want me to?' she said lamely.

'Only if you do.'

Trevor sat back on the wooden chair, and looked away to contemplate the crudely coloured travel poster of the white Parthenon set against a midnight blue sky on the wall at his side. Then he took her hand, as though she needed protecting from what he was about to say.

'We've always had fantastic sex, we haven't got tired with one another, we've never seen sex as a duty. Before I met you, I never thought it could be like this. What I'm afraid of is . . .' He paused, as though rearranging his thoughts into neat order. 'It's hard for me to say. It sounds so selfish.'

'Go on,' said Annie, trying not to seem pleased at his hesitation.

'I don't want us to change. With women, all right with my former wife, she lost all interest. Margaret only had sex with me because I wanted it. I knew she wasn't really interested. She didn't want me as a man any more, only as a father. And I couldn't give her what she wanted.'

'And you think that would happen to me?'

'I'm afraid it would. To be honest, I don't want to spend years being a liberated dad at home, I have enough of that at college. And I don't want to live with a mother figure. I love you for being Annie, for being wonderfully alive and responsive and funny. And loving your job. And being so sexy. But all this has nothing to do with how you feel. In the end, it's not up to me.'

'But you'd rather I didn't.'

'Darling, I know you'd prove me wrong. You usually do. As long as I didn't have to change nappies or watch you giving birth.'

Annie poured out a slug of Retsina, first into Trevor's glass, then into her own. He had made the decision. No tears, no anguish, no confessions, no dread. He had given her a way out, so that there was no need to spill out her remorse. At the time, it had seemed so natural. Not for one moment had she thought that one night could have changed her marriage. Now she promised herself that never, never would she allow herself to pretend that it hadn't mattered.

'I *do* love you,' she said, holding tightly on to the stem of her wineglass, fearing that at any moment she might tell him, release her guilt in a torrent of explanation.

'I know you do, darling,' Trevor replied.

'I care about you more than having a child. I'd be frightened if I had it.'

'Frightened? Why?'

Annie swallowed, and twisted the end of the napkin under the table.

'What matters is our marriage. It will always come first. It always has, it always will. I don't mind having an abortion. Really. I promise I won't go into a deep depression and blame you for destroying my life.'

'You mean that? It sounds so final. An abortion. You don't have to, Annie. I'll support you if you want to go ahead, as long as you don't blame me for forcing you into it.'

'No, no, I'd never do that.'

'Or blame yourself for making the wrong decision.'

Annie looked up with relief. She couldn't wait to destroy the evidence, it was a mistake, a mistake.

'If I wanted the child so badly, I'd have told you. I'm not like Kate. I don't have maternal dreams and look longingly into prams.'

Trevor pulled her hand towards him, and kissed her fingers.

'Darling Annie. Afterwards, we'll go away. Anywhere you like.'

'Greece again.'

'Right. Greece again.'

'Or even Southwold again. I don't even care if it's raining and cold.'

Six weeks later, Annie booked herself into the Huntingdon Clinic in St John's Wood, a white-painted house surrounded by flowering cherry trees where they asked you to consult the menu the moment you were settled into your white-frilled bed. The nurses gave understanding smiles when she rejected the counselling service. She remembered her tears afterwards, how she kept repeating, 'I wouldn't have done it if it was Trevor's. And I can't tell him. I can't tell him.' And she remembered Kate's words of comfort, as she sat on the end of the bed handing her sugared almonds.

When she came home, Trevor presented her with a pair of black silk, lace-edged knickers and two air tickets to Athens. Before Mel left the BBC, she would occasionally have a drink with him, but they didn't refer to their night together. It was one of the things Annie liked about being in television, you always went on to something else. Whatever happened when you were away would be quickly forgotten. That was sometime, when? Last month? Last year? It wasn't anything like the life most people led, determined by grey swathes of work and colour-snaps of holidays abroad and birthday dinners. No wonder they envied her.

Annie scarcely gave another thought to motherhood, until Kate became pregnant again, and this time decided to have her baby. For a week after leaving hospital, Kate was ensconced at Langton Villas in order to have a rest, tiny Dahlia flexing her beetroot fingers, wriggling in a quilted box. It could have been her instead of Kate, Annie thought, as she brought her cups of tea and magazines to the bedroom. She envied her the peace of achievement, envied the experience which she had denied herself and which Kate, she was sure, would be prepared to die for. Annie wondered if she had been a coward.

Then, observing Kate's total exhaustion, her aching back, her sore breasts, her constantly shadowed eyes, her willingness to be at the mercy of another for all those years, Annie knew why she could never allow it to happen. To give up her work would now be akin to giving up herself, and work for Annie was something you could never share, never water down, never pretend was just a way of occupying yourself. How could she leave in the middle of a shoot because her baby was sick? How could she not? And when the baby became a child, what then? Would she spend hours arguing with Trevor about whether to betray the ideals of State education in favour of a nurturing private school? Or who should stay at home to help with homework?

Annie could have changed her mind. She almost did, during a three-week holiday in Crete with Trevor, observing the exultant fathers with children astride their backs, wading deeper into the dazzling sea, smile-ringed tiny faces in floppy sun-hats careering down the beaches, or being lifted up towards the pendant fruits in the orange and lemon groves. Then, once back home, she shut the images away.

Looking back, there was no reason to regret her decision to have an abortion. She remembered thinking, There will always be another time. One day we'll have a child. You hoped it would happen by accident, but it never did and the moment was never right. Did Trevor feel but not admit, that she had refused to give him what all men wanted from the woman they loved? Could that be the root of his restlessness?

There was still time, just time. Suddenly the idea began to take root, the realization that she could still have a child. 'Love, let's think again about about a baby, before it's too late.' No, for a while, she would keep it to herself. She would have to grow used to seeing herself in a new light. Annie Griffiths, mother. Why hadn't she done so before? In an instant, she had planned out her life. A baby, companion for Dally. Kate could live with them. A visiting nanny. All it took was organization. She would carry on working, with a whole support system geared to the baby. She had really wanted a child all along, only she hadn't allowed herself to believe that she could cope. But Trevor, being Trevor, would want to be certain that she had thought it through, that it wasn't one of her wild impulses she would later regret.

The water in the bath was cold. Annie jumped onto the mat, briskly rubbed herself down with a towel, then ran to the bedroom where she hurriedly put on some unspoilable clothes. She had to prepare for Dally's arrival, having promised to look after her while Kate had a few hours off. Was there time to make a jelly? Was there some orange juice left? Biscuits? Did Kate allow her to eat biscuits between meals? Would it stop raining so they could go out? Did she need a rest? When?

'Don't worry, you'll be fine,' said Kate, as she deposited Dally's bag of toys and refreshments in the kitchen. 'I can't believe I'm having half a day to myself!'

Later that afternoon, when Kate returned, she found Annie with Dally over her shoulder, walking round the house singing 'Half a Pound of Tuppeny Rice' in a scratchy contralto.

'How's she been?' she asked, taking Dally and hugging her to her as though she'd been away for a year.

'Restless,' said Annie. 'Is she like this all the time?'

Kate laughed and set Dally on the ground.

'You get used to it. She's always excited coming here. I hope you're not too exhausted.'

Dally pattered over to the kitchen drawer where Annie kept an assortment of coloured pens and scraps of paper.

'She couldn't bear being without you,' said Annie. 'I couldn't fool her for a minute.'

'Oh, she's just being awkward. She's like that sometimes.' Kate pulled up a chair and settled Dally on a cushion into the drawing position. 'Darling, are you going to make a picture for Annie?'

'Awright.'

Annie watched as she clasped a fat felt-tipped pen in her hand, and then scrawled delicately over the paper, ignoring both of them. She took to pens and paper as naturally as her mother, who stood over her watching every mark.

'Kate, do you think forty-two's too old to have a baby?'

'Of course it isn't. Annie, have you been hiding it? Are you pregnant?'

'Calm down. I'm just thinking about it.'

'Oh, you must, you must.'

Kate abandoned Dally to create on her own, and went to curl up on the sagging settee, and Annie joined her, crouching on the floor.

'I'm wondering how it would be. Could you see Trevor with a baby slung round his neck, or pushing a pram? Has he ever picked up Dally? And suppose something went wrong. What then? I couldn't spend the rest of my life looking after a deformed child, not like Barbara. You have to consider that.'

'You must have all the tests,' said Kate, airily. 'And you're the healthiest person I know. Bet you can still run faster than me.'

'Would I have to breastfeed? How do you change a nappy? How would I manage at work? Come on, Kate. It isn't that easy.'

'You're scared, that's all. Quite natural.'

'I'm frightened about not having the choice any more. Of growing old, and never having had the experience you've had. I don't want to have to make excuses. Ah yes, but look at all I've done.'

'You can't think of it like that, you really can't. At first, every woman's worried about having a kid, wants it all over quickly, prays it won't leave scars and veins and saggy tits. Childbirth is a slog, but it just happens. Then you muddle along.'

'I wonder if wanting to be pregnant is just an instinct?' said Annie. 'Or maybe it's something I was born without. Why did you go ahead with Dally? What made you do it?'

'It's impossible to explain. I just wanted another me.'

'Another you? Is that true? Isn't one enough?'

'First time around didn't turn out too well, so I thought I'd give it another go.'

Annie continued talking while she went through the arch to grind the coffee, scraped it into the ancient French pot and put on the kettle.

'You're still the best designer I've ever had. God, Kate, it ought to be easier. If only I could find you someone decent instead of your TV bastards, someone who'd pay the rent and the baby-sitter and smile at you over breakfast, I'd force you into an arranged marriage.'

'It doesn't work, Annie. It's out of date. Could you see me asking for housekeeping money, or a few quid to buy Dally's shoes? How many Trevors are out there? How many decent, independent, intelligent, handsome nice-guys except in movies?'

Annie returned, placed a mug in Kate's hand, then shifted a space on the chipped marble fireplace to put down hers, dislodging the petals of some peonies which Kate had brought and arranged perfectly in a vase. She always had something tucked under her arm – some cakes she had made, a pot of jam – however broke she was. It was only with Kate that Annie was able to survey her life. Kate shone her light in dark corners, brought her up short.

'I suppose Trevor is a nice-guy. But isn't that because he does what he likes doing? Suppose he was trapped in some awful job.'

'He wouldn't be.'

'How do you know?'

'Because he's not that kind of person.'

'I'm not sure any more.'

'Sure about what?'

'Whether Trevor really has the life he wants. Something's changed. I don't know what exactly, but I feel that Trevor's restless, he needs to get out of the house. I never used to feel that. In my crazy moments, I even wonder if there's someone else. Or if he wants someone else.'

'If there was someone else, Trevor wouldn't hang about, he'd come right out with it. Has he started being mean to you?'

'No.'

'Or taken to staying out all night?'

Annie shook her head.

'Or stopped bothering in bed?'

Annie paused, unwilling to admit her fears. It would seem like a betrayal.

'When we're not both too tired.'

'Trevor's a proper, grown-up human being. Think of all his opportunities. Has he ever acted as though he's having secret meetings in some grotty pub? He's not that kind of man.'

'He has lunch with his students sometimes.'

Kate gave a disbelieving laugh. 'Big deal. What's come over you?'

'I know what Intertel's like. How would I know if some girl has set her mind on Trevor? And how could I ask him? Gavin's always surrounded by beautiful creatures. Why shouldn't one of them try out my husband?'

Kate gave Annie a pitying look. 'Honestly, Annie. One Sunday when he's out, suddenly he's carrying on a steamy affair! Ring up Gavin if you like. See if he's round at his house.'

'I wouldn't do that. Anyway, he's down at the cottage,' said Annie, crossly.

'Ring him there, then.'

'We agreed not to put in a phone, otherwise I'd never be off it. Trevor's been working as hard as me, he needs some peace. I don't want to bother him but it's just . . . he forgets things, and he never used to. And we don't see much of one another.'

'But, Annie, it's always been like that when you've had a long shoot. That's nothing new.'

'I wonder sometimes how long he'll put up with all my meetings, burying myself in work, all those phone calls I have to take at home. Mightn't he long for someone who has dinner ready and watches late-night movies with him instead of being dead as a dodo after eleven? I don't even know who any of his students are any more. He always used to tell me about them.'

'So suddenly you imagine he's cheating on you?'

'Not cheating. Hiding something, not wanting to hurt me. Who knows?'

Annie knew that Kate wasn't taking it seriously, screwing up her sunny face, wrinkling her nose like Dally when she was misbehaving.

'You know what? Your next production should be a nice soppy love story in a lovely location instead of all your ratty detectives sniffing around the backstreets. It's getting to you, it always does.'

'You think I'm making it all up? You can't see that Trevor's changed?'

'Has he taken to wearing gaudy shirts and unsuitable ties, or buying new underpants?'

Kate rattled it off, like a doctor listing symptoms of a common complaint, then she was distracted by a sharp scream from Dally. She went over to the table, and Annie heard her say in soothing tones, 'Lovely, darling. What a lovely doggie.'

By the time she came back, it was as though the conversation had continued without interruption.

'Did I ever tell you? I made Gordon the most outrageous shirt, I'd just found this fabric with bilious green cactus plants all over it and I dared him to wear it. He did. He's so sweet, he'll experiment with anything. I don't have such fun with anyone else. Isn't it stupid? We get on so well together.'

'I know.'

Kate refused to acknowledge that Gordon enjoyed his life as a divorced man about town, and was always trying to entice him back to domesticity. She made it sound as though he was a constant presence in her life. But he wasn't. Annie admired her, her ability to make so much out of so little. She should learn from Kate, Annie thought and stop dreaming up dissatis-faction like a bored holidaymaker on a deserted palm-fringed tropical beach, sitting under a straw umbrella, complaining that the beer was too warm.

'It's easy to imagine things. Just becuase Trevor's always worrying about the book, and whether he's been an academic for too long, that doesn't mean—'

'No, Kate. It's not that. I'm getting wobbly, that's all. If they don't like *Rough Trade*, if it isn't as good as I think it's going to be, then what? Suppose no-one watches it? Will Intertel allow me one failure? You bet they won't. But I can still surprise them. Imagine their faces! Sorry, Alan, no point in talking about my next project for a while, I'm taking pregnancy leave. Back in a few months. You can't be a failure with new life inside you.'

Kate leaped up from the settee, and began to rearrange the peonies in a more pleasing shape, then moved the vase along the cluttered mantelpiece and stood back to appraise the effect.

'I want to clear all this away,' she said, as though talking to herself. 'Everything's clashing, they look lost.' Then, as she rearranged some ornaments, she added, 'Annie, you're not thinking of getting pregnant because of Trevor?'

'No, of course not. Why should I?'

'Some women do, though they don't admit it. Even some of my friends who should know better. You know I'd be over the moon if you had a kid. But do you really really want one?'

Annie laughed.

'I don't know what I want at the moment. Apart from finishing *Rough Trade*.'

Annie screwed up her eyes, puffed on the glass of the cracked mirror over the fireplace and rubbed at a fingermark as though it would improve her image. Then she moved to the kitchen, and ripped open the Marks & Spencer salmon trout elegantly packaged with a beurre blanc sauce she had bought for Trevor.

'What's that?' enquired Dally, staring at Annie as she washed the silvery fish.

'It's a salmon. Special treat.'

'Don't like it.'

'Sweetheart, you love fish fingers. It's just like fish fingers only bigger.' In spite of Kate's ecstatic voice, Dally shook her head.

'I'll boil her an egg,' Kate said.

Annie sighed. Perhaps children should be spoiled, even though she wanted to tell Dally to eat the damned stuff or shut up and leave it. Trevor was right, she thought. I'm minus the maternal urge. I'd have to stop myself being a tyrant as a mother.

'Will Trevor be expecting supper later?' asked Kate. 'Shouldn't we have saved something? And what about Rick and Bryonie?'

'Just us today,' answered Annie. 'Bryonie's taken Rick off to visit her parents. And I haven't seen Trevor the whole weekend. Friday, he was seeing Gavin again. Why does he spend so much time with that bloody man? And why does he make such a song and dance about appearing for five minutes on Gavin's tacky arts programme?'

'Why not? I bet he'll be a wow. You're just jealous.'

'Me? Why should I care? I don't know why it stays on air. Who watches it?'

'Wait till the shoot's over. It'll be different then.'

'Then yesterday, Trevor called from the village post office, said he had an appointment with the plumber and would stay down at the cottage.Why does he never ask if I'd like to come?'

'You know why, Annie. Hasn't he told you that he wants to

get the cottage finished before we go to Greece? That he won't let you see it until everything's perfect?'

'Yes, yes,' said Annie, with a sigh.

'What's so strange about that?'

'Don't take any notice, Kate. It's just premenstrual Sunday blues. End of grouse. Let's eat.'

After supper, Kate and Annie eased into the tranquillity of a long summer evening. Dally fell asleep on the settee, wedged between Kate and Annie. A pile of dissected newspapers was spread around them on the floor, and the only sound was the excited chirp of birds sifting through the freshly turned soil from the garden next door.

'Kate, why don't we all go down to the cottage next weekend? So what if Trevor wants to wait until it's all finished? I'll persuade him. You won't mind if it's a bit rough and ready, will you?'

'Me? Annie, I've been longing to go.'

'I'll make sure Rick and Bryonie come along too.'

It was a couple of weeks later that the friends finally assembled at Honeysuckle Cottage. *Rough Trade* was almost in the can. Annie, just back from a shoot in Cornwall, like an actress making her first entrance, was waiting to tell her story to a hushed audience. They were all lying on the grass outside the cottage, Rick, Bryonie, Kate, Dally and Trevor, basking in the hazy August sun.

'How is everything?' said Trevor, bearing a laden tray.

'Trevor's been a darling,' announced Annie, as she handed round the burnt sausages and blackened tomatoes and under-done chops for their late Saturday brunch. 'He came back from filming for Gavin and did all the shopping. Without me even asking.'

'And I even remembered alphabet spaghetti for Dally. Are the tomatoes a little too brown?'

'Burnt to buggery, just how I like them,' said Rick.

'These are genuine Cumberland sausages. And the chops are organic, hope you noticed. The eggs are proper free-range, none of your farm-fresh. It's a good shop, Sainsbury's. You need a car, of course. But I understand there's a free bus for pensioners.'

With Trevor determined to elicit an evaluation of every item on the plate, Annie wondered if the others were as irritated as she was. And then, as he launched into an analysis of why he had chosen Kenyan coffee, rather than Colombian or Breakfast or Italian, she broke in to his monologue.

'Trev, it all tastes fantastic.'

He gave her an appreciative smile, which she resented.

'Glad you like it. I've got a surprise for you, darling. It's a late birthday present.'

'Wait till I've finished.'

'Aren't you pleased that I remembered?'

'Yes, love. Of course I am.'

'You won't believe what happened in Cornwall,' Annie began, now that her audience had satisfied the first ravenous pangs of hunger.

'Something always happens in Annie's dramas,' said Trevor. 'This time it wasn't a disaster, thank God. Filming with Gavin made me realize that on the whole, it's a tedious process. I feel happier in the studio. It really was a good experience, though, forcing myself to say something of value in two minutes.'

'Trev, do stop,' interrupted Kate, 'Annie was about to tell us about Cornwall. We want to hear.'

'Rick and I went to Cornwall once,' began Bryonie.

'Did we?' said Rick. 'I must have disgraced myself. Memory block, see.'

Annie sat up, biting into a fat sausage which she held between her fingers.

'The idea was, we have a skeleton crew, and shoot this fantastic chase scene, starting in a misty dawn, you just see a tiny moving speck along a winding road, like a ladybird running along a twig, then you get closer, wham, wheels throwing up grit, roar of engine, it disappears. A black figure emerges from behind a hut on an allotment, jumps onto this huge machine and starts off in the same direction. We follow the figure, faster and faster. Then it's in the mirror of the Porsche, all black. And the chase starts. Everything was set, road closed off for half an hour, no-one about. Then what happens? The bloke who was meant to ride the Harley doesn't show. Panic. Morley the stunt-man's let us down. We're just about to turn back, when this voice behind me says, 'I could have a go.' Guess who?'

'Has to be the electrician,' said Rick. 'Sparks always like big engines. And they're always little guys, have you noticed?'

'No. Wasn't him. And it wasn't any of the blokes. It was

Lucinda. She gets into the leathers, plonks on a helmet, calmly goes up to this monster, next thing she's bombing down the road. PA goes crazy, what about the insurance? But I said what the hell. I just wanted to see their faces. Then she comes back, circles round the car-park, takes off her helmet and says, 'Let's do it now. I'm ready.' She really is amazing that girl. We'd almost finished the sequence, and there's a bit where the guy on the bike has to zoom along the quay at Newlyn, swerving round the fishing nets, figure-of-eight stuff. She insisted on doing it, almost came off a couple of times. But she made it! Thanks to Lucinda, we got almost everything. Then, the moment we've finished, we all go back to the hotel to crash out for a while. There was no question of driving back that night, we were knackered. So I get some kip, go to Lucinda's room and she's not there. The barman hands me a note. "Didn't want to wake you. If you want more bike antics, I'm sure Tim will oblige. He's much better than me. Love L." Knowing Lucinda, she was probably in Tim's club, raving away all night.'

'Next time I see her, I'll ask to ride pillion. When I was covering the riots in LA, I met this girl who had the most amazing bike—'

'Yes, we know Rick,' said Bryonie. 'And you discovered she made 3-D lesbian porno movies.'

They all laughed, having heard the story before. Annie passed over to Rick the last remaining chop, and lay back on the grass.

'Listen, Trev, did you know that Sherwood Hall is only about fifteen minutes from here? Lucinda's staying down there this weekend and I was going to ask her to come over.'

'Oh? And did you?' asked Trevor, putting down a half-eaten sausage.

'No. I decided not to.'

'Thank Heavens. Now we can relax,' Trevor said.

'How about tea, she could always come for tea,' muttered Rick, through a mouthful of meat. Bryonie glared at her husband.

'I don't intend being on my best behaviour for anyone.'

'And I haven't got a tablecloth.'

Annie sat up and tapped Rick on the shoulder. 'How about making some more coffee?'

'No, no. That's my job,' Trevor insisted. 'But Bryonie's

right. We've come here to cut off, not to be on our best behaviour.'

'I'm sure she's not like you imagine,' said Kate. 'She sounds great to me. I'd love to meet her. She doesn't have to stay all weekend. Does she, Annie?'

'Why I mentioned it was that Lucinda did say she'd love to pop over, give us some ideas about what to plant if we wanted. She told me that Sherwood Hall had a fantastic arboretum and herb garden.'

'What the bloody hell's an arboretum?' shouted Rick, shielding his eyes from the sun.

'A garden with unusual trees in it,' said Bryonie. 'Ones which are difficult to grow.'

'Trust her. Give me the easy ones.'

Rick rolled over, and presented his grass-covered back to the sky. Trevor moved over to Annie's side and slipped his arm round her waist.

'I'm sorry I forgot your birthday, darling. But I remembered in the end. Come and see, I've bought you something.'

'Now?'

Trevor pulled Annie to her feet.

'Let's all go,' said Bryonie. 'Come on, Dally.'

Bryonie hitched up her long skirt, and ran across the lawn, her blond curls fanning out under her scarf, followed by Dally and Kate, who was squealing as her bare feet hit the dry summer stalks.

'It's bloody paradise here,' said Rick, strolling behind them with Trevor and Annie.

'Doesn't Bry look like an angel in a hurry? Not bad for forty-two, is she?'

'You should tell her, Rick,' said Annie.

'She might start getting ideas. Someone else might fancy her.'

'Why not?' replied Annie, gaily. 'Do her good to have a gentleman admirer.'

Rick snorted. 'Is that what you say behind my back?'

'Oh yes, we spend all our time plotting and planning. Didn't you know?'

Trevor pushed open the door of the toolshed at the back of the cottage.

'Christmas tree,' shouted Dally.

Standing proudly in a large earthenware pot, was a graceful tree, with slender branches covered in a bleached white bloom, pale sage green leaves delicately hanging from spindly stalks. Annie stood back and gasped with astonishment.

'Trev! It's beautiful. What is it? Where did you find it?'

'Willow. It's a willow tree,' said Bryonie.

'*Salix daphonoides*, darling. The proper name. Did you know, there are loads of different willows? This one originally came from the Himalayas.'

'From where?'

'The Himalayas.'

'That's what I thought you said. Is that what we call them nowadays?' said Rick. 'Him-arl-i-yars? Or is that posh botanical speak?'

'Trev's discovered nature. Next thing, he'll be on *Gardener's Question Time*. It took me eight years to be a doctor and he's got the ability to become an expert in weeks. Not fair.'

'I told you he'd be ideal for telly.'

'Do you like it?' Trevor said, taking Annie's hand.

'I love it. What made you think of a tree? It's perfect, love.' Trevor smiled.

'Let's plant it, shall we?'

Annie picked up the pot, the soft leaves caressing her face, and carried it round to the front of the cottage.

'He's never given me anything like this. It's the best present I've ever had. I've always wanted something which didn't break or wear out.'

'As it's a willow, it'll have catkins in spring,' said Kate. 'Dally will love those. Dancing catkins.'

Leaning on a spade, Trevor was having a grave consultation with Rick.

'I wonder if it'll need fertilizer, in the growing period?' said Trevor.

'Stick it in and let it grow, that's what I'd do. If the bugger can't survive, it's not meant for this world.'

Annie came across the grass, and placed the tree reverently by Trevor's side.

'You have to dig a hole first, Trev. Where shall we put it? Over there somewhere?'

'Where you can see it. So everyone can say, That's Annie and Trev's cottage, the one with the willow tree,' suggested Rick.

'How about at the side of the house?' said Bryonie.

'Just a minute. You can't put a tree just anywhere. It'll stay there for all of its life. Suppose it's the wrong place? Suppose it wants sun and you give it shade? Or it goes in a damp place and it needs dry? Or it hates wind and it's too exposed?'

'Bryonie thinks she's giving child-guidance lectures,' said Rick. 'What's wrong with moving a tree? Stick it somewhere else if it's unhappy.'

'No, Rick. It's got to be in the right place. Bryonie's right.'

'I know where I'd put it,' said Trevor. 'By the side of the house, it would soften the contour. But it's Annie's decision.'

'I refuse. You make the decision, Trev. I've had enough of that during the week.'

Bryonie stuck up her finger and tried to determine where the wind would come from, if there had been any.

'Where's the prevailing wind?' she asked.

'Let's toss for it. Heads it goes in the middle of the garden, tails it goes at the side.'

'We haven't asked Dally,' said Kate. 'Where do you think, sweetheart?'

'There!' replied the child, pointing at the sky.

The tree was planted at the side of the cottage, and then they all walked down the track to observe it at a distance, the tiny distinguishing mark which would one day spill over with a massive umbrella of weeping branches.

13

FRIENDS

The talk in the Grotto was centred round one event: Thelma
Poole had changed her image. Her mane of hair had upped
its blond rating and had peaked with Day-Glo silver, long
locks waving permanently around her plump shoulders like a
transvestite's wig. Jeff Walker, her partner as he preferred to
call himself, never husband, was seeking admiration from all
and sundry. Rick's gaze was not directed at her hair, but at the
breasts which struggled to make an exit from something lacy
and stretchy.

'Don't touch!'

Rick drew back his hand.

'I only wanted to see if they were real.'

'Of course they are. Do you think I've been hiding in a secret
Harley Street clinic?'

Jeff waved a hand to silence her.

'Rick, you're going to eat your heart out. Have we got some
subject for next month's series!'

'Don't tell me. I know, a searing exposé on the balance of
payments, cut to music.'

Smoothing back his tinted hair, Jeff attempted a sardonic
smile. 'Now this one, Rick, really *is* an amazing story. This is
serious, hard stuff. Something Thelma can really get her teeth
into. An exclusive, so keep quiet.'

Only when Rick gave a jocular roar, did Jeff realize that he
might have put it better. Thelma's teeth had been 'rearranged'
in the service of a ratings rise, as had her breasts, which were
less like a saggy bag of flour, more like one of those rounded
Stone Age nuraghi Rick had seen in Sardinia. She had to have
it done, but she was over-sensitive about it. Much better
to brazen it out, argued Jeff. Although she despised him in

public, Thelma took his advice in private. Even if he lacked an ability for bitchy repartee, his flair for obtaining publicity had meant that *Poole Reports* had stayed on the air for over five years, even though Alan had tried to axe it on several occasions.

'Go on. Cross my heart I won't tell,' said Rick. 'Or rather, I won't nick it unless I'm desperate.'

Jeff leaned towards Rick and spoke in a hushed voice.

'There's this pensioner living in an army retirement home in Hove. Wife died years ago. Puny fellow, long white moustache, never goes out without a cane. Breeds cats, Persian cats.'

'A cat molester. I knew it,' retorted Rick.

'He meets a gang of chums in a pub, and they persuade him to do the lottery with them. And then the bugger actually wins! But they don't get a penny. He's been listening to their system, going home and buying his own ticket each week without telling them. A million and a half he gets, all for himself. Guess the first thing he did?'

'Bought the retirement home, chucked out the pensioners and turned it into a cattery.'

'Wrong.'

Jeff looked at him stonily.

'He's having a sex change. At seventy-two. Doesn't give a damn that he might cop it. All he wants is to walk down the seafront in his dead sister's clothes, which he's kept for thirty-five years. And we're going to film him doing it for the first time. Isn't that bloody amazing?'

'I'm speechless. Jeff, that's a winner. It's a BAFTA cert for investigation of the year.'

'Thanks, Rick. I appreciate that.'

'And he's an absolute darling,' added Thelma. 'He'll say anything I want him to. The first time he told his story, I cried. I actually cried.'

'I just know it's going to be terrific,' Jeff replied.

Tiring of the mutual adulation, Rick quickly invented a pressing interview. If only . . . But Thelma grasped his arm and prevented him from pushing off.

'Rick. You're a friend of Annie's, aren't you? I mean a real friend, not just one of her hangers-on?'

'Wouldn't hear a thing said against her,' he said quickly. Thelma put a multi-ringed hand on Rick's shoulder and gazed up at him.

'The most awful thing has happened. I feel dreadful. I don't know what to do. But we've all got to do something.'

'Like have a drink?' suggested Rick, dreading an emotional confrontation. Who had Annie offended now?

'It's Lucinda Sherwood. She's doing it with Annie's husband.'

Rick gulped.

'Oh. Christ!' Then he recovered. 'Who's spreading that around?'

'Gemma, Gavin's PA. And she's not spreading it around, she told me in confidence. What's his name, Annie's hubbie?'

'Trevor.'

'That's right, Trevor. Trevor Watson. Isn't he a professor or something? Really bright, apparently. Brilliant talker.'

'He is a close mate, Thelma. Of course he's bright.'

Thelma hesitated, Rick was so touchy.

'Gemma told me that he was doing a location insert for Gavin, some plush hotel outside Plymouth, and she was asked at the last minute to book the bridal suite. Gavin said he needed somewhere private and comfortable to meet the artists. We all know what that means. Then, Gemma was having a late drink at the bar, and guess who turns up? Leggy Lucy, in a dress which left little to the imagination, so I gather. Lucinda says, "Hi. Did everything go all right? Sorry I couldn't get here earlier. Is Gavin around?" As though she was part of the production team.'

'Very good, very good. Sounds just like her. Hardly conclusive proof,' said Rick. 'No wonder you're not in current affairs. I'd stick her on the budget, too, if I was Gavin. Lucky bastard.'

'Don't be silly, Rick. It wasn't Gavin she was after. Next morning they had an early start, so Gemma went to wake up Trevor Watson, she always checks, and he wasn't in his room. So she went along to the suite and guess what? There was a tray outside the door. Empty champagne bottle, two sets of plates and glasses. It was obvious, as though he wanted everyone to know.'

'So? A quick screw, is that so unusual in this business?' Rick said, irritably. 'As it happens, I was down with Trev and Annie last weekend at their cottage. We all had a great time, they were around one another like a couple of lovebirds. Trev isn't a fool. So Lucinda decides to seduce him one night. That girl knows she can get anyone she wants. What's a man meant to do? Say, sorry I can't, I've got my period?'

'It's more serious than that, Rick.'

'Oh? Concrete evidence, have we? Were they kissing in the car-park?'

'Gemma lives a few streets up from Lucinda. She was walking up the King's Road the other day, and she saw them having breakfast together, in an Italian café.'

'Ever heard of a breakfast meeting?'

'Kissing over the croissants?'

'I'd do the same myself,' said Rick. 'Trevor is devoted. But human, thank God. He's like me, likes to flirt and go home to his wife. We men do that, Thelma.'

'Jeff doesn't,' she replied pointedly.

Rick didn't want to give the quick retort which entered his mind, no girl in her right mind would consider Jeff as bedding material, but neither did he want to pursue the topic.

'Even a starving hack wouldn't see that as evidence, Thelma,' he said sternly.

'Are you implying that Gemma's spreading malicious lies? Why should she? She's nothing against Annie. Or Trevor.'

'All right, all right. Look, there's only one thing to do. Two things. I'll talk to Gemma and say her job's on the line if she breathes a word to anyone. And you must promise—'

'Rick. You don't have to say. Don't you trust me by now?'

'You know I do. You're a good woman even with that hair.'

After giving Thelma a quick peck on the cheek, Rick made a decisive exit from the Intertel bar.

His first reaction, as a male, was 'Good old Trevor. There's life in the old sod yet. I'd do the same in his place. Wonder what's she's like in the sack? Bloody marvellous, most likely.' Then once he had left his Intertel persona behind, the hangover gloom crept up on him as he approached his territory, Langton Crescent. He had a vision of 14 Langton Villas with a For Sale notice, no more Sundays, no more amiable ramblings in the Langton Arms, removal vans, but worst of all, Trevor making a fool of himself with some long-legged, ice-coated aristocrat who would give him hell and leave him with egg on his face. He didn't want his mate Trevor to make a fool of himself, he didn't want him to let the side down. Silly git! Then he reassured himself. Once they got on the screen, people lost their bearings, but it was only temporary. Academic meets expense account and fame. It wouldn't last. Trevor was level-headed, Christ, he was level-headed. Rooted, like he would never be. Rooted like Bryonie, Bryonie a doctor doing something solid and worthwhile not like having a quick flash in front of millions, Trevor caring about words, caring about beliefs. Caring about Annie. He'd get over it.

When he arrived home, the house was empty, Bryonie had been called out. He picked up the phone, because he couldn't let it rest.

'Kate? What are you up to?'

'Making Dally a party dress. What are you up to?'

'I'm coming round.'

'We've had supper, Rick.'

'I don't want supper. I want to see you.'

'Have you been drinking?'

'Only one. One and a little one.'

Passing by the off-licence, Rick remembered the bottle of wine. White, gnat's dribble which Kate insisted on drinking. They both sat on the futon she'd picked up in some car-boot sale, leaning against the low open-plan divider, covered in Dally's smiling hairy suns and smiling hairy Mummies. They talked about the cottage, and what great times they all had, and how Trevor was leaping about like a teenager, and how good it was to see them forgetting everything, how lucky they were, all of them throwing off the ghastly week in each other's company . . . and then Rick relayed his conversation with Thelma.

'It's all fabrication, I'm sure it is, but I don't want it to get back to Annie. Or have those bastards sniggering behind her back.'

Rick fetched himself a beaker and splashed in some of the warm white wine he'd brought for Kate. Hateful stuff.

'Do you think it's true, Kate?'

'If it's true, it doesn't matter. It doesn't matter. It'll never last.'

'No, of course it doesn't matter.'

'I wish it hadn't been her.'

'You think it is her?'

Kate was staring at the floor.

'I thought there was someone. Maybe. But why did it have to be Lucinda?'

'If it was.'

'Annie likes her, for Christ's sake. Trevor's not mean, he wouldn't have a fling with someone Annie sees all day long, someone she gets on with so well. I wonder if it might have been Gemma?'

'Unlikely. No challenge,' replied Rick, gloomily.

'Trevor has changed slightly, but I suppose men do when they get older.'

'I hadn't noticed him being any different.'

'You wouldn't.'

'Insensitive Welsh nut-case, am I? Come on, be specific.'

'I can't. All right then. He fusses around all the time.'

'Trevor's always like that. Have you only just noticed?'

'But when he is at home, which isn't often these days, he never lets her alone. Annie, shall I do this; no, Annie, let me; I'll get something for supper; Annie, would you like this; Annie, would you like that; Annie, I'm just nipping down to the pub, back in forty-five minutes; isn't Annie marvellous? He was never like that.'

Did women have second sight? Extraordinary powers of perception, like a dog barking when it heard its master's car a mile away? Rick immediately wondered if Bryonie could tell who he had been eyeing up in the bar. Or whether women knew bloody everything like the Inland Revenue.

'You're making it up, Kate. Trevor's always been like that.'

'Has he? It's probably hormonal,' she added.

'Men don't have hormones. They were invented by women to excuse irrational behaviour.'

'You know nothing about women, Rick. But you might at least try and learn.'

'How about some evening classes? Cheer up, Kate. Is teasing politically uncorrect or am I being unbearably insensitive?'

'Don't, Rick.'

'All right, I'll be boring. Is the telly working?'

'The picture is either snowy or rainy. Dally doesn't mind as long as she hears the sound.'

'I'll have a look for you.'

Rick crawled along the carpet, turned on the small set which was sitting on a Dally-height stool.

'Rick, leave it. Gordon's going to find me another one.'

'Thought he was meant to do that months ago.'

'He's been busy. Rick, don't you think you ought to—'

'Say something?'

'To Lucinda. No, better have a quiet word with Trevor. Find out what happened. Ask him to meet you in the pub.'

'You do it, Kate.'

'No, Rick. You're better with words. And it's easier for a man.'

'How can I possibly? What do I say? Trev, by the way, I thought you ought to know . . . Christ, it's none of my business.'

'Don't say anything, then. Don't think about it. If it's true, it's a passing phase. Trev trying to prove himself. Gordon was just the same, except he told me about it. Gordon always tells me everything, he's so sweet. He said every man past forty wants to see if he can fuck a girl the same age as his daughter. Incest at one remove. Then, afterwards, he feels guilty and dreadful but if he's got any sense, he can laugh about it. It never lasts.'

'What if Annie gets to hear?'

'By the time she's back in her office, it'll have blown over. Really, it's better if you don't say anything. You know what it's like, someone invents a story for a lark. Soon, *Rough Trade* will have finished shooting, and we'll all be in Greece. Bet you it's all over by then. If we create a stink now, we'll make it all seem more important than it is. Let's wait, Rick.'

Rick laughed. 'It's not as though he's announced his divorce. We're being daft, Katie. Everything's going to be all right.'

'He should never have done it to Annie . . .'

'So what? Just for a night? A few hours before the call time? Annie'd never expect a man to be faithful for over twenty years. She'd just blow her top, give him a hard time for a day or so, then forget it. Whatever's happened to the good old days? None of us thought anything of it, we didn't have to. Remember that clap clinic? I used to get more stories from there than El Vino's.'

'And the Indian doctor who kept saying, "Very good, very good, now you must be very good"?'

'Sex has got too bloody serious, Kate.'

He looked round at the bright prints and glowing paints with which Kate had transformed her box-like council flat, and suddenly felt like staying.

'You and I should—'

'No we shouldn't,' said Kate with a sweet smile. 'We tried once and it was a disaster. Remember?'

'Too much beer, it happens.'

'You hadn't been drinking, Rick, not that night.'

'We could always try again. My foreplay has improved,' replied Rick, ever hopeful.

Kate pushed him towards the door, as she had many times before.

'Bryonie will be home by now. Why don't you tell her what's happened? She'll know what to do. Bry always does. Move your arse.'

'I can't, Kate. You know me. Let's do it together.'

Suddenly Kate's Colonel Bogey chimes, a joke from Gordon, bonged in the entrance.

'Is this a raid?' exclaimed Rick, instinctively buttoning up his shirt.

'It's only Gordon,' said Kate, as she ran to the door.

Rick took one look at his Bevis and Butthead T-shirt, his overblue eyes (coloured contact lenses) long blond hair pushed back over the ears, the bland, indentikit buddy-face of middle America – and wondered what the hell Kate saw in him.

'Hi, Gordon.'

'Good to see you, Rick.'

'I came to mend the telly. All attempts at rescue have failed, sad to say.'

'No problem, I'll get her a decent set. Hi, babe. I was in the neighbourhood, just came from Judd's party. Boring as hell. But I brought a rude balloon for Dally. Think she'll like it?'

'Oh, how sweet.'

Rick watched for a few seconds as Gordon puffed his cheeks and inflated a star-sprinkled scrap of blue rubber into the size of a dinosaur's penis.

'Have a fun evening. What's left of it,' he remarked as he headed for the door. The only satisfaction he could rustle up was that, although he didn't know it yet, Gordon was about to produce Intertel's darts championship autumn series and that all he had for sustenance, apart from Kate, was a third of a bottle of luke-warm Muscadet. Serve the bastard right.

At Intertel, Lucinda's popularity rating was at last beginning to soar. The motor bike episode had been reassuring. She had shown that she was more than some trust-fund bimbo who'd been brought in by Alan to curry favour with Sherwood. Gordon, who together with Thelma and Jeff had organized the Intertel Game for a Laugh Charity Marathon, had persuaded her to repeat her performance in public, do a few laps round the ring on a Harley in the grand finale. The other reason they now smiled at her when she made a rare appearance at the bar (spending all her time on that new show of Annie's) was that it was quite clear that Lucinda had told Gavin to get lost. Gemma overheard her saying she couldn't go to Rome with him, that she did happen to have a regular boyfriend. Lucinda kept everyone guessing, and remained a topic of conversation throughout the summer.

Annie hadn't been around for a while, but one evening she came into the bar, hair tousled, nut-brown face, success written all over her face. Benny, leaning gloomily against the bar, felt a twinge of envy for that production high he might never have again. It wasn't the same, endless meetings, hunting for formulas, sinking back into the well-tried furrows, keeping his pecker up, trying to pretend to the lads they'd got the next *Till Death* or *Porridge* on their hands.

'Well I never. How's things, Annie?' Benny said, taking his place at her side.

'It's all worth it. Everyone flat out, we're going to do it. I don't care what anyone says now, Benny.'

'Better than *Streetcred*?'

'Different. No, it'll be better. Tighter, faster. Not an inch to spare. It's so fantastic, reading a script and then it comes out how you want it. Only two more scenes to go, and we've done the hard ones. Clary Hunt is going to be a winner. And I tell you, it was a gamble. Little experience of acting, then come the crunch, it pours out. I just hope she won't be nicked by Hollywood. I want her for my next. Totally instinctive, Benny, the kind of actress who takes over the screen, even when she's in a crowd scene, you can't take your eyes off her.'

'You're the one who'll be nicked by Hollywood. But don't go. Stick around, Annie. They'd chew you into ribbons over there.'

'Don't worry, Benny. Could you see me sweating it out round the LA cocktail circuit? I'd go crazy.'

'They'd love you.'

'They love anyone who's a success. It doesn't mean anything. And besides, when Trevor and I went there a few years ago, he couldn't wait to get home. We're too old to transplant, Benny. Though I bet Lucinda ends up there.'

'Why don't you suggest it?'

'I need her at the moment. Though she's off on leave now. I'm thinking of producing her script. It would be something new for me, I'd love to have a go. How's it been around here? Anything I should know?'

'Gavin's going to be moved to a later slot. He's not well pleased. But he's planning some early-evening game show for the kids, so they say. It's good to see you, Annie. Will you have a look at the comedy series I've just signed?'

'Of course.'

'It's set in a garden centre. Gnomes play a big part. Desperation in the herbaceous border and cheating at the Chelsea Flower Show. Love and lust in the greenhouse. Should be a winner.'

'Jokes good?'

'Not bad, Annie. But you're not big on gardening, so you might not appreciate it.'

'Don't you be too sure. I've got a place in the country now. I'm learning fast. You could shoot some good stuff down there. It's in Wiltshire, pretty village near by, and a wonderful gay vicar everyone adores and tries to find a wife for. When I'm back from holiday, will you come?'

'You're on, Annie. Me dad had an allotment and me mum had me.'

'I've missed your jokes, Bennie. The crew have heard them all, I need a new one for tomorrow. Have you got one for me, before I go?'

'Heard the one about the owl and the pussy-cat?'

'In a pea-green boat?'

'That's the one. Owl is sitting there, opposite pussy-cat. Sun shining. Pussy-cat gorgeous in a bikini, getting a tan, gives a simper at Owl. Owl leans forward. "I've a confession to make," he says. "What, dearest owl?" she says, purring like pussy-cats do. And he says, "There have been other pussy-cats." Come on, Annie. Don't I get a laugh?'

'A smile.'

'You going out with the better half tonight? Hitting the high spots?'

'Not tonight. Trev's down in the country, loves it there. No point in him mooching around in London, when I'm hardly there. Fancy a bite to eat?'

Benny grabbed her arm.

'Annie Griffiths, is this a date? Is this my night?'

'I fancy Joe Allen's. A Caesar salad and a huge hamburger.'
'You should be married to me. I make a great burger.'

When Bryonie and Rick moved in to Langton Crescent, they thought they'd only be there a few years. When the baby came along, they'd need more space, even though Rick pointed out that the house was built for families, working-class families who thought nothing of putting three or four kids to a room. Bryonie, who had grown up with three sisters and a brother in a detached house in Richmond, large enough for her father's surgery, separate rooms for the children and even a nursery, found it difficult to imagine.

When they first married, and she was beginning to build up her practice, Bryonie had a comforting view of the future. When Rick was a father, he would cut down on his drinking and womanizing. Over the years, Bryonie's optimistic plans had settled into stoic acceptance. Her father had been against the marriage, but Bryonie always knew that Rick drank too much, that he eyed other girls even in the early days, she accepted what she was taking on. Rick had chosen her, from all the flashy girls he surrounded himself with as a young reporter. He made no promises, wrote no flowery letters, occasionally picked up something from the duty free as a present on his frequent trips abroad and was the most egocentric man she had ever met. But Rick was a socialist, the first person she had ever met who would fight for the inarticulate, the exploited, the weak members of a callous society. For that, Bryonie would forgive him everything.

The reason Bryonie was quieter now than she used to be was only partly that practising as a doctor had become harder, now that she had to steel herself for daily confrontations with the dispirited, the hostile or the grindingly poor. Bryonie's tranquil, seemingly passive exterior, her reluctance to rush into debate, was the consequence of coping with a surgery situated in one of the more wretched parts of London – her choice – living with the wild, unruly Rick and a mask for a deep-felt disappointment. They had never moved from Langton Crescent and the expected child had never arrived. It was strange, Bryonie thought, that she had come from such a fertile family, that her siblings became pregnant with carefree regularity. On a few occasions, when she had suggested that Rick might take some tests, he had flown into a rage. What was she trying to imply? That he was lacking as a man? He wasn't going to have some quack peering at his sperm through a microscope.

Bryonie's house was neat and orderly. The living room, separate from the kitchen, was lined with shelves, the books arranged by subject and author, her books. Rick's books, children's books she had bought for when Dally came. Throwing a provençal cloth over the kitchen table, she wondered if they would be expecting to eat. Kate said not to bother, but she never knew with Rick. He couldn't abide set meal-times, but had a habit of demanding food at impossible hours. Bryonie placed some slices of sausage and ham on one plate, and some cheeses for Kate on another. Then Rick came through the door.

'Bry. We're all going out. You can put that away. Kate's in the car and the brat's with a friend. So we can all get rat-arsed tonight.'

'No, you can't, Rick. You go with Kate, I really don't feel like going out.'

'You don't want me to enjoy myself, is that it? I've had nothing all day. One beer, that's all.'

'Don't shout.'

'I never shout.'

'You do, Rick. Take Kate out for a nice meal.'

Bryonie began to remove the plates from the table.

'I want you to come, Bry. Can't I take my wife out for a hot dinner?'

'Another time.'

'Then we'll stay here. I'll go and get Kate. I ate a big lunch out anyway.'

Having replaced the plates, Bryonie lit a couple of candles, surveyed herself in the mirror and decided to replace her surgery dress, heavy cotton with a peter-pan collar, for the Chinese silk one Rick had brought her from Hong Kong. It was far too tight, but she would wear it just this once. When she came down from the bedroom, Rick had opened a bottle of wine she had been saving, but tonight she merely shrugged. Kate would enjoy it.

'Come on, Kate,' said Rick, pouring out a wineglass up to the brim. 'Over to you.'

'Something's happened, Bryonie. We thought we ought to talk about it, together.'

'What's happened?'

'Trevor,' Rick began. 'Trevor is—'

'Seeing someone else.'

'You mean, he's having an affair with one of his students? Cheating on Annie? Oh, no, not Trevor? Are you sure?'

Suddenly Rick understood why patients grew tongue-tied in surgeries. He had no desire to interfere and a greater desire to hunt down the bottle of whisky hidden in his sports bag. He took a deep breath.

'Yes. But she's a former student. Annie's assistant Lucinda.'

'Does Annie know?'

'Unlikely,' said Rick, shaking his head. 'No, I'm sure she doesn't. Why he had to choose Lucinda Sherwood for a spree, it's beyond me. All those girls, and he goes and picks her. Or, more likely, she picked him. Trevor just doesn't have a clue what he's got himself into. Anyone who's regularly seen with Leggy Lucy will find his fizz in Dempster sooner or later. Seen coming out of Tim Sherwood's fashionable nighterie is Lucinda's latest escort, fifty-six-year-old Trevor Watson, making a sizzling début on—'

'They didn't write that?'

'No. But they soon could.'

'Does everyone know? Everyone at Intertel? Who told you? How can you be sure it's true?'

'Thelma, but she's promised to keep it to herself. She's all right, is Thelma. Sometimes she even gets her facts right.' Rick decided to tailor his story, there was no need to bring up Gemma's name again. 'She saw them all over each other, having an early breakfast in the King's Road. And a friend of hers saw them at a hotel together.'

'I think you should say something to Trevor, at least find out what's happening,' said Bryonie.

'To Trev? How could I? My oldest mate?'

'If it's true, he's sure to tell Annie, he doesn't hide things—'

'Don't be daft, Kate. He wouldn't do that, he's not like Gordon.'

'Me and Gordon, that was quite different,' said Kate, defensively. 'Everyone knew it was over with him and Audrey.'

'Audrey didn't,' said Rick. 'Let's be straight about this.'

'Are you criticizing me? Are you trying to say I broke up Gordon's marriage? That's unfair, Rick.'

'Hold on. We're talking about Trevor and Annie.'

'Is that what you really think? You're quite wrong, Rick. You think you know about everything, but you don't. You don't know about me.'

'Tell me, tell me.'

'Rick, lay off,' said Bryonie.

'I wouldn't have dreamed of hurting Audrey. Audrey's fantastic, we've got a lot in common. But you wouldn't understand that, would you?'

'I'm just a pig-ignorant reporter, Kate. Keep going. This is good stuff.'

'Shut up, Rick,' said Bryonie.

Kate's eyes had filled with tears.

'He didn't mean it, Kate.'

'I'm not upset because of me. It's Annie. What if Trevor's been having an affair for ages? Suppose she cracks up? And we've done nothing.'

'What Kate's getting at, Bry, is . . . well . . . We thought you might say something to Trevor. You'd know how to put it. Kate would burst into tears, and I'd probably end up saying what I thought.'

'And that is?' said Bryonie, looking straight at Rick.

'I'm just envious. Who wouldn't be? Every man at Intertel would give his right arm, or rather his left arm, to get into her knickers. Crude but true.'

'Would you, given the chance?'

'What do you want me to say? Darling Bryonie, I wouldn't dream of it, how could I destroy our happiness?'

'Something like that, Rick. Sometimes I need you to say why you're still here. Is that surprising?'

'Even if Lucinda took off her Chanel jacket and begged me to undress her, I'd say—'

'You'd say nothing. You'd go right ahead,' said Kate. 'Do you think you're different from the others?'

'I know I have the misfortune to be a man, Katie. But you're wrong.'

He leaned over and caught Bryonie's left hand.

'Look. My ring. She still wears it. Thank God Bry's never been converted by you lot.'

'I've never had time. But I'll get round to it eventually. I could get a BA in Women's Studies.'

'Womens' whats? You bloody dare!'

'You're the only person who can talk to Annie,' Kate said, wiping her eyes.

'What should I say? That you both knew but neither of you had the guts to have it out in the open? That I haven't either?'

'Don't give me that,' said Rick. 'You could stop a riot if you wanted to.'

'Do you think Lucinda wants to marry him?' Kate said to Rick.

'Why should she?'

'She might love him.'

'Dear Kate. I thought you lot believed that women had exactly the same desires as men. Or doesn't that include lust? I'd fancy Trev if I was her.'

'Even Lucinda Sherwood might have some doubts about screwing up the life of her boss. How do we know she isn't going through hell? Suppose Trevor is the first man she's ever fallen for? We don't know anything about what's going on.'

'Who's side are you on, Kate?'

'I don't want to be on anyone's side. That's what's so awful. Why can't we all live together and be happy?'

'Because, Kate, we have a dilemma on our hands.'

'It's not our dilemma. It's Trevor's. In the end, he'll do what he wants whatever we say.'

'That's defeatist,' said Bryonie. 'You can make people think.'

'Oh God, what if he's thinking of leaving Annie?' Kate gasped. 'You don't imagine he'd do that? Would he really move out? I couldn't bear it if they sold Langton Villas. What would happen to our holiday in Greece? Would Annie still come on her own? Maybe she'd like me to stay in the house, I could make it really nice. We could still have dinner parties, and Gordon could fix a few things, he's good like that.'

Bryonie suddenly got up and left the table.

'Where's she gone?' said Kate. 'Did I say something dreadful?'

'I think she's gone to sit under the crabapple tree.'

'I don't know what to think. I just don't know, Rick.'

'Want a whisky? I've got one hidden, emergency supply. This qualifies as an emergency.'

'No, it doesn't. And Bryonie will go crazy.'

'She won't. She probably knows anyway, bless her. I could always go to the pub.'

'On your own?'

'Bugger that. We'll go together, later. When the committee has reached a conclusion. What's up? What have I said now?'

'It's so awful, I never knew that Trevor was such a bastard. What else has he been hiding? Somehow, I never did trust him. It was Annie who was my friend, not him. You always try and like the husband, don't you?'

Rick began to feel even gloomier. It took such a little time for good friends to become bad friends, only one trivial event, he supposed it would be trivial in the end, to distort the years of comradeship and trust, to paint a different face over the one you knew, to build up a new character in a sinister mould. Still, Kate did have a habit of saying the first thing which came into her head. Lucky she wasn't in politics.

Bryonie came quietly through the garden door, and leaned against the table, facing Rick and Kate.

'I've decided what to do. I think we should wait until the holiday. Let's hope it doesn't blow up before then. I'll find a time to talk to Trevor. If you think I'm the right person . . .'

'Good. That's settled,' said Rick.

During the last week of the shoot Annie was summoned back to Intertel by Alan. She had been away from the office for days, reluctant to miss a minute of filming, pushing the crew, pushing the director. By now, her doubts had given way to exhilaration. She didn't want it to end, no-one wanted it to end, they were already talking about a second series. Annie had viewed the rough assemblies with the cast, the publicity machine was beginning to create expectation, her new lead would be the sensation of the autumn.

Alan was sitting behind his desk when Annie came in, clad in the skirt of the interview ensemble which had been jammed at the back of the wardrobe for months, topped by a jazzy *Rough Trade* T-shirt, but he made no sign of registering her playful gesture. There was nothing in his office on which she could fix her gaze, not even a silly executive toy, for all the surfaces were empty and gleaming. He didn't ask her about *Rough Trade*, only said, looking towards the window not at her, that the BBC was putting out a key comedy series at exactly the time he had planned for the first episode of *Rough Trade*. He wasn't in a mood to consider alternatives. *Rough Trade* would go out earlier, with cuts to moderate the language.

After half an hour of fighting her corner, trying to persuade him that it would make nonsense to castrate the first episode which was never meant for pre-news viewing, Annie was forced to give way. More work, more hold-ups, more agonizing over what to take out, what they could leave. More re-shoots.

'Look, Alan,' Annie conceded, 'I see you're in a hole. But I still don't see the BBC as competition, not for this. There's nothing in their autumn schedule which would be a threat to *Rough Trade*.'

'I can't risk it. We've managed to establish a healthy lead over the opposition and I want to keep it that way.'

'Right. But if I take out every four-letter word, it might as well be mimed. People use them. What am I meant to do? *Rough Trade* wasn't conceived as a funsy series for ten year olds.'

'You could try dipping the sound, overlaying effects, slamming doors and so on. We've done that before.'

It was becoming too absurd but Annie kept a straight face.

'Good idea, Alan. I'll see what I can do,' she said cheerily, which even the dumbest of actors would have taken as irony. But Alan couldn't understand 'thesps' as he called them, and didn't pretend to. Showing off and being paid for it, too much most of them.

'But you know I'm about to go to Greece. If I don't, I'll be splattered over the floor of some psychiatric ward.'

'How long for?' asked Alan, stroking his chin.

'Ten days,' replied Annie, knocking off a few days. A fortnight sounded excessive. Alan grunted. It was in her contract, that she could stipulate the date, if not the length, of her holiday.

'But you'll be by a phone, I assume?'

'Oh, no problem about that,' said Annie.

It was always easier to lie when you felt good. If the ancient moped was working, she'd get Rick or Trevor to putt down and see the architect from Athens who, last year, had just moved into a neighbouring village and was rumoured to have a fax machine.

'Incidentally, Annie, I hear it's possible in the States to edit by remote, pictures and soundtracks all sent down the line. You can even do a rough mix.'

'Fantastic idea. I'll investigate that. Mind you, the Americans have more incentive than we do. They'll do anything to stay glued round a pool. Too many fish genes in their bloodstock, that's the trouble. My lineage is definitely ape. Swinging from trees is much more fun, wouldn't you say?'

'You must take a look at our new natural history programme, Annie. When you get back. Four-way co-production, but it's turned out well, much to my surprise. We should recoup on the interactive video alone.'

'Great, Alan. Is there anything else to discuss? Will you come to the bar?'

'I'm seeing some Americans any minute now. Another time. I hear your shoot has gone rather well.'

'We'll see,' said Annie, turning towards the closed door. Alan raised himself from his leather chair. 'Don't get up, please.'

'Keep in touch, Annie. Just a moment. Have you my home fax number?'

Annie pocketed the large embossed card he had extracted from his desk-drawer, and hurried away.

In the bar, she found an unexpected ally in Gavin.

'Alan's lost his nerve,' he said, after Annie had fumed at the rearrangement of the schedule. 'He's done the same to me. My audience will drop by fifty per cent. *Splash!* is geared for ten-thirty, not eleven-thirty. At least you get peak-time.'

'And I get to butcher episode one. Plus a few thousand letters of complaint.'

'Of course, he could be giving in to pressure. That would figure. He must have known well before now about the BBC plans. Don't you think Sherwood might have had something to do with it?'

'Can't believe that. Are you saying that Alan's towing the Sherwood line? Is he that crass and feeble?'

Gavin gave a caustic laugh.

'Alan? He blows with the wind. Why he's stayed. His clean-up campaign will have enough window-dressing to look good in the annual report. I hope Trevor's going to blow the gaff.'

'That's a tough one. If he writes about what's going on, it'll come directly back to me. It'll make my position here impossible.'

'No, Annie. It'll make your position stronger. Everyone here will be right behind you if Alan causes trouble.'

'You've forgotten something, Gavin. How can Trevor appear on *Splash!* and slaughter Intertel in the press a few days or weeks later?'

'Who said slaughter?' replied Gavin. 'A little academic generality, so people can read between the lines. Isn't that what he's so good at? It's his decision, of course. Maybe it would make Alan watch my programmes for a change. I'm seeing Trevor in the middle of next week for a drink, I'll sound him out.'

'Next week? Are you sure? I didn't think he was coming back. He said he'd be staying down at our cottage till just before we go away. There was no point in his being in London, not when I'm knee-deep in finishing the shoot.'

'He did mention he had to come up to London for a meeting, I expect he'll be driving straight back, that's the impression I got, anyway.'

Annie made a quick calculation. Trevor had last phoned her from a call-box a couple of days ago, asked if she needed him to be in London, but she told him to stay down there. That would give him time to finish painting the back bedroom, he said. He assured her he wasn't bored, he'd discovered some local pubs, had dinner with Phil, the neighbouring farmer. He must have forgotten about the meeting.

'I suppose we'll have to get a phone, damn it,' Annie said.

'Forget it. It's good to be inaccessible at times.'

During the last week of the shoot, Annie was without Lucinda. She said it was far better if she took some holiday at this stage and returned to the office once Annie was back from Greece. Then she could help with the mountain of post-production correspondence, and make notes of the rough assemblies. When Annie asked her if she was going abroad somewhere, Lucinda said she hadn't made up her mind. She never organized her holidays, she said. Just took off at the last minute with a few things in a bag. Maybe spend a few days with Daddy and friends in Tuscany. Maybe join Tim in the Maldives. But she wouldn't go away with Jeremy, he was fine for skiing but hopeless in the sun, poor old Jeremy, absolutely refused to wear a hat and they always argued in the summer. Before they parted, Annie spent an evening with her, downing champagne, laughing about how they would change *Rough Trade* into a kiddies' programme, inventing crazy characters, the kind of silliness which happened after a long shoot, the good-time silliness born of slog and achievement.

Only one more week. Annie put aside an hour or so to gather together the holiday clothes, Trevor's ancient espadrilles he refused to throw away, the gaily patterned shirts and shorts and sawn-off jeans, the sun-hats, sarongs, towels, water bottles, all the paraphernalia which she kept together in a cupboard, collected over years, ready to be thrown into a couple of cases. And those sexy warm nights, naked golden skins against the coarse white cotton, getting up afterwards to gaze out over the moonlit sea, breakfasting on bursting figs spilling their crimson seeds. It only needed a few days, and Trevor would turn into a bronzed wanderer, Odysseus returning home, head lifted up towards the dark blue horizon, an expression of relaxed contentment when nothing mattered except reaching the straw-covered bar on the beach before the midday sun scorched the sand. Annie pressed her face into one of Trevor's shirts, the faded blue cotton one which covered his shorts. There was still a faint trace of Ambre Solaire, scenting the collar. Glorious summers, glorious Greece. Only three more days.

Annie's taxi arrived to take her to work, she would catch up on some paperwork on the way in, instead of fretting at the traffic in the Kentish Town Road. As she was about to fling herself in the back, she caught sight of Trevor's red Toyota parked on the corner of Langton Villas, right on a double yellow line. He must have been in a hurry. Of course, his meeting with Gavin. Why hadn't he come up the night before? Most likely because he disliked driving in the dark. And he wouldn't want a long drive after working all day. Why didn't he take the car into town? Of course, he loathed doing that, hunting around for somewhere to park. Annie hoped he wouldn't go straight back to the cottage. It would be such a treat, to have him in bed beside her, just a few hours, the warmth of his body pressing against her stomach, melting away the monthly cramps. 'Wait here,' she said to the taxi-driver. 'My daft husband's gone and parked where he shouldn't. I'll just move his car.' Annie ran into the house and collected the spare set of keys hanging from the row of hooks in Trevor's study.

At least he had remembered to pull down the hood. Annie jumped into the car. The interior was spotless, everything neatly in position, a new road-map and a bottle of mineral water wedged between the seats. Although he had had the car for several months, there was no sign of his occupancy, no sign of wear. Typical Trevor.

Annie jammed the key into the ignition but it didn't seem to fit naturally, and she had the curious sensation that she was in the wrong car. Then, as the engine fired, the sound was not as she remembered it. She peered round at the small back seat, and noticed a black umbrella tightly folded. That was definitely Trevor's. He came home with it one day in April, showery April. I need an umbrella made for two, he had said, since you always lose yours. She'd teased him, he'd always said he hated umbrellas, but for some reason he liked this one. But it still felt as though the car belonged to someone else. Annie sat motionless, with the gear in neutral. What was it? Then she gave a sniff, he must have polished the inside with some scented product. An air-freshener was dangling from the dashboard, so she put her nose close to it. That wasn't it. It was a strange fragrance, the kind which you associated with a particular experience, a particular place. He sometimes gave Kate a lift home. Was it Kate's perfume? Not heavy or assertive enough. Could it be aftershave? Trevor had taken to wearing it recently, he had managed to find one he liked which didn't smell like damp pine-forests, but it wasn't that. It worried Annie, that it was so familiar, and yet she was unable to place it.

The taxi hooted, she lowered her window and gestured to the driver to wait. Outside, a drizzle was beginning to cover the glass in fine dots, so she immediately pressed the button to close it again and turned on the de-mister. Then she moved the seat forward, adjusted for Trevor's long legs, and took hold of the gear lever. For some reason she couldn't fathom, the perfume was now more powerful than before, penetrating the blasting air inside the car. Glancing down over her left shoulder, she saw what she thought was a rag, which had been stuffed under the seat. She took it by one corner, and the rag billowed out, flapping across her face, fine almond-coloured silk.

'You have it, Annie. It suits you.'

Now she recognized it. Lucinda's scarf. Lucinda's perfume.

Annie stopped the engine, wrenched out the ignition key, and without locking the car, she jumped out as though she was about to be trapped in poisonous fumes.

'I haven't time to move it after all,' she explained breathlessly to the taxi-driver. 'I didn't realize it was so late. Go to Intertel by the quickest route, I don't care if you go by Waterloo Bridge as long as I get there by eleven.'

Annie felt as though someone had just punched her in the gut, leaving her breathless, and not only run off with everything she owned but her whole identity, leaving a zombie in her place. She pressed her face against the window of the taxi and tried to collect herself. The most far-fetched explanations crowded into her mind. Lucinda had left her scarf in Annie's car, Trevor had found it, meant to give to her, forgotten, it wasn't Lucinda's scarf, someone at college had one like it, Liberty's, lots of women bought scarves from there, the perfume was similar, not the same, similar. Or Trevor could have given her a lift home, they could have met at Tim's club, a favourite haunt of Gavin's. Or any number of fashionable places Trev was now being introduced to. Maybe he was drunk, didn't think to tell her, forgot, trivial, giving someone a lift home. Trevor was rarely drunk. He counted his glasses when he was driving. It was her scarf. Annie wanted to take back the moment when she had stepped into Trevor's car, wind back and press the erase button. Either it hadn't happened or there was a simple explanation. She wanted it now, the simple explanation.

'I've changed my mind,' she called out, and she heard her voice coming back to her, as though she was in a resonant cave. 'Go in the direction of Holloway. I'll direct you when we're near where I want to go.'

The taxi-driver tutted and shook his head, as Annie rummaged in her briefcase like a desperate air-traveller searching for a sick-bag. Finding no tissues, she let out a curse and failed to prevent a tear slipping down her cheek. Then she pulled out a sheaf of papers, and bent her head low over them, so that her hair swung forward, hiding her fury, her wretchedness, her despair.

Thank God, Kate was in.

'I must use the phone,' said Annie, already dialling the office.

'Anita? I can't come in today. Can I just go through what needs doing urgently?'

'Is anything wrong? You sound awful, Annie.'

'Nothing's wrong. Ghastly period, I get them sometimes. Get a message to the director, I'll be there later. Are you ready?'

After she had given her instructions, Annie pushed away the pile of toys on Kate's futon and leaned back, her eyes closed, trying to convince herself that it had all been a mistake, what had happened to her had happened to someone else, that nothing had been real.

Kate was bending over her.

227

'Annie. Are you sick? Do you want to lie down on my bed, it's more comfortable?'

Annie groaned and shook her head.

'Annie, please. Open your eyes. I'll get some brandy.'

Annie sat up, and threw back the contents of the glass tumbler, relishing the burn as the brandy hit her throat.

'I can't believe it, I can't believe it.'

'What, Annie?'

'I've just found Lucinda's scarf in Trevor's car. I know it's hers. She's been wearing it all summer.'

'What?' Kate repeated, as her legs turned to jelly and she sank down to the floor.

Annie knew, Annie knew. She prayed that she would find the right words.

'Trevor. There's only one explanation. He must be screwing Lucinda. His car stinks of her perfume. She's meant to be away, the bitch. Both of them, lying their heads off. Why? Why? I'm going to throw up.'

'It can't be true, Annie,' Kate said weakly, as she sponged down Annie's face in the bathroom. If only she had told her before.

'Why her? Couldn't he have found someone else? I'm going to move out. No, I'll get the bastard to move out, he can take every damn thing with him. I want him out.'

'Annie, Annie, how can you be sure?'

'Of course I'm sure. Why's he been staying down at the cottage all the time? What's happened to the bloody book? Nothing. He's been shagging rotten in my cottage. The bastard, the bastard. I'm going down there right now. See what they've got to say for themselves. "Don't know where I'm going on holiday," she said. The bitch. If they've been sleeping in our bed, I'll kill her. I don't care where they've been sleeping. He's just gone and fucked up twenty years. Twenty years. Without even giving me any warning. Not a clue. If he'd only said, "Annie, can we talk about it?" But he hasn't. He's behaved like any two-timing lout from the valleys. Except I've found out. Now, only now. I should have guessed, but I never thought. I never thought Trevor could behave like this. Kate, Kate, what am I going to do? What the hell am I going to do? I can't think of being without him. And I can't think of being with him.'

When Kate put her arms round her, Annie howled. Not

228

since childhood when she screamed and cried at her dad for refusing her what she had set her heart on, had she felt misery shaking her body, gasping for breath until her heaving pants gave way to hiccups, just like a kid. She lay on her stomach, her head buried in a cushion, torture-currents of spasm shaking her shoulders, hot blood gushing between her legs.

'Annie. You'll be all right,' Kate repeated, again and again. She wanted so desperately to tell Annie that she had made a mistake, Trevor wouldn't go off with anyone else, she had known so many unfaithful men, you always knew, they came out with the same excuses, Trevor wasn't like that. But she was unable to utter the falsely comforting words although she wanted to.

'Tell me it isn't true, tell me,' Annie sobbed, but Kate was unable to reply. 'And get a towel, quick. I'm flooding.'

Kate rushed into the bathroom, grabbed two towels and handed them to Annie.

'Oh, God. Hope I haven't made a mess.'

'Don't worry. Everything's a mess, Annie. But I'm sure Trev will come back. If he's made an idiot of himself, he'll come back.'

'Don't be stupid, Kate. He hasn't gone,' Annie snapped, forcing back a sob.

'I'm sure he still loves you.'

Annie suddenly sat up, staring at Kate.

'I'm right, aren't I? He is fucking that girl, isn't he? And he's been doing it for ages, I know he has.'

'I'm not sure. I really don't know, Annie.'

'You think I've gone mad, I know you do. Just because I found Lucinda's scarf in his car.'

'No, no, I don't, Annie. I'd feel the same.'

'Am I inventing all this?'

'I don't know,' repeated Kate, trying to keep herself from screaming point. 'Annie, I can't give you proof. You must talk to Trevor.'

'But you suspected?'

'Not really, Annie.'

'Nothing, nothing at all?'

'I thought, well I thought being on Gavin's programme had gone to his head a bit.'

'Oh Christ.'

229

Annie's tears subsided and she lay on her back, as though floating in a solitary sea.

'I'm going to find Trevor and tell him to come round here. I don't care if it's the right moment or not. I want to hear it from him. I want to know how long it's been going on.'

Kate went to take Annie's hand, then drew back. She was still in shock, it was like seeing someone you had last met at a riotous evening, lying trapped by tubes, motionless in a hospital bed.

'Annie, finding Lucinda's scarf in his car, it hardly means they've been at it for months. I mean, perhaps he saw her walking along, gave her a lift home—'

'Don't be daft,' said Annie. 'He would have told me by now.'

Kate went to the tiny kitchen area to make coffee.

'Does it matter so much? I mean, it's not as though he's suddenly announced that he's moving in with someone else. People do have short flings. Look at me and Gordon. We started going out when he was married, but he didn't leave Audrey because of me. He left because his marriage wasn't working, hadn't worked for years. People don't walk out when they love someone.'

'Have you got some tissues?' Annie called out.

'Loo roll in the loo,' said Kate.

'You should get some work, you really should. You can't go on living like this, Kate.'

'Don't start that,' said Kate.

'Sorry. I'm upset, damn it.'

'I know.'

'Do you think it's all round Intertel? Do you think everyone knows except me? Do you think Gavin knows?'

Kate concentrated on pouring the boiling water in a steady stream into the small cups. 'Annie, how can I tell? I never go in there. We'll find out.'

'I don't care if he loves me or not. I can't bear him being deceitful, that's what really hurts. I'm not against sexual freedom, you know I'm not. But if it's not open, where does that leave us? Covering up in public, screaming at our husbands in private? Oh, Christ! Kate, what should I do? Get rid of Lucinda? I can't have her in my office. But what can I say? "Lucinda, you're having a scene with my husband. Get lost." I'm Controller of Drama, how can I? How dare he make me feel such an idiot? How dare he! And besides, I like her. I do.

I don't blame her, I blame Trevor. He's meeting Gavin for a drink. I'll ring Gavin's office, find out where they're going. Right now.'

'Annie, don't.'

'Why on earth not?'

Kate came over with the cups and put one in Annie's hand. 'Let's work out what to do. Let's try and be sensible.'

For hours they talked, as though there was a solution which was waiting to be found, and they only stopped when Kate realized she had to collect Dally from school. It was then that Annie caught sight of herself in the mirror, peering between the brightly coloured stickers, a face like a disaster victim caught by an intrusive camera.

'Christ, I look awful,' Annie said, rummaging for her make-up bag amongst the papers in her briefcase. She attacked her face with powder, trying to hide the charcoal circles under her eyes.

'Kate, have you any lipstick? And a hairbrush?'

'Of course.'

Annie began to draw a hesitant outline round her lips.

'Do I look better?' asked Annie.

'Great.'

'You think what we've decided will work?'

'What's more important, Annie? You have to finish *Rough Trade*.'

'Yes.'

'Nothing else matters. It's going to be the best series you've ever done. And no-one's going to spoil it.'

'They're shooting in Enfield today. I should just make it.'

Before she left, Kate took out an ancient iron and restored Annie's crumpled shirt so that by the time she met up with the actors and crew, no-one could tell that this was not a day like any other. When Annie arrived back at Langton Villas, she looked up at the windows. Everything was dark. When she listened to her messages, there was one from Trevor. 'Hope you don't mind, but I decided to drive straight back. There's a lot to do before we go away. You'll love it when it's done. Hope the shoot went well, darling. See you soon. Lots of love.' Hearing his voice, she could feel tears of anger welling up in her eyes. She rewound the messages, switched on the television and lay on the settee, eyes blank, hearing nothing. Then Kate rang.

'Annie, are you all right?'

'I think so. Yes, yes, I'm all right.'

'Would you like to come round here?'

'Trevor went back to the cottage. I'm going to have a stiff brandy and go to bed.'

'Ring me tomorrow, don't forget.'

'I don't want to have it out with Trevor till we're in Greece. I'll wait a few days till we get out there. Is that sensible? I don't know what's sensible any more. I can't talk to him when I'm so full of hate.'

'You're right, Annie. In Greece, we'll all be there. You mustn't do it alone.'

'I was lying here wondering why I wanted to spoil the perfect marriage. If I say nothing, would it be better?'

'No, Annie. You aren't that kind of woman.'

'If I came round tomorrow night, would you mind? Only it's going to be a tough day. For the cast, I mean . . .'

14

ANNIE AND TREVOR

Iannis's villa was identical to several others scattered over the terraces of the hillside, forming the southern part of the island which had been christened Paradisos by Annie and Trevor, although that was not its real name. When they first rented the single-storey traditional house, fearing that the supply of deserted, unspoiled Greek islands would soon be exhausted, or that the members of some braying villa party company would take over, they had sworn one another to secrecy and invented the code-name Paradisos. Tiny island, very basic, nothing there, they would reply when questioned. Iannis took off each summer to Stevenage, home of his English wife's family, and had been doing so for several years. In common with other islanders who had graduated from barter, to cash, to credit cards, bank accounts and corruption in the space of a mere five years, he had discovered that you could earn twice over by letting your home in the summer season and working in England. Since none of his earnings would be declared, Iannis was now rich and the father of three fine boys who would soon go to boarding-school in England. Judicious bribes had enabled him to enhance his family land by building a wire fence around rather more than its legal boundaries, and by constructing a small, randomly shaped Californian-style swimming-pool with terrace, whose shallow depth and faulty construction could not be detected in his summer brochure.

Annie and Trevor used to say they preferred the way it was in the early days when they first rented it. Then the family would relocate to a neighbouring plot and move in with cousin Dionysus, but they had now added another floor onto the squat, rectangular building and updated the simple wooden furniture with a three-piece suite, plastic stacking chairs and gilded standard lamps to make the British feel at home. The front of the house was unchanged, the vine still crawled unimpeded along the ancient supports of the wooden pergola, the fig tree spread its broad-fingered leaves to shield the afternoon sun, and the people they had grown to know still congregated at the nearest bar, unmodernized and unfrequented by the tourists cramming the Excelsior, the Grand, or the Plaza which had spread like nettles in the north of the island, multi-roomed hotels whose uncertain foundations and erratic plumbing failed to live up to the expectations of their names.

Once they had selected their rooms, there would be a minimum of organization, a rota for cooking and shopping, the cleaning and laundry would be taken care of by Agata, Iannis's aunt – and so far the only argument had been to determine who would have the best bedroom with the balcony and adjoining shower-room. The suitcases were still leaning against one another outside the front door. Dally had set off like a firecracker, running off over the dry grass, pursued by Kate.

'No, you have the balcony bedroom. We had it last year. It's your turn now, Annie.'

'Why not Kate and Dally?'

'She'd fall off,' said Bryonie.

'I really don't care. I'm going to get into the sea. You decide.'

Annie tipped over her case and pulled out a black swimming-costume, while Trevor looked on, not daring to disturb the sardine-layered wedge of flattened clothes.

'Where are my trunks, darling?'

'Swimming things in there,' said Annie, pointing to a large holdall.

Then she set off, running down the path, towards the low sand-dunes forming the hinterland of the beach. Soon she was a small black dot in the blue sea, striking out with a vigorous crawl towards the rocks at the western end of the beach. A few minutes later, Trevor set off in pursuit, a tightly rolled towel and frayed beach-mat under his arm.

'We'd better decide on the rooms,' said Bryonie, after Rick and Kate had paced round the house, noting the new additions. 'Who's going to have the best one upstairs?'

Rick flipped a coin and caught it on his hand.

'It's ours, Bry.'

'I still think Trev and Annie should have it.' Then Bryonie said softly, 'Under the circumstances.'

'They might prefer the twin beds in the downstairs bedroom. I would.'

'They were fine on the plane.'

'Annie was asleep most of the time.'

'She was leaning against Trev. Didn't you notice? He had his arm round her.'

'Did he? Who knows? Perhaps they've had it out already.'

'It's so awful, watching all the time, wondering.'

'It's their business, in the end,' said Rick.

'Come on. Help me unpack.'

'Do that later, Bry. Get out my beach stuff.'

Rick moved the bags into the ground-floor bedroom and left Bryonie sorting the clothes into neat piles. She never felt happy until everything was in its place, even on holiday.

By the time Kate arrived at the sea's edge, Annie was already bone-dry, spreadeagled face-upwards to the sun on a towel. Dally, in a bright turquoise sunhat was poking with a stick amongst the seaweed and Kate set out an array of bottles beside her, contemplating which sun-factor cream should be applied to which portion of her body.

'My tummy's still saggy,' she said, smearing a thick cream over her belly button. 'The bright sun makes you see things. Half an hour, Annie, don't overdo it. Look at Trevor and Rick, miles out.'

'Remember when we used to sleep out all night on the beach?' said Annie. 'Shame they don't allow it any more.'

'We can still make a fire, though. Have an evening barbie. I wonder if Panos still has his guitar?'

'We'll stop by later.'

'Melina must have had her baby by now.'

'And wasn't Nikos going to start renting out proper motor bikes?'

'For God's sake, Annie, don't let Rick loose on one of those.'

'Why not? I'm sure he and Trev will want to go off somewhere. Then we can take out the old wooden boat with Bry, and go over to Lion Island.'

Kate swivelled round and looked towards the dunes.

'What's Bry up to? Shall I go and find her?'

'She won't come until she's unpacked, you know what she's like.'

'Then Rick will mess everything up. I don't know why she bothers. God knows what she'd do if she had a child. On holiday's meant to be the best time. Wouldn't it be fabulous if they managed it? Roll over, Annie. You need some cream on your back.'

Annie allowed herself to be smothered in thick goo, then stared out to sea, leaning on her elbows. At this moment, she wished Trevor would go on swimming and swimming, and disappear into the indigo horizon.

'I wish I could have a room to myself,' said Annie.

'Once Dally's asleep, you can come into my room. I'm sure Iannis could find an extra bed.'

'I can't do that,' Annie replied. 'Trev would go wild. Part of me wants to wake up one gorgeous morning and find that everything is all right again. Trevor keeps touching me, I can't bear it. Then, if I don't let him make love, it's even worse. So I turn over and wait for it to be over when all I want is to kick him out of bed. I can't believe it, I've stopped fancying him, just like that.'

'It'll come back,' said Kate, soothingly. 'Have you said anything yet?'

'No, I haven't. I'm going to enjoy some holiday first. Why shouldn't he feel uncomfortable for a while? He keeps asking me if anything's wrong. As though I'd say there was. Why should he have the satisfaction of making me drag it out of him?'

'But what will you do about, about her?'

'Benny's doing a comedy series in Glasgow. I'll get her transferred up there when she comes back.'

'At least she won't be lurking around here.'

'No-one to make a proper cocktail, darling.'

'And what does one do in the evenings?'

'Find a hairy Greek and roll on the beach.'

'Oh, too too ghastly.'

'I hope she picks up something nasty and tropical and contagious in the Maldives, something which turns you yellow preferably,' said Annie.

'Or horribly spotty,' added Kate.

Soon they heard the sound of male splashing, as Trevor and Rick waded through the shallows and headed in their direction.

'How about an ice-cream, Dally?' said Annie, springing to her feet as the two men approached. 'Let's go and say hello to Dionysus.'

Ignoring the enthusiastic waves from Trevor and Rick, the

two women ran off down the beach, with Dally in hot pursuit. For the rest of the day, Annie succeeded in creating a distance between herself and Trevor, scarcely registering his presence.

Next morning, they paired off for their familiar duties. Kate and Annie caught the local bus to the small town where they hired bicycles each year. Rick went hunting for something more powerful and mechanized. Trevor and Bryonie set off for the local market, which was little more than a few trestle-tables set up against a stone wall. Local growers were standing behind jumbled piles of aubergines, courgettes and peppers, wilted lettuces, scraggy chickens and pungent sausages.

'There's much better produce in the local shop,' said Bryonie, fingering a wizened courgette. 'They're worse than last year.'

Catching her expression of disapproval, a young man in Ray-Bans, replied in perfect English, 'For this year, it's good produce. Quality. We had little rain.'

Trevor nodded sympathetically. 'A kilo of courgettes, then.'

Before Bryonie could stop him, he had added several brown bags of onion, cabbage and split tomatoes.

'Nothing wrong with these,' said Trevor, as they sat under the awning of a bar. 'Kate will love them. And we are supporting local effort. Having a place in the country has made me realize that nature is imperfect. You tend to think that everything grows like the picture on the packet. I can quite see myself developing into a gardening bore. The apples on our tree will ripen while we're away. Isn't that sad? We should have sprayed them, apparently, so half of them will get eaten away I suppose.'

'I don't spray my crab-apples. They seem to do all right.'

'They wouldn't dare do otherwise!' said Trevor, smiling at Bryonie.

'I don't have the time, that's all.'

Breathing in with contentment, Trevor stuck his feet on the chair opposite. 'Rick seems on good form.'

'He'll be fine for a couple of days, then he'll go spare hunting for a newspaper. Dionysus said he'd bring back some from town, but he only goes twice a week. It's like an addiction with Rick.'

'I like being isolated now, even though I never used to. Another beer?'

Bryonie nodded.

237

'Though I'm not sure Annie does. I had to stop her making an attempt to contact the office. She's still a bit edgy, it might take her longer than usual to wind down. Understandable, after weeks of filming.'

'She might have a reason to be edgy, Trev.'

'Well, I know she's been getting these awfully heavy periods. She's probably got one now, poor girl. But she was swimming all the same, typical Annie.'

'It's quite safe,' remarked Bryonie. 'The water's clean.'

'Last time I asked her if that was why she was down, she snapped my head off. So now I don't ask. But I'm pretty sure that's the reason. Makes her go right off sex, but I suppose that's normal. Is there really nothing she can take?'

'A stiff drink. Or aspirin.'

'Nothing better than that?'

'A changed husband?'

Trevor grinned. 'Don't worry, I never make a fuss about it. There's nothing worse than going through the motions if you don't feel like it.'

Fumbling in the brown bag, Trevor brought out a rock-hard, pale tomato, and turned it round in his hand.

'We mustn't forget the wonderful Greek olive oil,' he said. Bryonie was looking far too serious for Paradisos. 'I try to be understanding. But then, sometimes I forget. Annie has always been so incredibly strong and healthy. You have to be, to work in television. In fact, I'd say it was one of the main criteria, staying power. Annie's certainly got that. And if she does feel bad, she's not one to moan. I suppose it couldn't be the menopause, could it? Don't some women get it early?'

'I doubt if that's the reason.'

'You're not suggesting it's some internal trouble she hasn't told me about? You would tell me, Bryonie . . .'

Bryonie took the tomato from Trevor's hand, and placed it back in the bag.

'I know it isn't my business. But Annie knows, Trevor. About Lucinda.'

'Lucinda?'

'Your girlfriend. Or is it mistress? She must qualify for that word by now.'

Although Trevor had rehearsed countless times what he would say if Annie confronted him, he was taken off guard. Bryonie sounded concerned, not angry, which made it worse.

'I'd call her a friend, a very close friend. Yes, Lucinda is someone special, I can't hide it, she's someone—'

'Annie was very upset. When she found out.'

'When did she find out?'

'Before you came away.'

'What idiot told her? That was the last thing . . . I was so careful, that she shouldn't hear about it from someone else. I took enormous trouble, we both did, to keep it private. It sounds so coldblooded, but it wasn't.'

'Has it been going on long?'

'Does it matter? A few months. In all, that is.'

'But you saw a lot of one another?'

Trevor paused. It was as though he was being forced to make a summary of something which couldn't be summarized.

'Yes, I suppose we did,' he said, reluctantly. 'Does everyone know at Intertel? I suppose they're all sniggering behind Annie's back, turning it into yet another seamy little episode. But I don't expect anyone to understand. Don't you try, for God's sake, don't try. How did Annie find out? How long has she known? Was it someone at Intertel? Was it Rick? Or Gavin? It couldn't possibly have been Gavin . . .'

'It wasn't any of them, Trevor. Lucinda left her scarf in your car. Annie discovered it when you came to London last week to meet Gavin. She put two and two together, you staying down at the cottage.'

'I don't believe it, I really don't.'

'She recognized the scarf, so Kate said. And your car was reeking of Lucinda's perfume.'

'Kate? She told Kate? Why didn't she say something to me?'

'Annie's not like that. I think she'd expect you to mention it first.'

'When? In the middle of shooting? How could I possibly?'

'At least Rick doesn't flaunt it under my nose.'

Trevor shifted his chair into the shade, as a trail of sweat trickled down his neck.

'I was going to tell her, find a right moment while we were here. But I had to let her recover first, I couldn't just spring it on her. And I had to work out in my own mind what I felt. It just isn't simple. If only it was.'

'If only . . .' said Bryonie, with a hint of irony.

'How can I talk about it? I can hear the tone of condemnation in your voice, Bry. It's natural you'd be concerned for

Annie. Didn't you think I might be concerned too?'

'It's good that you can admit it.'

'Admit? What are you talking about? You make it sound like a crime. Lucinda is someone who came along. I had no intention of getting involved, no intention of hurting Annie, but I had no control, I couldn't understand what was happening. I still can't.'

'But it's finished now?'

'Now, this minute? Yes.'

'And when we get back?'

'I don't know, Bryonie, I just don't know. The usual rules, they don't apply with Lucinda. That's what attracted me to her, I suppose. She's always surprising me, she's so spontaneous, affectionate. Nothing else matters, her background, her friends. Somehow when we're together, none of that matters. Everything feels right, I've found someone who's shaken me up, made me see new colours around me—'

'You're in love?'

'I do love her, yes.'

'Rick never pretends to be in love. But if you really are, go off and live with Lucinda. Tell Annie you want a divorce.'

'Divorce? I haven't thought of it, not even for one moment.'

'Wouldn't that be honest? If you feel as you do . . .'

'It isn't that simple.'

'So you keep saying. Of course it isn't, when you can't resist going to bed with someone. Did you bring Lucinda back to Langton Villas?'

'Do you really imagine I'd do that? Don't you know me better? Why do you jump to the conclusion that it was only sex? If that's all I wanted, nothing could be easier.'

'It was quite convenient, though, that Lucinda persuaded Annie to take a cottage near her house in the country.'

'It isn't her house, it's her father's. She isn't there that often.'

'Are you saying you never met up there when Annie was away?'

'Sometimes we did, yes.'

At that moment, Dionysus passed by, advertising his presence by opening the throttle of his brand new Suzuki bike.

'You coming to eat with us?' he shouted, before freewheeling down the hill. Trevor waved, then began to collect up the bags. Bryonie remained seated.

'Didn't you think Annie might have guessed?'

Trevor sighed and sank back into his chair. The facts were being twisted – or was it refocused – into a version he had so far refused to recognize. From the outside, admittedly, his behaviour could seem shabby, underhand and indulgent. He could only see Annie's shocked, angry face.

'What could I do? I had to wait until the situation was resolved. I knew it would be resolved, eventually. If Annie hadn't been working so hard, I would have told her, obviously I would. And I hoped it wouldn't be necessary, that by now Lucinda and I would have gone our separate ways. But I never had the slightest intention of pretending it hadn't happened. I respect and love Annie too much for that.'

'I'm glad you can talk about it. I'll get a couple more beers.'

Bryonie hurried inside the bar, leaving Trevor to reflect on whether confessing could make it more or less bearable. By the time she came back with two more glasses, he had decided to forestall the questions which still remained to be asked.

'I never wanted this to happen, never dreamed it would last more than a couple of weeks. And I often felt terrible afterwards. Quite sick, when I was driving back to London. But the last thing Lucinda wanted was to break up my marriage. It's just a very dear friendship.'

'*Is*, Trev?'

'It would be dishonest of me to say "was" when I'm just not sure. I want to say "was". So, Rick knows?'

'Yes. But I made him swear to keep it to himself.'

'And Kate, of course.'

'Yes. Do you realize what you're doing, Trev?'

'Don't make it worse. Can you imagine what I've been through? It wasn't something I went looking for. And it wasn't sordid, Bry, it wasn't a quick score by a fifty-something year old. There is a quality between us which is, well, indescribable. Which I've never experienced before.'

Bryonie the doctor was eclipsing Bryonie the woman, she was reacting with an expression of reigned-in sadness at human frailty.

'Perhaps you think I'm too old to have a new experience?' he said with a smile, but Bryonie didn't respond.

'Everyone says that. Didn't they say that about LSD? Indescribable. What does it mean? A temporary altered state. I took LSD once when I was a student, for medical reasons we told ourselves, and was terribly sick, vomiting all over the carpet. Everyone else was so entranced by their experience, they started seeing visions in my vomit, streaming flows of coloured lava, diamond-encrusted crowns drifting down a tangerine river. I wanted them to help me, but the words wouldn't come out, so I staggered out into the street, found my car and sat there for half a day, staring out of the window, trying to make the streetlamps stand still.'

She reached forward, and rested her hand on Trevor's. 'My father would have said, Pull yourself together, man. But we can't say that any more. He was probably a better doctor than I am.'

'I doubt it.'

Bryonie looked at him questioningly.

'So what are you going to do?'

'Did Annie take it badly? No, I shouldn't ask that. I've no right. I'll find a way of discussing it.'

Bryonie rose from the plastic chair and placed a pile of drachmas on the table. Then she pulled on her straw hat, and smiled before putting on her sunglasses.

'I think you should. The sooner the better. Yes?'

'It's not fair on her, when she's so exhausted. I'll wait until she's recovered.'

'Annie recovers in a day out here,' sighed Bryonie. 'I wish I could.'

'You don't think I should wait until Annie brings it up?'

'Why don't you two go off on your own? I can organize a fishing trip with Rick and Kate. We'll be out of your way.'

'It's so difficult, putting it into words.'

'Say you're sorry.'

'Just that?'

'What more can you do? She'll accept it, I know she will. Why don't you try? So far, you haven't given her the opportunity to understand what's happened. No wonder she feels bitter.'

'You don't think she'd ask for a divorce?'

'Is that what you're frightened of?'

The idea, until now, hadn't crossed Trevor's mind. How could you divorce someone you loved? There was no question of it. It was only women who were traditionally meant to think that way, all or nothing. Her or me. They didn't think like that any longer, surely? Ending a marriage because of infidelity, it was an outmoded idea. Never again setting foot in the house? Acting like strangers? Pretending indifference? No, it was inconceivable. But if Annie threatened divorce, would he have to give up Lucinda? He did feel fear, the fear of being forced into making a choice.

Could he bear to go through it all yet again? Another letter, written on the same terrace, at almost the same time: Lucinda, it just can't be . . . Why had he kept to his resolution last year? Why was he unable to now? Had she changed him? Did people change? Had Annie stopped loving him? Was it a look of contempt she gave him as she dried herself on the beach, or had he imagined it? He would rather brave her anger than her contempt, he decided. Bryonie was right, it wasn't fair on Annie. However much he was dreading it, he would answer all her questions, tell her what she wanted to know. It wouldn't be like last year. There would be no letter. The right moment would surely arise when he could tell Lucinda. You couldn't plan these things, she had taught him that.

'How do other couples manage?'

Bryonie smiled, reached for her hat and pulled it down over her eyes.

'They get to be tolerant, I suppose. And we're not like swans, mating for life, are we?'

'I love you in that hat,' Trevor said.

'It's coming apart, the straw's splitting. Rick bought it for me in Karpathos. He actually bought me something I wanted. So I can't throw it away now. Let's find the others, Trev. They'll be expecting something for lunch.'

'Do you realize, this is our ninth year in Greece? Next year, we'll have to have a celebration, invite the whole village. Wouldn't that be marvellous? Annie would love it. A thank-you for being so good to us.'

'Why not?'

Bryonie set off gaily down the hill, her hips swinging with abandon, while Trevor gathered up the provisions and swiftly followed her. There was a quality in the warm thyme-scented air which was full of promise and he felt almost happy.

A couple of days later, Rick and Kate were on kitchen duty, preparing for supper. The chores roster had been handwritten by Kate and the words had faded by now, blotched with tomato sauce and olive oil though still legible and the sheet of paper was held together by yellowing Sellotape. It was a reminder from the past, and each year she stuck it up on the wooden door.

'What do I do with carrots? Peel or scrape?' asked Rick.

'Peel. Look, these ones are old and woody.'

'I don't have an affinity with vegetables like you do. Let's swop and I'll peel a few spuds. I wonder if Greek men have started peeling spuds? Bet they haven't.'

'Then it's time they did,' said Kate.

Rick grasped a mud-laden potato and started to hack into it with Kate's Sabatier knife, part of her Greek essentials like the lotion bottles.

'You have to wash them first. Can't you find the potato peeler?'

'That's for sissies. I'm going to use a knife.'

Annie was preparing the table in the garden when Kate came out with the salad. Bryonie was reading a story to Dally by candlelight, her voice backed by a pair of crickets.

'Why can't we have stars like that?' said Kate, craning up to scan the sky. 'It looks as though someone's polished them, they're so bright.'

'Something's boiling over,' shouted Rick, leaning out from the kitchen door.

'Turn it down then,' Kate shouted back. Then she grinned at Annie. 'No wonder Bryonie bans him from the kitchen. Where's Trevor? Wasn't he going to get some more wine?'

'I've no idea,' said Annie.

'He's probably stopped off at Dionysus' bar. We won't have time to chill it if he doesn't come soon. The fridge is working today. Isn't that spectacular?'

'Trevor's bound to be at the bar. Since it's the nearest place with a phone.'

'Annie, give him a chance. You can't go on being suspicious all the time.'

'Can't I? Well, I can't go on like this. I'm just not up to it. I wish he wasn't here. If he wants to be with her, why doesn't he bloody go?'

'Because he wants to be with you.'

'Is that why he went off on his own all day?'

'You don't have to be together all the time.'

'For Christ's sake, Kate. Just let it drop. I'm fed up thinking about it, I want to enjoy my holiday.'

'I still think you should have it out with him,' Kate persisted. 'It would clear the air for you and for all of us.'

'Fine. If that's what you all want. Trevor and I will have dinner on our own tomorrow. I'm sure Dionysus will have some suitable Greek sayings to trot out over the moussaka. And I'm sure we can find a flight home for Trevor the next day. Because I'm staying here. I found this place after all.'

'I must put Dally to bed now,' said Kate.

Bryonie was changing when Trevor knocked on the door.

'Bry? I've put the wine in the fridge. Can I come in?'

'Sure.'

Bryonie was pulling up a long skirt, naked from the waist up. Trevor looked at her pale, small-nippled breasts, only Bryonie resisted the lure of the sun. They all knew one another's bodies, there was an intimacy which flourished only in the warmth of Greece, but disappeared once they returned to London.

'I'm taking Annie out to dinner tomorrow night. She's been avoiding me all the time.'

'We noticed, Trev.'

'I think we should talk, don't you?'

'Yes. That would be a good idea,' replied Bryonie, as though it had not been mentioned before.

'Then we will. I'm determined that we won't have a row. I'm so bad at rows. Would you mind not eating at Dionysus' place tomorrow night? We ought to be on our own.'

'Of course you should. I'll take Rick, Dally and Kate off somewhere, don't worry. And don't have too much Metaxa,' said Bryonie, with a smile.

Propping open the rickety wardrobe, Trevor pulled out his silk shirt, the one which appeared in the photographs they all took each year and threw into a drawer until the next time. It was a little creased, faded from dark blue to slatey blue, going under the arms, but he liked it. Annie used to like stroking it. Should he say it, right at the beginning? We'll be calm and say what we feel and then it will be over. We won't refer to it again. If we say things we don't mean, that's possible, we won't throw them back at one another. If Margaret had been able to talk reasonably, they might have stood a chance. You couldn't plan out what to say, like a lecture, although the temptation was there. This is what happened. There should be an order to the conversation. You talk. Then I talk. And then it would be over. If it was over, they would make love again. He had been tempted, seeing Annie wandering round the room naked, to hurl her onto the bed but that was through frustration, not love. He longed to slide his hands over her hot body, sensing the night breeze breathing through the open window, to come slowly inside her so that she melted towards him.

Annie was on the balcony, holding a glass of wine, staring at the turquoise pool below. I'll just let him talk, she told herself. He can do the bloody talking. All he had to do was to regret what he'd done – and apologize. What more could she ask? Then it would be over. They had never gone without sex for so long. Weeks, she had lost count. A vital communion had been lost, she hated the coldness it brought. How could you live for years like that, pretend it didn't matter?

Why had she reached for that dress, the one with the puffy sleeves and sash which tied at the back? Laura Ashley's sale, bought when she was at the Beeb, a girly dress. She had taken it last year and not worn it.

'Why are you taking that off?' Trevor asked, watching Annie groping down her back for the zip. He wouldn't help her with it, she might regard it as an insolent gesture. Over-familiar.

'I never liked it.'

'I did. Still do.'

'Can't think why I put it on.'

'We'll be late.'

'Everyone's late in Greece.'

'I'll be downstairs in the garden.'

When Annie appeared, she had apparently changed her mind and put the dress back on, but Trevor didn't comment. They walked to the restaurant in silence.

'Dionysus must be doing well,' Annie commented as they went in, struck by the white cloths on every table, and the posies of orange and white carnations arranged in apricot-glazed pots. They were the first to arrive, still observing the early eating habits of the British. It was, after all, only nine o'clock.

'Greetings, my friends! I say to myself, When are the Watsons coming to eat? We knew you were here, of course. Is everything all right at my cousin's villa? Everything to your satisfaction?'

'Everything's absolutely fine,' said Trevor, returning his beaming smile.

'And Mr and Mrs Evans? And the girl with the beautiful baby? They are busy tonight no doubt?'

'They've been off for the day. But they'll be in soon. We all will, you can be sure of that. You've done a great job with your taverna. Congratulations!'

'I say to my wife, We must make a proper restaurant. Now we have the fountain. Next, we will have a painting, painting on the wall, how you say?'

'Mural.'

'Exactly. Mural. An artist is coming, very important in England, a friend of Iannis. He has a picture in the Academy of Art in London.'

'Shall we order?' said Annie.

'Ah, excuse me. I bring the menu.'

Annie raised her hand.

'We'll have your meze first. Like we always do.'

'No prawn cocktail? No smoked salmon? This season, we have a different menu. Very very good.'

'Maybe another time,' said Trevor, bowing to Annie's wishes.

'Meze and fish and a bottle of local wine now. White,' added Annie, firmly. Dionysus wheeled round, walked with a relaxed strut between the tables and waved away a young waiter who was standing with shoulders stiffly back, notebook at the ready. The Watsons were too important to entrust to a village lad, even though he was dressed in a dazzling white shirt and real Levis.

'He's gone and spoiled this place. Who wants a mural?'

'Never mind, darling. He looks so proud and happy.'

'So what? We're the customers.'

Trevor's heart sank. He could see that Annie was building up for confrontation, that she wasn't going to settle for anything, and he was dreading the sudden, uncontrollable explosion.

'Annie.'

'Yes?'

'Don't make it harder than it need be. This is our holiday.'

Annie grimaced, and unfolded the cotton napkin with a flourish.

'I'll pretend we're having breakfast at the Savoy. Or should it be the Happy Eater? When do we talk? After the fish or before the fish?'

'Whenever you want to.'

'As long as I don't have to pretend I'm here for a jolly meal. Because I'm not. But don't worry, I won't go anorexic on you. Not yet.'

'Annie, please.' Trevor went to take her hand across the table, and drew back. 'I never wanted this to happen.'

'Wine first,' said Annie. 'You never talk business until after the first glass of wine. Women in Management, I think it was the last lecture. I'm meant to ask you about where you live, if you play tennis, whether you have a garden and enquire if you're a member of the local Rotary Club. See, I did learn something. If it was a drama, the door would burst open and I'd say, "Where the hell have you been?" Then I'd throw things at the wall and we'd shout and scream. I wish we had. Christ, Trevor. Have you any idea of the humiliation?'

'Annie, the wine's coming.'

Dionysus came over, pacing his steps carefully, and removed the bottle from the silver ice bucket. Annie examined the label.

'Anything wrong?'

'This isn't local wine. It's a *vin de table*. French, supposedly.'

'I could ask for some Greek fizz.'

'Why don't you?'

Trevor got up from the table, just as another couple was entering. Annie heard enthusing northern voices and hoped they were only passing through. When he came back, he had a long face.

'Dionysus' wife has had another baby. Apparently the hospital treatment was appalling, I couldn't believe it. From what I gather, she was close to a nervous breakdown. Even Greek women have them now, he tells me. Anyways, he's sent her back to England.'

'She should have married a Greek who lives in Camden Town. Then she'd have the Royal Free to go to. What was it? Boy or girl?'

'I didn't ask, Annie.'

'Bound to be a boy. English girls who marry Greeks always have boys.'

'I'm so glad they're doing well. Dionysus has built some extra rooms at the back, they're going to take paying guests. Sandra's going to take care of that, apparently, it'll be her business. That's progress, isn't it? Most wives around here are still kept indoors. With any luck, when Sandra comes back and meets

248

her friends, they'll start wanting change, they'll want to do something apart from spoiling their children. I'm beginning to think that's worth more than a hundred militants. I can say that, now Kate's not here.'

'It's the telly which changes things. Not a few women gossiping in the square. If they had a decent soap, campaigning for enlightenment, you wouldn't have Sandra being packed off to England. And maybe they'd do something about that hospital.'

'You're right.'

'I wonder if *Rough Trade* would go down well in Greece? Maybe I should shoot something here.'

'Excellent idea, Annie.'

'I always wanted to keep away. But there's no point in laying off, any more, is there? Or keeping quiet about Paradisos. Before long, it'll all be taken over by Allied Carpets and Ikea and theme bars and burger chains.'

'And decent roads and decent hospitals, and more work.'

'And crummy executive housing estates amongst the olive trees, and land being bought up by foreign developers, but there's always another island somewhere, if you look hard enough. I'll start looking.'

Dionysus reappeared behind his young waiter, directing the different plates for arrangement on Annie's and Trevor's table. Trevor took a small stuffed vine leaf, which trickled tomato over his fingers. Automatically, he grasped the cotton napkin and wiped them clean.

'You can suck your fingers,' said Annie. 'Why should we change our habits? Or have your habits changed anyway? I suppose you're having to adapt. What my mum would call "refined behaviour". Don't you find it tiresome?'

Annie took a piece of sausage in her fingers and stuffed it into her mouth.

'Oh, Christ, look. There's a coach outside, it's going to park right by the window. I want to leave.'

'We've ordered now, Annie. If we walk out, how can we come back again? And there's nowhere else to have dinner.'

Annie craned her neck as a disorderly file of men and women gathered outside the restaurant. Dionysis rushed out to greet them and a lot of kissing took place.

'They seem to be Greeks. So they won't be asking for bangers and chips. All right, I'll stay. Do you want me to stay?'

249

'Yes, Annie.'

'Why didn't you tell me?'

'It's better if I start at the beginning.'

'I don't care about the beginning. I don't want to know when it started. Yes, I do. I do want to know. I want to know the beginning, the middle and the end. If there is an end. Is there an end, Trevor? Or do I have to wait till we get back to London for Trevor and Lucinda part two?'

'Nothing happened when she was my student. She was just one of a bunch of attractive girls, they all are at that age.'

'You've sampled them?'

'Annie, let me speak.'

Annie rested her elbow on the table, curling her fingers over her mouth, and fixed her eyes on Trevor.

'You know she sent me her script.'

Annie nodded.

'We met once for lunch, to talk about it. That was all. It was just an ordinary lunch, I don't remember much about it really. The next time I heard from her, she told me she was going for an interview at Intertel. I hadn't intended to meet her again, but she insisted, in fact I thought, for some reason, she sounded extremely anxious. So we met again and . . .' Trevor hesitated, wondering how he could soften the blow.

'Then?' said Annie, sharply.

'I went back to her house.'

'How many times? How often?'

'We did have sex a few times, Annie. I can't deny that.'

'Just sex?'

'Just sex, if you put it that way.'

'You fucked her.'

'Yes.'

'And you went on fucking her. After she'd got the job.'

'Sometimes, yes.'

'You fucked my assistant, knowing she was sitting in my office all day, knowing that we had become close, knowing that it would get all round Intertel. But you didn't tell me. That stinks, Trev.'

'I know, I know. I keep asking myself why? When you're dazzled by someone, you don't think.'

'Have there been others?'

'Annie, I'm not Rick. I don't make a habit of recharging my ego by chasing women.'

'What's she like in bed? Does she give you something I don't? Did you buy her a black suspender belt and lacy undies, or does she buy her own?'

'A couple of paperbacks, that's all I gave her.'

Annie gave a contemptuous sniff. 'And she's beautiful. And sexy. And if she was here, you'd be off like a shot. Come on, Trev. Be honest.'

'Yes, I suppose Lucinda is beautiful. Most people seem to think so, anyway.'

'So you met her down at our cottage – our cottage, Trev – and said how your wife didn't understand you, or did you say something more original?'

'Annie, I never talked about you in that way. It was her idea, to come over while she was staying at Sherwood Hall. I'd never have suggested it. Listen, you're not interrogating a suspect, I regret it but it happened.'

'And you made love in Honeysuckle Cottage. How romantic. Shame there's no honeysuckle.'

'We did have sex, yes.'

'In our bed, by any chance?'

'Where, is not relevant.'

'In our bed?'

'No. Not in our bed.'

'Good. I didn't want to chuck it out. And I won't have to hunt for stains on the mattress. It's more comfortable than the one in London, I always sleep well in it.'

'I'm sorry about the scarf. It was a lousy, pathetic way to find out. But you were away a lot, Annie, I didn't have a chance to tell you. Not that I would have done, not while you were shooting—'

'No, certainly not then. You had pressing engagements at our cottage. Who told you I'd found the scarf?'

'Bryonie.'

'At least you had the guts not to deny it.'

'Annie, I've no intention of denying anything.'

'I'm impressed, deeply impressed. Did they all know, my good friends Rick and Kate and Bryonie? Were you all in it together? And what about Gavin? He must have known. Sorry, Gavin, can't stay for lunch. I'm meeting Lucinda down at the cottage.'

'There's no need to bring Gavin into it.'

'She was meant to be away on holiday, the bitch.'

Trevor took a deep breath, trying to quell the momentum of Annie's anger.

'Lucinda may be thoughtless, and of course I was flattered. And I suppose I felt paternal about her. But she is not a bitch. She was always concerned about you.'

'Fucking great. I'm thrilled about that.'

Annie quickly got up. Trevor watched her anxiously, then saw her heading for the skirted sign at the end of the restaurant. He had said enough, he thought as he refilled her glass. the coach-load of Greeks had filled up most of the taverna, and he was drawn to the sun-cracked voices, the large heads of the women, puffed out hair and strings of tiny gold chains, the straight chests of the jet-haired men as they dominated the ranks of dishes, like Greek commanders standing over the troops.

'Is everything OK?'

Dionysus leaned over Trevor.

'Tonight is very busy. Excuse me if I don't have talk with you.'

'As good as ever,' replied Trevor, hoping that he would refrain from commenting on the barely eaten plate of meze. 'Another bottle of wine?'

'No problem. I go.'

'Are you all right, darling?' Trevor said, as Annie sat down again.

'When was the last time you saw her? Did you manage it twice for Leggy Lucy? That's Rick's name for her, I'm sure you know.'

'I didn't.'

'Well, did you?'

'Did I what?'

'Do it more than once?'

'Annie, this is ridiculous. We've never been one of those voyeuristic couples who get turned on by recounting their sexual exploits. I really don't think this is necessary. We never did in the early days. Why do it now?'

'In our early days, everyone was fucking everyone else. The point is, Trev, they're not doing it now. Only you, apparently.'

'I'm sure that's an exaggeration. My students take precautions when we didn't, that's the only difference.'

'Ah. So you know. That's what research means, silly me I should have guessed.'

'Annie, please.'

'Did she invite you to Sherwood Hall? Did you meet Daddy? Did she take you for a ride on Tim's motor-bike? Have you met Jeremy yet? Lucinda's fond of Jeremy but she isn't sure if they'll get married or not. Rich background, of course, but she does find him a bit boring. Lucinda likes chatting about her life, gives me glimpses of the *Tatler* world. Useful, if I ever start making those hooray dramas the Americans love. You have to get the detail right nowadays. Tell me, I want to know more about your seedy soap. I might even stick it in the development file, who knows.'

'I don't know anything about Jeremy. Lucinda's life is her own, I never question her.'

'What a relief. Has sex got boring, too, or do you need more time to find out? Let me know, Trev. So I can put it in one of my diaries, you know how forgetful I am. I need a tissue. Give me a tissue.'

'I don't have one.'

'Well, I'll use this serviette then. Or is it napkin? You should know by now, I never remember.'

'Here comes the fish.'

The waiter removed the platter of meze and Dionysus set down a dish of red mullet, strewn with herbs and thick chunks of lemon. Then he brought the second bottle of wine.

'Compliments of the house. To enjoy your meal.'

'That's very kind,' said Trevor. He waited in silence until he saw him take a seat at a neighbouring table.

'Annie, I know I've hurt you and I should have told you earlier. I'm sorry. There's not much more to say, there really isn't. There's no point in excavating the past, I shouldn't have got involved.'

'Before you came away, did you tell her you'd see her when you got back?'

'I said I'd talk to you, that I didn't know what would happen—'

'Waiting for me to make the decision? Is that it? Her or me?'

'No, no, not at all. She knows I love you, Annie, she's never resented that.'

'Thank goodness. So generous. What a decent girl she is. The perfect mistress, following all the rules. Isn't that quaint!'

'Annie—'

'What, dear?' said Annie sarcastically.

253

'I know I've been stupid. But now you have to trust me. Let's put this behind us. Wouldn't that be best?'

'I'll never be able to enjoy anything with you again. That's what you've done. I don't care about the screwing, but I care about the deceit.'

'Can't you see how impossible it was? What was I meant to say? Sorry, Annie, I'm off with Lucinda tonight? I didn't have that kind of control, and if I did, I'd have been a bastard. I love you, Annie.'

'Don't say that, don't say that.'

'What should I say?'

'For Christ's sake, don't say that. It doesn't mean a bloody thing,' Annie said, her face drained of all expression. Then she started to rise from her chair.

'Haven't we been together long enough for it to mean something? Annie, listen—'

'Why should I? I'm going home.'

'Stay, just a little longer. I'll tell Lucinda it's over, that we won't see each other when I get back.'

Annie sat down again and leaned towards him.

'Then do it now. This minute. Phone her in London, leave a message if she's not there. I want to hear you telling her that it's over.'

'Annie, you have to trust me.'

'I don't care if you say how much you miss her, how unhappy you are, but I want to hear you say it's finished. Then I'll try and enjoy my holiday.' She looked over her shoulder, towards the cloakroom, half hidden by a lattice screen. 'No-one's using the phone. Have you got some change?'

Before Trevor could answer, there was a burst of sound. Three bouzouki players and a singer had taken up a place at the side of the taverna, and had begun the introduction to a folk song. After a few bars, a strapping voice filled the room.

'Isn't that the motor-mechanic, Andreas?' said Trevor.

'No, it's his brother. The one who sings in the local church. It must be someone's birthday.'

'Did you know he was going to sing tonight?'

'How could I have done?'

Annie picked at the fish, and replaced her knife and fork on her plate. She was racking her brains but the questions had stopped coming. She stared vacantly at the singer, who was putting on the booming voice of one character, then tripping up the scale to a whining falsetto while the Greeks heaved with laughter. Even if she had learned more than a handful of Greek words, she wouldn't have been able to understand this gabbled dialogue. A handsome young Greek leaned across from the table nearest to them, and addressed Annie.

'You are German?'

'English,' said Annie crossly.

'Good. I speak English, a little. This song, a naughty song, is about a baker who is making a bread in the shape of the bosoms of his mistress. His wife gets up early one morning. He takes out a bread from his oven and they have argument.'

'Thank you. I'll watch my husband when he's baking bread.'

'Your husband? Baker?'

Annie laughed and he laughed back. His white shirt was open, black hairs nearly up to his neck but they weren't thick, and his skin was walnut brown. There was a slim gold chain round his neck, and a heavy Japanese studded watch on his wrist.

'What's he saying?' said Trevor, leaning across Annie.

'What's a nice girl like you doing with a man like that?'

Trevor glared. 'Want me to say something to him?'

'Why? He's only being Greek.'

'Are you all right, Annie?'

'No.'

'Shall we go home? Or out for a walk?'

'Neither. You can go if you like.'

She could see that Trevor had no intention of moving. There was more to say, but Annie was tired of questions, tired of answers. The bouzouki music had paused for the singer to make a few comments, as he wandered round the tables, bending over the ladies to whisper what must have been obscene, by Greek standards. It was a good way to spend a birthday. The birthday girl was a woman of forty, fifty, sixty, hard to tell, in a scoop-necked floral dress, with tiered frills over a full skirt, bangles up her arm like a gypsy. Her black-moustachioed husband was beside her, putting on the appropriate expressions of outrage and good humour which were expected of him. The song ended with a burst of clapping, hands held high in the air, shouts of congratulation. Trevor and Annie had both turned outwards from their chairs, facing the musicians. More songs followed, with the audience joining in the lusty choruses. Then there was a pause, while the guests regrouped, the waiters pushed back the front tables and the bouzouki players picked up glasses of sparkling wine.

'We should have come on another night,' said Annie.

'They don't seem to mind us being here. But they don't make the distinction between private and public that we do.'

'Miserable bloody English sitting in a corner saying nothing, I bet that's what they're thinking.'

'Why don't we go back now, Annie?'

'I haven't had my Metaxa. Besides, we might as well wait until the others have gone to bed. Perhaps the world will have changed by breakfast-time. Do all couples go through this? The surveys always contradict one another. Have you noticed? One in ten, one in five, one in two. But that isn't surprising. Why should anyone tell the truth? I think one in three sounds about right for the extra-marital bonking statistic. What do you think?'

'I really don't have a clue.'

The bouzouki players turned to their chairs, lovingly picked up their instruments, nodded at one another and plucked out a fast waltz rhythm. The moustachioed man accompanied his wife to the front of the taverna, placed his gnarled hand on her back, and with one nimble step, propelled her into a furious dance, puffing out every inch of her skirt as he whirled her round. Annie couldn't take her eyes off their thick-ankled feet, his in a pair of heavy black shoes, hers in high-heeled bulging courts, each following the other in delicate steps, turning, sweeping in a straight line, turning again.

'My grandmother, she dances good, better than my mother,' said the young Greek who had talked to Annie earlier. 'My name is Michael and I have four brothers and two sisters. Your name, please?'

'Annie.'

'Will your husband mind if I ask for a dance?'

'I'll dance with you, when everyone else is on the floor.'

'You are here on holidays?'

'Yes and no.'

When he took Annie onto the floor, he clasped her like a young fiancé alone with his intended. He desired her, he wanted her to feel it, pressed close against her. Suddenly sensation returned, she was a woman again, basking in the embrace of a man who, although he said nothing, swept her along as though he would soon take her with him, out to the moonlit dunes. The room swam round her, they were clapping out the rhythm, and when the music stopped, Annie let him hold her. Then he kissed her hand.

'You are beautiful,' he said. And then he walked away, his head held high, and stood next to two girls who shared his black eyes and black hair, hanging in a thick bush down their backs. Annie stood watching him. The island was so small, it was out of the question, but she allowed herself to imagine him lying naked beside her, listening to the gentle rush of white-edged waves curling onto the shore.

Trevor glanced up mournfully as Annie came back to sit opposite him.

'Dionysus has brought you a tumbler of Metaxa. If they stop playing waltzes, we could have a dance.'

'You have to make a phone call.'

'Annie, I haven't forgotten.'

Annie saw the first couples linking arms, then more joined them until a snaking line of Greeks began to hop joyfully round the tables, hands clutching waists, old and young, one or two taller, the majority with the short stature of the islanders. At the end of the line, now a cohesive whole held together by tightly linked arms, was a hand waving like a tentacle. And the hand grabbed Annie as Dionysus shouted, 'Come, come with us!' A girl with ribboned plaits took hold of Trevor's belt, and they were hurtled out of the taverna as more joined them and the music went faster and faster. Having reached a climax, staggering to remain upright, gasping for breath, the dancers suddenly came to a halt, ending in a giant circle on the stony forecourt outside. They all raised their hands, shouting, clapping, as the shuddering engine of the coach started up.

Annie walked off a little way into the night, looking up at the moon which was creating filigree patterns from the olive trees lining the dusty road. The tears she had held back all evening streamed remorselessly down her face. She could hear no footsteps behind her, so she sat on a low wall which enclosed a tumble-down shepherd's house, goats tethered near by, tossing their heads so that the metal bells round their necks clattered impatiently.

Taking a corner of her dress, Annie wiped her eyes. Could she really bear to stand beside Trevor while he attempted to call Lucinda? How could she treat her husband like an in-competent actor? What right did she have to humiliate him? Didn't she remember what it was like? With Mel? Hadn't she

257

kept that hidden from him? Gloated over the memory in secret? Never admitted that the child wasn't his? Even if the affair had been brief, mightn't she have jumped into bed again if the opportunity arose? She got to her feet, and strode back to the taverna.

'I wondered where you'd gone,' said Trevor, a dark silhouette against the glass. Inside, the lights were low, as they cleared the tables and pulled down the streamers.

'I'll do it now, if you like. Make that call.'

'Let's get back. I'm exhausted,' Annie replied.

15

ANNIE

Annie felt for her plastic card amidst the debris of her bag, wondering why she was unable to see anything other than a blur. Only when she failed to see the slot in her office door, did she realize she was still wearing her Greek sunglasses. She let herself in, rushed over to Lucinda's desk and flung open the drawers one after another. What was she expecting to find? Ribboned sheafs of love-letters, tiny mementoes, dried flowers from a country field? Contraceptives sealed in an envelope for the sudden escape?

Anita had phoned her at home the night before. While she was away, the rat-pack – couldn't call them press could you? – had been phoning every day, offered her lunch at the Ritz, a free weekend in Paris but she told them, excuse my language, to stuff it. She wasn't talking to anyone and neither was her boss. She'd find everything on her desk in a brown folder marked Urgent.

Trevor had been listening to the conversation.

'Something happened?' he asked, as Annie slapped down the phone.

'How could you have been so bloody stupid? Your little idyll is plastered all over the *News of the World* the *Express*, the *Mail*, probably didn't make the *Sunday Sport*. Of course, they're all interested in her. They don't reckon you're worth much lineage. Now what? Any suggestions?'

Ashen faced, Trevor sank back into his chair.

'Christ! Why didn't Anita leave a message with Dionysus? Couldn't she have let you know?'

'She didn't want to spoil my holiday.'

'Why on earth did they bother? Why would anyone be remotely interested?'

'Because – maybe it's because Lady Lucinda looks good in the pics. Decadent aristo creates havoc in TV. One more to add to the list. Now all they need is a few comments from me. And you. Of course, the story won't stand up without Lucinda, they'll have to speak to her. What do you suggest, Trev? Any ideas?'

'Stupid bastards! God, I hate the press! Why can't they leave us alone?' Without thinking, Trevor moved towards the phone.

'Don't you bloody dare!' shrieked Annie.

'Calm down, calm down. I was about to contact Rick.'

'What do I say? I stand by my husband? Like hell! For God's sake, Trevor, I'm the one who's got to deal with this. What do I do? Make a statement? Saying what? I've got a series to put out, extra shooting to do. I can't cope. I can't cope.'

'There's no need to cope with anything, Annie. Leave it to me. Why don't we go to the cottage till it's all calmed down? The press will be bored after a week or so. But you do understand, I'll have to talk to Lucinda first. We need to know if she's giving any interviews, she'll be under a lot of pressure to talk. We need to get together on this.'

'No we don't. I'm the person to talk to Lucinda. And then I'll have to face them all in the bar. Show them all that Annie Griffiths can take the knocks. What a fucking mess.'

'We'll work out what to do. If you think it's best to go in, I'll come along with you.'

'No,' said Annie wearily. 'I'm on my own now. Thanks to you, my love.'

'Who on earth could have talked, I wonder? Rick promised Bryonie he wouldn't tell a soul. How could anyone have known?'

'Well, someone did, didn't they? Maybe Jeremy got to hear. I expect I'll find out soon enough when I go in tomorrow. Lucinda will be back, I'm sure she'll have some ideas.'

'Don't go in, darling. Wait a while.'

'What, go into hiding? Don't be silly, I've got work to do. Why don't you go down to the cottage?'

'Would you rather I did?'

'Yes,' said Annie.

His head throbbing, unable to stir from the kitchen table, Trevor listened to Annie's angry footsteps as she walked up the creaking stairs to the bedroom. He knew he couldn't join her, he would sleep on the settee. Remorse was something to suffer in isolation. Above all, it made him seem inadequate, which then made the words dry in his throat. He knew he had been the cause of anguish for Annie but it was almost worse, the harm he had inflicted on Lucinda. Worse, because he could give her no comfort. Even now, it pained him to think of her confronting the insulting scandal, confronting her father's rage, without his support. He couldn't tell her now that he was unable to see her again. How could she take another rejection? And how could he bear to have her last memories of him clouded with hate? Would Annie, in time, accept that he had to bear some responsibility for Lucinda? That he couldn't just cut himself off because of what had happened?

Tonight, there was nothing he could do. Tomorrow? Tomorrow he would rise early, escape to Honeysuckle Cottage, better for Annie to have him out of the way. He was behind with the book. The garden needed attention. He might drop down to the pub, listen to farmers talk of harvests and set-aside plans for the winter. There was no reason not to stay there a few more days until the beginning of term.

Annie spread the cuttings all over her desk and swiftly devoured the contents. *Express, Mail, Standard*, and a couple of Sundays. It wouldn't have been a story, not without the long-lens shot of Her with Him at country love-nest. Her lying topless on the grass, Him bending over her. They had discovered that Lady Lucinda was engaged to marry Jeremy Logan-Wilkes, whose father was a friend of Lord Sherwood's. So Jeremy was the son of a Cabinet minister. 'We're not exactly engaged. Lucinda and I are just good friends. She has her life, I have mine,' said the loquacious Jeremy from the doorstep of his Fulham house. They all had something to say, Amanda Armitage, old school-friend; brother Timothy, the biking club-owner; Jaspar Huntley and countless others who professed to have shared flats, or stayed at Sherwood Hall. The *Standard* had even quoted from a script she had written. Lady Lucinda bonks drama-chief's hubbie, porno shows in stately home, screamed the *News of the World*. There were brief references to Trevor Watson, University prof trying to make it in TV with occasional appearances on *Splash!* the controversial youth programme.

'It'll blow over. They'll get bored,' Annie kept repeating to herself, trying to ignore the sick lumps of anger threatening to explode in her throat. It was still early, just after nine. Benny would be in by now, reading the papers in his office. As she expected, Annie found him lying stretched out on his white leather settee, holding *Variety* at arm's length.

'Don't get up,' she said as she settled into the matching armchair. 'I've just caught up on last week's junk. All of it. Can you recommend a private clinic?'

'You can stay at my place. Bring a Rottweiler if you like, that'd put off the slimy bastards. I know a good lawyer.'

'I don't want a bloody lawyer. I want a good scream. I don't care about her. Or if all her friends gets a buzz out of having five seconds of fame. I don't give a damn about that. Who's interested?'

In spite of her determination, the tears erupted in sobs, and she pressed her hands tightly against her face.

'I just can't think what to do. What's best? Lucinda's coming in later, she left a message with Anita. Why the hell didn't she stay away?'

'Say nothing, love. And come over here. Cup of tea?'

'No tea.'

Annie was enveloped in Benny's arms, and he stuffed a clump of tissues into her hand.

'Cry if you want. Then we'll talk.'

'I must get back, Benny. So much to get out of the way. You know the worst part?'

'Having the bitch in your office. Get her out, Annie. Even if she is under contract, we'll deal with that.'

'It's Trevor. I can't bear him being made to seem such an idiot. He isn't, he really isn't. He just didn't know what he was getting himself into. Do people really think I've been married to an idiot all these years? Trevor's not like that. They make out he's some kind of publicity-seeking academic who's out to front his own show. It's not true, Benny. Trevor never intended—'

'Don't upset yourself. You going to talk to the girl today? Get her out. Get your priorities sorted. You and your show, that's what matters.'

'Has Alan said anything?'

'Not for the last year, not that I've noticed. He's been in Ireland, should be back today.'

'I'll see him. Mind if I make a few calls?'

'All yours,' said Benny, gesturing towards an onyx, gold-rimmed telephone.

Having booked a conference room, Annie looked up towards Benny.

'It would make things easier if I could offer Lucinda something to do in another department. I can't sack her for having an affair with my husband.'

'Why not? There's no need to put it that way. You can always tell her that you've had to make cuts in staffing levels.'

'That's not how I operate, Benny. Why should I cover up how I feel? But I don't want to screw up her career, I don't want her to blame me for throwing her off the series. One day, she'll do something good.'

'Think so?'

'She has got talent, Benny. When all this has blown over, I'd like to produce her script.'

'Who are you trying to convince? If you say so.'

'She needs to get experience in other departments, to widen her scope.'

'Widen her scope? She's got enough to sink a battleship.'

Benny grunted, then blew his nose trumpet-fashion to clear his brain.

'What about Gavin's show? I'm sure he'd take her. Made for each other, I'd say.'

'No, then she'd be London-based, I can't have that. Didn't you say you were shooting one of your series up north?'

'Glasgow.'

'Thought so. Would you try her out?'

'Ooh, now then. I'd have to think about that, Annie. I'd have to think about what she could do. I don't see her in comedy, not really. Not the type. I don't want Pa looking over my shoulder all the time, couldn't handle that. Would she be any good on the PR side? We need all we can get on this one.'

'She wouldn't buy that.'

'Script consultant?'

'You can have her on the drama budget. Attachment to comedy. How about that, Benny?'

'Script consultant then, another useless script consultant. You're on. It's a deal. I couldn't promise to keep her, not if it didn't work out. But I'll keep her busy for a few weeks, if it helps.'

'Thanks, Benny. You're a darling.'

'You know where to come, if you fancy a Caesar salad. You

must see the new motor, it's a white Roller. They can put me in there when I've gone, it's big enough for a hearse.'

When Annie entered her office again, she found Anita giving the finishing touches to an autumn flower arrangement, assessing the ox-eye daisies and copper leaves which were standing high and mighty, precariously balanced in small, thick-glazed pots. She greeted Annie with a flustered smile, unable to decide whether to give vent to her feelings or to downplay the whole nasty business.

'Good holiday, Annie? How was Greece?'

'Wonderful. As always. Those flowers look great.'

Noticing that Annie's eyes were glistening and red round the edges, and that she was thinner after her holiday when everyone else was fatter, she got up to pour her a cup of coffee. It wasn't fair, for it to happen to someone like Annie, all those sordid goings-on. Until now, she had imagined that her boss was immune from the messes that everyone else got into, rather like the Queen. Best to wait until Annie brought up the subject.

'You're in early. I thought you might be. The coffee's ready.'

'Thanks.' Annie paced round the office, as though reassuring herself that nothing had changed. 'How was your Spanish art course?'

'Very nice. Rod didn't like it, well not much. He kept going on about wanting to see a bull fight, but they didn't have them, not in the part of Spain we were. There wasn't much in the shops but I thought those pots would go nicely in the office.'

When Annie had settled at her desk, Anita brought over a mug of black coffee and some chocolate biscuits which were left untouched.

'Has Lucinda come in?'

'Not yet, Annie.'

'Perhaps she'll get run over by a bus.'

Annie grinned, and Anita immediately felt better.

'You'll find the important stuff at the top. Or what I thought was urgent. I didn't stick the cuttings in the book, not those ones.'

Annie hardly gave them a second glance, merely pushed the small pile to the back of the desk.

'I saw them earlier.'

'They do write drivel,' said Anita, removing the offensive scraps of newsprint. She was dying to ask whether she was going to boot Trevor out, but Annie, quite rightly, wasn't giving her a clue. Such dignity. Most people would be blubbering all over the desk by now.

'Thanks for sorting everything out, Anita. We'll do the written replies this afternoon. Is Alan back yet?' Annie asked, beginning to go through the three piles left for her attention, faxes, letters, notes of calls.

'He'll be in the office today, that's what he said.'

'I'll be in conference this morning. When she comes in, tell Lucinda to see me immediately. I'll be in Room C. While we're in there, you'll be able to clear her desk. I'm moving her to Benny's department. He's desperate for an extra hand, and we don't need her here.'

Only now did the strain show in her voice.

'Shall I confirm it in writing?' replied Anita.

'Yes, you'd better. A brief memo to Benny.'

'Mind you, I never thought she suited our department but you can't always tell at the beginning. Some people fit, and some don't. If you ask me, she didn't have a clue about television.'

'There's no need to discuss it,' said Annie. 'I'll see what she has to say and then she can go. We've got a series to put out.'

Once Annie had left the office, Anita began to take the practical steps necessary for Lucinda's departure, gathering together the contents of her desk drawer, Estée Lauder skin freshener, nail file, herbal gel, little silver brandy bottle, earrings, little drop pearls, real pearls, silly to leave those there, lots of those fancy Japanese pens she liked, bought those herself, and a leather writing case with Sherwood Hall notepaper in it, crest as well, tiny one, book by someone called Nin, sounded Japanese and when she flipped it open, it was pure filth. She gave the inventory over the phone to Gemma.

'You aren't allowed to keep scripts, are you? No, thought not. Security risk. I'll lock them away in the filing cabinet . . . No, she isn't. Annie's being absolutely wonderful, you'd never know. All she said was, "Benny's desperate for an extra researcher, so Lucinda's going to comedy. I think she'll fit in well there." Just like Annie, never thinks about herself. Lovely person . . . I know, I know . . . If it was me, I'd have sacked her straight away, but they always sack the wrong people at Intertel. Annie must be feeling awful inside, but you'd never guess . . . That's right. The show must go on. Annie's always like that . . . No, of course I didn't ask. But we all know what she's feeling. It's like someone's mother dying really. What can you say? How awful for you? . . . No, she's just getting on with things . . . Seeing her in a conference room . . . Yes, better that way . . . It wasn't as though there was any real work for that girl in the first place. Couldn't even type her own letters properly, two fingers, useless. Not as though she needed the money . . .'

Conference room C was chilly and smelt of cigar smoke mixed with the sickly aroma of Summer Glade. Annie settled herself in the armchair at the head of the table where someone had laid out large pads and pens, a decanter and water glasses, even a calculator. She was trying to order her thoughts. She would be brief, to the point, this was not the occasion to follow her natural impulses. The Controller of Drama was taking a meeting. It helped, they said, if you counted your breaths, ten in, ten out. The telephone was by her hand. Shivering in the blast of air conditioning, she went over to open the window. Warm, muggy September air, laden with the build-up of summer pollution. Stress management. The mantra they had intoned, was it day two or day three? I am in control, I am in control. Wouldn't it have been better to be fretful, pulsing with rage? Suddenly there was a firm knock on the door.

'Where shall I sit?' asked Lucinda.

'There will be fine,' said Annie, pointing to the chair opposite her.

'I didn't bring the production file. Shall I get it?'

'This isn't a production matter. I thought we should talk.'

'I want to, Annie. That's why I came in.'

'At least you had the good sense not to bare your soul to the press. Under the circumstances, I thought you were quite brave to come back to the office.'

'They've been ringing up at the Hall all weekend. It's been absolutely ghastly, all those inventions and lies. I couldn't do anything about it. People I thought were my friends, people I was at school with—'

'You needn't tell me the details. They concern you, not me. Trevor has apologized and that's good enough. If you live with someone for over twenty years, you confront these kind of situations. It's painful, but you do. I'm not a saint, I was hurt and angry, but it's over now. And you needn't think it's changed anything, because it hasn't. It came as a surprise, though. And I don't know why you didn't tell me earlier.'

'Annie, I couldn't. I just couldn't.'

'Why not?'

'It was between me and Trevor.'

'At least you don't deny it.'

'What did you expect me to do? Say it never happened? I'm not like that, Annie.'

'Why Trevor? That's what puzzled me. Of all the people you must know, you light on him. You could have anyone you like, Lucinda. Why did you choose an ageing academic who'll soon be thinking of retirement? Or have you always gone for older, married men?'

'Annie, it wasn't planned. Do you think I wanted to fall in love with your husband?'

'I don't care whether you did or not, as it happens.'

'There was never any question of our running off together, not on my part anyway. Did you ever imagine there was?'

'It did cross my mind. Does that surprise you?'

'Just because you love someone, it doesn't mean you're out to break up a marriage. It wasn't a problem for me, I never considered it for one moment. I knew you didn't have that kind of marriage, anyway.'

'What kind? What are you talking about?'

'The usual, boring, keeping-tabs-on-each-other marriage. You must have had other people sometimes, after all those years.'

'Is that what Trevor assumed? Is that how he justified behaving like a shit?'

'There's no need to see it like that, Annie.'

'How am I meant to see it? Poor Trev, getting a bit dreary in bed, needs a leg-over to pep up his libido? You expect me to say thank you? Do you see yourself as a sex therapist for flagging husbands? I know some girls do.'

'That's ridiculous. The sex part wasn't that important.'

'Oh, so Trev let you down, did he? I am sorry. That's very unlike him. So what was that important? Tell me. Come on, that's the least you can do.'

Annie rose from her chair and walked over to the window, standing with her back to Lucinda.

'Take as long as you like,' Annie added. 'I won't repeat anything you say, not to anyone. This is between us.'

Turning to face her again, leaning back against the window, Annie looked down at the biscuit-tanned, flawless oval face with perfect arching brows, the blonded hair screwed back in a ponytail and tried to imagine her puffy-faced and dumpy. If she had looked like Anita, this conversation would not be taking place. It seemed an age before Lucinda broke the silence, staring at the glass decanter on the table, hands clutched together. Her words were hesitant, as though she hadn't voiced her feelings before.

'I'd never been with someone who didn't talk about himself all the time, who took my work seriously, who took me seriously, who made everything come alive, who was just absolutely wonderful. Trevor's helped me to grow up.'

'I thought fathers and mothers did that.'

'Not mine. They never even tried to understand me. Sometimes I used to wonder if they liked me. Now, I don't think they do, not specially. Trevor was the only man I've ever met who cared about me as a person. He listened to me. We talked about real, important things.'

'But it was better to talk about them in bed. Are you trying to pretend it was some deep spiritual relationship? You were screwing him, for God's sake. Sneaking off to fuck my husband. How do you think that makes me feel? I don't see marriage like your set. Maybe you get a kick out of seducing other women's husbands. Don't tell me it's the first time.'

'Do you honestly believe that I'd behave like some of the ghastly girls around here? You know I don't think like that. You know I couldn't possibly.'

'Thinking doesn't seem to come into it.'

'I trusted him completely and I never trust people. I never wanted to take him away, Annie. All I wanted was to be with him sometimes, to talk, to share things. Why should it matter if your partner sleeps with someone else occasionally? I can't see why two people should be locked into one another for a lifetime. Can't we enjoy the company of different friends? Does it really matter if it ends up in bed? Trevor still loves you. You're not a conventional, ordinary wife. I never thought you'd mind so much, really I didn't. Is it so awful that he's important in my life as well as yours?'

'He *is* important? What's that supposed to mean? Are you saying that you intend to go on seeing each other? Is that what you're saying?'

'I don't know. What do you want? Do you expect me to say I'll never see Trevor again?'

'Yes. I do. Or even try to see him.'

'I can't promise that, Annie.'

'So what's your solution? Carrying on working with me, scooting off when you feel like it to get between the sheets with my husband? The odd weekend in my cottage perhaps? Do you expect me to go along with that? Are you that dumb?'

'I don't see it like you. Trevor's my friend and your husband. And we're friends, too, aren't we? What's wrong with that? Why should having sex make any difference?'

'You don't see a bloody thing. This isn't a script, it's my life, Trevor's life. You can theorize all you like, pretend you're making rational decisions, but you're fooling yourself. I'll tell you how it is. Two people live together a long time, love and respect each other, then there's something called loyalty. You put one another first. You often do things you don't want to do, without thinking. It's nothing to do with going spare about an odd kiss with someone else at a drunken party. It's about living together in a civilized way. It's not about saying, Sorry, darling, can't see that movie tonight, promised to see Paul; sorry, darling, too tired tonight, working too hard; sorry, darling, must carry on with the book. Once you start those shitty lies, it's all crap. If you live with someone one day, you'll find out. That's how you grow up, Lucinda.'

Annie returned to her chair, and stood with her hands firmly placed on the leather back.

'I'm sorry, Annie. Sorry if I mucked up your life. I didn't mean to.'

'No, you've mucked up yours.'

'I do love him.'

'Is that meant to make me feel better?' said Annie, staring angrily at Lucinda. Looking down to avoid Annie's gaze, her brow began to wrinkle.

'I understand if you want me to leave. My father would be delighted. He thinks I'm wasting my time and he also thinks that Trevor's a bad influence. Politically, that is. I'm an embarrassment to him. Maybe I am. Isn't that what artists are meant to be?'

'Artists?' In spite of herself, Annie smiled. 'But you enjoy being an embarrassment. Sticking up two fingers at anything and anyone. Listen, Lucinda, I've no intention of sacking you.

Not because of your father, certainly not because of your paltry little affair with Trevor, but because you'll be a producer or a head of scripts some day. I've never screwed up talented people, even my enemies can't say that.'

'Thanks, Annie. For being so decent.'

'I'll see what's going in other departments. But there is a condition.'

'Yes?'

'You don't go behind my back ever again. Will you promise?'

'I will, Annie. Of course I will.'

Annie got up from her chair, and walked slowly over to the open window.

'Benny's shooting a comedy series in Glasgow. He needs someone up there. You'll be starting in a couple of weeks and until then, you can take paid leave.'

'But I don't know anything about comedy. I'd be hopeless, Annie.'

'When I started, I knew nothing about drama. You'll learn. If you drop into Benny's office, he'll find some scripts for you. Anita's clearing your desk, she'll bring along your things. Benny's a good person to work with. Now I must get on. Close the windows, would you?'

'There's something I wanted to ask.'

'What? I've got another meeting.'

'Are you still considering *Grains of Evil?*'

'We'll talk about that another time.'

'You might produce it next year? You haven't changed your mind?'

'I've had other things to think about, Lucinda. Why should I change my mind?'

'I just thought—'

'That I'd only go ahead if you stopped seeing Trevor? You really are unbelievable sometimes.'

Alan came forward to greet Annie, standing genially in his outer office then taking her hand and leading her towards two green leather chesterfields facing one another in an attempt at intimacy. A newly framed picture of his numerous children waving from the deck of a modest yacht reminded Annie that he was a family man. Intertel was a family station.

'I'm aware of the situation,' he said. 'It must be difficult, coming back. But I want you to try and ignore all this . . . all this ridiculous nonsense. If Lord Sherwood had kept his mouth shut, none of this would have happened. While you were away, a couple of reporters turned up at Sherwood Hall, hunting for Lucinda. He was furious, big family row apparently.'

'I'll talk to anyone,' said Annie. 'But only about *Rough Trade*. And in the presence of our Controller of Publicity.'

'Very good. That's very brave of you.'

'It's not brave, it's common sense. I want the publicity on this series to have a long fuse, so critics don't forget it's on our screens. I don't see why Trevor making an idiot of himself for a few weeks should force me into purdah. It's ridiculous. Would anyone have been the slightest bit interested if there had been a male Controller of Drama? Of course not. It goes with the job, doesn't it? Let's talk about the sex on screen, not fumblings off it. What's happening, Alan? Do you still want me to make those cuts?'

'I know how reluctant you are. I've given it a lot of thought. What I'm aiming for now, is to start you in the eight o'clock peak slot, and then put episodes four to six at a later time. Say nine.'

'But not after the news.'

'No, no. I'm putting *Splash!* on then.'

'So there'll be only small scene changes in episodes one and two.'

'That's right.'

'And it's fixed? We still go out on 19 November?'

'That's your first show-date.'

'Thanks, Alan. So, from what you've seen, do you think we could start thinking about the second series?'

'No harm, Annie. Obviously, it depends on audience response.'

'You build audience response, Alan. I think Clary Hunt is going to have them glued, she'll carry another series easily. I want to tie her up before she gets hauled off to make a forgettable film in Hollywood.'

'If you can do a good deal, go ahead.'

'I did a good deal with you, didn't I?'

Alan gave a slight smile.

'It makes such a difference, seeing you so confident. You're a real asset to Intertel, Annie.'

Annie shrugged off the compliment . . .

'I've also been thinking ahead,' she went on. 'One of our

one-off drama slots for next year. There's a script I've been sitting on for a while. With some rewrites, it'll be stunning. Don't say anything for the moment, but I know it's a winner. Guess who wrote the treatment? First attempt from Lucinda Sherwood. Of course, it's all over the place at the moment, but once I get my hands on it—'

'Annie, are you sure about this? Is it a wise move?'

'It's not a move, Alan. I believe in it. I wouldn't bother with it otherwise, you know me.'

'I hope it's low budget. We'll have to spread ourselves a bit thin next year.'

'I know, Alan. Don't worry, it can be made for a song. Nearly all location in East Anglia, only two star parts, small cast, find some stunning unknowns . . .'

'Sounds promising, very promising. If you think you can cope.'

'I wouldn't have suggested it otherwise.'

'Have you mentioned it to the Controller of Scripts? Have you said anything?'

'No. It's too soon. I'll will when I'm ready.'

Next day, Annie marched buoyantly into the Intertel bar. The evening before, she had been visited by Jake. It was his idea, to cut her hair short in a wispy, gamine style. Greater versatility, and hair-pieces for grand occasions. Her head felt lighter, her neck longer. When the shearing was completed, she had sat at the kitchen table, drinking in Jake's sympathy – they never leave you in peace, terrible, he did understand – enjoying his chatter about the private lives of famous clients who'd gone through even more dreadful times.

Annie was feeling an almost tangible sense of achievement, as though overnight she had added inches to her stature. Tomorrow she would take the whole day to view *Rough Trade*, book the actors, organize the re-shoots. In a matter of days, everything had been settled. She would enjoy the breathing space before the next crisis. Thelma was giving a frenzied wave, then she left the table where she was holding court with Jeff, together with one of the three broad-chested male researchers reserved for *Poole Reports* in the uniform of tight T-shirts and jeans, and a couple who could only have come from outside Intertel, the kind who thought you put on Sunday best to come into a television station.

'Annie, nearly didn't recognize you.'

'That's the idea!'

'Who did your hair? Absolutely gorgeous. Turn round.' Annie half turned her head. 'Where did you go? I must know.'

'I didn't go anywhere. Jake came to the house. I didn't feel like exposing myself to the public in Galvin's.'

'I know exactly what you've been through. We all think you've been fantastically discreet, Annie. I couldn't have been like that. When I wore that tight strapless dress for my rape programme, and said no girl ever asked for it, remember the stink that caused?' Annie nodded. 'Those evil bastards wouldn't let me alone. I had to get my phone number changed. All day and all night.'

'It wasn't as bad as that,' said Annie.

'We were all thinking, How dare that girl come back? But in she comes, as though nothing had happened. I'd have slapped her round the face, well, you know what I'm like. Best thing that could have happened, putting her in comedy. That'll sort her out. Glasgow, isn't it?'

Annie grinned. 'News travels fast.'

'That kind of news. We just can't work out who it was—'

'One of Lucinda's friends probably. It doesn't matter.'

'Did you manage to have a good holiday?'

'I guess so.'

'It's no good making a song and dance, is it? Just get on with the job.'

'Quite.'

'Did you see my programme on marriage, the one last year? Had a tremendous impact. We had more letters about that than anything else, well, apart from the rape one. It's amazing how many people stay married. That was the marvellous thing. Single parents just get all the publicity, that's all.'

Annie surveyed the bar and gave an apologetic smile.

'Sorry, Thelma, I must go. Some things to discuss with Gavin.'

Gavin was waiting, which he indicated by lowering his finger in the direction of an empty chair.

'I'd really like you to come over to my place next week. Just a small drinks party for David Mamet. But I thought you two should meet. Great guy.'

'I've too much on, really. Why don't you ask Trevor?'

'I wasn't sure if you two were—'

'A couple? Being seen together? Everything's all right now, between us anyway. We sorted it out on holiday.'

'Good for you, Annie. Great, fantastic. Such good news, really. It put me in an impossible position. I did suspect that there was something going on with Trevor and Lucinda. But what could I say? How could I tell him how to behave? And then. I just assumed your marriage was fairly relaxed, open, I didn't think it was that important.'

Annie flashed a deliberate, flirtatious smile.

'No, I'm sure you didn't.'

'Shame the press started sniffing around, shame Lucinda wasn't just another spotty researcher from Essex University – but there you go.'

'But she isn't.'

'So what is she? A hip chick who fancies herself as a writer, likes a fun time and happens to be Lord Sherwood's daughter. She's used to having attention, but she's still a kid. I always said she should have come on *Splash!*. But you wouldn't listen, would you?'

'If she'd gone to you, how would that have changed anything? Trevor would have still have met her.'

'Ah yes, but I would have got there first.'

'I don't think she fancies you, Gavin.'

'That often makes it more interesting,' he said, with a dismissive laugh. 'But it would have meant trouble. Trevor couldn't handle Lucinda, but I'm not sure I could either. He's well out of it.'

'Out of it? When he comes home to a great press reception? It wasn't fun for either of us, Gavin.'

'I know, I know. But no-one takes it seriously. You don't, I hope?'

'Oh no, Gavin. I love every minute of it.'

Gavin kept a smile on his face, and decided to drop the subject. Over the weeks, he had been stepping up his campaign to win over Lord Sherwood. All it took was a series of quiet meetings at his Albany flat, briefing sessions over a few glasses of Scotch about what was really happening at Intertel. And they got on rather well. Sherwood liked bright young men, as long as his daughter didn't marry one. Gavin thought he'd better mention that Annie Griffiths, whose drama they both agreed was an unnecessary drain on Intertel's resources, was having trouble with her husband. His name, unfortunately, had been linked to Lucinda's, usual rumours. Shortly afterwards – the timing had to be right – Gavin met a Wapping media correspondent for a quiet drink. Before he left, he dropped a little item of gossip, knowing it would be passed on. Sherwood went spare when he read the story a few days later.

Being a straightforward working-class lad, which was how Gavin saw himself, he was surprised at how easy it all was. He was getting quite good at the politics game. Sherwood said the Tories needed someone like him. One day, Gavin thought, he might even give it a try.

'When am I going to see *Rough Trade*, Annie? I was thinking perhaps of doing something on it, just before it goes out. November, isn't it?'

'November 19.'

'I could bring in a couple of heavy fems, discussion on the male identity crisis, the blurring of gender roles, that kind of stuff. How does that grab you?'

'Can't you find a different angle?'

'Sure. Let's talk nearer the time. Any ideas, let me know and I'll pencil in a slot. Call me any time. I'll be in Chicago for a week, then Brussels . . . Jesus, I'd forgotten about the Berlin trip. Must rush, Annie. Great to see you. Ciao.'

By mid October, *Rough Trade* was as near perfection as it would ever be. The title music irked her, every time she heard it she saw that black-and-white room, but it was too late now, too expensive to change. She no longer hurried away from Intertel, her spirits lifting as she was driven towards Langton Villas. The Saab was in a garage somewhere, it saved time using an Intertel driver, and she rarely took it out.

'I live for my work. I want to be at it when I'm eighty,' was in the cuttings book kept religiously by Anita, although she didn't remember saying it. There had been so many interviews, she hadn't kept count, a spate of features on Annie Griffiths, *Rough Trade*, articles giving her views on current social issues, new drama, Hollywood cinema, the return of power dressing, retrospective, talks at the National Film Theatre and of course, an extended profile on *Splash!* By now, the Controller of Publicity had impressed on all the hacks that Annie Griffiths refused to touch upon her private life. With a woman in her position, there was precious little of that. Her husband supported her in everything she did. What had happened in the past was not their concern. It was not newsworthy. Lucinda Sherwood was out of London, working on a new show. She, too, would talk to no-one.

Annie wasn't aware that her behaviour had changed, any more than she was aware that she was either working or meeting people eighteen hours a day, except when Trevor said, 'Annie, stop asking me questions all the time.' Then she apologized. It was something she said automatically, she realized that. You never got over it, some women said. Something had gone, something was numb. Neither she nor Trevor had mentioned Lucinda again, but Trevor had suggested they went away somewhere different next year. Annie was non-committal. She was sinking into an ordinary marriage, a tetchy exchange of information, routine enquiries about domestic matters, one person coming in, another going out, food's in the fridge, video's on record, don't forget your dental appointment, be back late, don't wait up, I'll be late as well. Annie hadn't invited anyone round for a meal for a while, she could never manage a free evening and, besides, Kate was supervising the building of the new kitchen, now once more walled up. The furniture from Bonham's Out of Africa sale was still smothered in polythene, carved black stools and benches, the honey-gold wicker chairs and settees piled up beside them, waiting for the final touches in the living room. Kate had finally decided on African décor, warm oranges and greens, black torsos balanced against the wall, zigzag patterns in hangings, and specially dyed matting, yellowy brown like autumn grass. When it was completed, they'd have a party, but it was taking a long time and Annie couldn't think of parties, not for a while.

One night, Annie dreamed that the cottage had burned down. Trying to rid herself of the image of leaping flames and charred rafters, she woke Trevor.

'What does it mean?' she said in panic.

'You're worrying about *Rough Trade*,' Trevor murmured, his eyes still closed. 'You always have bad dreams before a series goes out. Don't you remember? Nothing will happen. Go to sleep.'

'I want to go down there,' Annie said emphatically.

'Then we'll go, darling. Even though it'll be cold.'

At the last minute, Annie asked Kate and Dally to go with them, but Kate excused herself, Gordon said he might drop by. Annie no longer added him to her invitation, she could no longer bear Kate's brave disappointment when he promised, but failed to turn up. Then she asked Bryonie, but Bryonie said she had friends staying, and she, too, declined. Trevor caught her as she was phoning some other friends they hadn't seen for a while.

'Annie. Let's go down on our own. Why do we have to have people all the time?'

'They're not people, they're my cousins,' said Annie, aborting the call. 'They're Dave and Anna. I told them ages ago we'd invite them down.'

'Not this weekend.'

Annie looked surprised. 'What's special about this weekend?'

'I want to be with you. Just you, Annie.'

'I've got some work to do, I'll have to take that down. And I haven't time to do the shopping. There aren't any warm clothes down there, either. We need some extra duvets. Really, Trev, I just haven't time to think about it. By the time we get there, we'll have to be starting back. Or I will, at any rate. And it's bound to be damp.'

'I'll get some eggs and bacon from Gillian.'

'Gillian?'

'The farmer's wife, you remember. And some fresh creamy milk. Then you can wake up to your favourite breakfast. Wouldn't that be good? And we can walk across the fields, the weather's going to be fine they said, but even if it isn't—'

'I'm not sure if I feel like going.'

'Annie,' said Trevor gently. 'I do. And I would like you to come.'

'Oh, all right,' replied Annie, grudgingly. 'As long as I don't have to bother with anything. I can't leave until after six.'

'Then we'll leave after six. I'll drive.'

'No, I'm not going in that thing,' said Annie, vehemently. 'We'll take the Saab. I'll drive.'

By the time they approached the cottage, night clouds were swirling across the moon, and a wind was creaking the trees. An animal had just scuttled across the road.

'What was that?' Annie said, pushing her foot down on the brake.

'Looked like a hare.'

'How do you know?'

277

'Larger than a rabbit, long ears. They have them in this part of the world.'

'I've never seen one.'

'You would, if you came more often.'

'What's that meant to mean?'

'Nothing, Annie. It was a simple statement of fact. I'd slow down if I were you. You turn off to the left, after the next bend. The trees look different now, it's easy to miss.'

'I know where it is.'

Annie accelerated and bumped down the track until she saw the dim white walls of the cottage. When they stopped, Annie kept in the warmth of the car while Trevor strode up to the entrance, illuminated by the beam of the headlights.

'It hasn't burned down,' he called out. 'No-one's broken in. Doesn't the willow tree look beautiful? It's seems to like it there, at the side of the house. Are you coming?'

Annie switched off the engine, stepped out of the car and ran up to the porch, shivering. Inside, she was assailed by the dank, musty smell of closed doors, damp rugs and lack of habitation. She stood with her Burberry raincoat wrapped round her, as Trevor methodically laid the fire, small twigs, firelighter, newspaper and then applied a couple of matches. The fire roared up, and gobbets of soot scattered from the chimney.

'When were we last here? I was trying to work it out,' said Annie.

'Oh, just before you finished shooting, I think. Some time around then. Aren't you glad you came? There should be a couple of bottles here somewhere.'

The fire warmed into a blaze and Trevor turned off the lamps. Suddenly Annie jumped, she could hear a phone ringing.

'They've connected the line,' said Trevor hurriedly. A moment later, she heard his feet pounding up the wooden stairs. Sounds were amplified in the country, they seemed to disregard walls and ceilings. Now she heard his feet crossing, going to their bedroom, but there was no answering voice. Annie came to the bottom of the stairs.

'I thought the idea was not to have a phone. Why, Trev?'

'One day, when I was here on my own, it just crossed my mind. Supposing anything happened? I'm afraid I do think of these things, now I do. It was reassuring to know I could call a doctor, that's all. I told you I was going to.'

'You didn't, Trevor.'
'Don't let's argue. Maybe I forgot.'
'Who was it, anyway?'
'A wrong number.'

Annie aimed a small log onto the fire from where she was sitting, and watched the sparks firing up the chimney like tracer bullets. A cork detonated in the kitchen, and she could hear a thud as it hit the ceiling and bounced down again. Then Trevor came rushing in, and decanted the champagne into two tumblers. Suddenly he did something from years back, he raised his glass upwards, then swept it towards her and put it to her lips. They used to cross glasses like that, in the days when he used to light a cigarette in his mouth, remove it slowly and put it in hers. Annie reluctantly completed the gesture and took a sip. Then they both lay on their sides in front of the fire.

'Aren't you glad you came? Isn't it wonderful, darling?'
'Yes,' said Annie.
She had hoped so desperately that the numb feeling would retire, like a tiresome visitor, that the excitement would return, blood coursing round her veins. It was like waking up one morning and finding yourself ten years older, everything moving slower, the world moving faster out of reach.

'Are you happy at Intertel?' Trevor began.
'Everything's fine,' said Annie.
'We haven't talked about it for so long. Well, you understand why.'
'Yes,' Annie repeated. 'Everything's fine.'
'You made the right decision. I know it was hard to do. And I understand why you didn't want to talk about it.'
'Who told you that? Did she tell you or was it Gavin?'
'Neither. Rick told me. He was impressed, Annie. You've no idea how he admires you.'
'He certainly never lets on.'
'You know Rick. Actually, he said if it had been him, he would have sacked her.'
'Maybe I should have done.'
'No, no, Annie. Absolutely not.'
'I've always tried to do things, go along with my instinct. But I'm beginning to think it holds you back. Remember when everyone said the whole power structure would change when

279

women fought for their rightful place? It doesn't work, Trev. If you aren't how men expect you to be, one of the club, they'll knock you down.'

'That's not true, darling. Look at what women have achieved, fighting for themselves.'

'What, exactly? Am I where I am because of the women's struggle? Did Margaret Thatcher stand on the shoulders of the feminists? And where are the women on the board of Intertel?'

'That will come, Annie. They'll follow your example, but give it time. The ideas of Christianity took hundreds of years to permeate. Socialism, feminism, these ideas are like tiny infants still. I know it's easy to forget this, working in a place like Intertel. But don't get disheartened.'

'It must be all these interviews I've been giving. After a while, you stop believing what you say. But you have to keep on saying it.'

'It only seems like it . . . Isn't it time we went to bed, darling?'

'I thought we were talking.'

'We can talk in bed.'

'The mattress will be damp.'

'Not up there, it won't. I put the fan heater on.'

Annie let Trevor's hands criss-cross her body, stroking across her breasts, along her thighs. The rush of the fan-heater recalled the wind sighing through the rushes on the dunes at Paradisos. There was a candle on a stool beside the bed, the flame dancing this way and that in the draught. He wanted to see her body, he said. She wanted it dark, but said nothing. All the while, he was murmuring to her, how he longed for her, how much he loved her, loved her, loved her. Drawing his hair down her torso, licking down her belly, he parted her legs then touched her lightly with his hot tongue, then again until she began to twitch.

'Come to me, come to me, my love,' he whispered, while he waited for the quivering to break out into a shudder, for the first signs of orgasm to respond to his touch. But she was unable to respond, the release she hoped for was always just out of reach.

'I can't, Trev,' Annie said, pushing away his head with her hand.

The words he had whispered were strange, new, uttered by someone she did not know, she had never heard them before.

The first glimmering of pleasure had turned to a searing frustration.

'What's that?' Annie exclaimed. Something was tapping against the window.

'A butterfly trying to get out.'

Annie sat up and saw black fluttering wings hurling against the pane.

'It's a moth. Do open the window.'

Trevor jumped out of bed, and then she could see his body, outlined against the window, buttocks tensing as he pushed up the uneasy sash. It reminded her of something, another occasion, her lying in bed, a naked man pushing up a window. Mel. Panting with heat, sweat pouring over them both, opening the window to let in the cool air in that hotel where they stayed. She could recall him by the window, but couldn't remember what the room looked like. His shoulders were broad, unlike Trevor's, fine dark hairs down his back, muscled calves and sturdy feet. Annie shut her eyes and tried to bring back that frenzy, his jumping inside her, then rolling over and over on the floor, until she was dizzy. She tried to superimpose that image from the past, but she failed to remember how he smelt, or why he had sent her reeling into the warm darkness.

'Lie back, Annie. Let's try again. Feel, I'm so hard. Aren't you proud, that I'm still like this for you?' Annie lay back, motionless. 'Don't you want to, darling? Let me come inside you, I don't mind if you lie still, there's no need to rush.'

She tried to tell herself how patient he was being, how hard he was trying to please her, but her transient moment of desire had changed into a longing to flee to Kate's bedroom, to be alone in that little narrow bed.

'Or if you don't want me to touch you, touch yourself. You know how I love that, watching you stroking, with your eyes closed. You're so beautiful, lying there. Annie, let me love you.'

'I can't,' she said again. 'I just can't.'

She could see him in the gloom, his head rising to look down at her, and tears welled in her eyes. Then he lowered himself to lie down over her, his hands cupped round the back of her head. She closed her eyes, knowing that his were open, trying to trace every flicker of emotion passing across her face.

'It shouldn't matter, my love. I'll never feel for anyone what I feel for you. I wish I could prove it.'

'I never asked you to prove anything. Why do men have

281

to prove things?' Annie murmured. Then, succeeding her frustration came a wave of anger, though Trevor would only see her eyes, wide open now, large black pupils shining in the candlelight. With one hand, she closed her fingers tightly round the base of his cock, opened her legs and pushed in the soft tip. Then she flung out her arms, stretching towards each side of the bed. Trevor was clutching her waist, pushing deeper and deeper, and then he rolled her over.

'I want you to come with me,' he said. His hand was holding her buttocks as he drove himself inside her, and then his finger was stroking down the divide. He was nearing his climax, panting, grunting and Annie too was beginning to pant, the moisture lapping round his cock. He used to put his hand over her mouth when she laughed, squelch, squelch, but she wasn't laughing now. And then his finger was inside, furrowing down her anus so that the unexpected pain, the alien gesture, fuelled her rage, and she screamed and flailed and cursed, swept out of herself by an angry release and buried her head in the pillow.

'Annie? Are you all right?'

She lay still for a couple of minutes, breathing in the smell of stale, damp feathers. She imagined that she could detect that strange perfume on the night air, coming from afar, seeping up through the bedclothes, gaining in intensity with the heat of their bodies. You could have the memory of a smell which lingered in your nostrils, even when it wasn't there, it could be recalled like the bars of a song.

'Is there any hot water?' she asked, as she turned over on her back.

'Not yet. Give it an hour or so, darling. Do you have to have a bath? I didn't hurt you, did I? Did you like it like that?'

'Not particularly.'

'But you came. And we both wanted to.'

He placed his head on her breasts, deep breaths of content-ment, his legs between hers.

'I love you, Annie. And I want to make love to you more often.'

'It makes me tired. Although it seems to have the opposite effect with you. I wonder why? Nature wanting me nice and quiet so the egg won't be disturbed? So the sperm won't be shaken out?'

Trevor laughed.

'It doesn't work like that.'

'You're heavy on my breasts, Trev.'

'Here.'

Trevor changed his position, lay on his side and pulled Annie towards him.

'Are you still on the Pill?'

'Yes. Why?'

'Would you rather not be?'

'I'm not having a coil again.'

'I didn't mean that. Darling, would you like . . . would you consider having a baby? I was thinking, it's been a very one-sided decision, a selfish one on my part. It's taken me a long time, but I feel I could cope with it now. I had a letter from Edward, he's coming over from Australia, wants to see me before he gets married. He wants us to sort things out. But Edward is only part of it, Annie. At long last, I feel ready to be a dad again. I'd help, I'd make it as easy as I could.'

Annie sat up abruptly, switched on the bedside light and stared at Trevor in disbelief.

'Really? You really want a child, Trev? I'm forty-two.'

'There's no need to look so alarmed. Lots of women have babies when they're over forty. Look at Kate, she was nearly forty, wasn't she, when she had Dally? There were no problems, as far as I remember. And you're much stronger and healthier than Kate.'

'I can't take time off, Trev. It's not possible.'

'Darling, you mustn't think like that. Just let the idea sink in. Intertel haven't the right to dictate whether or not you should get pregnant. And since *Rough Trade* is bound to be a success, isn't this the right moment to rest on your laurels for a few months?'

'Maybe.'

'I never forgot about the abortion. And I understood why you never talked about it. Looking back, we probably made the wrong decision.'

'I didn't want to have a baby. Not then.'

'It's easy to say that now. But you can't just root out maternal instincts, I recognize that now. I may not have showed it, but I was extremely upset when you had the abortion.'

'Were you? I didn't realize. I don't remember feeling devastated. Perhaps I never had maternal instincts in the first place.'

283

'Of course you did, darling. Only you repressed them.'

'Did I repress them? I didn't notice.'

'Look, I'm not forcing you. I wouldn't dream of forcing you. But I'd be happy to be a father, Annie. In some ways, being older is an advantage. Darling, I want you to have our baby.'

'What did you say?'

'I'd be so happy if you got pregnant.'

'I don't know. Oh, God, I don't know. Trev, do you mean it?'

'I'd help you, support you, we'd do it together. You'd be a wonderful mum, you know that?'

'Big-bellied Annie. I can't imagine it. Suppose it came out with some horrible disease? Or three eyes or something? What would we do then?'

'And suppose it came out as a beautiful, rosy, black-haired baby with slate-grey eyes?'

'Suppose it did.'

'I don't want you to be afraid. Kiss me, Annie.'

Annie put her lips delicately over his, but he thrust his tongue into her mouth, pressing her head down into the pillow. Then he took her in his arms, her head resting on his chest, and they both fell into a profound, dreamless country sleep.

Annie was awakened by a ray of the sun which had escaped through a parting in the curtains, and Trevor failed to stir when she jumped out of bed to survey the rolling landscape, the brown stubble of the fields, and the bare branches of the trees surrounding the farm. Glancing back at Trevor, she pulled on her jeans and a thick sweater. Then she ran out at the back of the cottage and jogged along the side of the field, jumping over the ruts, occasionally throwing her head back to wonder at the pale blue sky. It was just after nine, but even on a Sunday their neighbours would have been up for a couple of hours. She found Gillian feeding the chickens in a yard at the side of the farm.

'We've not seen you for a while,' said Gillian, continuing to scatter the feed in the yard. She was a handsome, round-faced woman who was never still, the kind of farmer's wife who could turn her hand equally to a tractor or a pie.

'We're just here for a day. Trevor's still in bed, so I thought maybe you could give me a few eggs and some milk. I can never find eggs like yours.'

284

'Go into the kitchen. I'll be there in a minute. There's a pot of tea on the table. Help yourself.'

Annie was planning their breakfast. If he was still asleep when she returned, he would be woken up by spitting bacon and sizzling eggs. She had never thought it could happen, the return of that kind of love. It was only when she saw the morning sun, that she realized it. He wanted a child. As yet, there was no voice saying 'yes, yes, now' but that didn't matter. What mattered was what he had said, what he had meant. As though they had travelled thousands of miles since that summer, the summer of distress, and they had reached a place to settle.

'You look well, in spite of London,' said Gillian, stomping in with mud-caked boots. 'You'll be retiring down here soon, I s'pose. Getting out of it all. People retire early nowadays. I went to London in June but it was too dirty for me.'

'I'm not ready yet,' replied Annie, with a grin. 'Right this minute, I'm starving.'

'What do you want?'

'Six eggs, a few slices of bread if you have some.'

'Milk and bacon, I expect.'

Annie nodded, enjoying the lack of ceremony, the simple attention to needs.

'I saw you had some friends from London a short while back. My husband was passing, they'd left the headlights on, full on mind. He thought they'd be dropping in, asking for a lead. But they never did. Battery must have been flat, though.'

'Doesn't sound like Trev, to do that. Was it a red car?'

'I'll ask Phil. Phil! You in there?'

A ruddy, unshaven face appeared round the door.

'Hello, Annie.'

'That car you saw down at Honeysuckle Cottage with the lights on, was it a red one? Only she was wondering.'

'Black one. Saloon. German car, Audi or Mercedes, something like that, or it could have been Japanese, can't tell the difference me, they all look the same.'

'Do you remember when it was? Only we don't always know who stays. Trevor gives keys to people sometimes, and doesn't bother to tell me.'

'Oooh, difficult to say. A week, ten days? Could have been a Wednesday or a Tuesday. They didn't stay long. Must have got it started somehow, it wasn't there when I passed by later.'

Gillian handed Annie a plastic bag.

'Careful with the eggs. It's all in there.'

Annie returned along the path skirting the field, remembered she hadn't offered to pay, and decided not to turn back. By the time she reached the cottage, Trevor was up. She greeted him cheerfully and presented him with the breakfast she had promised, sending him back to bed. She knew she would never do this again, it was like a last rite in honour of the past. Trevor praised the colour of the yolks, the taste of bacon he remembered as a child, joked about the crumbs in the bed, said it was time they had clean sheets, he'd change them before they left. Annie said, don't bother.

'Darling, we haven't said anything since Greece. Or rather, you haven't said anything. I feel it's only right for me to tell you how things are. I don't want to hide behind us both being busy, not the right moment and so on.'

'I'm listening,' said Annie, leaning hard against the brass bed-head. She took the tray, leaned over and placed it on the floor without rattling the cups, though it was an effort. Above all, she had to force herself to remain calm. She must listen, consider his point of view, knowing what he would say. It was over. She would practise it being over, as though they had just met after a long period, for friendship's sake. You had to prevent your ex-husband becoming an enemy, even before the lawyers heated the cauldron.

'I'm still seeing Lucinda.'

'I thought so,' replied Annie. 'Rather, I guessed.'

'Do you want me to talk about it?'

'That would be best.' She was trying to sound reasonable, the reasonable wife.

'It has everything to do with us – and nothing. I meant all I said about the baby, about wanting your child. This is very difficult to explain. It will seem bizarre, maybe it won't make sense. But I can't live without Lucinda. And I can't live without you. I do so need your help. We have to reach the right decision, together.'

'How, Trevor?' Annie said, looking him in the face but he was staring at his hands, gently resting on the duvet.

'To resolve the situation in the best way possible. I think there is a solution, but I don't know whether you will, whether you could accept it. It's only a suggestion, an idea.'

'What kind of idea?' asked Annie, smiling sweetly.

'I love you. And I love Lucinda. I can't do without either of

286

you. What's the point of destroying what we all have with one another, for the sake of convention? There's no reason why we couldn't all be happy.'

'Living together?' asked Annie. 'Is it a *ménage à trois* we're considering here?'

'No, not at all. That's far too calculated. This would be three people relating to one another, who care about one another, who like one another . . .'

'Go on, Trev.' Annie held her breath in amazement.

'Not necessarily in the same house, but near.'

'And which days would I have?'

'I know it must sound strange.'

'I'm listening. Tell me.'

'I see it more as houses with open doors. If we wanted to do things together, we would. If we wanted to be alone, fine. Sometimes we'd eat together, sometimes we'd see movies together, if you were working, there'd be one of us caring for the child.'

Annie looked at Trevor, perplexed. Then she decided it was a game. Trevor's game to test her out.

'Oh, I think I'd want to have an au pair. I wouldn't want the child to be a burden. After all, you and Lucinda will both be working. Isn't that right? Or do we all go off and live in the country?'

'We'd have to work that out, between us. I know I'm asking a great deal of you, darling, or perhaps I'm not.'

'What does Lucinda think of this idea? Have you discussed it?'

'I mentioned it a couple of times, in a light-hearted way. We never went into detail.'

'About sex, for example.' Annie managed a giggle. It was becoming so absurd, she was beginning to enjoy planning out this fictional ménage. 'As long as I don't end up with Mondays. I hate Mondays. But I quite like Saturdays. It's awkward, that there's seven days in a week. Or would you like a day off?'

'Look, in the end, would it be any different from being a friend, like it is with Rick, Bryonie and Kate? Except that sometimes I'd go to bed with you, sometimes with Lucinda. Could you accept that?'

'It would take some getting used to, I admit. Specially for a little Welsh girl from the valleys. I don't think we've had a *ménage à trois* in the Griffiths family.'

'I know it sounds ludicrous if you start talking about it in the abstract. But I think it could work and we'd make absolutely sure that it was a discreet arrangement. There's no need for any but close friends to know.'

'Who gets to take your shirts to the laundry, Trev?'

'Oh, I'll do that.'

At that point, Annie burst into giggles. At least Trevor had the grace to smile.

'What if I said no to the arrangement? What then?'

'I couldn't promise not to see Lucinda.'

'I tell you what. Why don't you see as much as you like of Lucinda, then we'll discuss it in a few weeks. When *Rough Trade*'s on the road. I promise I won't be difficult, and I won't ask questions. Perhaps I'll get used to the idea, little by little.'

'That's a lot to ask of you.'

'No, no. I mean it.'

'Annie, darling, you're the most generous person I've ever met. And I love you more than ever.'

'Do you fancy a walk? A good long one? Or shall we get down to the garden?'

Crunching over the dry stalks of the field, Annie barely felt them scratching her ankles. The wind was making her eyes water, but she didn't notice that either. And she kept a few steps ahead of Trevor so that it was difficult to maintain a conversation.

On Monday morning, the Location Controller at Intertel received an unexpected memo from Annie Griffiths. 'Have informed cast and crew to be on standby for one day *Rough Trade* insert. Place and time to be announced.' He was puzzled, since *Rough Trade* had finished shooting weeks ago. Typical Annie Griffiths, changing her mind. Hastily taking a copy of the memo, plus a print-out of the latest budget statement for *Rough Trade* and enclosing both in an envelope marked 'Confidential', he delivered it by hand to Gavin's office.

16

TREVOR

'How did Annie react? What did she say?'

'I think she was excited by the idea. It was my fault, that she'd put it out of her mind. She was obviously thinking about it but she didn't refer to it. Do you mind my talking about this?'

'No. Why should I?'

'I don't want to keep anything from you. And it's what I love about you. I can speak freely. It did help, Annie knowing that I'd been through it before.'

'With Edward.'

'Yes. Though it will be a totally different experience. I can't see Annie being child-bound.'

'Absolutely not. She wouldn't be one of those ghastly women who talk baby all day. And she wouldn't drag it around on location and make a thing about heaving out her breasts. I don't think babies should be stuck with their mothers all the time. We weren't. We were just left to get on with it. How can you be independent otherwise?'

'Of course, you can't always tell what will happen. Annie's much more bound by the narrow tradition of the Welsh valleys than she'd care to admit. If she'd stayed in Wales, she would have been perfectly happy bringing up kids, looking after a husband. In some ways, she's conventional. I think you have to be, at some level, to work in television.'

'How can you possibly say she's conventional? Annie, of all people.'

'She's getting that way. Wearing a jacket and skirt, for example.'

'Honestly! If I was Controller of Drama, I'd do the same.'

'And she never wants to go too far from what's expected. Give it a new slant, perhaps, but without rocking the boat.'

'I don't believe that.'

'Why not, sweetheart?'

'If she was like that, how could she accept us being together? If people are honest, Annie takes them for what they are. And she never pushes her views if you don't agree. That's why actors love her, she listens.'

'It did come as a surprise, that she was willing to consider the idea. But then Annie has always been practical, unlike me.'

'Annie's a sharing person. And we'd both be getting on with our work, helping one another. It's the most wonderful way to be. The artist is always trying to escape isolation. And it's not as though we'd be sharing the kitchen, it wouldn't be like being stuck in some ghastly commune. But you know I couldn't possibly live in Kentish Town? That would be dreadful, I'd curl up and die.'

'I know, I know. But we could always move.'

'There are loads of houses up for sale near me. I never said we had to live in the same place. As long as you're near by. But I couldn't bear living with a yawling baby.'

'I suppose I could get used to living in Chelsea. And Annie might get to like it, eventually. Do they have good nursery schools in Chelsea?'

'You couldn't have better. Annie will love it.'

'How about you? I worry about you.'

'I've told you, it's the best thing that could happen. I'd be really, really pleased.'

'It wouldn't upset you, that she was having something I couldn't give you?'

'You give me everything I want. And I don't want you to give me nappies, thank you very much. As long as we can still go away together, and eat together, go to movies, and parties, and talk and have amazing sex—'

'Darling, you make it so easy to love you. But are you sure you don't mind that Annie and I, that we'd still—'

'Have sex? Why should I mind? I know married people do it occasionally.'

'Very occasionally.'

'But not like we do it.'

'No, not like we do it.'

'Shall we do it again?'

'Can't I have a rest?'

'You've had at least five hours' sleep.'

'In a little while, then. There's no hurry. We can stay till tomorrow if you like.'

'Great! I thought you'd be driving back.'

'What about you? Can you stay, my love?'

'They can do without me. It's such a bore. I thought it would be a laugh, being in comedy. But they take it all terribly seriously. And I could write better jokes.'

'I'm sure you could. I must remember to call Annie, to let her know I'll be down here another night.'

'Sure. Later, we can go to the Hall. Daddy's staying in town.'

'You're sure that none of the family will be there?'

'There might be a couple of staff around, that's all. Anyway, everyone's used to us bringing our friends. Tim might be around, he's screwing some awful PR girl at the moment. You really do want to be a father again, don't you?'

'I'm getting round to quite liking the idea. Of course, there's always the fear that you'll produce a very average child. Edward was bright, from what I remember, but not enormously intelligent. He resembled Margaret more than me. I'd like you to meet him. Eventually.'

'I hope he's not too good-looking. I might fall for him.'

'Far too young for you, darling. And besides, he's getting married.'

'Then he'll be too straight for me. I can't stand people who marry young. It's as though they can't think of anything else to do. Should we get up? Go for a walk, come back to bed again?'

'Let's stay in bed for a while.'

'We could always walk over to the Hall this afternoon. Or I could get someone to drive and collect us.'

'Do servants have cars nowadays?'

'You're being a tease. You know they do. Anyway, they're not servants.'

'What are they?'

'I told you, they're the staff. And they have nice little studio flats, they're not forced into a freezing garret, or stuck below stairs in case you thought that.'

'Sweetheart, I don't have a clue about your father's domestic arrangements.'

'Everyone at Intertel imagines our whole family changes for dinner every night and natters about television over the port and stilton. We don't even do that when we're all at the Hall. We live just like everyone else.'

'Of course you do . . . Ow! That hurt.'

'I know you think I'm a spoilt bitch. There! I like pinching you. And then—'

'Just you wait.'

'I'm going to make a teeny bite—'

'No, no. You can't do that.'

'Yes, I can. Just here, on your bottom. So you'll think of me every time you sit down.'

'You won't get away with that, my girl.'

'I will, I will.'

'You think you can do just what you like? Is that it?'

'Anything I like. So there. No, no, don't pull my hair. I don't like it.'

'What else don't you like?'

'Having my bottom smacked.'

'Then that's what we'll do then.'

'No, no. Don't do that.'

'Please. Say please.'

'Please don't do that. No, no, no,' she cried, as his hand came crashing down on her taut, pebble-smooth buttocks, precisely aimed on the lower part, where the flesh rounded neatly into the top of her thighs. After a few strokes, she tore herself away and threw herself at him, squeaking, scratching, biting so that he had to hold her wrists in a vice-like grip. He threw her on the bed, pinning them behind her back, and with one hand covered her mouth. With the other, he arranged her underneath him, and stroked the damp inner side of her thighs. Once he had penetrated, he rolled over on his back, she had stopped struggling now, inserted his finger in the pulsing hole, and began the slow rhythm towards climax.

'Oh, God. You're so fantastic, Trevor. A dreamy lover. But I knew you would be, right from the start.'

'How did you know that?'

'The way you walked. The way you held your head. Your eyes had a kind of concentrated look as though you wanted to eat me.'

Her lips were fluttering over his, small pecks all over his face.

'Kiss me properly.'

'I'm doing it properly.'

'No, you're not. Let me show you.'

He put his mouth over hers, pressed open her mouth, and kept his tongue inside, swirling round, sucking, licking, feeling her tongue, the hot wet walls of her cheeks. She began to grunt as he pressed and then when they were both breathless, she moved onto her back. Their act was over, she wanted to lie with a tiny space between them, a few inches for recollection, he understood that.

'Trevor, I thought I heard something outside,' she said, after a few minutes of silence.

'Don't worry. Annie won't be coming. I told you, she went to Wales to see her mum, staying over till this evening. And she said she might stay longer. It'll be our neighbour coming over with some eggs and milk. He often does, if he sees a car outside.'

'I hope he's not nosy.'

'Phil? Hardly. He says very little. That's one of the things I've learned to like about the country, they accept things.'

'It sounds like shuffling feet in the grass.'

'Maybe some cows got in. Don't get up.'

'I'm curious.'

Lucinda drew up her legs, swung down off the bed and walked over to the window.

'Nothing but empty field. And it's going to rain. Do you mind walking in the rain?'

'Not with you. And I've brought our big, black umbrella.'

She smiled as Trevor watched her face, a languorous, after-sex smile. Then she tilted back her head, listening.

'Trevor, I can hear a car.'

'Are you sure? If it's not the farmer, it'll be the vicar. He sometimes drops by. If he knocks, we'll ignore it.'

'I'm going to have a look.'

'Put a towel round you, in case he looks up and thinks he's seen the devil.'

She laughed, took a towel which was hanging from the brass bedrail, and began to dry herself between her legs, one leg propped up on the bed.

'I'll do that.'

But before he had time, she had wrapped the towel round her chest and left the room. Now he could hear it, the sound of a vehicle whining in second gear. There seemed to be another behind it, a heavy form of transport like an army of builders on the move. For one terrifying moment, Trevor had a vision of the cottage being demolished, knocked by swinging concrete weights into a pile of supine rubble. Lucinda came running back into the bedroom.

'I can't believe it. Come and see, come and see.'

Trevor pulled on his underpants and followed Lucinda into Kate and Dally's room at the front of the cottage. Lucinda pressed her face to the pane and stared out in disbelief. A large van, emblazoned with the Intertel logo, was backing into the tractor turning-point leading from the track. Two Mercedes estates were parking on the rough verge which flanked the track, nearer the cottage. Behind them were two others, then a third.

'My God!' said Trevor. 'What the hell is happening?'

He backed off from the window, and viewed the scene a few feet back, his stomach churning.

'They're getting out equipment. There's the director, Hugh, I recognize him. Look, it's a shoot. Annie's going down the path to meet them. Has she been downstairs all this time? Didn't Annie say anything to you? Didn't you tell her you were coming down?'

'Of course I did. We agreed I wouldn't hide anything.'

'Gosh! I wonder how long she's been there? Do you think she heard us?'

'Get back from the window. Keep quiet, we might find out what's going on.'

They both retreated to the edge of Kate's bed, legs tightly together, Trevor's arm protectively round Lucinda's shoulders.

'What should we do, Trevor?'

'We don't have to do anything.'

'Supposing someone comes up? How do we explain that you're in your underpants and I'm dressed in a towel?'

He was holding her hand, gripping it tightly.

'We're not criminals. This is my cottage. I didn't give them permission to come here. Annie must have forgotten.'

'I ought to get some clothes on. Someone might come upstairs.'

'Better to wait a little. We shouldn't move around, you know how creaky the boards are. I can't understand. She knew I was coming down.'

'Did you tell her I was coming?'

'I didn't say you weren't.'

'That's not the same, Trevor.'

'There was no need to spell it out. I just don't understand.

It can't be deliberate. Something must have happened, you know how Annie is. You suddenly need a certain shot, she would have suggested coming here, without thinking. Annie's like that sometimes.'

'But she knows we're here. She'll have seen our cars.'

'You're right. So why didn't she come upstairs, to check if we were here?'

'Perhaps she did. When we were at it. Oh, Trevor, how awful. You can hear everything in this cottage.'

Lucinda was biting her lower lip, an embarrassed flush tingeing her neck, her cheeks. Trevor was quiet for a moment. It was not like Annie, to come sneaking around. There was nothing to be ashamed about, she knew they had sex. He felt humiliated, then irritated. If Annie wanted to make it worse, to hurt herself, this was the way to do it. She might not have heard the squeaks but she would have heard the slaps. He was upset about that – he didn't want Annie to think he harboured secret perversions when he didn't.

'I think the best thing to do is to sit here for a bit.'

'If they're doing exteriors, they won't be long and they won't be coming in. I'll take another quick look.'

'Sh. Keep your voice down. Stay here. Let's listen.'

They could hear the sound of shouting voices outside, coming from the garden, by the shed, all around the cottage.

'We'll get some sun in a minute. The cloud's moving.'

'Won't be for long.'

'Quick. Bash some light on the wall.'

'Where's Clary?'

'Make-up.'

'Get her out here. It's only a silhouette, we won't see her face.'

'Where the bloody hell's George?'

'Getting another mike.'

'This is a guide track, for fuck's sake.'

'Take it easy, Ned.'

'It's coming out. Move your arse. We've got three minutes at most. Get the artists in position.'

Lucinda was now sitting cross-legged on the bed and she suddenly repressed a giggle, placing a hand across her mouth before whispering to Trevor.

'It suddenly struck me. It's really rather amusing. Us sitting on the bed and waiting with no clothes on. Why don't I find somewhere to hide? Like under the bed? And you could go in the wardrobe.'

'No, no. We can't hide.'

'Then why don't we go downstairs? I'll say I dropped over for tea.'

'Who's going to believe that? They'll see through the windows that we've suddenly appeared downstairs. It'll be obvious.'

'Let's be obvious. I don't care. I bet we have a laugh about it afterwards.'

At that moment, they heard footsteps shuffling around outside the front door.

'It's open.'

'Super place. Just right.'

'Which bedroom for the set-up, Annie?'

'The back one's best, overlooking the fields. You should get enough light in there. I'll wait outside. There's not much room, as you can see.'

'Come on, move, folks.'

What seemed like a contingent of the SAS began to storm the stairs.

'Mind the walls.'

'OK.'

'Which one?'

'No, not that one. This one. The back one.'

'OK, squire.'

Then a voice from downstairs.

'Ready for artists?'

'Not yet.'

Trevor could feel his heart pounding against his chest. Lucinda went over to a small wooden wardrobe pasted over with Dally's artwork and opened it out. Inside, was a pair of child's dungarees hanging from a Peter Rabbit hanger. From the floor of the wardrobe, Lucinda picked up a pair of Kate's jeans.

'Could you get into those?' she whispered, still giggling.

'No. Not possible.'

'I could.'

'What would you wear on top? There's only one thing to do. Get into this bed, I can go in the wardrobe. Pretend to be ill or asleep or something if someone comes in. I'll wrap myself in this ridiculous rug.'

Trevor pulled off a woollen patchwork rug from Kate's bed and attempted to knot it round his waist.

'This is a drama crew, they won't have a clue who you are.'

'Sh. Someone's outside the door.'

They heard a click, then a loud voice from the main bedroom.

'Standby for insert scene three five six A.'

Outside the door, someone was intoning, as though in church.

'*Rough Trade* insert. Guidetrack. Scene three five six A.'

'Action.'

Shuffle, shuffle.

'Cut.'

'What's up?'

'Mistake in continuity. Clary's dress wasn't buttoned at the neck.'

'Well spotted, Gemma.'

'I can't see the bloody dress, not in this light.'

'Best not to risk it.'

'OK. Standby.'

'Running.'

'Action.'

Trevor was beginning to sweat. He rose quietly from the bed and crept towards the window. Lucinda followed him.

'There's no-one out at the front at the moment,' he whispered. 'We could climb out of the window.'

'There's no foothold. Too high. Anyway, I can't go running off in a towel.'

'You're right. How about the bathroom? We could creep in there, lock the door. Stop them coming in, at least.'

'Good idea. As soon as they've gone back downstairs, we'll do that.'

Suddenly the bedroom door slipped from its jamb and gave way. An irate sound-man found himself rolling backwards, clutching his precious machine to his chest.

'Shit! Bloody door!' George shouted, struggling to his feet, clutching the door handle.

Trevor waved frantically to Lucinda and whispered, 'Under the duvet, quick.'

'Beg pardon,' said George, startled once again. 'Didn't know you was in here. Sorry for the disturbance.'

'There's a sick girl in here,' said Trevor.

297

'Sorry. We're shooting a film. Won't be long. Thought they'd have told you.'

'They didn't.'

'Thoughtless, some people. Mind if I leave the door open? There's no room out here. Never enough room, if you ask me.'

'What's happening? What's happening to sound?' called a voice.

'Door collapsed. OK now.'

'Is it damaged?'

Gemma came tripping out, and was face to face with Trevor. It took her only a second to register that there was a human figure underneath the Mickey Mouse duvet.

'Professor Watson, hello. We thought you were out for a walk, well, we saw the cars, naturally, terribly sorry—'

'Just a moment,' said Trevor, pushing the sound-man out and closing the door. 'There's been a terrible mix-up. Annie forgot to tell me. I hope you're not going to be long.'

'Oh, there's only a tiny scene to do in here. Clary, that's our lead actress, wonderful she is, she just has to walk in, she's looking for someone, then she goes out. Simple. It'll only take two ticks. Were you asleep?'

'No. Not exactly. Resting. Trying to get some peace and quiet.'

Gemma smiled in sympathy.

'I'll ask the director if we could do the scene in another room. They're doing the mute cut-aways at the moment. Didn't I see a third bedroom?'

'No good. It's full of junk.'

Then Trevor had an inspiration.

'Gemma. Could you do something for me?'

'Course.'

'Did you notice some clothes over a chair in the back bedroom?'

'We left them. The director thought it looked right, he hates rooms with nothing in.'

'Could you bring them in here?'

'Certainly. When we've finished. Can't disturb them now otherwise we'll be here all night.'

'Gemma!' called a voice. 'What the hell are you doing? We need you in here.'

For what seemed like hours, but was only ten minutes,

Trevor waited in silence, staring at the bump in the duvet. Then there was a knock on the door.

'Here we are!' came a cheery voice.

Gemma was standing with two pairs of jeans, one cashmere sweater, another thicker one, draped over her arm. 'This what you wanted? I found some shoes. Thought you might need those.'

She placed them gingerly at the end of the bed.

'My lips are sealed!' she said, nodding at the bump.

'Did Annie say anything?'

'No, nothing.'

'She's down in the kitchen. You could slip out of the front door.'

'There's no point. Not with our cars stuck out there.'

'Wait up here, then. We'll all be off soon. Annie's going back to London straight away, with the director she said.'

'Thanks a lot, Gemma.'

'No problem,' she said, as she tip-toed out of the room, carefully closing the door behind her. Lucinda's head emerged from the Mickey Mouse duvet.

'They gone?'

Trevor listened.

'Sounds as though they're out of the bedroom.'

'Dying for a wee, Trevor.'

'Get dressed first.'

'Can't wait.'

Trevor opened the door a fraction. There was no sign of cables or lights.

'Off you go.'

Hanging on the door of the bathroom, was an old, faded cotton dressing-gown.

Lucinda threw it on and cautiously opened the door. Suddenly she froze, her hand still on the door-knob. At first, she closed the door again in panic, then opened it again, realizing that she must try and make a pretext of normal behaviour. Annie was standing in front of her, silent for a moment as she registered her dressing-gown, the one she was going to throw out but thought she'd leave, which only reached to Lucinda's knees. Then she stared at her long tanned legs, perfectly painted toe-nails, and the tousled hair.

'Hi, Annie,' said Lucinda, pulling the dressing-gown tightly round her.

Annie stood in front of her, barring her way.

'Lucinda. Get out. Now.'

'But, Annie, I thought you understood. Trevor said—'

'Out.'

Then Annie put her hand firmly round Lucinda's neck and frogmarched her down the stairs, past the silent crew who were waiting by the front door. Still pushing her, she only let go when she had reached the black BMW.

'This is it, Lucinda. We won't meet again. What Trevor does is his own affair. You've made a fool of him, but you're not going to make a fool of me. Now get in.'

Annie opened the car door and Lucinda climbed in, tears streaming down her face.

'I thought you understood. Honestly I did.'

Then Annie slammed the door and walked back to the crew.

'There's still some clearing up to do, Annie,' said Gemma. 'Have you got a Hoover somewhere?'

'Leave it. The cottage will have to be cleaned, before it's put on the market.'

The director approached, tentatively. 'Annie?'

'Yes, Hugh?'

'I'll tell them it's a wrap. We can skip the next scene. It's not essential.'

'You sure?'

'I am. Thanks a lot for letting us use your cottage. It was perfect. Sorry, we should have checked to see if anyone was in. My apologies.'

'Don't apologize,' said Annie. 'I'm glad you got that scene in the can. Is that it?'

'Should be.'

'Let me know if something isn't right.'

'Don't you want to view the rushes?'

'No, I'm sure they'll be fine. I'm thinking about what we'll do for the next series.'

'Great! Any idea when it'll be?'

'No, not yet. Alan will have to give the go-ahead. But you'll be the first to know.'

'Can't wait, Annie. See you at the press show. Will you be all right? Do you want to drive back to London with me? I can drop you home, it's no trouble.'

'No, thanks all the same. I feel great. It's like cleaning out the drains.'

300

'She's disturbed, that girl. Delinquent, I'd say. No-one can stand her in Benny's department.'

'It's sometimes quite a good idea, not to keep things private. Don't you think?'

'I couldn't have done it. I'd have blown off her head with a shotgun.'

'Of course you wouldn't. Only actors in my series do that.'

When they had all left, Annie made herself a cup of tea, then put her portable computer on the kitchen table. New file, new letter. What was the name of the estate agent? Anita would hunt it out, find the address. When she had printed it out, she took a set of keys for the cottage and wrapped it round the letter. She could even offer it to Lucinda first. Honeysuckle Cottage, conveniently near to Sherwood Hall, ideal as a guest house or knocking shop. View by appointment only.

Trevor came in, looking white and distraught. For a brief moment, she felt a welling of sympathy for him, wanted to take him in her arms. There, there, it's all over now. Out of the corner of her eye, she watched him take the kettle, fill a mug to overflowing, then open the doors of each cupboard in turn.

'The tea-bags are in there,' she said, pointing to a drawer. 'Milk's in the fridge. I brought some. She's gone off, in case you're wondering. That chair's the broken one. Try the other one. I need to be back in London by nine, I'm expecting a couple of calls from LA. I decided not to go back with Hugh. We'll . . . I'll take your car. You can come back with me if you like. Or stay here. Whichever.'

'Annie? What came over you?'

'What do you mean?'

'It won't do either of us any good.'

'It did me a lot of good.'

'Did you actually plan it? I can't believe that.'

'Believe what you like.'

'You're quite right to be angry.'

'I'm not angry, Trevor.'

'I am. There was no need to humiliate me. That doesn't solve anything. I was trying my utmost to find a solution. Annie, you'll have to face up to how things are.'

'Oh, I have, don't worry, I have.'

'I don't want to have a row. We won't get anywhere if we start going for one another.'

'No, quite.'

'There's no point in talking when you're angry.'

'I'm not angry, Trevor.'

'I can see you are.'

'It's about time we . . . it's about time I started off. Where are the car keys?'

'I'll come with you.'

It must be like having a bad pregnancy, Annie thought. Each painful moment seemed raw and unforgettable, as the warm interchanges were suddenly stifled and the flow of feelings became sour trickles. She'd heard that all the awful minutes would sink into the trough of memory until they seeped away, leaving only the residue of a brief time which could be dismissed in a sentence. Bad times shrunk when you recalled good ones, like saying after a disastrous holiday, 'It was marvellous.' She longed to tuck it all into the past, to file away the disappointments, the gnawing reminders of deceit, and worst of all, the silence. But the present inched by, like the second hands marking out a shoot.

What would she remember? How she couldn't find the key to the back door but wouldn't ask Trevor where it was? How she couldn't get the wet-warped window in their bedroom to close, it was beyond her strength, but had left it open? Throwing the bedclothes into the bin, waiting until he could see her doing it? Pulling the phone out of its socket, throwing it into a sack of fertilizer in the shed? The tears in her eyes as she carefully folded Dally's duvet, then rolled up Kate's rug, and swept clear the rickety little wardrobe covered in smiling suns?

'Why are you doing that, Annie?'

'It's obvious, isn't it? I'm clearing the cottage. It shouldn't take long to sell.'

'Couldn't you do that another time? I thought you wanted to get back. We'll have to drive back in the dark.'

'*I'll* have to drive back in the dark. There's still some things of yours in the back bedroom. The drawers need clearing. And I haven't touched Rick and Bryonie's room yet. Why don't you start in there?'

Before he could reply, Annie ran out of the cottage, glancing up at the sky, the grey fading light, then at her watch. Rummaging in the toolshed, she found what she was looking for, pulled on the gardening boots encrusted with yellowing weeds and summer earth and turned back to the cottage. Trevor ran after her, panting with fear.

'Annie, what on earth are you doing?'

'Stripping honours. You can be given a medal, then years later it can be taken away. That's all. What's done can be undone, I believe that's the idea. You didn't think I'd leave this, did you?'

'For heaven's sake, go inside. It's cold out here.'

Annie was attempting to saw vigorously through the slender young trunk of the willow tree, the rusty teeth scarcely penetrated the damp wood.

'Useless bloody piece of equipment,' she muttered to herself. Then she threw it down into the trampled grass, memento of the crew, and went back to the shed. From the upstairs side window, Trevor saw her returning.

'Annie! What the hell . . . ?' he shouted.

She was swinging an axe by her side as she walked, with an air of triumph. With legs apart, she swiped at the trunk. One gash, two gashes, and shaken by the blows, the few remaining golden leaves whirled away, caught by a gust of wind. Now divorced from the knee-high stump, anonymous like an abandoned bean-pole, the willow lay at her feet. Annie dropped the axe, picked up the tree and swung it over her shoulder. It was lighter than she had expected but it was only young. When she reached the wire fence bounding the field, she slung it as far as she could across the ploughed furrows.

Trevor, tightly belted in the passenger seat, winced as Annie crashed through the gears.

'I'll be glad when we get back to London. We'll be able to talk then. Hey, watch that junction!'

But Annie barely slowed down. She had been driving for all those years, never had an accident except scrapes and bumps as though she was protected by some African God of the Road. They both stared ahead in the darkness, then Annie pushed in the button of the radio. For mile upon mile, there would be flashing headlights, dipping headlights, accompanied by droning voices discussing the future of the nuclear power industry.

'Are there any cigarettes in the car?'

'No, Annie.'

'She doesn't smoke, of course she doesn't. As though I could forget.'

'There are some peppermints somewhere.'

'I never eat peppermints.'

'Would you mind changing the station?'

Annie said nothing, and pressed one button, then another. Passing over a Mozart piano concerto, she settled on the loud banter of a local rap station.

'For God's sake, turn that off. It's very childish, Annie.'

'Childish? I thought you liked little girls. Or is that only in bed?'

Trevor took a deep breath and switched off the irksome sound.

'Annie, listen to me. We're both angry. We've both made mistakes. I wanted, I really did think, that we could resolve things differently. What do you want me to do?'

For another half-hour, Annie was silent, and Trevor attempted to doze, to give himself respite from the debate which was raging in his head. Occasionally, Annie gave a slight turn, enough to see that he appeared to be sleeping. He would not be sleeping beside her again. She knew she had to stop the tears which were building up behind her eyes, her lids were heavy like laden clouds. If she cried, she might have to stop, he would take her in his arms, she would be pulled back into the past, obliterating the trauma, forgiving him, if there was anything to forgive, perhaps it was her fault. She should have taken him at his word. Perhaps he was right, that she refused to recognize that there were other ways of loving. Had they come to the end? Was there a turning, a way out, which she had refused to see?

What was it Kate had said once about Gordon? I'd rather have part of him than all of anyone else. Did she really think that or had she persuaded herself? But she had never been married to him. Maybe Kate was lucky to have avoided marriage. Annie Griffiths, Controller of Drama, having a time-share husband. How could she have allowed him to even suggest the idea?

A powerful saloon was coming up close behind her, head-lights searching through the back window. Annie imagined the shot. Woman bolt upright, driving. Man slumped back against the window, asleep. Seen from the back, outlined in black like shadow puppets on a candlelit screen. Then the lights moved round, the car was overtaking, staying parallel, a foxy malevolent face flicking sideways, then back to the road, trying to draw her attention.

'Stupid bastard,' said Annie. Sexual provocation, driving at a hundred and ten. Fast in a car, fast in bed. Typical male, to make that assumption. She slowed down to ninety. How could he sleep like that? Had she tired him out? Squeaking like a new-born kitten? What had they been up to? Was it different, the upper-class lay? An acquired taste, like oysters? What had they been talking about?

Then the realization dawned. What a brilliant, satisfying, creative solution! How he would have welcomed it. She should have thought of it before, but she hadn't.

'Of course, after my first wife Margaret had the baby, she went off sex. Completely. It's quite common, I believe.'

How convenient. Annie has a child. Annie is a mother. Annie loses her desire. In steps Lucinda to complete the triangle. Wife and mother, mistress and man. No doubt it was the accepted solution, in her circle. And Trevor would be so decent, so understanding, so liberal, that she couldn't possibly object.

There was a sudden jolt as Annie put her foot on the brakes.
'Sod off.'

She knew the driver couldn't hear her, but he would see her spitting the words out, through the glass. With a roar of acceleration, the grey saloon took off in the fast lane. About a hundred and thirty, Annie guessed. Damn. No portable phone. She had forgotten she was in Trevor's car, no phone, no cigarettes. He could keep it, she wouldn't take back that heap of junk. Trevor was awake now, she was aware of him shifting to an upright position but she kept her eyes firmly on the road.

Annie waited until they had arrived back at Langton Villas. Trevor had gone straight up to his study. The car was still loaded with possessions she had gathered together, but she would leave them there, send someone to collect the shabby remains of a simple country cottage. She had managed to avoid looking at him, she was making the effort to imagine that he was gone, it was easier that way. Sipping a brandy at the kitchen table, stale cigarette burning on a saucer, sitting alone, hunched in front of her computer, she began to attack the keyboard.

It's easier to write it down. Isn't that what you do, with people you don't trust? And then you put: *WITHOUT*

305

PREJUDICE. Which means, I assume, Don't throw it in my face afterwards, don't give it to the lawyers. Well, don't give it to the lawyers.

I suppose you thought I would go along with it. Yes, Trevor. I really did think that you had changed your mind. I even surprised myself. It's the first time someone had ever asked that. Will you have my baby? It's not that I was desperate to have a child. But all these years, I was hoping that you might say that, just as I was trembling with expectancy when we first met, waiting for the first time you said, 'I love you.' You forgive anything from a man who says those two things. He loves you. He wants to have a child with you. For a short while, I was mad enough to believe you, to believe that you really were ready to start a new life. Annie and Trevor, part two. Annie and Trevor plus one. I thought about it, having my belly swell up with your child, taking time off. I never doubted I'd get pregnant, I still thought it would be easy, like the first time. We'd have a wonderful night together, and then afterwards I'd know it had happened.

But you hadn't just said, I want your baby. I had to make a bargain. You have our child, which we both want, but I want Lucinda as well. Do you know, I actually considered it! I really did begin to wonder if it was a way of making our marriage survive. I still felt I had to fight though I never believed you fought for a marriage. You're together because you want to be, as I see it. Although I hated your lying and deceit, I thought at least all that would end if there was nothing to cover up. I even thought, why not Lucinda? I'd know who it was, and wouldn't be worrying about which strange girl you were screwing, not like poor Bryonie. And Lucinda kept insisting that she'd no intention of getting married, didn't need to. So it could have been a possible arrangement. Lots of people do it discreetly, successfully, without getting into the *News of the World*. Why shouldn't we?

If you hadn't jumped the gun, if you hadn't assumed that I'd already given my assent, I might never have reached the obvious conclusion. I can't imagine why I didn't. It was staring me in the face. I suddenly realized who you really were, and what must have happened with your first marriage. It was a fully worked-out plan. It had nothing to do with how you felt for me. You wanted me to have a child because it was convenient.

OK, Trev. I've written enough for the moment. You can pack tomorrow, I intend to get some sleep tonight. I'll ring Pickfords and get them to move the heavy stuff. Just put everything in your study. But take the clothes out of my house. All of them, winter and summer, otherwise they'll go to Oxfam. And arrange for your mail to be forwarded. And I won't be taking over your phone line, so I'll discontinue your number and get a new one. You can leave it to me to tell Kate and Bryonie that you've moved out. You can tell Rick, though. If he starts spreading it round Intertel, I'll make sure he really does lose his job. Is there anything I've forgotten? If there is, I'm sure I'll remember in the morning. Don't wake me up.

ANNIE

Cautiously Annie pushed open the bedroom door a fraction. The bed was empty. Then she checked the spare room, and saw him sprawled across the bed, still dressed. She put the letter on the table beside him and went to take a bath.

17

ANNIE

The transmission of episode one of *Rough Trade* was commemorated by a tribal gathering in the Chief's hut, with all the cast and crew – wives, husbands and friends – crouched or sprawled over the rough matting, eyes riveted on a giant mounted screen which was obscuring the marble fireplace. The room was so crowded that even if Trevor had been there, Annie could easily have avoided talking to him all evening. She attempted to put out of her mind the previous occasions, previous first episodes, when she and Trevor would take off to a grand hotel and watch it in a stately bedroom. Tonight she was dressed in a clinging emerald green dress, a colour he had always disliked.

As the end-titles rolled, they all burst out clapping and shouting. *Rough Trade* was now public property. There was always the irrational fear that the screen would remain blank, that someone would make a mistake in the control suite or a giant electricity failure would darken the whole country. It still sent her spirits dancing, to imagine all those millions who had just seen what they had seen. Someone turned the sound down as *News at Ten* bonged out its signature. Kate was the first to hug Annie who was standing nervously at the back, pressing her fingers round a glass of champagne.

'Annie, it's spectacular, the best thing I've ever seen. And Clary is knock-out. She looks amazing on screen.'

'Did you think it moved fast enough? You didn't think it was a bit slow?' said Annie.

'Perfect. Where on earth did you find that music? Fantastic, I loved it.'

Annie grinned. 'I didn't like it much but I thought it worked.'

Everyone began to rise to their feet, Annie moved across the room to embrace the director and then climbed up onto a chair and clapped her hands.

'Well done, everyone. Thank you for all being so smashing and working so hard, every single one of you. I think we've won the gold!'

More cheers, more hugs, more kisses. There was enough love and affection generated to drive out the emptiness for a while. Benny crushed Annie to his rounded belly.

'Don't know how you do it. She's a corker, that Clary.'

'I can still pick stars, then?'

'You bet.'

Annie released herself and beckoned to Clary, who was still sitting on the floor. Even in the simple movement of rising to her feet, she commanded attention. Clary was dressed in stone-coloured jeans and a black, low-cut spangled top which showed off her long neck encircled with some gaudy beads. Her face reminded Benny of the young Twiggy, tilted nose and those great greeny eyes like a chinchilla cat.

'You ever done comedy?' asked Benny, looking up at Clary. He liked tall girls.

'Nah. I done modellin' then I done some commercials. Then Annie said I could do *Rough Trade*. Good, innit?' Then she turned to Annie. 'We on for a second series, then?'

'There'll be a second something, you bet your life,' replied Benny.

'Me bloke's gone missin'. I said I wanted a dry martini. Don't know why I said that, I never 'ave dry martinis. See ya.'

'Sit-com. A natural for sit-com,' said Benny, keeping his eyes on Clary's rear as she moved off, she had a way of moving each buttock separately like a dancer.

'I've got her next lined up already,' said Annie. 'Precocious fourteen year old.'

'I'd go for that. See she doesn't get some voice coach ironing her out.'

'You always worry they'll start moving down the production line and turn out like everyone else. Still, they couldn't do that to Emma Thompson. Maybe Clary will have the guts to stick out.'

'Only trouble is, she'll have to learn not to be a one-part girl. She's great in *Rough Trade*, part's made for her, but will she develop, Annie? So many of them don't. You think she likes hamburgers? She looks like a hamburger girl to me.'

'Why don't you ask her?' replied Annie, with a grin.

'No, mustn't. Not my age-range any more. Time I stopped making a fool of mesself. Every morning, I look in the mirror and say, "Who'd go for that? Silly geezer." Have I got thinner? The doc says I've got to lose a couple of stone.'

He opened the bottom button of his shirt.

'Here. Give a squeeze of that. Tell me there's less of it.'

'How can I tell?'

'Go on.'

Annie gave the folds of skin a light pinch.

'Coming along nicely, I'd say.'

'You look good, Annie. Sure you wouldn't like a replacement? I'd be a good lodger, tidy round the house—'

'Hold on, Benny. He's only been gone a few days. Give a girl a chance.'

'Loved it, Annie, just loved it. Gemma was falling about every time she told the story. All the girls were calling you Right-On Annie. I wish I'd seen it. Annie Griffiths taking Leggy Lucy by the scruff of the neck. Bet that took her by surprise. But I can't understand why the daft bugger did it in the second home. I'd have gone to a hotel – or a boarding-house depending on the bird.'

'My husband likes home comforts, and recognizing the furniture. Besides, he only went to hotels when it was on expenses.'

Benny clucked disapprovingly. 'Mean with it. You deserved better.'

'He can be generous – when it's his idea. He always organizes marvellous anniversary dos. And he's fantastic to his students. No, Trevor's not mean.'

'He'll be back, then, knocking on your door. And you'll say, Come in, darling beloved, all is forgiven.'

'I bloody won't.'

'Just testing.'

'If only I could get some kip at nights. That's the worst part, Benny.'

'Move into a single bed. That's what I normally do. Then you don't have to look at the next-door pillow. I tried it with Paddington Bear, but it didn't work. Never thought he'd snore all night, that's the trouble with bears.'

'How about a large dog?'

'Now you mention it, that's what Julie did. She walked out

310

and got herself a Great Dane. A lot of work around the house, dogs are.'

'Like men?'

'I'm easy, doll. Too easy, that's my trouble. Anything to eat in the kitchen?'

'Kate's made some wonderful African specialities—'

'Wot, no bangers? No bangers on sticks?'

Annie pushed Benny through the newly streaked, ebonized door – Kate's latest skill was perfecting *trompe l'oeil* wood effects – and left him prodding at patties and sniffing bowls of unfamiliar cereals. Now that it was over, she could get full-blown, reelingly, gloriously, swimmingly drunk. The noise of Annie's triumph would be heard all down Langton Villas, but she didn't care. She thought she heard an insistent finger on the front bell a few times, after someone had turned the music up. At some point in the evening, she found herself lying across some man, warm arms round her shoulders, an animated buzz of conversation continuing somewhere over her head before everything faded to black.

Still floating on the aftermath, she had somehow managed to stagger up to their bedroom, no, her bedroom. When she came to, it was light, only eight in the morning but she was fully awake. All those weeks of filming had made her gear up to an early full alert. Flinging on a robe, she moved cautiously down the stairs. Several bodies were stretched out on the floor, on cushions, like bags of mail waiting for collection. She stepped over a jumble of bottles and bags and flung open a window to banish the odour of cigarette smoke, a few must have been smoking dope, and spilled alcohol. A proper party, she hadn't given one since she was a student. Kate was the only person she could see who was on her feet.

'Hi, Annie. Wasn't it great? Dally slept through it all. Hope you don't mind, I borrowed one of Trevor's old shirts when I took off my party dress. He'd left it in my room.'

'What? Oh yes. He slept in there when he came back from the cottage. Keep it. It's better on you.'

Kate had cleared a space on the kitchen table and was observing Dally's attempt to eat cornflakes with chopsticks. Annie surveyed the debris around her, wondering whether to make a start.

'If Trevor could have seen this, he'd have gone berserk. What, you've only just redone everywhere, you're crazy! He'd

311

have said that afterwards, but at the time he would have enjoyed it. He was good at parties. Is good at parties.'

'You'll find someone else who's good at parties. And who isn't out to screw your guests.'

'Trevor never did that, what are you talking about? Even if he was chatting up someone, he'd always come back to my side, just at the right moment. He was good like that.'

'Why are you sticking up for him all of a sudden?'

'I can see his good points, can't I?'

'No. Because then you'll start wanting him back.'

'I don't want him back. He can do what the hell he likes. But he's not going to make me sell this house. He can find himself somewhere else. Perhaps he'd like to buy Honeysuckle Cottage. No, that's stupid. I found it.'

'Annie, you mustn't think of selling everything. You can't do that.'

'I wonder where he'll go. He hates Chelsea.'

Kate placed a steaming cup of black coffee in front of Annie.

'He could always move farther out, near me. Nice working-class area, real working-class neighbours. Why don't you suggest it?'

'No, don't. Lucinda would move in, and North Holloway would end up like Notting Hill. Full of girls like her stepping round winos and saying how real it is. You wouldn't like that, would you?'

'It wouldn't worry me.'

Annie watched Dally stuffing cornflakes into her mouth with her fingers.

'Does she want a spoon?'

'She's happy. Aren't you, darling?'

Kate moved the tempting sugar bowl out of reach, and began to sort through the randomly piled-up dishes.

'It can wait. Don't bother,' said Annie. 'If I did decide to sell this house, I could move into one of those Soho lofts. I've always fancied that, a great open space. I suggested it once to Trevor, but he said if you're living with someone, you need separate territories. He thought it wouldn't work.'

'Oh, Annie, I thought you liked the way I'd done the house.'

'I love it, Kate. I do.'

'He's gone and you want everything to be different.'

'At the moment, I want to be on my own, I couldn't bear it to be otherwise.'

She threw off Trevor's shirt and stepped carefully into a long, tight skirt.

'I mean it.'

'Don't be silly, Annie. You can have any designer you want. Who's heard of Kate Roberts nowadays? Anyway, I'll most likely do something else when Dally's older, something quite different. I might even go to university and study philosophy.'

'That's a daft idea. What on earth made you think of that?'

'I might discover I've got a brain. I've always admired people who know how to think properly, like Trevor. I can listen for hours, seeing how one idea develops and fits into another.'

'But why throw away something you're good at? Something you enjoy?'

'Anyone can be a designer,' replied Kate, defensively.

'I couldn't. Rick couldn't. Gordon couldn't. And Trevor certainly couldn't.'

'You could do anything, Annie. You know you could.'

'I wish you'd stop admiring me. All I do is work hard. Like you.'

Kate gave a disbelieving laugh. 'You don't know how brilliant you are.'

'I deliver the goods,' replied Annie.

'Dally's going to be the talented one. She'll be a great artist one day, and then I can go along to her exhibitions and be a proud mum. I'd be quite happy with that. I've never been ambitious, Annie, I'm not like you. It's only men who think it's wrong not to have ambition. Everything's got so competitive. It was different then, sitting around and coming up with ideas, trying them out, scrapping them if they didn't turn out right. You couldn't do that now.'

'Give yourself a chance.'

'When Dally's older, maybe. Here, your turn now.'

How did she do it? Kate pulled and tucked and threw things round Annie until she felt like a figure from Harvey Nichol's window pageant. Then it was Dally's turn, she was jumping up and down, crying out, 'Me, me, me. I want a pretty dress.' As they left the house, Annie could hear the phone ringing but she ignored it.

'Trevor hasn't told me where he is,' Annie said, as she was demolishing the sausages, mushrooms and eggs. 'But I suppose he's gone to Chelsea.'

'It doesn't matter where he's gone.'

'He'll hate her house, but he'll pretend he likes it. He'll pretend he likes everything about her. Poor Trevor.'

'Annie, he's been a shit.'

'I shouldn't have done what I did. He was just confused. Oh, Kate. I want him back. If he walked through the door, I'd fall into his arms. I miss him, I bloody miss him. I want to know what he thought of *Rough Trade*. I want him to burn breakfast. Oh God, I want him to be mine again.'

'I know, Annie.'

'You don't.'

'All right, I don't.'

'Am I meant to be sisterly and loving and invite Lucinda to dinner? Is that what one does today, Kate? Christ, I've no idea what to do.'

'You needn't do that, not now. Later on, perhaps, you could all meet up.'

'If I did invite her over, she'd probably come, the silly girl. Why don't I give a dinner party and we could all get together? Margaret, me and Lucinda?'

'Margaret? Which Margaret?'

'Wife number one. The one we forget about. I keep wondering how Margaret felt. At the time, I never did. If only I could compare notes. Or just say, "I'm sorry it happened." I asked Trevor to describe her once. Ordinary, he said. Quite pretty in an ordinary way, the kind of girl you'd see at a Prom concert. And when I asked him why he'd married her, he said he'd got used to her. Wouldn't it be bizarre if she looked like me? I've often wished we could bump into one another.'

'Gordon's good like that. He can't see why everyone can't be friends, it's so sweet. He doesn't mind me seeing his ex-wife, not at all. He's pleased we get on so well.'

'Supposing you hadn't liked her?'

'It's only men who think women don't like one another.'

'It works because you don't see her as a rival, Kate. Now that Gordon's on his own, there's no-one fighting for him.'

'If no-one wanted to marry anyone else, we could all be free. And society would be organized so that children would be looked after by people who really wanted that job.'

'Women, you mean.'

'If it was paid properly, men would do it too.'

'If. It's a big if.'

'You've got to believe that things can be different, Annie.'

By the weekend, the house was restored to perfect order and it pleased her, the wicker chairs and stools arranged at precise angles, the pictures and hangings straightened. The cleaners had even polished the inside of the cupboards, now tidily stacked with plates piled on plates, saucers on saucers instead of the usual jumble. Over all those years, Trevor had put up with Annie's neglect of housework and assumed that she associated creativity with muddle. That wasn't so, she decided. She had hated cleanliness and order because they were the outward signs of the repressive town and family against which she had rebelled. Chaos was the natural state for revolution and change, though Trevor in that respect was more like Lenin than Trotsky. He liked everything to be planned and worked out. Or was he merely reacting to her? And was she merely reacting to youthful aggression? Had she fixed Trevor in a mould which she had created? Was he quite different with Lucinda? Had he been different with Margaret? Could he be different with her? Could they both be different?

Kate had gone home, and Annie had returned to bed. In the middle of sifting through a pile of newspapers, skimming the TV reviews, Trevor rang. Her heart beat faster when she heard his voice, but she wouldn't let him know how it pleased her.

'Hi, Trevor.'

'Annie, how are you?'

'Fine.'

'Congratulations, darling. I was amazed. *Rough Trade* was quite exceptional, I wanted to tell you. When the dust has settled, I predict it'll be a landmark for television drama, even if the critics are incapable of seeing it now. Typical Godfrey West, to say that Clary Hunt has taken her part from the bottom drawer of drama-school clichés. What a pillock! All he seems to like on TV is football and *Splash!* But then he is a friend of Gavin's.'

'I haven't seen the papers yet,' said Annie, drily.

'Oh, I thought you would have done. Since it's nearly tea-time.'

'I was having a lazy day, doing exactly what I wanted. I'd forgotten what it was like, not to be woken up by you at some ungodly hour.'

'Are you all right? I do worry, Annie. I wanted to call you, in case you were upset.'

'Upset? What am I meant to be upset about?'

'The reviews. I know you always take them badly.'

'It was watched by twelve million. Intertel hasn't reached that for at least six months. Alan sent me a note, an effusive note for him. I don't give a damn about reviews, it's a waste of time. Anita does the cuts, I'll have a scan through tomorrow.'

'You always used to. You always used to get the first editions.'

'I had a great party last night. At least a hundred people. Lots of them stayed till morning.'

'That's good. I wish I'd been there.'

'I don't know why we stopped having parties. I must do it more often. A great success.'

'I'm glad. Anyway, I might as well let you know where I'm staying. I'm not with Rick and Bryonie any more.'

'So I gathered.'

'I'll be at Danvers Street for a while, until I've sorted out somewhere to live. The phone number is—'

'I know the number.'

'It doesn't seem right, being in the Sherwood family home. We'll be looking for a flat somewhere. But I'll let you know when we move.'

'I can't wait.'

'Annie, there's no need to feel hostile. Obviously, I was furious at the way you handled the situation at the cottage. But I don't blame you. Not now.'

'You should blame me.'

'It was just unfortunate that we happened to be there, embarrassing for all of us.'

'I planned it, Trev.'

Trevor gasped. 'You didn't, Annie. You couldn't have done.'

'Gillian was very helpful. Whenever you were coming down, she said, you phoned up to ask if she'd drop by and put something in the fridge. For guests. Does Lucinda get hungry in the country? Usually, she eats like a sparrow.'

'I can't believe this of you. Why didn't you say something to me? You must have known we were going to the cottage, I never hid it from you. I thought you'd come to terms with—'

'It did have its funny side, don't you think?'

'So you enjoyed humiliating us. That's cheap, Annie. Not like you at all.'

'I thought it might stop you making an idiot of yourself.'

'Am I meant to be grateful then?' Trevor burst out. 'What you absolutely refuse to see is that I love you. And I love her.'

'What about Margaret? What about her? Do you still love her as well? And how many others are grouped together in your little love file?'

'Annie, this isn't getting us anywhere. You've closed your mind, I can't talk to you any more.'

'Damn you, Trevor, you can talk to me when you've something sensible to say.'

Annie sent the receiver crashing down on the cradle. Again, she thought of selling the house. He still talked as though he was part of her, as though he was privy to all her habits, all her reactions, every inch of the well-worn road of marriage. More and more, she resented him knowing her. From now on, she would work at being a stranger so that he could say, 'I was married to Annie once; and no-one would believe him.

Annie kept trying to conjure up what he had said, when they first knew they would be together for years and years even though he was married to Margaret. She remembered days when he used to turn up at her student digs as though he had been on a long, exhausting hike.

'We had a row. Don't let's talk about it.'

She never asked him the cause, he insisted that was his affair. He would sort it out. Margaret was being difficult. Margaret was being obstinate. Difficult and obstinate Margaret Watson. It was time they met. In an old address book, Annie had kept the names of their old friends. B for Bristol. Harry and Mary and Sheila and David and Monty and Gwynn, written down in Trevor's spidery writing.

Harry still kept in touch, he and Margaret sang in the same choir together he told her. Edward would be getting married in the church where Margaret had had her wedding. A good opportunity for another reunion. Didn't Annie know that Trevor had been married in church? Everyone did, in those days. Someone said that Trevor was appearing on a television programme, but they couldn't get to see him, it being London region. He should make a trip to Bristol, both of them should, it had been too long. Margaret had gone on some course, she was a careers counsellor now, never went on about the past, not like some women. She was trying to persuade young kids there were jobs out there. Still, she enjoyed it. Annie wrote down the address and assured Harry they'd be down soon.

'Give our regards to Trev, won't you?' he said, before he rung off.

How long would it take before every time she heard someone else say his name, she felt as though it was she who had betrayed him? How long before she could say, 'We aren't living together any more,' and accept the expressions of regret and sympathy without dissolving into tears? She tried to compose a letter in her head, an all-purpose letter. There would be no ready-made cards for what she had to say, no tacky rhymes, no flowers, no joky bears, no black-edged borders or silver bells. Dear Blank, Just to let you know that Trevor and I have split up. We must keep in touch. My phone number is . . . Trevor's phone number is . . . You're welcome to stay, any time you're in London. After she had typed it out on her computer, Annie sat staring at the screen, her eyes glazed, and then she pressed delete.

18

ANNIE

Dressed in her old jeans and the black leather jacket she had discovered in a heap at the bottom of the wardrobe, Annie sat in her car, studying the map. She had given no warning of her visit. It would be better if she appeared to be passing through, making a casual call. She had no idea of Margaret's appearance, Trevor kept no photographs. He thought it was a primitive idea, keeping snapshots, approximate records as though you had a faulty memory. She's nothing like you, he said. He had never described her adequately, which Annie found strange with someone you'd lived with for several years. Edward was two when he left. Her character not his, even at that age, so he said.

There was a blank face somewhere in Bristol, waiting to be filled out like the first impression of a photofit artist settling on the shape, hunting for clues to give the blank an expression. Annie hoped it would be an attractive face, or perhaps pretty. How would she react if the figure which confronted hers was dumpy, a cosy-mother shape, like Auntie Gwen? Wearing a pinny? Then she realized that the guilt she had gaily discarded so long ago was still there. Why would it be more bearable if she was pretty, striking, beautiful even? Would that be a justification? A fair exchange? Would she still be in the same house, the house to which he always returned, after he had rushed out of her digs, leaving the guttering candle, the scent of joss sticks, the jumble of the unmade bed? The address which Harry had given her was unfamiliar, but if Trevor had told her, which she doubted, she would have forgotten after all this time.

It was dark by the time Annie reached Hampstead Gardens, Bristol, a long terrace of Victorian villas. She had once dropped Trevor somewhere in this street, now it came back to her, when she had her first Citroën. Hampstead Gardens, Bristol. Margaret had a right to the house, but he confessed that it made him bitter when a rise in property prices had increased its value threefold. Annie was unsympathetic. It was the price of their love, that Margaret should keep her home. What did property mean? When Britain had a real socialist government, all property would disappear. Property was a dirty word, the hallmark of the grasping, capitalist Tories. You would sooner admit how much you earned than mention that you owned a house. Trevor and Annie did neither. They were waiting for the revolution, they and their friends in Bristol.

Having driven slowly down the length of the street, Annie turned the corner, went round the block and parked the Saab, conspicuous amongst the ailing Datsuns and Escorts cramming the street. She walked briskly down Hampstead Gardens until she reached number eighty-two. There was a standard lamp in the front room, glowing through the net curtains and someone was seated at a table, head bowed over a pile of papers and books. Annie pressed the bell. It was as though she had an appointment years ago, and had only just remembered. She could not think what she would say. If they disliked one another on sight, she would have a brief conversation, and invent someone else to see.

'Hi. I'm Annie. Is this the right address? I'm an old friend of Margaret Watson's. Does she still live here?'

The young woman who greeted her looked blank, but not unfriendly.

'She's in the kitchen, I'll get her.'

'Who's that, Joan?' came a voice from down the hall.

'It's Annie.'

'Annie who?'

Margaret came towards Annie from a room at the back of the house. She had grey hair, cut squarely round her face, and she was wearing an emerald green smock over black tights. Annie had never imagined her hair would be grey, or that she would have left it grey. There were tight lines round her mouth, but the blue eyes were alert, intelligent, looking straight at Annie.

'Should I know you?'

'I'm Trevor's wife. I wanted to meet you.'

Margaret's severe features dissolved into an astonished smile.

'Good heavens! That Annie! Come in.'

'I'll watch the saucepan,' said Joan, as she squeezed past them in the narrow hall.

Annie followed Margaret into the front room, and when she had motioned Annie to sit down, she suddenly burst out, 'You haven't come because . . . Something hasn't happened?'

'He's still alive and well.'

'You're nothing like I imagined. Why did I think you had blond hair?'

'Isn't the other woman always a blonde?'

They both laughed, staring at one another.

'I hope you don't mind me coming. But I was in Bristol and I thought, Well, why shouldn't we meet?'

'You wouldn't be likely to bump into me in London,' said Margaret. 'I'll turn up the gas fire. I expect you're used to central heating.'

'Don't bother. I'm used to cold. I was born in Cardiff, after all.'

'So you were. But I never knew much about you. I knew you were awfully clever, been to university. But I've caught up with you. I completed a degree course in sociology last year.'

'I do admire you. I'd be hopeless at studying now.'

'Don't you do something in television?'

'Yes. I'm in drama.'

'I'm sure I saw an article in the *Guardian*. You don't call yourself Watson, do you?'

'No. Griffiths. Annie Griffiths.'

'I'm Miz Watson. Mrs isn't allowed, not where I work. Let me get you something. We're in the middle of making chutney, it's getting to the crucial stage, I expect you can smell it. Just a moment.'

Margaret went to the door and called down the hall. 'Joan? Is there any elderflower wine left?'

Annie couldn't hear the reply, but soon Joan appeared with a couple of thick glass tumblers.

'This is Joan. We share the house. Well, to be honest, I need to. Edward went to private school, then to university. Trevor didn't pay for any of it.'

'No, of course.'

'And I didn't ask him to. He never believed in private education. But I wanted to give Edward the best. Trevor only wanted the best for other people, not his son.'

323

A large ginger cat appeared from behind Annie's chair and leaped onto her lap.

'Chunky, get down. Off!'

Margaret grasped the cat by the scruff of the neck, set him on the floor and clapped her hands.

'He always jumps on people who dislike cats. I do apologize. You're not allergic, by any chance, are you?' Annie shook her head. 'They're like children, cats, always doing what you least expect. Did you, do you have children?'

'No.' Annie shifted nervously in the leatherette chair. 'Somehow I never thought you'd stay in Bristol,' she said, quickly. 'I assumed you'd want to get right away.'

'I intended to go back and live in London, but somehow it never happened. I don't miss it now, but I did then. I don't know why, but I always dreamed of living in Hampstead. That could be why we chose this house, because of the street name. I'd never thought of that before. All our friends who made it were living in Hampstead. I thought it sounded so glamorous, so exciting. And here I am, in Bristol. They all come to this street, you know, the divorced women with grown-up children. We call it Settlement Street. But I've always lived here and I don't miss London, not at all.'

'And you're near the most wonderful country.'

'Indeed, yes. I go for walks with Joan. Joan's a serious walker, she always carries a compass and a map in a plastic sheet. She walks in the rain.'

Annie took a sip of the sickly wine.

'I came to tell you that Trevor and I have split up. I thought you'd want to let Edward know, now that he's getting married. I wasn't sure Trevor would say anything, you see.'

'Oh, Annie. How awful. Did it happen recently?'

'Yes.'

'I'm very sorry. You don't know what to say, do you? I really am sorry. I could have murdered you at the time, not literally, but I wished you'd, oh never mind. It was only later I saw it wouldn't have made any difference. But you always want to blame someone in the beginning. You loved him, didn't you?' Annie nodded. 'I loved him, too. But I loved him because I thought he'd be a wonderful father. Then, when Edward came along, he became a different person. He couldn't bear to be in the house, always shouting at me. I couldn't do a thing right.'

'Didn't you ever think that it might have been a temporary

reaction? Trevor likes time to adjust, to think things through.'

Margaret gave a slight smile.

'He couldn't cope with babies. I kept hoping he'd change, but he didn't. He just wasn't interested, then when you came along—'

'It must have been at the worst possible time. I had no idea, Margaret.'

'Perhaps we should have met then. To be honest, I hoped it wouldn't last, yes, that did make it worse when I heard that you two had got married. I used to pray that Trevor would wake up one day and see you beside him and say to himself, "I might just as well have stayed with Margaret." Silly, I know.'

Annie had drained the tumbler and was about to put it down on the floor beside her.

'Oh, let me take that. I'm afraid that was the last of the elderberry wine. Joan made it from some berries she picked on one of her rambles. She's a great walker.'

Annie smiled. 'So you said.'

'I prefer looking at the great outdoors through a window, with a roaring fire in the grate, not that we've got a roaring fire, of course, but Joan always manages to drag me out. Would you like some tea? Or coffee, instant coffee, I'm afraid?'

'No, don't worry. I'm fine. Can I tell you what happened? Would it upset you? Only, I'm still trying to make sense of the last few months.'

'Please do. I'm used to listening. You can ask me anything you like.'

'I've begun to wonder, if there were other girls before I came along. When you were married . . .'

Margaret chuckled and leaned back, her eyes raised as she conjured up the past. Annie could see the attraction of her face, now that the blue eyes had come alive, and she saw how she must have been as a pretty, peachy-skinned, wholesome young girl.

'He was always surrounded by female students, well he's a handsome man is Trevor, he was at any rate. All bright and healthy, springing about like new-born lambs. They used to say all the pretty ones went to Bristol University.'

'And did he take any of them to bed?'

'His students? I doubt it. Some of the other lecturers used to have affairs, but Trevor always disapproved. He used to say it would be like a therapist going to bed with a patient. He did feel responsible for them, and I remember once he had a huge row with a promising girl who'd flunked her exams and run off with her boyfriend. It's silly, but I sometimes thought he cared more about what happened to them, than he cared for me. I did feel jealous, sometimes, all the attention he gave them.'

'But you never worried he might be unfaithful?'

'We were married, Annie. In those days, you believed in happily ever after. But I'm not saying he couldn't have changed. Some men do. I can't imagine him with grey hair. Once you have grey hair, the world looks different, it does to me anyway.'

'So, when we were seeing one another, you never suspected?'

'It was a long time ago, Annie, and I had my hands full with Edward. He was a difficult child. But it doesn't matter now, does it? No point in bringing up the past, that's my advice. Sorry, I'm used to giving advice. Joan's always telling me off about that.'

'I know the girl. That made it worse,' said Annie.

'And was she one of his students?'

'At one time, yes. But nothing happened then, not as far as I know. She came to work for me after she graduated, a stunningly beautiful girl in her early twenties. He started having an affair, and tried to hide it. It went on for months.'

'Oh dear. And you hoped it wouldn't last—'

'A year ago, we had our twentieth anniversary. We'd had twenty fantastic years together. I couldn't understand why his affair went on for so long. And you couldn't imagine anyone more unlikely. We tried to talk about it, but Trevor wouldn't see reason. He refused to stop seeing her. I never thought I would, but I threw him out after that. Then the day after, I was dying for him to come walking back. But he never did. He's living with her now.'

'Her?'

'The girl.'

'What's she called? It helps, saying the name, I found that anyhow.'

'Lucinda.'

'Pretty name.'

'I couldn't fathom it out. We were happy together.' Annie put her hands over her eyes. 'I wanted to know if you were happy together.'

'I thought we were.'

'Once I'd found out, that was it. He didn't even try, he just went on seeing her as though nothing had happened. And then had the nerve to suggest . . . to suggest that I share him with . . . with her. Did he ever say that to you?'

'No.'

'When Trevor left you to live with me, did he give an explanation? I wish I knew what was in his mind.'

'Trevor never left. It was me. In the end, I didn't want him near my child. Once, I went out to the shops and I found Edward screaming his head off, real awful screams, he'd somehow got his head between the bars of the cot – while Trevor was writing away. He said he hadn't heard him. In the end, I was glad he went to live with you.'

'But didn't you regret it, that Edward never really knew his father?'

'When he was older, he said Trevor had never tried to be a proper dad. I couldn't persuade him that he might have changed, to give him a chance. He absolutely refused to see him.'

'How did you cope, bringing up a child on your own?' said Annie.

'It was hard at first, being Mum and Dad in one, but when Joan came along . . .'

'It was easier, I suppose,' said Annie.

Margaret gave a rueful smile. 'Not for Trevor. I'm sure he was convinced that Edward would turn out to be gay. Why should it matter? In spite of what he says, Trevor finds it difficult to accept, well I suppose what some people might call unconventional situations.'

Annie was taken aback, and tried not to show her surprise.

'You think so?'

Margaret rose from her chair, collected up the tumblers and put them on the mantelpiece where Annie noticed some clip-framed photographs of mountain views, small grinning figures with rucksacks posing in the mid-distance.

'It must be so interesting, your line of business,' Margaret continued, returning to sit opposite Annie. 'How did you start?'

'As a secretary.'

'You must be so clever. I thought you must be. Trevor liked girls with brains. I don't quite know how we ended up married. He wanted to save me, I sometimes thought.'

'Save you from what?'

'My family. They were working class, you see, but they voted

327

Tory. Did he see red, so to speak. You should have heard the arguments with my dad. Dad thought if you worked hard enough, then you could keep the womenfolk at home. That was his dream, to have a wife who didn't have to work. And there was Trevor saying women workers were the future. "Conduits of the revolution." That couldn't have been it, sounds like a sewer.'

Margaret gave a slight, embarrassed titter and resumed. 'Well, you'll know all about that; I don't know why I'm wittering on like this.'

'So how long were you with Trevor?'

'Five years and two months. Would you care to stay for supper? Nothing grand, macaroni cheese, but there'll be enough for three.'

'That's very kind, but I have to get back to London.'

'You must meet Edward. He looks just like Trevor, same smile, the way he walks . . . Don't feel you have to go. I'm sure we can talk about other things.'

Margaret got up and went towards the open door. It was only then that Annie noticed her thick thighs and hefty legs.

'Joan!' she called out. 'There's no need to hide. Come and meet Annie, Trevor's second wife.'

Joan, in a long striped apron, emerged from the kitchen, the kitchen at the end which would once have been the scullery.

'I've put the chutney in jars.'

'Has it set?'

'Yes. But don't move it yet, leave it on the draining-board. We've got about ten pounds.'

'Wonderful, Joan. I don't know how you manage it, I can never get the stuff to set.' Margaret glanced at Annie. 'Joan's incredibly capable, she really is, and she makes the best macaroni cheese I've ever tasted. I think it's the mustard, she puts mustard with it. Little imaginative touches I'd never have thought of.'

Joan shook Annie's hand, the hand grasping hers felt rough.

'I'll get back to the kitchen.'

'Stay and talk for a moment. Annie works in television.'

'Oh, does she? What kind of things?'

'Drama,' Annie replied.

'Everything's drama. That doesn't tell me much.'

'She's just left Trevor, came to tell me.'

'I hope he rots,' said Joan.

'That's not a nice thing to say.'

'What am I meant to say? Tough luck?'

'Joan always says what she thinks.'

'About men. Why not? We don't miss them.'

'I read a survey at work the other day,' said Margaret. 'They asked some schoolgirls what their aspirations were. Most of them said a good job, somewhere decent to live and a baby later on.'

Joan continued, as though she had been neatly edited into the conversation.

'No mention of marriage. And when they were asked, "Do you see yourself living with a man either within or outside marriage" ninety per cent said no. That's encouraging, isn't it? Best thing I've heard in ages. Like some tea? I've just made a pot.'

'We'd love some,' said Margaret.

'Joan's a counsellor too,' continued Margaret, when she had left the room. 'But she specializes in cases of sexual harassment. Fascinating job, she travels all over the country. It's pioneering work, she gives seminars to alert the workforce, to show them the warning signs. Stroking bottoms is not part of the contract. That's one of the points Joan raises. Some of them don't realize that. And the *Guardian* have asked if they can interview her. You must watch out for the article.'

Joan returned to set down two mugs of tea, strong like a workman's brew, and disappeared back to the kitchen.

'Have you lived together a long time?' Annie said, politely.

'About nine years. It doesn't seem like it. Joan's a little blunt sometimes, but she's been wonderful to me, and a real friend to Edward. She's coming to the wedding, of course. I can't believe my son's getting married, I'm so excited.'

'Trevor's pleased, too. He hasn't said much, but I know it means a lot to him that Edward wants him to come.'

'Oh, he really does. Now he does. I think Janine made him see sense, she sounds a wonderful girl. Edward feels much better now about meeting his dad. It's time to forget about the past, don't you think? It's a shame, if all this hadn't happened, I'd have asked you as well.'

'I would have come, of course I would,' said Annie, with a sigh.

'Have I been any help? I really haven't said much, but I know

329

what you're going through. It'll be so much easier once you're divorced.'

It was the first time Annie had heard the word. The logical end to her marriage hadn't occurred to her. Margaret caught her startled expression.

'There's no hurry. You'll have lots of time to think it over.'

'Supper's ready,' called Joan.

'You're sure you won't have some macaroni cheese?'

'I've got to have dinner in London. Business dinner, unfortunately.'

'If you want to catch the train, I'll need to call a taxi. The bus isn't very reliable.'

'My car's parked not far away, thank you, Margaret. You've been very kind.'

'You must come again. That settee pulls out to make a bed, it squeaks a little but I sleep well on it, you're always welcome. Are you appearing in anything at the moment? Anything on television?'

'Not at the moment,' said Annie, with a smile.

'Never mind. Something will turn up. I'll look out for you. Joan! Come and say goodbye. Annie's got to go back to London now. She can't stay.'

They stood on the front step, kissing Annie first on one cheek, then on the other. Annie assumed it was a gesture to make her feel at home, the showbiz embrace. Margaret had built up a picture of the actress Annie Griffiths all these years, no wonder she thought she was blond. She started up the car, and drove slowly down Hampstead Gardens, fixing the image of the matchbox windows, some hidden by wicker blinds, some whose lit interiors allowed her to see the occupants through patterned lace curtains. They were mostly women, many alone, quietly watching the garish ill-registered pictures from dated television sets, clutching mugs of tea or fragments of knitting. But for an accident in her career, she thought, she might have been sitting there too. Hampstead Gardens, neither Hampstead nor possessing anything which could be called a garden, street of disappointment, reduced circumstances – and divorce.

19

TREVOR

Trevor was out of breath. Fortunately, the lights were so dim that his heaving chest would not be noticed, and he was able to give a surreptitious wipe to his streaming brow as he walked away from the dance floor. Flinging himself onto a velvet-covered chesterfield, he observed Lucinda through half-closed, moist-lidded eyes. It was easier to take in her movements at a distance, to imagine that she was giving a private performance especially for him.

Every now and again, the strobe lights picked up Lucinda's silver shift, flaring way above her knees as she twisted and turned, and then she would undulate upwards like some underwater serpent drawn to the light above, palms together, the top of her breasts glistening with sweat, mouth open with highlighted purply white teeth. She was laughing at her brother Tim, gyrating on his heels in front of her. Gavin, too, appeared to be tireless, moving in a slower, more studied fashion on the dance-floor taking one turn to her two, brushing his hand against the back of a near-naked girl in a glistening tube. She was throwing her head from one side to the other, occasionally giving him an expressionless, sideways glance. Suddenly, Gavin abandoned the green pool of the underlit dance floor even though the music was still frenetically thumping, while his partner carried on dancing, oblivious that he had left, merging into a forest of long legs and glittering shoes.

'Hi, Trev. How are you doing?'

Trevor was growing used to communicating by short sharp shouts, clearing through the music, adapting himself to noise. There was a lot of noise in his life now.

'Thought I'd take a break.'

Gavin extracted a small cigar from the breast pocket of his

shiny hound's-tooth jacket, lit it and puffed langorously in Trevor's direction.

'Think it would work, to do a show from here?'

'Sure. If Tim agrees. I'm calling it *Room at the Top*, it has the right retro feel.'

'Any idea of the content yet?'

'Something sexy and provoking.'

'So what'd be different?'

'An audience grabbie. Who did you sleep with last night? How did you meet? How did you do it?'

'I'm not sure about the title.'

'Hey, Trev, don't quibble.'

'Setting it up might be tricky.'

'Nothing simpler. What do girls always long to tell? What they did the night before. Otherwise, what do you talk about over lunch? Sole topic of conversation. What could be better?'

'I don't think it's *Splash!* material. It sounds like Cilla Black gone *Tatler*.'

'It all depends on Lucinda's interview talent. We'll soon see. Not as easy as it looks.'

'I'm not happy about it.'

'Mind if I ask her? It's her decision still, isn't it?'

'Yes.'

'Good. No agent, is there?' Trevor shook his head, annoyed that Gavin was already regarding her as a two-bit performer. 'Look, let her do the test, I'll do it impro, no big deal, nothing scripted. Don't discuss it. If you think it's a crap idea, that means it's a cert.'

'She'd be too self-conscious on camera. Not her natural medium.'

'Hang about, Trev. You're not going possessive on me? Are you jealous, by any chance?'

Trevor pushed back his hair, growing long at Lucinda's insistence – short was yesterday – and gave a puckish smile.

'Just trying to keep your standards at street level. This idea is gutter level.'

'I doubt if Alan is able to see the difference any more. The name of my game is survival, Trev. Ratings falling below the horizon.'

Trevor pondered. They both knew that however fiercely he attacked plummeting standards in television, it was now being argued that television should be given back to the people.

People's choice, people's programmes. A dangerous argument, Trevor thought.

'Anyway, it's not a good moment. For Lucinda.'

'Why not?'

'There's something big she's involved in, looks like happening. We can't say anything yet.'

'She's coming over. Leave it to me. We haven't talked, OK?'

Lucinda draped herself on the low couch beside Trevor, and ran a finger down the side of his face.

'Get me another drink, will you? My throat feels like the Nevada desert.'

'Put it on my bill,' said Gavin, catching Trevor's moment of hesitancy. An evening at Tim's club could run into hundreds. Lucinda leaned down towards her tiny Chanel bag, just large enough to hold eyeliner and lipstick, a gold card and a silk handkerchief. She handed the silk handkerchief to Trevor.

'My back's hot and sweaty,' she whispered hoarsely in his ear. 'Wipe it down for me, would you?'

She raised herself up, presenting her back to him, her face turned towards Gavin. Gavin shifted his armchair nearer to Lucinda and leaned back, clasping his hands loosely in his lap.

'Something's come up which would be right for you. Just an idea I've been kicking around. I think you might be able to handle it.'

'I'm in comedy, Gavin. I'm rather enjoying it, actually.'

She was smiling, head leaning back against Trevor, enjoying the gentle circular caress passing over her shoulder blades, along her spine.

'I'd like you to do a test first. Like to try?'

'I might. Depends what it is.'

'Quick interviews. Getting the essential out in thirty seconds. Right up your street.'

'My street's busy at the moment.'

'Up to you, Lucinda. I'm not asking you to stay awake at nights—'

Trevor interrupted. 'I don't think it's a good idea, sweetheart, for the moment anyway. You've got a lot to be going on with.'

Lucinda tossed her head, dismissively.

'Come on, Gavin. Spew it out.'

'You'll hate it, absolutely hate it. Trevor hates it too.'

'How do you know?'

'Daddy would go spare, but that's usually an advantage. Still, he'll be tucked up when it goes out.'

'What's my father got to do with it? Why does everyone think I have to ask his permission for everything I do?'

Trevor frowned at Lucinda. Gavin was playing the television game, but she didn't yet know the rules. Lucinda continued, tossing back her hair in annoyance.

'I do wish people would stop it. I'm quite capable of making my own decisions. You might treat me as an adult, Gavin.'

'That's exactly what I was going to suggest. What I'm going for, is a new approach to human sexuality. We've had the boy-scout jolly approach, had the arse-achingly tedious confessions to camera, had the endless comparisons with the animal world. But what have we learned? Nothing that you couldn't leaf through in WH Smith's. What I'm looking for is telling it like it is. Real people telling us real experiences, without wrapping it up in jargon they've borrowed from their shrink. I want to put the fun back into sex. Fun but deep-down serious. That's how I see it.'

'And what's my role in all this?'

Lucinda was winding the chain of her bag round her finger, Trevor could sense that the antagonism was a thin mask for attraction. In a moment, Gavin would suddenly switch from indifference to flattery. At least he knew him well enough to know his moves.

'Asking questions. I've noticed you're good at that.'

Then came the expected smile, the wait for her response.

'I'd like to, but I can't, Gavin. Maybe later on, but I've a good reason.'

Lucinda swivelled round, so that she was at Trevor's side.

'Should I tell him?'

'I'd wait a while.'

'Oh, do let me, I must tell someone. I've had a letter from the Controller of Scripts. Intertel have decided to go ahead on *Grains of Evil*. Remember, the script I gave you?'

'I have a confession to make. I haven't read it yet,' Gavin said. Then he added, 'God, I hope it's not another epic of the upper classes.'

'I'm having a meeting about it soon, they're going to fix a date. I never dreamed it would happen, I never dreamed Annie would say yes. I mean, it's unbelievable, after all that happened. But don't say anything at the moment, will you? Annie could still change her mind. It was Trevor's idea, he suggested I sent *Grains of Evil* to Clary Hunt, but I said she wouldn't even look at it. She must get hundreds of scripts. Anyway, I sent one off. And guess what? She did like it, really liked it. In fact, she loved it. Said she'd cancel everything to do it.'

'Well done, well done,' said Gavin, genuinely impressed. As yet, Clary hadn't agreed to a frank interview on *Splash!* – difficult girl – but now it was looking possible.

'Bright move, Trev, sending it to Clary. Very bright move.'

'When I saw her in *Rough Trade*, I just knew she'd be right. Trevor said if she approved, I'd be more than halfway to production. Isn't that right, darling?'

'We were both knocked out, when Clary wrote a note, saying she'd like to meet the author. But I keep telling Lucinda not to get too excited. It's early days. Well, Gavin, I don't have to tell you.'

'Has anyone talked budget?' asked Gavin.

'They must know it's not something you can knock off in a studio,' Lucinda said, indignantly. 'If that's what they've got in mind, they can jolly well stuff it. I'd rather it wasn't made at all.'

'Yes, yes. But you've got to understand that every time Intertel throws money at drama, it means less for other programmes. We can't be top heavy on drama, it's not good for the company.'

'Why should I worry about that? I'm not running Intertel.'

'I worry,' said Gavin. 'I always worry that the arts will be marginalized out of existence. But I'll fight to see they aren't. As it is, I have to bow lower than I want to, to accommodate popular taste. Still, that's my problem. Have you a figure in mind for . . . what's the name of it?'

'*Grains of Evil*,' said Trevor. 'We have a rough idea, of course. We'll talk figures when the time comes. I'm just concerned to see that they aren't going to push for a mountain of changes. And that we have a say on casting. Crucial, with a script like this.'

'What's this, Trev? Are you acting as Lucinda' agent?'

'Just giving advice from the sidelines.'

'Trevor's being modest. I couldn't have gone ahead without him.'

'Do you think that's wise? Negotiating with your estranged wife?'

'We wouldn't be doing that directly. In any case, I trust Annie. She's the only person I know who can be fair and objective – when it comes to drama. Apart from anything else, she was enthusiastic right from the start. She read the script ages ago. She won't let the difficulties in our private life stand in the way. She'd be crazy if she did.'

'Did you know she's off to the States soon?'

'Annie goes every year,' said Trevor.

'All I'm saying is, it might be a while before anything's decided. Depends on the take-up in LA,' said Gavin. Then he turned to Lucinda. 'Think about it. If you want to make a name as a movie scriptwriter, it'd be a good start, getting your face on TV.'

'I'm not interested in publicity. All I want is to see actors speaking my words on the screen.'

'Good luck. I mean that sincerely, Lucinda. I do understand writers, you know. Being one myself. Or doesn't poetry count?'

'Of course it does,' she replied, crossly.

As Gavin left again to trawl around the dance floor, Trevor put his arm round Lucinda's shoulder, but she shook him off impatiently.

'Is anything the matter?'

'No. Yes. I don't like it. It feels as though everyone is trying to take me over.'

Trevor tried not to betray his anxiety.

'That's not so, sweetheart.'

'Gavin thinks he can just pick people up when the mood takes him. And it's obvious, why he wants me on *Splash!*. He could just as well have asked Tim. All he wants on the screen is the Sherwood name. He doesn't care who I am, what I've done. I don't know why you see so much of him.'

'Gavin's bright.'

'Not that bright. I want to go somewhere else. How about going to the Black Hole? I haven't been there for ages.'

'Do you really want to? I should be getting back. I've lots to do tomorrow. Today, rather.'

'There's a really good gig on tonight. Live music. And there won't be anyone boring in TV, just a load of my friends. Come on, Trevor. Let's enjoy ourselves.'

'Just for half an hour, then.'

'If it's good, I'll stay. You go when you want to. I won't mind.'

Lucinda leaped to her feet, and Trevor picked up the bottle of champagne nestling in an ice bucket.

'Look. Half left.'

'Gavin can drink it. Come on.'

'Wouldn't you rather see a late-night movie, sweetheart?'

'I don't feel like sex.'

Trevor laughed. Some films would never be the same again.

'I feel like dancing. Proper dancing, not like this place.'

When Trevor called a cab from the Black Hole a couple of hours later, he was a little drunk and achingly, jumpily tired. Why else would he have given the wrong address, and only noticed once they were skirting Regent's Park that he was following the familiar route to Langton Villas? Hastily correcting his instructions, he felt in his pocket for his key, leaned back in his seat and promptly fell asleep. The next thing he knew, someone was shouting, 'Which number, mate?' After he had rid himself of his remaining cash, he pushed his way into Lucinda's house, and dragged himself upstairs to the living room. The remains of a half-eaten pizza and a bowl of wilting salad was on the floor, a reminder that Lucinda had suddenly felt the urge to eat, just when they were ready to leave.

The house, which came to life in her presence, now seemed cold and uncomfortable. He noticed that she had left a window wide open on the first floor, the battery of made-to-order sound systems clearly visible from the street. When he'd complained once, she'd looked amazed. 'If anything gets nicked, I can buy some more. Stop fussing, Trevor.' He felt like fussing. The fresh food he had bought on his way back from college was still wrapped on the draining-board. She didn't like to bother with cooking. Either you ate out in a proper, expensive restaurant, or you snacked. She was mystified by Trevor's delight in eating at home. It was difficult for him to say, 'Shall we go home?' But he would get over it. They had only been living together for a matter of weeks. Small adjustments, essential to forming new habits, might take years. He could accept that.

Trevor still hesitated about taking the final step, trying to fathom out if the time had come to inform his close friends of his change of address, still harbouring the hope that in the near future, Annie might change her mind so that he could divide his time between Kentish Town and Chelsea. He wished that he hadn't arranged for the Post Office to forward his mail. Picking up the mail would be one excuse to see her, to maintain the contact which had dwindled into a curt discussion of practicalities. Why was she so reluctant to tell him what she was doing with Langton Villas? She might have told him earlier, that she was knocking down the wall of his study, with the intention of making more space for a playroom and bedroom for Dally. Last time they spoke, he had lost his temper, then tried to ring her back to apologize but she left the phone off the hook. It was as though she was deliberately trying to create hostility between them, which was quite unnecessary and petty. Annie could easily have reached him at college, but she made a point of phoning him at Danvers Street. If Lucinda answered, she would say curtly, 'Is my husband there?' Not only unnecessary, but childish and gauche, not like Annie at all.

Lucinda said she could always tell, even without listening, when he was on the phone to Annie, just by the expression on his face.

'What did she say this time?'

'Nothing much. Actually, it was difficult to hear. It would be easier without the competition. Don't you ever listen to music at a normal level?'

'Honestly! I turned it right down. Go to the top of the house, it's quiet there.'

No wonder Annie accused him of being difficult and thought he was trying to avoid her. How could he sound friendly and relaxed when he had to walk round the house with Lucinda's mobile phone, trying to find a quiet corner away from the exuberant music belching out from countless speakers which sprouted in the most unexpected places, even the lavatory?

'What did you say? This is a bad line, Annie.'

'The wall's coming down.'

'Then there's nothing I can say, is there? I'm not sure it's a good idea, though, Kate moving in.'

'Trevor, that's my decision. Mine and Kate's.'

'Like knocking down the wall.'

'Right. Like knocking down the wall.'

'I just thought you could have asked me. We've always gone fifty- fifty on the mortgage, remember?'

'I know. I'm aware of that.'

'I'm not pushing it, but I do still have some say in what gets altered. You do realize it's now a three-bedroom house, not a four-bedroom house.'

'What the hell does it matter? You're not living here. And I've just spent twenty-five grand on one thing and another.'

'The market value in Kentish Town is beginning to rise. And about time. That house with four bedrooms would be worth at least three hundred thousand, I'd say. Less with three bedrooms.'

'What's this? What makes you think I'm selling?'

'I'm merely reminding you of what it's worth, Annie, that's all.'

'I'm not selling the house, Trevor. I AM NOT SELLING THIS HOUSE.'

'Annie, darling. Calm down. I'm not asking you to sell the house. But I may need to release some capital, to get a place of my own.'

'All right. Take back your bloody capital. Take back the five thousand you put in. Is that what you want?'

'We'll talk about it another time. It would be far better if we met. I'd like to see you, Annie.'

'I'm too busy. Masses to do. I'm about to go to the States.'

'Before you go, would you consider doing something for me?'

'What now, Trevor?'

'Edward's arrived in England with his fiancée, Janine. I'd really appreciate it if we could meet him together before the wedding. I didn't feel I could tell him about us, not at this stage, it would be too upsetting. The news that his long-lost dad . . . well, you can imagine what his reaction would be. He's had a pretty unstable life with his mother, I would imagine. It would mean a lot to me, if you came. I'd fit in with your plans, if you'd tell me when's suitable.'

'Who said I was going to the wedding?'

'We talked about it, before.'

'Before. Now it's after. Look, you've moved out from here and you've moved in with Lucinda. Your life has nothing to do with me any more. Why pretend that nothing's changed? Why do you always have to pretend, Trevor?'

'I'm not pretending. I'm just asking you to make a simple, human gesture. For Edward's sake.'

'The answer's no. I can't.'

'Is it because you don't want to meet Margaret?'

He heard her give a slight laugh.

339

'Well, Annie?'

'The simple fact is I haven't time.'

'That isn't the real reason. You're saying no to be awkward and difficult. If only you'd stop hating me.'

'You can go to the wedding with Lucinda. I'm sure she'd love to meet all your relatives from Nottingham.'

'Annie. If I go without you, I assure you I'll be on my own. I wouldn't dream of taking Lucinda. She's not part of our life, and never will be.'

'Good. That's a relief. For her anyway. Anything else to impart, Trev? I should be in town by now.'

'Annie, listen. When you're away in the States, don't forget to call me if you have problems, anything which bothers you. Who are you seeing by the way?'

'One or two producers.'

'I meant *seeing*. You must be seeing another man by now.'

'Must I?'

'After being married all that time, I wouldn't expect you to be celibate.'

'Although it's fashionable, it doesn't appeal to me. As you used to say, the denial of sensuality is the English disease. I never knew how right you were, Trevor.'

'You haven't answered my question. I suppose it's foolish of me to expect you to be sleeping alone.'

There was a pause before Annie replied. 'Are you happy with her?'

'Yes. Very very happy.'

'Good. At least one of us is.'

'Lucinda was knocked out, getting the letter from the script department about *Grains of Evil*. I know how difficult it must have been for you. But I think you've made the right decision. It's just the right moment in your career, to do something like this. All the same, I do admire you, Annie, I don't think I could have done that.'

'I had little to do with it. We had a drama department meeting and I said it was time we did something completely different, that's all. So the Controller of Scripts sifted through a load of stuff and *Grains of Evil* was in the top three. He thought Clary Hunt might be interested in it, sent a copy to her agent. Even before we heard back, he recommended going ahead. Once we'd budgeted out the other scripts, they were out of the running. Simple as that.'

340

'I know it wasn't. It can't have been easy. Do you think you can cope?'

'With what, Trevor?'

'Seeing Lucinda again.'

'She won't be working with me. As far as I'm concerned, her script is just one of next year's package. I'll get the right director and let everyone get on with it. By the way, I found your Greek bag of summer things when I was turning out. If you want it, I'll send it over in a cab. Otherwise I'll throw it out.'

'You know how I hate chucking things away.'

'I'll send it over then.'

'I'll be thinking of you, Annie. Hope you have a successful trip. When are you leaving?'

'No idea. I really don't know. Goodbye, Trevor.'

In spite of Annie's cold response, Trevor failed to experience the usual leaden feeling after his calls to her. It made such a difference, admitting to Annie that he was happy with Lucinda. Although he had said he was in love with her, being happy implied something more permanent, something which couldn't be dismissed as infatuation. Love and happiness rarely kept in step. But he was not only in love, he was happy, in varying degrees, whenever he was with her. They were right together, even though they were so unlike one another. Perhaps Annie and he had been too similar, too complacent. He so disliked comparing them, but the guilt would be unbearable unless he could justify, if only to himself, why he was now with Lucinda, and not with Annie. Although he was unable to blame Annie in any way, he did sometimes wonder whether she had brought it upon herself, by not remaining open to new possibilities.

Lucinda was always open to new possibilities. Had that been the root of his attraction, right at the beginning? Her openness to experience, the way she refused to box in the different parts of her life? The ease of her relationship with family and friends, both bound together in a loose, confident alliance, so unlike Annie who groaned at her twice-yearly visits to Cardiff, duty calls on mother and relatives she would never discuss? Having overcome his conditioned hostility, Trevor had come to respect Lucinda's friends, slightly envied them perhaps – not because they were landed and upper class, but because they were so tolerant, so friendly with one another, so independent yet respecting one another's individuality. Now he could see the

341

attraction where once he had condemned through ignorance. The upper-class tradition, he now admitted to himself, did have something of value. It was part of the England he loved.

One day, when her father was abroad, Lucinda took him to visit Sherwood Hall. She longed for him to share her past. 'You have to know me, really know me,' she said. 'I want you to know everything.' They were both on edge with excitement, as she led him down the long corridors, peering into one room after another. He imagined her playing in the giant doll's house in the nursery, gazing at the posters of pop-stars still pinned up in her bedroom, doing homework in the holidays, bent over her small desk, occasionally looking up at the row of china dolls with dangling legs ranged on a shelf above it. He wondered at all the childhood mementoes from past and present generations, the old rocking-horses and leather-bound scrap-books, the lawn which had sprung up year after year, immune to children and rampaging dogs. He almost felt he could have belonged there, as he sat in the library, scanning the rows of leather-bound books.

They were chatting haphazardly in the conservatory of Sherwood Hall, where an ornate Swedish stove was throwing out the heat denied by the weak winter sun. It was one of the most glorious weekends Trevor had ever experienced. He had kissed her fingers, and held them even when they were brought coffee by one of the household. He had become used to the quiet footsteps of the staff, padding down corridors bearing linen or trays or boxes of cleaning materials, and no longer felt the need to give an embarrassed smile to acknowledge their presence.

That's one of the things I adore about you, Trevor. You take everything so seriously. No-one does around here.'

'But your father would take it pretty seriously, if we were married.'

'I suppose so,' said Lucinda absently. 'But I've told him I'm not going to get married until I'm well over thirty.'

'Couldn't you change your mind?'

'Trevor! Are you proposing?'

'I wouldn't dare, sweetheart. Just putting the idea in your head, so you know that one day I might ask you.'

'When you're an old, old man. And I would light up your declining years. Hey, wouldn't that be a great movie idea? Or

342

maybe it should be a gay guy. A gay guy meets this old man in some decadent resort, South of France or Italy—'

'Been done, sweetheart.'

'Damn. Really? You always say that. I won't listen. Don't tell me. All right, just a moment. Another idea. I thought of this at school. A convent girl buys a crucifix in a shop selling religious antiques, falls in love with the old guy who owns it and he locks her up with statues of the Virgin Mary and gory Christs. It would be a statement about sex and religion.'

'Mm.'

'You don't like it?'

'Why don't you make your next script a feminist western? The John Wayne character is a woman.'

'Are you pulling my leg? Trevor, it's amazing. A super idea. Lots of dust and galloping horses, bullets screaming into the dust – but she'd be more Clint Eastwood than John Wayne. Kind of reluctant, cool, pigtails and a divided skirt, lolloping along on a little grey mare. She gets into town and wow!'

'We could write it together.'

'Go away to Nevada and live in a motel with a big whirry fan.'

'I'd have to dig out my old portable typewriter. Let's get this right.'

'Would you? Would you just take off with me one day?'

'Into the sunset with a fiction treatment.'

'Better than boring old Greece. When *Grains of Evil* gets raves in *Variety*, and the calls and faxes are queueing up, then we'll just disappear. And come up with my next.'

'Don't forget, I hate being in Hollywood.'

'But you haven't been with me, have you? I bet there's a hip scene you never even saw. Tim's got some super friends out there. We'd have a great, great time.'

'It would have to be in the vacation. How about next summer?'

'Bad time. Autumn is better. And I know someone who knows someone who knows Arnie. We could meet Arnie!'

'Arnie?'

'Schwarz-en-egger, silly.'

'Give me a kiss.'

Lucinda jumped onto Trevor's lap and pecked round his lips. 'Proper one.'

'No. Not till we're in Hollywood.'

It was not long after they returned from their visit to Sherwood Hall, that Trevor received a note from Edward saying that he was in London. It was the day before Annie was leaving for Los Angeles, and he appreciated that she had other things on her mind. If nothing else, he could reassure himself that he had done everything he could.

'What did she say this time?'

Lucinda was in the bedroom, dying her eyelashes, straddling a black chair in her underwear, staring imperiously into the mirror, reminding Trevor of the famous photograph of Christine Keeler. Tonight they were off to Covent Garden, sharing a box with Gavin, who was interested in securing an adagio solo from one of the principal dancers.

'She absolutely refuses to meet Edward.'

'Oh, honestly.'

Lucinda flicked a tiny, spiked brush through her lashes, and widened her eyes to gauge the effect.

'I'd hoped she might have second thoughts. But she didn't. There was no way of persuading her. She said she had no intention of making a special trip back to London once she was in Los Angeles. I said I'd buy the air-ticket, but she wouldn't listen. I wish she'd see that it's not for me, it's for Edward.'

'Annie is very stubborn sometimes, isn't she? What difference would it make? She doesn't know him. It would be no different from chatting to a stranger in a bar.'

'Hardly. Edward probably blames Annie as much as me for what happened.'

'But that was eons ago. I bet he doesn't even remember anything about it. He was only a baby.'

'Babies remember, subconsciously.'

'What on earth makes you say that?'

'Freud, for example.'

'No-one takes him seriously. Only Americans.'

Trevor sighed, unwilling to embark on an evaluation of psychoanalysis.

'Don't be so down, Trevor. Why don't I come? I don't mind meeting Edward.'

'Darling, that's very sweet. But out of the question.'

'Why? I thought you didn't want to hide anything from him.'

'I don't.'

344

'Just me, you want to hide me.'

'You know that's not true.'

'If Annie did come, you'd have to tell him eventually. Then he'd trust you even less. Why not be frank about what's happened? No-one lives with another person for ever any more, he must know that. If I was Edward, I'd much prefer it that way. OK, so he might be upset for a bit, but so what? Anyway, we might have something in common. I'm only a little older, aren't I?'

'I'll think about it.'

But Trevor had already made up his mind.

Edward was staying in a newly renovated hotel on the edge of Earl's Court. As they entered, Trevor was assailed by a sweep of brilliant red and blue acrylic carpet, and plaster columns sprouting in unlikely corners, around which plastic creeper crawled in regular spirals. The large mahogany bar, which stretched the length of the high-ceilinged room, was covered in notices in Gothic script, announcing the delights of Happy Hour cocktails. A group of Americans in check trousers of various hues, with stomachs protruding like pumpkins, were consulting maps and commanding the attention of the girls behind the bar. The other occupants, a seated gathering of Japanese businessmen, were silently holding large plastic bar menus in front of their faces.

Lucinda, conspicuous in a short, low-necked black dress clinging round her buttocks with a cream gaberdine jacket thrown over her shoulders, was attracting curious stares. Trevor had decided not to comment on the large black-lensed glasses which she had put on as she left the house. She went straight over to the bar while Trevor hung back for a moment, examining the various corners of the room for someone who might be his son. Edward had told him he would be wearing a blue denim jacket. Janine had curly red hair, he couldn't miss them.

'I don't think they're here yet,' he said to Lucinda.

'Your son is over there, I believe.'

'Where?'

'The other end of the bar.'

Trevor saw a large figure bent over a magazine.

'Are you sure? He isn't wearing a blue denim jacket.'

'It's him.'

345

As he was looking, a strapping girl in an ample, floppy blue felt hat, embellished with large white felt daisies, a huge patterned sweater, a long skirt and cowboy boots, said something and sat beside the man. Now they were all looking in the same direction. 'Look, Trevor. He's got your nose and your hair.'

Trevor masked his reaction with a smile and strolled over towards Edward. Lucinda was exaggerating, for he bore absolutely no resemblance to his father, fat bloated face, small chin and long arms. Trevor stretched out his hand.

'Edward?'

'Dad? Pleased to meet you. And this is my fiancée Janine. Janine, meet Dad.'

His voice was the confident sound of Sydney.

'Pleased to meet you,' said Janine.

She was plump, with a sprinkling of freckles on her beaming face, and a full mouth outlined in lipstick the colour of a kid's orange lolly. As she shook his hand, the blue ear-rings shaped like dolphins bobbed round her face. He wanted to hug his son, had imagined some manly reunion, but instead he clasped his hands together in front of him.

'It's so good to see you, Edward. This is my friend, Lucinda.'

Lucinda merely nodded, without smiling.

'I'll find us some seats,' said Edward.

Then he strode off towards some empty chairs, but was waved away and returned.

'All taken. Never mind, we'll talk on our feet. That suit you?'

'Sure,' said Trevor.

'Isn't he just like his pa?' said Janine, turning to Lucinda. 'I thought he would be.'

'There's some people leaving back there.'

Lucinda began walking towards a table partly obscured by a rubber plant, and they followed her in single file, like a party of tourists following a guide.

'Edward doesn't drink, he'll have a juice, and I'll have a beer,' said Janine, when they had all settled round the table.

'How about champagne?' suggested Lucinda.

'Yeh. Let's go high life. That's cool.'

Despairing of obtaining the attention of a waiter, Trevor went over to the bar, followed by his son.

'The girls can talk amongst themselves,' said Edward.

Now that he was next to him, Trevor felt almost dwarfed,

346

although Edward couldn't have been more than a couple of inches taller. Six foot one, something like that.

'I hope we can have some time to get to know one another,' said Trevor. He had to keep himself from staring, studying Edward's face like an unfamiliar map, and tried to ignore the ring hanging obtrusively from one of his ears. 'I always had this nightmare, that we'd have met in the past, and I wouldn't have recognized you.'

'You haven't changed, not from the photo I found in Mum's drawer as a kid. What do I call you? I don't have to say Father, do I?'

Trevor smiled. 'Dad if you like.'

'I think I'll call you Trevor. That OK? Everyone calls me Eddie.'

Trevor ordered the drinks, and Edward turned down the offer of a tray, as though it was an insult to his masculinity.

'Here, I'll do this,' he said, grasping the bottle of champagne and the flat-rimmed champagne glasses in one hand, a glass of orange juice and Trevor's beer in the other.

'I was a waiter once. Done it all, I have. Now it's a desk job, bit of travel. You got a computer, Trevor?'

'Haven't got round to it yet.'

'I sell them, see. Around Sydney. Janine makes hats. We're saving up so she can get herself a shop. Great girl, she is. We weren't going to bother with getting hitched, but now she's got one on the way, well, you have to.'

'So I'm a dad and a grandad in one go?'

'S'right. You pleased?'

'You bet.'

Trevor glanced quickly at the girls, hoping that Janine would omit to mention that she was pregnant in front of Lucinda. Trevor Watson, grandad. It was an unwelcome reminder of his age. He was relieved to see that the girls were obviously discussing one of Janine's creations, as the felt hat with the daisies had temporarily changed owners. Lucinda could never resist a hat.

He followed Edward to their table. Janine was holding up a handmirror while Lucinda manipulated the brim, bending it first up, then down.

'Looks wonderful on her, don't you think, Janine? Could have been made to order,' said Edward, as he set down the drinks. 'That one's my favourite.'

347

'Eddie always says that. He's going to be my salesman. Eddie could sell fridges to Eskimos, Eddie could!'

Trevor had expected Edward to gaze in admiration at Lucinda but he was looking at the hat. It only needed one accessory, only one slight change, for him to realize again how beautiful she was. With that hat, any man ought to be on his knees. Her eyes had changed hue with the shadow of the brim, and were dark shadowy blue like the rocks below the surface of the sea in Paradisos bay. One day, he would take her to Greece.

'Will you make one for me? I must have a hat like this. Isn't it super, Trevor?'

'Stunning, sweetheart.'

'Our first export order! Do you think we'd sell in England?'

Lucinda removed the hat, and examined the inside, parting the felt seams with a long nail-glossed finger. Then she gave Janine a whole list of places and people to try. Janine extracted a crumpled bill from the body belt concealed under her sweater, and noted them down while Edward peered over her shoulder.

'Great stuff, woa, that'll do,' said Edward, suddenly noticing that Lucinda was topping up his fruit juice with champagne. 'Well, Trevor? Who'd have thought that you'd bring along a girl who knows all about hats? It's made Janine's day. Now it's my turn. Mustn't let the girls hog the pitch.'

Trevor gently rejected Edward's offer of a computer package with academic software, instead advising him to send some brochures to his college. Undeterred, Edward then took a couple of packets from his pocket, and proceeded to cover the table with high-gloss photographs of a bungalow taken from every angle.

'OK. Now let me show you something. This is our little place. And there's a spare room for when you come out to Australia.'

'You haven't thought of settling in England?'

Edward grinned, one side of his mouth lifted slightly more than the other like Trevor's.

'Aussie suits me. It's a good life out there. Good mates, fantastic beaches. What have you got here?' Then he bent towards Trevor. 'That your girl?'

'Lucinda? Yes. We're living together.'

'Good on you, Trevor. Mum said you'd split from Annie. Isn't she a famous actress now?'

'I didn't tell your mother.'

'Mum gets to know everything. She's going nuts with excitement. Can't wait for the wedding. She and Janine get on like a house on fire. Mum's coming out as soon as we've saved enough for the ticket. Fifty hats and we reckon we're there.'

'That's marvellous,' said Trevor.

'You didn't have kids, that right?'

'Right.'

'One was enough? We want two, Janine and me, we got it all planned out.'

'Very wise,' said Trevor, hastily.

'Why don't you bring Lucinda out to Aussie?'

'Perhaps I will. I'll do my best.'

'You still a prof?'

'Still a prof. Come and visit me in college, before you go back.'

'Sure will. We've got really high-level universities in Australia. Computer science departments better than here, so they say. There's nothing second-rate, you know, nothing second-rate about Aussie.'

'Lucinda tapped Trevor's arm.

'We'll have to go.'

'Hey? Could you get us seats for *Miss Saigon*? Is it as fantastic as they say?' said Janine, sticking the hat back on her head and puffing up her curls.

'I'll do my best,' said Trevor. 'I hear it's excellent.'

'That's the only thing I envy you, all those fantastic theatres. Shame you've got to go. Eddie and me are going to hit the Greek. He just loves Greek cuisine, pitta bread and fish paté, that kind of stuff.'

'I like it too. Another time.'

Trevor took Edward's hand again and was taken aback when Janine planted a wet kiss on his cheek.

'Bye, Trevor. You're a good guy. See you soon.'

Lucinda had given a slight wave, a cool smile and was already by the revolving doors. She said nothing until they climbed into a cab and Trevor prompted her.

'Well?'

'Her hats should go down big in Sydney. And he hasn't got your nose, I decided.'

'So what did you think of Edward?'

349

'What am I meant to think? I'm sure he's wonderful with computers.'

He left Lucinda at Gavin's dinner party at Christopher's, where she had discovered a lot in common with a young Irish film director, already the subject of numerous newspaper profiles. Yet again, he heard her narrating the plot-line of *Grains of Evil*. Gavin had heard it more than once, but was reacting as though it was the first time. A tight band was pressing down on Trevor's eyes which he supposed was a migraine. Annie had them very occasionally, she used to lie on the bed and he would put a wet towel over her forehead. He slipped out of the restaurant, with the excuse that he was feverish, some virus. Lucinda didn't enquire further, she seemed unconcerned. When you were young, physical ailments were only a temporary barrier to enjoyment. Nothing was ever serious or incapacitating. Why was he conjuring up a brain tumour, a pea of decay lodged somewhere in his head? He was in hospital, bandages swathed round his head, Annie bending over him, willing him to live . . .

'You OK?'

Lucinda found him fully dressed lying on the floor of the drawing room with a flannel over his eyes.

'Slight headache.'

'God. I thought it was something serious, you rushing off like that.'

She sat cross-legged on the floor beside him and began to elaborate on her conversation with the Irish genius.

'Sweetheart, could I hear another time?'

'Sure. I thought you'd be interested.'

'I am. But I need to talk about Edward. What did you really think?'

'About your son? Not quite what I expected. Perfectly nice.'

'The terrible part is, I felt exactly the same meeting him this time as I felt when I walked out. As though he had nothing to do with me, yet he's obviously mine. Thank you for being so pleasant.'

'Was I? Her hat wasn't bad. Not right for here, but I told her to drop into David Shilling, if she wants to see how it's done.'

'There was so much I wanted to say, about being a father, about how painful it all was, about how I wanted to begin again.

350

And then, somehow I couldn't. Never mind, it'll be easier meeting up on our own.'

'You're jolly lucky he's going back to Australia. He'll be perfectly happy with all his perfectly boring friends and his perfectly boring job in that perfectly boring country. It was the luck of the draw, that he took after Margaret, isn't that her name?'

'Yes.'

'Want a coffee?'

'No thanks. I've still got a slight headache.'

A couple of weeks later, Trevor and Lucinda had their first disagreement. He hadn't the heart to say that he really wasn't up to it, not tonight. He ought to have said something while she was getting changed into a dress he had chosen for her at Vivienne Westwood's, but he couldn't bring himself to spoil her anticipation.

'Isn't it absolutely gorgeous? I want to hang it on the wall,' she said, holding against her body the boned, skimpy crushed-velvet number with a brilliant pink satin train.

Trevor's eyes were fixed on the gossamer thin suspender belt, the sheer black stockings and high shiny heels as she turned towards the mirror. She had given up wearing the teddies or bodies or whatever she called them, sexless objects with idiotic buttons under the crotch he had to fumble with to release. Just as she was stepping into the dress, he said, 'You look stunning. But I really can't go out tonight, darling. I've too much to do. I know I'll be dreary if I come. And you can't stand me being dreary, can you?'

'I'll go on my own then.'

'Do you want to?'

'Of course I don't. I want you to come.'

'I can't go to bed late every night.'

'You went to bed early last night.'

'It wasn't early.'

'You're bored with my friends. Why don't you say so?'

'I prefer having you to myself sometimes. Why don't we have something to eat here, watch a movie and talk? What's wrong with that?'

'Nothing. Except I told Amanda we'd be there. It's her birthday.'

'You go.'

351

'If I do, will you be grumpy?'

'No. But it would be nice if there was something to eat in the house. And if the phone wasn't ringing incessantly. And I do need one room I can work in where I don't walk in and find it's occupied by one of your friends. My room, without your things all over the place. I thought you said you knew someone who could let us have a flat?'

'Did I? Why do you keep going on about getting a flat? What's wrong with this house?'

'I want to contribute something, I want us to have somewhere which is ours. Can't you see that?'

'Why are you so bothered? Why would life be any different in some dreary place in Fulham? Anyway, it doesn't matter where we are. I don't want to move.'

'You told me you did.'

'I've changed my mind then.'

Until now, Trevor had deliberately held back from bringing up the subject of finding a flat, or mentioning Lucinda's friends. But he was tired, and this was not the occasion to engage in debate.

'We'll talk about it another time, sweetheart.'

Lucinda was going through a difficult time, he had to keep reminding himself. The longed-for meeting with the Intertel script department had been delayed, then postponed until sometime in the New Year. He tried to reassure her, that was the way things happened in television. Even the biggest hits had rocky beginnings, nail-biting periods of despair, for no-one made quick decisions, not any more, not with committees run by accountants who would have turned down *Gone With the Wind*.

Although she would never admit it, Trevor sensed that she wanted to go out only to forget her disappointment for a few hours. Every time they went to Tiger Tim's she bravely enthused over her script, parrying the questions from envious friends. They would start shooting next year, she told them all, her eyes sparkling with imagined success. One evening when he came back, he found Lucinda in tears. She had tried calling everyone she could think of in the drama department, but the right person was never available. Then she charged straight into the script office and was fobbed off by a secretary who told her smugly that 'everything was in hand' and that she would be hearing shortly. It was all Trevor could do to stop her sending a letter saying she was taking her script elsewhere.

'I bet Steven Spielberg doesn't treat writers like this,' she wailed. 'Or Coppola. Or even Stephen Frears. I hope they all rot in hell. I hope Intertel gets taken over. I hope they all get the sack. I never want to go in there again.'

Trevor saw it would only enrage her more if he tried to calm her down. She was lying on the floor, bellowing into a cushion. It was the only time he had seen her hysterical, but he put it down to her constant diet of late hours and champagne. Or perhaps she had been helping herself to Tim's cocaine. He had questioned her once, but she dismissed his concern airily. 'God, Trevor. Everybody does. Everybody of my age anyhow.' He was planning to take her out of the city, some quiet country hotel by the sea. That night, she would not allow him to touch her, she wanted to nurse her grief. In vain did he assure her that if Annie had given the go-ahead, it would happen, he knew Annie, she didn't muck people about, that she must try and be patient.

Their first row was over something so trivial, whether Tim's friend Freddie should sleep in the small guest-room which had been cleared out to become Trevor's retreat, or whether he could kip for a night in the drawing room.

'If it's only for a night, why can't he sleep on the settee?'

'The sofa, you mean.'

'All right. The bloody sofa. I need that little room to myself, Lucinda. Is that so much to ask?'

'It's my house.'

'I don't care whose house it is. We're living together. Together.'

'Sorry. I hadn't noticed.'

'Stop being childish.'

'You're so uptight you wouldn't know how to be childish. No wonder Edward never wanted to see you. I don't blame him.'

'Lucinda, you have no right to say that. This has nothing to do with you. You know nothing about it.'

'You've talked about it enough. Edward, Edward, Edward. You must have been beastly to him. I bet you were ashamed of him, because he couldn't read at three. I bet you gave him a terrible time.'

'Just because he isn't a spoilt brat like you.'

'Spoilt brats get places, that's what you don't realize. You hate it because when I was a kid I had things you didn't. Well, I'm glad. I'm jolly glad I had everything I wanted. And I'm sick of hearing about people who don't. All your leftie friends, all they're after is to have what we've got. They don't give a damn about other people. Life is unfair. What's wrong with that? You worked hard, you made it. So why can't they?'

'Lucinda, is it really impossible for you to understand anyone other than yourself? Can you only see what's outside your window? If you want to write for films, you'd better start learning.'

'I will, but I don't need your help, thank you very much.'

'I hadn't noticed you turning it down, all the time I've spent. Lucinda, let's stop. We're both saying things we don't mean.'

'You only like me in bed. I know that. I don't know why we're bothering to talk.'

'Don't be stupid.'

'OK, so I'm stupid. You didn't think so once. Just because I don't agree with you all the time.'

'For God's sake, girl, can we change the subject?'

'No, no, I won't. You never let me speak. You never let me do things for myself. Now I know why.'

'When do you ever do something you don't want to? When have I ever asked you to alter your plans because of me?'

'All the time. I turn down invitations every week. I used to go out every night, I'd be away with friends most weekends.'

'Would you? So why don't you ask me to come?'

'Honestly, you know why.'

'Would it be different if we were married?'

'Yes. I wouldn't get asked.'

'You mean, they'd feel threatened by having me in the house.'

'That's not true. But you might say something, oh, I don't know. They're not used to people who read the *Guardian* and the *Independent*.'

Trevor burst out laughing.

'You can't be serious?'

'Sort of.'

'What would they do? Hold me under the Prevention of Terrorism Act?'

'I don't want to talk about it. It's boring.'

'What? That you'd rather not be seen around with someone

354

whose family doesn't even manage a couple of inches of Debrett's?'

'That's a perfectly stupid thing to say.'

Next morning, having slept alone for the first time, Trevor went out to find some fresh croissants, made his usual pot of coffee and carefully pushed open the door of the drawing room. The blinds were down, and a table lamp still lit even though it had been light for at least an hour. A crumpled rug lay on the couch, the pillow was on the floor, but she was no longer there. He waited for a call from Lucinda at college but none came. For two days he fretted, for two days he was unable to trace her. On the third day, he was making himself supper when she walked in, a large soft leather bag hanging from her shoulder.

'Hi.'

'Have you been somewhere?'

'Yes. I needed to get away.'

'Couldn't you have told me? Left a note?'

'Why? You knew I'd be back. Do you need to have a record of all my movements?'

'Of course not. But I was worried.'

'I can't bear you fussing all the time.'

'How did I know something hadn't happened? You were in a state, it wasn't like you. All you needed to say was, I'm going away on my own for a couple of days.'

'Then you'd have asked me where. You always ask me where I'm going. Did you do that with Annie?'

'No. She used to tell me.'

'And I suppose you phoned each other up every day?'

'Usually.'

'I think it's ghastly, keeping tabs like that. It's worse than being at school. Did you give one another exeats? Darling, you can go out now. But back by ten, don't forget. If that's what being married means, you can stuff it. I'm not accountable to you. I can do what I like. And so can you. I don't ring up every minute of the day, do I? Well, do I?'

'Why are you so angry? What on earth's happened?'

'None of your business.'

'Being hostile won't help anything. What do you want, Lucinda?'

Suddenly her tone changed. 'I want you to move out,' she said, levelly. 'I want you to move out now.'

355

'And your reason?'

'I don't need a fucking reason.'

'You don't love me, then. You've suddenly decided you don't love me any more.'

'Honestly, Trevor. There's no need to make a drama out of it. I just want to be on my own. For a while.'

'Very well. But I wish you wouldn't take out your disappointment on me. I know it's been tough, I know what that script means to you. But you must be patient.'

'Patient? You're out of your mind. When your wife kills my project because she wants to get at you?'

'Lucinda! That's complete nonsense.'

'I suppose your friend Gavin's lying then.'

'What did he say?'

'Only that Intertel weren't going ahead, what a shame, poor Lucinda, he'd heard it was so marvellous, blah, blah. Someone in the script department said Annie had changed her mind just before she went away. The reason was fucking obvious. I hate television. I'm going to get out.'

'Listen, do listen. I know that Annie will stick by her decision. Someone has got it very wrong.'

'Oh, for Christ's sake, Trevor. You know nothing about television.'

'That's what Annie used to say.'

'And Annie is always right, isn't she?'

'When did you talk to Gavin, by the way?'

'None of your business.'

'Have you been out with him?'

'He was at Tim's, if you want to know.'

'When?'

'I was stoned out of my brain and I wasn't looking at my watch. So there, Professor Watson.'

As Trevor went upstairs, he heard her clattering in the kitchen, the creak of the fridge door, a bottle popping open. When he heard the slamming of the front door, he called up Bryonie. It didn't take him long to pack.

20

ANNIE

The tanned male faces of the executives seated round the open-air breakfast table at the Bel Air Hotel were all turned towards Annie. Even though it was impossibly early, 8.15 a.m., she had been up since six. Body massage, facial and cosmetic application had been part of the service, one way of acquiring an American gloss which was needed for successful communication. Annie felt good, hair glistening with rare and natural oils, her lips newly full and coated, face given a hint of Hollywood bronze as though she'd already put in time around the pools. She looked the part, in a pants suit of pale beige gaberdine, with a vicuna coat flung over her shoulder. It was only the jewellery, she decided after nitpicking her appearance, which betrayed her origin. The Victorian jet pendant which Trevor had bought her to wear at an awards ceremony needed to be replaced by something chunkier, muted not shiny gold, the kind displayed on black velvet necks in Rodeo Drive.

The people who mattered, high-ups from the network, marketing bosses, were prepared to bite. *Rough Trade* with its strong female lead, had taken their fancy. Annie was getting near to realizing the impossible dream, a network television sale. The tiny trickle of British films had begun to make an impact now that the great American public was getting used to the strange accents. Clary Hunt had good diction, they'd understand mostly. Annie had left *Grains of Evil* until last, mentioning it casually when conversation flagged at one of her lunch meetings with Jerry Last, a top agent who had given her this month's highs and lows and was guiding her Hollywood trip. After she had outlined the plot, he nodded his head vigorously and said several times, 'Yeh, could be substantial minority interest.' Next morning, having read the script, and

357

taken in all of it because he knew what happened in the middle, he called to suggest a breakfast meeting with some people who'd be strong on the TV movie/video angle.

Annie shifted away from the sun, drained her fresh-pressed juice, and was cued to present the plotline of *Grains of Evil*. A strikingly handsome young man, in the darkest despair following a disappointed love, has turned to the Church and taken up residence in a small village. A gang of girls, daughters of workers at a neighbouring chicken farm . . . yeh, yeh, Annie, we get the idea, Jerry's pro the concept. Let's talk working scenarios. Then Jerry took over, talking about possibles, boxing *Grains of Evil* into a category which would be instantly recognizable, but not yet to Annie. The hunter's eyes round the table were sniffing round Jerry's possible. They began to argue over the concept, the concept being the location, the cast and the budget. The baseline was, big movie or small movie? Or, as Al Gorbetsky put it, what was the title saying to us? What the title was saying, Annie insisted, was big movie, big concept, big director. Mini-series? They were swilling this idea round, along with the veggie-juice cocktail. There was one man whose position or creative function in the hierarchy was difficult to place, he had been introduced as Lance Fielding. She was meant to know who he was. He could be an actor, legs casually crossed, sexy eye contact, the only man who would get a five-star rating in *Vanity Fair*'s Man of the Month. Bob Morione, who was a deputy network chief, was sitting back with arms folded, occasionally moving his jaw as though he was chewing a phantom toffee.

Jerry addressed his remarks to Bob, whose function, Annie guessed, was like the figure of Christ on the altar. Everything was directed towards him but he was not expected to reply.

'As I see it, *Grains* needs a more directional approach. Focused. OK, we buy the country idea, some hicksville place, sure. But it still needs some big-town action. What *Grains of Evil* says to me is: Here's this guy, believes in good and finds bad.'

'Story of my life,' said Hal, the rubbery-faced man who was the top-shot director of one of the major independent production houses. Marla Blech, who was a script consultant, added her husky voice and clasped the back of her neck as though giving herself a massage.

'Great concept. Let's think this through. At the moment, it's too localized. Where's it set? Anyone got a map?'

Jerry opened the script, licked his finger and pushed back the title pages.

'England. East Anglia. Corn-belt country,' said Annie. 'It's all flat and windy, big skies, stunted trees, marshes, remote villages. Where they say you don't cross the road to marry.'

'Rednecks,' explained Jerry.

'I like skies,' said Lance. 'Sounds like Montana.'

Annie tried to concentrate while the animated conversation raged round her. The ball was out of her court, she would wait till it bounced back.

'I said who is he, the writer?'

Annie gave a slight cough, and was immediately handed a glass of Agnès B. spring water.

'Lucinda Sherwood. She was a junior, working in my department, it's the first thing she's done. That's why I thought I'd give it a try. You don't often find a script like that, one which sticks.'

'You mean this is written by a kid?'

Annie smiled. 'She is quite young, I suppose.'

'Terrific!'

She knew why Jerry was looking so delighted. It would boost the promotional story, young English girl writes first script, they'd go wild when they discovered she lived in a stately home, daughter of a lord. That still meant something. Annie began to wish they could change the subject.

'How long's the option, Annie? How much time we got?' said Bob, pursing together his fleshy lips in the shape of a reluctant kiss.

Annie came to with a jolt. She had never considered that the Americans would give *Grains of Evil* anything more challenging than a polite refusal. It was a make-weight project, the kind of tool you mustered when the heavy negotiations had begun and a difficult agreement had been made so your partners could have the satisfaction of turning something down. Always bring something they can turn down, Annie had learned long ago. *Grains of Evil* had made its way into the Annie Griffiths Hollywood portfolio so that it could be dropped. Annie had already drafted the fax, and was about to send it to Anita: Dear Ms Sherwood, Unfortunately *Grains of Evil* failed to attract any interest in Hollywood, despite strenuous efforts on the part of Intertel. We are returning the script and wish you every success elsewhere . . . It was a mean stroke which Annie was beginning to regret.

'You're not going to believe this,' she said brightly, grinning at Jerry. 'But I was handed the script at the last minute, just before I left. I wasn't going to show it to you, then I thought, Well, maybe it's got a chance. So it hadn't got to the option stage.'

'Terrific,' said Jerry. 'I was hoping you'd say that.'

'Who's the agent?' asked Al.

'I'm ninety-nine per cent sure she doesn't have one . . .' Annie picked up one of the scripts, scanned the title page, then the last page and dropped it back on the table. 'If she had one, there'd be a name on here. Sorry about this.'

'No problem,' said Jerry.

The situation was becoming farcical. Annie Griffiths with a script she was trying not to sell and suddenly everyone was interested. The only off-putting factor would be budget. Great concept, skyhigh costs, no deal.

'I'll be straight with you, though. Lucinda might give us trouble.'

'What kind of trouble?'

'She's likely to ask a ridiculous figure for an option, comes from a wealthy family. And if we went ahead on a co-pro, I'm not sure I'd want to work with her. I had to get rid of her after she'd been in my department a few weeks. Lucinda's hero is Spielberg, she thinks TV movies are made of millions.'

'That so?' Jerry winked at Annie. 'This is looking good.'

Marla rattled her serried rank of gold bangles.

'Are you thinking what I'm thinking?'

'Could be. What's your take on this?'

'Fatal Attraction?'

'No, honey. They did buy an option, at the start. Then this guy kicks up because they changed his lousy story into a worldwide hit. Any of your writers work on that?'

'A couple,' said Marla with a nod.

Annie took advantage of a momentary pause for reflection.

'What *Grains of Evil* has going for it, apart from the story, is that it touches on something which is very, very English. I don't share your confidence that it would take hold on the American market. Though I'm prepared to be convinced.'

Jerry gave Annie an admiring glance. So English, so appealing, that way of holding back your interest when you only held one card.

'Listen to me,' said Jerry, even though everyone was clearly listening. 'The story's good but it needs a good writer, someone like Leo Mossberg.'

'*Laughing All the Way*? That guy?'

'Al's right. It needs a good writer. Leo'd do a great job.'

Annie suddenly interjected. 'But I think it's very impressive. The dialogue's unexpected, you never know what's coming next. A little alteration maybe, but it's the quality of writing which makes it.'

Jerry took a large unwrapped cigar from his pocket, sucked it and put it back again which was the nearest he came to nicotine stimulation.

'Mind if I disagree, Annie? Can I be straight. It's too clinical. We need more background, more about this guy's sister, a warm gut feeling about him. And the girls, well, the girls—'

'No under-age girls. Sixteen minimum. We can't have our hero seduced by under-age chicks.'

'*Lolita*?'

'*Lolita* was an art movie. And don't talk to me about Kubrick.'

'What difference does it make? They're at high school. What's in a couple of years?'

'Look, Annie, the script we can handle. And it's a good story. We all think it's a good story. Set in the States and it could take off. Really take off.'

'Richard Gere for the lead?' suggested Al.

'And Lillie Dart as the number-one girl.'

'Who's that, Jerry?'

'Talent like you wouldn't believe.'

Al gave a knowing grin.

'One of yours?'

'Yeh, yeh. It'd go big on video, done right. Your main guy, what's his name?'

'Jaspar,' said Annie.

'OK, for the moment Jaspar. We change the name later. This is a reversal situation. Jaspar escapes to find the good simple life in Montana. What does he find? Evil and corruption. So then he goes back to the city, falls in love and finds humanity in the mean streets of New York, or Chicago or wherever.'

'Know something? It's beginning to sound good, really good,' said Marla.

'Terrific. You know Leo Mossberg's commitments?'

'I'll find out.'

Marla disappeared to make a call.

'Just Leo's kind of thing,' said Jerry. 'He'll love it. You in town tomorrow, Annie?'

'Yes.'

'We'll get together with Leo. Well, Lance, what's your take on this?'

Lance tipped back in his chair and opened his leather jacket. Definitely an actor, Annie thought, the studied movements, the deliberate turn of the head.

'I'd like to see a first draft.'

'Sure, sure. Leo's a fast worker. He'd get you out something in a month. But in principle, it's a yes?'

'I'm pretty booked up but I'm sure we'll work a way around it.'

'You'd do a great job, Lance. And I say this without hesitation, you are number-one director choice. Number-one. No-one else could handle this. No-one.'

'Thanks. I appreciate that.'

Annie gave a small sigh of relief. Now she had placed everyone round the table.

Lance rose to leave, and Annie felt a mixture of relief and regret that his place at the table would be empty. As he shook Annie's hand in a warm grasp, he said, 'Where do I find you? If we need to talk?'

'Right here.'

'It's been great meeting you, Annie. Bye, everyone.'

Annie steeled herself not to watch him going out.

'Everything Lance touches turns to gold,' said Bob. 'I hope he lasts.'

Al gave a broad grin.

'Why not, Bob. I represent him, don't I?'

The meeting was almost over, and the assembled company stood up as Bob glanced at his watch and made his way to the next appointment. Shortly after he had left them, Marla came prancing out onto the terrace, holding out her notebook.

'I've gotten hold of Leo's schedule. He can manage a half-hour tomorrow, if that's OK with everyone.'

362

'I'll take tomorrow,' said Jerry. 'He and I can throw around a few ideas, then we'll go from there—'

'I'd like to be present,' Annie broke in.

'You will. We're counting on you, Annie,' Jerry replied.

'You do realize, I hadn't considered changing the whole script around. I'd need to see what you two have in mind.'

'Sure, sure. But that's how it goes here, Annie. You see a thing one way, and in comes the creative talent and suddenly your eyes are opened. Instead of a mouse you got a lion. You and I are after big game. Is that right or isn't it?'

'Give me time, just a little time to consider. I do already have a casting commitment, Jerry.'

'Why didn't you say? Come on, don't tell me you've pulled in Hugh Grant?'

'Not exactly. Clary Hunt, from *Rough Trade* . . .'

'Nice girl.'

'Wants to play Debbie. She'd be fantastic in that role.'

'An English girl in Montana? We'd have to put that one past Leo. I'm sure we can find her something, Annie. No trouble.'

'I still need time. It's a big decision.'

'OK, tomorrow night after you've heard what Leo has to say. Let me know tomorrow night.'

Annie sat at the bar, a morning cocktail would help drive her through the remaining appointments. She suddenly felt as though there was a great space around her, that she was invisible to the strangers congregated at her side. She had an overwhelming desire to rush back and find Jerry. It's not how we do things, she would tell him, I can't go along with this. Then she asked herself, would she have behaved the same way if *Grains of Evil* had been written by someone else? If Lucinda Sherwood's name had not been spread across the title page in bold italicized letters? Was she doing the very thing she had guarded against all these years? Would she have acted the same way a year ago? Annie Griffiths, Controller of Drama. Stole someone else's idea. But there were always stories like that. Who really discovered DNA? Who really wrote the plays of Bertolt Brecht? Was it really a scientist and mother working on her kitchen table who discovered the existence of black holes in the universe? Was Emeric Pressburger the hidden genius propping up the achievements of the fabled film director, Michael Powell? It happened all the time. What mattered were the achievers. What mattered was what remained behind. She had to stand by her decision. If challenged, she would deny that she had ever read Lucinda's script. Wasn't it true that seemingly original ideas often surfaced from different sources at similar times? She might even bring a smile to Alan's face. Yes, they're keen on buying *Rough Trade*. And, by the way, we'll be co-producing a movie, some idea we developed together. She had forged the link which every executive in British television would kill to achieve. A space on American network television was the biggest prize on offer, and a made-for-TV feature thrown in. Her reputation was unassailable.

Annie began to roll the plot over in her mind. By tomorrow, she would have her own ideas in place, let them think it would go all their own way, then carefully shift the emphasis. An English mother, it would work, Jaspar could have an English mother. Character part, Glenda Jackson might, might, might. She and Trevor had supported her causes, waited in street vigils in Hampstead standing out against the developers, fighting against the closure of the old people's home.

After another quick drink in the bar, a quick check on her reflection in the mirror, Annie strolled out of the hotel into the sparkling sun, warm in December like an early summer day in England, to find her waiting limo. Her mind was icy clear as she stepped elegantly into the air-conditioned interior and waited for the door to be softly closed. She would spend two hours lunching at Morton's, then take in three more appointments. As they rolled unctuously down Rodeo Drive, she glanced at the shimmering windows of the shops which Trevor had refused to enter. He had recounted the history of Los Angeles, pulling her away from the unobtainable displays, in the days when you never saw a black face in this rich man's ghetto. Even when black directors began to make mainstream films, he said they were still slaves in Hollywood, refused to take them seriously. It was the first time she had thought of him for days. Annie wondered if he was thinking of her at that moment, if their old trick of fortuitously picking up the phone to one another at the same time, still had its magic. Now he would be waiting for Lucinda's call. Annie clicked open her new Hermès briefcase, pulled down the little drop-flap table in front of her and began to take notes of the morning's meeting.

*   *   *

In Hollywood, every second was planned like a prize-fighter's régime. Meetings all day, then you gave yourself to the ritual of revival – sauna, swim, Jacuzzi, shower, quick collapse into the hands of the masseur, blanking the mind to prepare for the next burst of super-charged dialogue. Annie was on the masseur's table, eyes closed, conscious only of the oiled hands stroking down her back, pressing her buttocks, preparing herself for her début at a Hollywood party. There would be half an hour to collect her messages, one hour to transform herself into what they would expect. Tonight would be the skin-tight silk cocktail suit with the tailored jacket, worn without a blouse and with a personality smile which Annie had been perfecting in the mirror. Lance Fielding had sent a gilded invitation to her hotel, together with one huge-budded, close-petalled, scentless dark red rose.

In her hotel room, Annie pulled on a black lacy chemise, unpacked the new sheer black stockings kept back for such an occasion, stroked the fine kid high-heeled shoes which pushed her forward and gave her the semblance of breasts. Then she stood by the mirror, appraising the new, made-over Annie. The shoes pinched, her toes felt like peas about to burst from a pod, but she would master them. Long ago, when she was sixteen, she had saved up to buy herself a similar pair. Taking pity on her tears of pain, her mum had come to the rescue. For two days she had stuffed a pair of thick socks into Annie's shoes and worn them around the house, waiting until the cheap leather had stretched enough to stop the torture. They had had a violent row afterwards. Why? She suddenly remembered, the shame of it. After this sublime example of motherly love, Annie had insisted that the shoes didn't go with her dress and refused to wear them.

The phone rang several times. Lying back in exorbitantly expensive underwear, with champagne on ice at your side, making and refusing appointments, was just how it was meant to be. Tonight she was going to talk to the right people, then bop the night away. Annie's voice was developing a childish giggle which she couldn't repress. Never mind, she'd take one more call.

'Hi. Annie Griffiths speaking.'

It was Trevor. Annie took a huge gulp of champagne.

'My LA voice. Do you like it? I'm just going out to party. *The* party. I have been a triumph. You called at the wrong time

365

but now it's the right time. I knew you'd phone me. All my admirers are calling this evening, one . . . after . . . another. But I'm staying cool, extremely cool. God, how cool.'

'I thought you said no-one drank in LA.'

'I do. Can you tell? Three thousand miles away and you're going to ration my champagne. Fourth glass, love. Or is it the fifth? The hotels are big but the glasses are small. How are you doing? How's life in little ole Chelsea?'

'I'm not there any more. That's why I rang, to let you know.'

'Listen, listen. They're going to buy *Rough Trade*. Network viewing. Have you ever heard of such a thing? No-one'll believe me when I get back to Intertel. Hello, Alan. Have you got it in writing, he'll say? Check it out, Alan, just check it out.'

'Wonderful, Annie. Great news. I knew it would happen.'

'Thanks, Trevor. I get a first, and you say, of course, we were all expecting it.'

'I'm pleased, very happy.'

'Good. I am, too. So where have we moved to, then? Wait, I'll write it down. And the phone number, if you don't mind. I think I've the right to talk to my husband, I've decided. Are you really in London? Sure you're not in Bel Air? You sound so close.'

'I'll call you tomorrow. I don't want to spoil your evening, Annie. I'm glad you're a triumph.'

'No. I'm in a chatty mood, Trev. Tomorrow I might not be. Tons of engagements, diary full. So many people. Speak to me now. This is where we say what we mean, on the phone. You have a meeting, on and on, and then afterwards you phone each other up and say everything important in five minutes.'

'I'm staying with Rick and Bryonie, for the time being.'

'Oh? Change of plans?'

'It wasn't fair on Lucinda, moving in on her as I did, so I decided it would be better to leave. And it would make it easier for us to meet when we want to.'

'I might decide to stay here. I love it, I love it. Permanently lying in a warm bubble-bath of positive thinking. I can't tell you how much I needed this. And the men! I have to say, I'm changing my mind. I feel like a girl of twenty, choosing between dates.'

'It's impossible, saying what I want to like this.'

'You could never stand LA. Poor Trev. Dragging around every year.'

'Rick and Bryonie send their love.'

'How is Rick? You're still seeing him, then?'

'I didn't, for a while.'

'I bet she doesn't approve of Rick. Far too loud, darling.'

'He's drinking less. For the time being anyhow.'

'And Bryonie? How is the saintly Bryonie?'

'She's been wonderful.'

'Bry is always wonderful. You should have married her.'

'Kate still in the house?'

Annie leaned over the bed, and emptied the remains of the champagne into her glass.

'Annie? Are you still there?'

'I must get dressed. I don't believe it's appropriate, to go to The Party in one's underwear. I'm not yet famous enough to be that outrageous.'

'It's so good to hear you.'

'Are you miserable? You sound down.'

'Not now.'

'Is she giving you a hard time?'

'No, no, nothing to do with Lucinda. Though she is in a state at the moment. Intertel refuse to say whether they're going ahead on *Grains of Evil* and she thinks it's some kind of conspiracy. I told her that when you get back, you'd let her know one way or the other. Lucinda still has strange ideas about how television works.'

'Do you want an answer? Now? Is that why you called?'

'Of course not. Look, Annie, you don't have to say anything. I just thought I'd mention it.'

'I'm afraid Lucinda will be disappointed.'

'I was beginning to suspect.'

'I tried, Trev, I really did.'

'I knew you would, I kept on saying, "Once Annie likes something, she doesn't let go . . ." '

'There wasn't a glimmer. No interest whatsoever. You know immediately if there's a chance, but they won't touch anything British which isn't either a thriller or a comedy. Blank faces. If she can get John Cleese as Jaspar, and turn it into a hayseed romp, I might reconsider. Or they might.'

'That's sad. Really sad. But I think someone should let her know, the letter doesn't have to come from you.'

'I'll try and remember to give Anita a call, to remind the script department.'

367

'Is that what really happened? They must have said something more?'

'Not for us. That's what they said. Not for us, Annie. I wanted the script to happen as much as she did. But quite frankly, I knew it wouldn't stand a chance over here.'

'So why did you put it forward?'

'To show that Intertel isn't totally hooked into American culture, that we have some ideas of our own. Anything wrong in that?'

'Have you thought of it for the British market?'

'My God, I'll be late! I have to get changed. Don't we have to meet sometime? My diary's crammed full till Christmas and next year is getting booked up as well. Oh yes, you wanted to talk about the house. I haven't changed my mind. I've found a good lawyer, by the way. She said it's better to try and sort things out ourselves first.'

'We'll talk about it.'

'Are you still doing things for Gavin?'

'Not a great deal. Apart from teaching, I'm getting on with the book. I'd like your opinion, on what I've done so far.'

'Hang on. The other phone's ringing . . . I'm supposed to be ready. My face isn't even on. Thanks for the call, Trev. Bye.'

She knew that she should have pretended to be drunker than she was, that it hadn't been a convincing performance. Had he guessed? She couldn't remember when she had lied to him before, but it suddenly seemed easy, now that her marriage was a past event, finished, drained of its reason for being. If only it was on paper – Annie Griffiths, divorced, the guilt removed, the hope removed, the anger removed, the whole thing out of the way.

Annie lowered the window of her limousine as a slow queue of identical vehicles wound their way up the drive. In front of her was a floodlit folly, the residence of Lance Fielding, nearer to a palace than a house. Pink and grey marble Doric, Corinthian and Ionian pillars stood against the great house, which had no need of their support. Their function, Annie supposed, was to bring added solemnity to the façade which mocked every pretence of European taste and style, with its Bavarian small-paned windows, the Italianate casements, the square-paned Georgian windows and the Norman crenellated slits which haphazardly broke up the massive rectangular shape. Black cypresses, scarlet maples and oleanders, floodlit in theatrical patches, were dotted down the surrounding slopes. She could just make out a luminous, electric-blue swimming-pool, partly shielded by a mammoth white trellis covered in red roses, plunging downward in luxuriant cascades.

Annie followed the crowd into a vast anti-room, where conversations were taking place around Greek statues interspersed with great stone urns overflowing with creepers and roses. She craned her neck to look at the azure ceiling, awash with clouds and cherubs and trumpeting angels. If Kate had been there, they would have shared knowing giggles at the awfulness of it all, but here no-one would know why she was smiling to herself.

'Isn't it too, too beautiful?' said a voice at her side.

'Indeed it is,' Annie said, without looking at the source of the gravelly actor's voice. She had suddenly noticed Lance, his mane of long, soft curls standing above the rigidly coiffured heads. He was dressed informally for some reason Annie could only guess, perhaps to distinguish himself from those around him, but he looked more splendid than any of them, in a white silk open-necked shirt, sleeves rolled up over powerful arms, and his eyes were fixed on her. Lance detached himself from a cluster of black ties, luminously white ruffled shirts, black bows and heaving breasts, and strode towards her.

'You on your own? So glad you could make it, Annie, so good to see you. Molto chic. I do love that English style. Come and say hi to a few people.'

Annie was amused that he had noted her failure to hit the Hollywood nail on the head. Didn't she look just like those other women bearing down on her, dying to be introduced? She made a few appropriate comments, yes, having a marvellous time, very productive, very positive, looking straight into all those faces with bleached-white teeth, long swinging blond hair, black hair, aggressive cleavages parting manufactured breasts, velvet bows with rhinestones nestling in flowing locks.

'Loved the way you took that meeting,' said Lance. 'Have you time to come out to Montana?'

Annie shook her head. 'I'm off soon.'

'Shame. Maybe I could persuade you to hang out a while longer.'

'Lance never persuades, he doesn't know what it means. Lance gives orders. But he's a honey, really he is.'

'This is Mary-Lou. She a top-shot at Warner's.'

'For now, Lance, only for now. And only if you stay directing my movies.'

'And you stay clear of sending me bum scripts.'

'He's a tease. And tough to work with. But we manage, don't we?'

'Most times.'

Mary-Lou flashed the dazzling teeth at Annie. 'But watch out. He has a reputation for going for strongminded ladies.'

'Want me to show you around, Annie? I've just had my place done over by Benino. The Michaelangelo of Tinseltown.'

'Later, Lance. I'm going to wander around first, see who I bump into.'

'Here's my suggestion. Everyone knows you're here, that you're my honoured guest. Tomorrow the whole town will know I'm doing your movie. Big piece in *Variety* should be out then. You just come with me.'

Without protesting, Annie allowed him to grasp her hand, and pull her away.

She made a mental note of those she recognized, storing up the details for Kate before faces and places disappeared in a mist of champagne. They crossed the gently sloping lawn and Annie heard the sounds of a Latin American combo drifting out from the white silk marquee set up at a distance from the swimming-pool. After following a path which wound round a Mediterranean rockery crowned by a portly-bellied Pan spurting his jet across the rosemary and thyme, Lance led her through a copse. Through the branches, she could just distinguish a miniature tower standing at its centre. Lance stopped in his tracks, surveying the outline.

'That tower is my design. This is where I'm private. You've always gotta have one private place.'

'It's fabulous,' Annie said, coming nearer to peer up at a pair of gargoyles leaning out from a stained-glass window.

'You think so? I think it's crazy, crazy like Hearst Castle. They can make it part of the Hollywood tour one day. My contribution to history.'

'Lance Fielding lived here. And they'll say, "You mean, *the* Lance Fielding?" ' said Annie, repressing a giggle.

'Fame doesn't bother me,' he replied.

Annie tried to keep a straight face by changing the subject.

'Directors don't make this kind of money in England. It's lucky you made it out here.'

Lance laughed, an exhuberant open laugh, and unlocked the low studded door.

'Come in, Annie. And mind your head. I don't want you sueing me for brain damage.' She clung on to the brass rail but the steep climb was defeating her, her feet were on fire.

Annie pulled off the offending shoes, swore to herself she would never wear them again, and as her stockinged feet hit the cool stone, she let out a sigh of relief. After more fitness-testing stairs, Annie hoped her panting breath would not betray her. She wondered how many other Hollywood lovelies had leaped up effortlessly before her, showing off their gym-honed prowess. He might have provided a wire, she thought, so that she could be hauled gracefully to the top without a struggle. She heard a door being unlocked, and his voice came from inside an echoing chamber.

'Annie? Just take a look at this.'

Now she had recovered enough to stroll through the Gothic arch, she tried to find some words of appreciation she hadn't used before. Medieval was not her favourite, all that dark panelling and gloomy tapestry and metal candle-holders discreetly wired up to give a simulated flicker.

'Very beautiful, Lance. It's divine.'

'This is my eyrie. A monument to the wages of sin, I guess. Commercials. That's how I started. Pepsi and Levis paid for all this. Plus a little investment and the odd TV series. Money's just a joke to me. I could move out tomorrow and live in a hotel room. Maybe I will. Can you recommend some place in London?'

'Do you plan to move? Is that the idea?'

'No. I'd come over to see you. You never know someone when they're visiting. They're too busy figuring out how they should be. Especially here.'

'You might be disappointed. I spend most of my time thinking of nothing else but what I'm doing.'

'Me too. That's movies, though. I wouldn't want it any other way. Come over here.'

Lance walked over to a long, dark-stained wooden table where a computer had recently spewed out a pile of type-written pages.

'This is the only place where I can free my mind. Here's a script idea I'm working on.'

Annie reverently picked up a page.

'You write as well?'

'We all do. But this is going to be special. I'll tell you about it some time. The hero's a white rhino.'

He had come up behind her, and slipped his hands round her waist. Then she could feel him lightly stroking down her thighs, nuzzling her neck.

'You married, Annie?'

'Does it matter?'

'No. As long as it doesn't to you. Whoever it is, I hope he's a good guy. Is he in the movie business?'

'That's private. That's Annie in England.'

'You're right. No more questions. And I promise not to ask you about the size of your salary cheque.'

'Or my tits!'

'You're great, Annie, you're great. You really are. Know what? We should eat muffins in bed. You like muffins, blueberry muffins? Know something? I'd get you anything you want. Am I crazy?'

'Only relatively.'

'So what's it to be?'

'First, I'll join the party. Then—'

'Then?'

Annie parted his fingers to free herself, and picked up her shoes.

'I don't have to go back to my hotel.'

'We're going to have a scene, Annie. I know it. Maybe now, maybe later.'

'Isn't it just too corny? The producer sleeping with the director?'

'What could be more romantic? I love your smile, Annie. You can't keep me out of bed, not with that smile. I like you. I like you a lot.'

It was an expert kiss, a lingering kiss, a kiss which promised slow, luxuriant love-making, but when he slipped his hand under her jacket, and onto the catch of her bra, Annie took a step back.

'There's no rush. You come to me whenever you're ready, Annie. If you want to go join the party, you do that.'

'I think I will, Lance.'

'Meet you by the pool. An hour be enough?'

'Can you find me a swimming costume? I want to say I've swum in a Hollywood pool.'

'Sure.'

'Follow me, I'll take you back to the party.'

Annie floated down the circular Gothic stairs, with Lance behind her and into the courtyard which was filling up with guests spilling over from the hall where they had first congregated. Then she gazed up into the sky, beyond the marquee, where lofty trees formed a dense barrier.

'It's so beautiful, to have a house built in the middle of a wood,' Annie said. 'Is that what you liked about it? All those beautiful trees?'

'Oh those. My landscape artist's idea. We had them flown in.'

'What, the trees?' Annie giggled, but Lance was looking serious.

'They're not natives, so we had to. We had a few problems of rooting stability, but most of them have taken. You need privacy around here. Though I've hired in extra protection for tonight. That guy over there, one of the best.'

It wasn't long before Jerry's group caught up with her. 'Annie darling, great to see you,' bursting forth as though she had last seen them years ago, instead of hours before. The same clique would stand together, Jerry and Al and Marla, now with resplendent deep-tanned spouses, briefly bringing into their circle the few to whom they would pay court – Annie spotted Jack Nicholson and Barbra Streisand, the centre of guards orbiting fussily like fireflies. Jerry had seen the first cut of Nicholson's latest.

'They're having trouble,' he said, in a low voice. 'I told them they should have got Leo for the script but they wouldn't listen. The movie's a mess.'

'Fifty million dollars so far. That's one helluva mess,' added Al.

Annie made an effusive excuse and walked away towards the flare-lit marquee, where the more anonymous guests were taking small decorous steps over the wooden floor. It wasn't smart to dance, not at a party like this, Annie decided, and certainly not in bare feet. Still clutching the shoes she had determined to master, which now defeated her, she wandered off down the deserted path which led to the pool. Lance found

Annie with her skirt pulled up, dipping her toes into the balmy water.

'Hi, Annie. Still want to take a dip? One of the girls has left you a costume and a robe over there. In the changing-rooms, first one on the left.'

Annie made her way towards a row of changing-rooms masquerading as gazebos, shielded by pink-starred clematis. Inside, she found a giftwrapped black costume, shiny, stretchy black satin, a towelling bath sheet and a white robe embroidered with LF. When she emerged she found Lance leaning over a new arrival, a small girl in a cerise ruched dress stretched tightly over her impossibly full breasts, tapering to bird-like hips, her face half-hidden by a sheet of silvery blond hair as she stared intently into his eyes. As she pivoted on her heels, Annie caught sight of a long, silky brown back. Flawless perfection in miniature, for the man who has everything.

Annie plunged into the water with a great angry splash and hurtled up the pool with a powerful crawl. Then she dipped down beneath the surface. On the illuminated base of the pool she could make out the glitter of gold mosaic which at first she mistook for sand, the golden sand of Greece. Pushing herself to the surface, she lay on her back and began a slow backstroke, gazing up at the stars scattered above her, glittering silver, everything was glittering, silver lights in the trees, as though she was on some space set, waiting for lift off. As she swam to one end of the pool, a tall figure came into her range of vision. Lance was standing right at the edge, waiting for her to climb up the pool steps.

'Great seeing you swim. We'll be clear in a while.'

'Who was that beautiful girl? Someone I should know?'

'You couldn't tell? I'll let him know. He'll be thrilled.'

Annie gasped.

'Really? You serious?'

'Just made his first movie as a woman. But the bazooms are *de trop*, don't you think?'

Annie immediately revised her previous resolution as he wrapped her in a towel and led her towards the changing-rooms. It seemed as though all the guests had been given a cue, since they were all streaming out of the marquee, away from the lawn, towards the main entrance.

'Did you tell them all to leave?' asked Annie.

'Oh no. They know to leave. If every party turned into a

marathon, no-one would give them. And besides, we all have to work in the morning.'

Alone in the small cubicle, Annie hesitated once more. Should she step back into her suit, reapply her make-up or merely get dried and emerge in the white robe? They both knew that she was going to stay the night. It had been so long since she had followed the ritual of holding off until the last moment, teasing with a yes one moment, a no the next, the look which said 'I might or I might not'. How did you make a graceful, sexy entrance as a successful woman in Hollywood, rather than a bouncy teenager in late-Sixties Cardiff hoping for a late night grope in Dad's garage with someone you fancied? Was this a date or a lay, a one-night stand, a thank-you for a lovely party or the Beginning of Something Big? Annie was confused. She no longer knew the language of the first encounter. It was easy with Mel, with Mel it was going to bed with a friend, a colleague, someone who already knew how you would be over breakfast even before sex, and how to take the outbursts of temper, how to put everything back onto an even keel. But she knew things had changed since Mel. Date-rape, AIDS, the fear of sex was something she had observed but not absorbed. You didn't, not when you were married. Now she would have to imagine herself back in single days. She would invent her own rules.

'Would you like to hear some music? Have a drink? Be alone with me, Annie?'

Annie smiled up at Lance. I just want him, she thought, as she slung on the robe, made a roll of her suit and underwear, and followed him towards a side entrance of the house.

Now for the Hollywood bedroom. Benny would have placed an instant order for an exact reproduction, all those thick-swagged satin curtains, the thick-pile, spotless straw-coloured carpet, the gigantic circular bed covered in black satin, fitted tightly as a condom. Annie glanced away from the heavy charcoal sketches of distorted, copulating couples framed on the wall, as Lance approached her bearing a heavy crystal glass.

'Take a sip of this, Annie.'

'What is it? Some aphrodisiac I should know?'

Lance held the glass like a sacramental offering.

'It's beautiful. Try it, just a tiny bit first.'

He brought the glass to her lips, and a thin trickle of liquid burned its way down Annie's throat.

375

'Tastes like Arak,' she said.

'It doesn't matter what it is. I have a friend who imports it specially for me. Isn't it special? Now you just sit down there, make yourself comfortable.' Lance pointed to a low couch with scrolled ends. 'I want you to have a unique experience, Annie. Something I'm going to do, just for you.'

Annie pulled her robe tightly round her and sat with her feet tucked underneath her while Lance dragged forward a heavy low table with a glass top, and moved it next to where she was sitting.

'Hold your glass, Annie, don't put it down on there,' he said.

'I can drink it, though?'

'Of course you can. Now I'd like to play you some music. If it's not pleasing to you, press the silver button by the bed. Make yourself at home, Annie. I'll be back soon.'

Annie couldn't imagine anything less like home. She gave a reluctant shiver, burying her hands in her pockets. Lance seemed to be preparing for some kind of elaborate, theatrical ritual. It was a relief not to hear Gregorian chants coming from the concealed speakers, and for a moment Annie wondered if Lance's inclinations were religious, not sexual, but there was no mistaking the red-blooded beating of drums, like the Rio Carnival, pumping their beat softly round the room. She had a strong craving for a cigarette but there was a greater chance of finding a hypodermic needle in this sandalwood-scented boudoir. It was on the tip of her tongue, to make her casual request, when Lance appeared again. He was standing by the gilded door with his hands over his head in some clasped, Indian position, staring blankly at her like a temple god. Around his hips, was a sky-blue sarong, printed with yellow moons and billowing out over a powerful erection, but otherwise he was naked. His body was gleaming with some kind of ointment. Then he began to sway his hips, like a belly-dancer's prelude, walking forward as he did so.

He reminded Annie of Nureyev, whom she had once seen on the stage, the way he held his head, the proud, self-absorbed expression. She had never seen a body like it, not overmuscled like a Chippendale, but firm and lean. To the rhythm of the drumbeat, he stepped up onto the low glass-topped table. He seemed to be willing her to keep her eyes on him, as he began to display his prowess thinly concealed under a scrap of silk, beginning with slow, pivoting thrusts. The beat quickened, and suddenly stopped. Lance flicked off the sarong and Annie had the low-angle view of a giant, veined Priapus wavering expectantly, upstaging its owner. She had to look, keeping a smile on her face, as though she was waiting desperately for the end of some audition, waiting for the actor to disappear before scoring through his name.

The drumbeats began again, in a slower tempo. Lance stroked down his belly, then put one finger after another round his cock, encircling it, beginning a languid motion, up and down, up and down. Having moved forward so that he was directly above her, all she could see now was this enormous hand, stroking the upright phallus.

'Annie. Stroke yourself, to keep up with me. This is for the two of us.'

When she did nothing, he made no comment. The beat quickened, but his movements slowed down. A bead of white appeared at the top, and Annie leaned back, trying to catch his expression, but his eyes were closed. Suddenly, the bead exploded into small milky white droplets, falling onto her hair. Lance panted, and said, 'Oh, Jesus, oh Jesus', then jumped down and sat on the edge of the table.

'Oh, Annie. I'm so sorry, I'm so sorry, I fucked up, Jesus, I fucked up. Did you like the first part?'

'Beautiful, Lance. Just incredible.'

'You're so sweet. But I really screwed up. I wasn't meant to come. That is the whole idea, not to come. I really am out of practice, or maybe I want you so much it couldn't happen. Oh well, I'll go take a shower. You like the music?'

'I do.'

'It's Brazilian, not quite right but it's a favourite of mine.'

Annie finished off the potent glass and went to try out the bed. As she suspected, it was rock hard, more suited for gymnastics than sex. She hoped she wouldn't end up with her legs over her head, cramped rigid in some Kama Sutra tangle. If he would only divest her of the towelling robe, her desire might return. Why hadn't he thought to undress her? Or was she meant to do it herself, make an exhibition like a stripper, drawing off the garment inch by inch? Annie closed her eyes. She wanted to be back in England.

'Hi, Annie. You asleep?'

Annie opened her eyes to see the perfect body loosely

wrapped in a towel. She felt better, hearing her name on his lips.

'No. I was just waiting for you.'

He came on the bed and lay full length next to her, one hand resting on her hip.

'One time, when I was shooting in India, I met this fantastic princess, lived in one of those crumbling Raj palaces. I used to meet her whenever I could and she promised to initiate me into the arts of love they practise out there. I spent hours, she was real fierce, but by the end I passed the test. You keep on and on and on, always on the edge. And the women learn that, too.'

'Sounds time-consuming,' said Annie.

'That's the trouble with the West. We're obsessed by time. Obviously, when you make movies, you have to, but outside of that, I try to put myself in a no-time situation. Notice I've no clocks or watches in here? And no phone, no fax, no TV?'

'That wasn't meant to be a serious comment, Lance.'

'OK. But this is serious, I really do mean it. I can never understand why the British didn't import that wonderful philosophy from India, after all they were out there a good few years.'

'I suppose they left sex to the natives,' said Annie.

'Is that so? You're a very clever lady, I know that. I love the way you say things. Now wait, just lie back and relax. This part will be wonderful, I promise.'

Lance opened Annie's robe.

'Beautiful, just beautiful. Back in the pool, I knew it. What a great body! Does this feel good?'

As she lay on her back, he kissed down her neck, trailing down to her belly, then kissed down the inside of each thigh.

'Tell me what you like, Annie,' he said, moving his hand up and running a finger down the scant parting of her breasts. Then he pinched her nipples, quite hard.

'That good?'

'I'd rather you kissed them,' Annie said.

As he licked round and round, flicking his tongue over one nipple, then the other, all Annie could feel was a burning in her cunt. Now she knew. With a stranger, she wanted a quick entry. She expected him to know, like Trevor knew, when to plunge inside, when to delay. Annie grasped his hand, his large hairy hand, and pushed it downwards.

'I'll do that later,' he said. 'I like taking things real slow. It's

378

better that way, believe me. Just relax, Annie. This is going to be fantastic, you see.'

She felt herself being lifted up as a pillow was put under her head, then her arms were raised. Lance was determined to find every erogenous zone, truffling under her arms, rubbing her back, stroking her neck, licking her feet, sucking her toes, pushing his tongue into her ears. When he had completed his investigation, he suddenly kissed her violently, passionately, then pulled away, crouched down on his hands and knees and gazed into her eyes.

'I love you, Annie. You make me wild. I could do anything with you. But you're not saying anything to me. Say something, Annie. Annie. Beautiful name. We speak the same language, that's so beautiful. We mustn't be afraid of words, Annie. There's something I want to do, Annie. Something I really really want to do. Close your eyes now.'

Her legs were parted, lifted up in his arms, and then he furrowed between her legs, nibbling, sucking. If only he would touch the right spot with the right pressure, but Annie knew she couldn't tell him. There was one language they didn't speak. She was on fire not with desire, but staying on its surface, longing for it to be over.

'Beautiful, Annie. You're so responsive,' he whispered, as he came up for air. 'We'll keep it like this, you're doing fine. Just let yourself go. Trust me, baby.'

Her cunt was feeling sore, her labia swollen and surfeited, the moisture between her legs was drying in the sterile air. Then she gave a jolt as he thrust his fingers inside her, stirring round and thrusting high up until she squealed.

'You like that? You like that? You coming, Annie?'

She squealed some more, forced herself to shiver and shudder, to pant louder and louder, to flail her arms, reaching her climax with a piercing cry. At last she could lie back. Lance held her tight, too tight in his arms. Annie laughed with relief. She had done something she had never done, something she never thought she could do, her Hollywood first. Simulated orgasm, she had seen it often enough in rushes.

'You could have come inside me, Lance,' Annie murmured. 'I'm on the pill.'

'I couldn't ask to see your AIDS test, not on the first date. We can talk about that later, Annie, I'm clear, by the way. Isn't it better this way? We've had the most fantastic sensations, we've got to know one another. Penetration is anti-human. What does it achieve? Nothing. Women have been conditioned to believe they need a cock hammering around inside them, but that isn't true. The lesbians in the gay movement have taught us the most valuable thing of all. Penetration sucks.'

'I'll think about that,' said Annie. 'Could I have something to drink?'

'What you need is herbal tea. I'll get some. Camomile or peppermint?'

'Mineral water?'

'Sure. Anything you want.'

Annie drank the whole bottle, as though she had just walked over the Hollywood hills in the heat of the day. Then she curled up, slipped one hand under the satin pillow, and prepared to sleep. Lance was still stroking her back as she imitated the deep breaths of slumber. And then her body was her own, he had rolled over to the other side.

It was a couple of days before Marla caught up with her, before the female gossip circuit had registered that drama supremo Annie Griffiths had landed up in bed with the best lover in town.

'Is it true? You stayed all night?' said Marla, repainting her perfect lips in the washroom of Campanile, after an excessive lunch of charcoal-grilled king prawns and frisée.

'I slept at Lance's place. Yes.'

'How absolutely gorgeous. And was he? Like they say?' Marla waved a finger upwards in the air.

'I wouldn't know. I only slept there.'

'Come on, Annie. Some girls out here would pay a million dollars for one night. They say he's out of this world. We're pretty frank here, don't be offended. It's just being sisterly. And we want you to have a good time.'

'I enjoyed the party.'

Marla sighed with exasperation.

'Oh, never mind. He probably isn't as great as he's made out to be. But since most of the guys you meet aren't hot shots in bed, there isn't much competition.'

'Maybe he's saying that about me.'

Annie gave a winsome smile which appeared to give satisfaction.

'Oh, Annie, really? That's great, absolutely great. I'm so

pleased, I am, really really pleased. Tony wants to know if he should invite both of you to his soirée tomorow. If you'd like Lance to be there, that is. And if you're still here Friday, we've a Top Girls get-together. We'd love you to be our guest, tell us a few things about the female executive role in Britain, share your experiences, nothing heavy. It's basically a good-time get-together, catching up on the male opposition.'

'I'll have to say no. I'm flying back Friday.'

'Shame, Annie. Any time you want a room at my place, you're always welcome. And I've every office facility, secretary, anything you want.'

Lance had given her some tapes of his work and a gold silk saree as a leaving present, Kate would make something of it later. They had met again, but she had not returned to the bedroom. She said it was better this way, that she couldn't handle a relationship, not now, not when she was in the throes of divorcing her husband and setting up a movie. But he didn't seem to mind. And he sent a huge bouquet of roses to her hotel, so sad he couldn't make it to the airport. She could call him any time, any time at all, his secretary would always pass on messages from Annie Griffiths.

On the plane back to England, Annie glanced through her American notebook, crammed with contacts, marked with keep-in-touch stars, neatly cross-referenced. Then she went through the pile of newspapers and magazines at her feet, and tore out the pages where she appeared in print or photographs, ready for the cuttings file. Brit series for TV network, Griffiths the new hot property. Annie Griffiths, drama chief from British TV, escorted by Lance Fielding, rumoured to be directing her next movie; Annie Griffiths makes a splash on the *Oprah Winfrey Show*. Annie Griffiths says Wake Up, America, the Women are Here. Griffiths, seen at this week's party with Jack Nicholson in Lance Fielding's mansion. Then she gave a great yawn, stretched out her legs clad in the Ralph Lauren jeans she had bought in Rodeo Drive, covered her eyes with a rose-scented moisturized patch and decided to give the inflight movie a miss.

21

ANNIE

The dustmen had laid an adventure trail of debris, making their progress down Langton Villas, and the furious wind had taken up the challenge, pushing polysterene chip boxes, discarded rags and coke tins across the pavement, through the front-garden gates and sprawling discarded video boxes into the street. Someone had vomited against the wall of the house next door and shiny bright yellow signs proclaimed that the introduction of residents' parking was imminent. As she kicked against a milk crate, spilling over with grimy bottles, Annie cursed and attempted to open the door, struggling with the key.

'Allow me.'

Her driver gave a few expert twists, then carried in her luggage, expanded with two extra suitcases. By mistake, she had tipped him a handful of dollars instead of pounds, but he ran off down the steps, apparently content. Annie heard Dally's scream, and then Kate came running towards her.

'Annie, you're back, how wonderful! I thought you were coming tomorrow.'

'I caught an earlier plane. I'd seen everyone I wanted to and I've piles of work to catch up on.'

'You should have let me know. I'd have come to meet you. Dally's so good on the tube, she loves it. Glad to be home?'

'Not yet. I need a bath.'

She stopped Kate from lugging her cases up the stairs, and glanced up at the toy cars, whistles, dolls and balls, strewn from top to bottom.

'Dally had some friends round. They had a marvellous time. How was it?'

'A good trip.'

'We've got some food for you, if you're hungry.'

'I'll have a drink. A gin and tonic would do nicely.'

The bathroom, unlike the stairway, was less crowded than before. Failing to find her favourite bath oil, Annie rummaged through the cabinet which was depleted of the array of expensive creams and lotions in heavy jars and bottles which she had left behind. Most had been sampled, some almost emptied. Hanging from the door was a furry bundle resembling a grubby moorland sheep. Annie fingered it gingerly, and supposed it to be a dressing-gown, something Kate had picked it up from somewhere. She should have told her that she wanted the gin and tonic while she was taking a bath, but she was tired. The water was lukewarm and the undigested soap lay in scummy trails on the surface. Heaving herself from the bath, Annie attempted to find a towel with newly washed freshness, but without success. As she dried herself quickly on the first one which came to hand, she realized she was still in room service mode. Then she rubbed off her remaining make-up with a scrap of cream left in the Lancôme jar and went into her bedroom. There was no reason why Kate shouldn't have slept there, but she wouldn't have minded so much if the bed had been made. She picked up one of her black lacy nightdresses from the floor, and stripped off the sheet. Her cashmere dressing-gown was still on its hook, and she took it down, wrapping it tightly round her.

'Won't take a second. We're just tidying up.'

Annie slumped into a chair as Kate dragged a black rubbish bag across the kitchen, throwing into it the potato peelings and eggshells accumulated in the sink. Then she heard the sound of the Hoover from the sitting room.'

'Surely the cleaning lady isn't still here?'

'No,' said Kate. 'That's Luke. He's helping out.'

'Luke?'

'Don't you remember, he came round one day looking for work and you said he could do the garden?'

'Did I?'

'Tall, fair hair and glasses.'

'I'm sure I didn't.'

'Honestly, Annie, that's what you said. I asked him in for coffee one Saturday morning.'

'Oh yes, the scruffy one with the posh accent.'

'He's terribly nice, and very cheap. He'll do everything, make a terrace, put in the plants, do the maintenance, even odd jobs round the house – and he only wants two hundred a week.'

'I can't think about that now. What's happened to that gin and tonic?'

Kate stopped piling up the dishes.

'Did you bring back some duty free? Only we've run out, there's some sherry though.'

'Never mind,' said Annie, with a sigh. 'Make it coffee.'

'Sorry about that. And I'll tidy up the bedroom. I meant to do it today, but I had to take Dally for a check-up and it took hours. Don't worry, everything will be back to normal in no time. Trevor's been round a couple of times. With Bryonie and Rick. You know he's staying there now.'

'Yes, he did inform me.'

'It was so wonderful, seeing them again. I made them all supper.'

'And Rick cleared the drinks cupboard?'

'Well, he had one or two. It was so good, being together. Trevor really wants to see you, Annie.'

'We've got to discuss what to do about this house. I've been thinking about finding a place nearer the centre of town. There's no point in making this journey every day when I spend most of my time at Intertel.'

'Yes, that does make sense. But wouldn't you miss not having a garden?'

'No, Kate, I would not.'

The hoovering had stopped and Luke came into the kitchen.

'Hi, Annie. Remember? I'm Luke. Kate, could you make me a coffee, too? How was the States?'

His friendly, familiar tone irked her. In Los Angeles, they had fought for the privilege of saying Hi. He could only be around thirty, Annie guessed. A weathered young face, open and pleasant. She tried not to sum up his character by the old ribbed sweater rolled up above his elbows, the torn jeans, the tattooed dragon on his forearm.

'Your house is great. And you must see what I've done in the garden.'

'Later.'

The doorbell rang and Annie glanced at her watch.

'That'll be my driver. Tell him I'll be ten minutes.'

'You're not going out now?' said Kate.

'For God's sake, Kate. I've got work to do. I haven't been swanning round the States on holiday.'

'No, I do know that,' said Kate, placatingly. 'I just thought that you'd need to rest.'

'Is your friend staying, by any chance? Or is he just working late? How many other people have I got lodging here?'

'Luke lives a long way away, in south London. I said he could stay for a month, to see how it goes. He's been working so hard all day.'

'Thank you for being so kind on my behalf, Kate,' Annie snapped.

'What's wrong? Did something awful happen?'

'I didn't expect to come back here and find a bloody mess, that's all. And some unqualified deadbeat you've taken pity on. Don't you think I've enough to cope with, without having to deal with this?'

'Just say, if you want me to go. I know you're exhausted, but you don't have to take it out on me. I thought you might have been glad to have someone looking after your house.'

'I've got my own life now, Kate. I'm under pressure, and I live with it. All you have to worry about is getting to the doctor's on time and whether Gordon will make it this week. It's not the same.'

'That's a cruel thing to say. You never used to be like this. You never minded about having the place neat and tidy. Why does it matter? Just because you're got a high-powered job, you're starting to act just like a man.'

'Is that the worst thing you can think of? Have you started to believe in sexual differences? Or is it back to sexual stereotypes now? What you mean is, I don't fall into your definition of a woman. You expect me to be caring and loving all the time. If you want that, go and live in some bloody New Age commune. They still have them, I believe.'

'You're tired, you don't mean that.'

'You don't have a clue, Kate. You've lost touch with how it is out there. All that talent gone to waste, it makes me weep. Don't you want to fight any more, to get back where you were? Don't you want to have a decent life?'

'I have got a decent life.'

'I'm sorry, really I am. I was only trying to make you see sense.'

'I'm happy as I am, and so is Dally. You can't accept it, that all that matters is my daughter. Dally comes first, Dally will always come first. If I was working, she'd end up stuck in front

385

of the TV eating junk food with a dim childminder. I wouldn't inflict that on her, never.'

'No-one's asking you to. You've made a stunning success of being a mum. Because I know I couldn't do it, perhaps I'm a little envious.'

'You?' Kate said, with a laugh. 'Why should you be envious of anyone?'

'I've got what I wanted, in my career. But they didn't say on my management course how you stay human. Since Trevor's gone, all I think about, all I care about, is my next move at Intertel. I'm frightened that I've become what they all expected, a hard-nosed bitch who gets results. Maybe that's what I am. Maybe it's an inevitable part of the job.'

'You're not like that, Annie. I know you're not anyhow. I'll clear up the bedroom, change the bed. And don't worry about Luke. He doesn't have to stay, there'll be someone round here who needs a gardener.'

'Of course he can stay,' said Annie. 'Help yourself to anything you want. I must get going.'

Having rushed upstairs and checked that her Intertel car was still waiting outside, Annie pulled on an angora dress and some boots, grabbed her briefcase and escaped from the house. As she applied her make-up in the back seat, barely registering that she was back in London streets, she began to think of changes she should make. The drama department needed a new image, more suited to the style and pace of Los Angeles. Once in her office, she gave Anita a brief resumé of her trip, scanned the faxes and mail in silence, signed some letters and told her to see the Controller of Office Management as soon as possible. She needed a larger office, somewhere more appropriate to receive visitors. Gavin's office, for example. He never used it for production meetings, why did he need all that space?

'Did you have time to buy some gorgeous things?'

Anita smiled expectantly, and Annie regretted not having brought anything back for her. Usually she gave her a bottle of something, some perfume, but she hadn't thought of it.

'There was nothing you couldn't get in London.'

Before leaving the office, Annie wrote in her notebook computer: Anita – Interflora. It was bad, to forget details.

*   *   *

Around the bar, there was some event in progress. Someone leaving, someone getting married, someone celebrating promotion, judging by the number of bottles spread around on the tables, and the packed huddle at the bar. Annie paused at the entrance, and had almost decided to go to Harry's Bar for a light supper, when Rick, dishevelled and exuberant, came up to her, mouthing a kiss.

'So glad you could make it. Darling Annie, knew you would. Good of you to come back specially, very much appreciated,' he said, squeezing her waist with a hug, and giving her a breathy taste of whisky. Annie refrained from asking him the reason for the celebration. Was it his birthday? What excuse this time?

'I can't stay long,' said Annie, forcing a smile. 'But we'll have a bottle of champagne.'

'I don't drink champagne. Surely you know that by now? Triple Scotch for me.'

'Could you get the drinks, Rick? I'm not up to fighting for service, not at the moment. Put them on my tab.'

Rick cleared a small space at the end of the bar, displacing a couple of accounts supervisors from *Global Highway* with exaggerated apologies.

'Go well in the States?' asked Rick. 'Were they falling all over you?'

'Very successful,' replied Annie. 'Network sale for *Rough Trade*. I was amazed.'

'Another major *coup* for our Annie. I'll make a special effort and drink to you, all night.'

'They'll try to screw us, of course, but I'm going to bring in some decent lawyers. Way beyond the legal department's expertise. I'll have a word with Alan about it. Have you seen him? Is he around?'

'Not exactly. I don't know where he is. No-one's seen him for a while.'

'Have you been away as well?'

'Hasn't Trevor told you?'

'We only spoke once when I was away. About practical details. I gather he's moved in with you and Bryonie. I can't say I was surprised. Poor old Trev, he's not good at coping with change, not at his age, though he'd hate me to say it. He should find himself a nice quiet girl to look after him.'

'Course he should! Then she could look after us both.'

'You do all right, Rick. So tell me what's happening?'

'I'd got too expensive for *Global Highway*, they were unable to finance my alcoholic preferences. Regretfully, I said, I will have to take my leave. The bastards took me seriously, would you believe? My desk is now occupied by someone called Jeremy who is stepping out with Leggy Lucy. He's being taught how to read the prompt. His speciality is financial reports and rumour has it that he's some crackpot degree from the States in economics, but who cares?'

'Have you talked to Alan? I'm sure he'd find you something. There's no-one with your experience left.'

Rick gave a bitter laugh. 'Who wants experience except in bed? No, Annie. I'm out. In a way, I'm glad. At last I'm free to devote my amazing ability and talent to something worthwhile. Bry's words. Fuck the lot of them. Courage under fire, that's me, with a little help from my friend the bottle. New career in the offing.'

'So what's it to be?'

'I'm thinking about politics. I've all the right qualifications except one.'

'Which is?'

'I'm not good at changing my views in the face of expediency. Grave disadvantage. But it can be learned, oh yes, it's never too late to learn. And my manipulative talent with expense claims should be a major qualification, don't you agree?'

'What does Trevor think?'

'That I should write a bestselling thriller. He's looking out a plot, dear old Trev. And he misses you, Annie. He'd have you back tonight, like a shot.'

'Have me back?'

Annie snorted, then glared at Rick.

'Who behaved like a swine and moved out?'

'Moved out? Well, he had to, since you gave him the elbow.'

'So now it's my fault, is it?'

'I won't hold it against you, Annie. Fancy coming round to supper with us?'

'You're impossible. I presume that's not a serious invitation. But you and Bryonie must come over to me. I'll ring up and fix a time with her.'

'Do that, Annie.'

'I won't forget. I'll make a note. When I've got Christmas over. Will you be free around mid January? I'm afraid I can't make it until then.'

'Next year is a long time in television,' said Rick, looking intently at Annie.

Her face had changed, it could have been the subtly applied make-up, the shining hair, the clinging but perfectly tailored jacket. Her shape was smooth, slimmed down, the kind of woman he would have avoided if he had met her now, as though she'd been done over by a Tory image-maker. They had them in the Labour Party now. Keep your distance. Just like Lucinda Sherwood.

'If you and Bryonie don't mind late supper, I could do it this week,' said Annie, relenting.

'Up to you, see how you're fixed.'

Annie followed Rick over to his table, making it clear that she was *en route* to somewhere else, just there to show her face for old times' sake.

'Annie, darling!' cried out Thelma. 'Lovely to see you. For an awful moment, we thought you weren't coming back. Thank goodness, someone with good news. Jeff said you'd taken LA by storm. Now he's saying I should go over there . . .'

While Rick was clearing a few glasses from the table, anticipating another round, Jeff got to his feet and took Annie aside.

'Don't say anything to Thelma, but the bastards haven't renewed. She thinks we're still negotiating. Six months to run and then kaput. I'm getting her to write the book of the show, keep her busy, get her on the chat slots.'

'But I thought Alan loved *Poole Reports*? His wife's a great fan, too. What's the reason?'

'Search me. Twenty per cent fall-off in the ratings. What's twenty per cent? And the appreciation index, thirty per cent up. Some fool made an alternative suggestion but I told him to stuff it. No way. Could you see Thelma fronting an afternoon health show for the mature viewer, consumer reports on hip replacements? Someone called Harry or Tom or Dickhead is now Controller of Contracts, only last year he was checking the figures on expense claims in the accounts department. Alan must be out of his mind.'

'Something will come up, Jeff. I'll find Alan, have a word.'

'You'll be lucky. No-one's seen him for weeks. Advising on some government report on broadcasting, so they say. Still, there's always Sky.'

'Keep in touch, Jeff,' said Annie. 'We need *Poole Reports*. I'll see what I can do.'

Benny didn't rise when Annie came over, she assumed he was still recovering but his face was golden, a November cruise, he knew how to look after himself. Mandy, with breasts heaving out of a sweetheart neckline, had one arm draped round Benny's neck.

'Hello, Annie. Did you have a fantastic time in LA?'

Annie nodded, with a brief smile.

'Glad you're back. Thought you'd run off with a soap-stud.'

'Too many to choose from, and it's tough, speaking a different language.'

Benny leaned back, eyes narrowed, lips pursed, then nodded with approval as Annie sat down beside him.

'Didn't recognize you. I knew the Di before, now you're the Di after. Mandy, persuade Roy to dig out some decent champagne and find Annie a chair. This lady has the sweet glow of success. She's just sold to the network.'

'How did you know?' said Annie.

'Your fax to Anita. It's pinned up in the eighth-floor corridor.'

Mandy gradually uncrossed her legs and prepared to shift forward onto her fur-trimmed, stiletto ankle boots.

'Don't bother, Mandy. I can't stay long. Just a glass of champagne will do.'

Benny watched with rapt attention as Mandy sidled over to the bar, then smiled knowingly at Annie.

'Strictly a working relationship, but I'm not letting on,' said Benny. 'I'm relating, she's working. Lovely little bum. I'm fit. How are you?'

'You can see, Benny.'

'Got rid of the husband yet?'

'That's the next move.'

'Wise girl. Get a much younger one or a much older one. That's what Mandy tells me and she's the expert now. Meet the new star of *Going for a Bong*. How does that grab you?'

'It doesn't.'

'Me neither. But it's a forward concept, Annie. Forward concept, that's the feller.'

'So what's the angle?'

'Quiz game with a strip-off penalty. Only Mandy doesn't strip off, more's the pity. But the pilot had them rolling.'

'Christ, Benny! I thought you'd be able to steer clear of that kind of crap. Come on, that was never your idea.'

'Bought in from a games-show franchiser. What do you expect? Gives me time to go on a cruise, put in a new bathroom, play a few rounds of golf. Who's complaining? Not me, not at my time of life. Sherwood will raise the moral objection, we'll cash in the cheques, and . . .'

Mandy edged round Annie and set down a glass of champagne.

'I spilled a bit. Silly me. I'm going for a sushi with Thelma and Jeff. Want to come?'

'Can you do without me for one night?'

Mandy tittered, and abandoned her boss with a flounce of her skirt. Annie moved her chair closer to Benny.

'Why is everyone letting it happen? You, of all people, Benny. I can understand Gavin, he's just out for the main chance, but what about everyone else? Don't they care any more? We should be breaking new ground, putting out some things which you can watch for more than thirty seconds without knowing what'll happen in the next thirty seconds.'

'We have wildlife, Annie. That's unpredictable. Guess when the tiger pounces. It's gripping stuff.'

'You know what I mean.'

'Have to say that your old man has a go, now and then. He had a bit in *The Times* the other day, thunder style. He was saying what you're saying, funnily enough. He can do that, now that Gavin's dropped him. Or he's dropped Gavin.'

'How did that come about?'

'The latest figures, Annie. They're down and the board are screaming for blood. And I think it's going to be Alan's on the carpet.'

'Hope you're wrong, that would be disaster. Who would we get in his place?'

'Oh, someone with a good accounts background in British Gas, I expect.'

Annie gave Benny a fleeting kiss, and picked up her briefcase.

'I really must go, I've a meeting at nine. Looks like I've a feature to see through after the next series.'

'That's good news, Annie. And this will please you, doll. Your girl has upped sticks and left me in the lurch. Pissed off, she was.'

'My girl?'

'Given in her notice. You're not surprised, surely?'

As Annie was about to leave, she heard Rick in full voice bellowing out a Welsh rugby song. She waited while a couple of the bar staff heaved his arms onto their shoulders and half carried him towards the door. The remaining crowd had all turned away as though nothing untoward was happening. Taking evasive action by using the back stairs, Annie hurried out of the building. She kept thinking of Rick, she should have offered to take him home, insisted even. What if she had arrived an hour late? The Controller of Drama could arrive whenever she wished, the producers she was due to see would wait. Appointments were merely rough guides as to when she might appear. And then she admitted to herself, that she didn't want to be seen in the company of a drunk, even it was Rick, as though his failure would infect her, tarnish the image she was carefully building up without realizing it. Annie Griffiths, triumphant Annie. She didn't want Rick Evans to spoil it. And she was tired. When you were that tired, it made you mean.

When Annie arrived back home, she passed by the living room and found Luke reading poetry to Kate by the light of a candle.

'I'm not answering the phone,' was all she said, before stumbling towards her bed, head spinning, eyes like lead. She tossed her jacket and skirt on the floor, and pulled over the duvet. When she was awoken by the soft beep of the phone by her bed sometime in the middle of the night or it could be morning, with December it was impossible to tell, she felt a lump on her thigh, and realized she still had on her suspender belt, stockings and the padded Wonderbra. The beep was insistent and she reached for the receiver automatically, eyes still closed.

'Oh, it's you. Trev, I've just got home. Trying to get some sleep.'

'I phoned your office. Anita said you were back.'

'Can I tell you later? I'm not thinking straight, my brain is scrambled.'

'I'd rather talk to you now.'

'What's so urgent?'

'Rick. He's in a terrible state. Last night he got wretchedly drunk and he refuses to get out of bed.'

'What time is it, for God's sake?'

'Around one, Annie.'

'I'm meant to be in the office this afternoon. Thank God you woke me up. I'll ring you from there.'

'Annie, all I want is the name of that clinic where David went, the one in Warwickshire somewhere.'

'How should I know? I'll get Anita to find it.'

'You've heard what happened?'

'He's been fired. We knew it would happen. I'd have thought he'd be prepared by now, he talked about it often enough. It's a relief more than anything.'

'It wasn't only that. I insisted that he went for a fertility test, for Bryonie's sake really. In the end he agreed. They found his sperm motility count was so low, it was unlikely he would ever father children. He got the letter this week. Bryonie's devastated.'

'I'm sorry. But what do you expect me to do? I won't have my feet on the ground until after Christmas, even then I'll only take off a day to see my mother. I'll try and visit him in the clinic, if you can get him there.'

'Bryonie would like you to see her, Annie. She needs someone like you at the moment.'

'She doesn't need me to hold her hand. And she should know what Rick is like by now.'

'Annie . . . oh, never mind.'

'What now? What are you trying to say?'

'You can't just cut people off, you can't pretend you haven't been part of our lives.'

'Trevor, I don't need your lectures any more. Why do you think you've the right to criticize my behaviour? You, of all people.'

'I'm not criticizing.'

'You bloody are. I don't want to hear it. I just want everything sorted out so I can get on with my life. And we must meet to discuss the house. I think we should both start next year with everything settled, don't you?'

'If you insist.'

'It needn't take long. We can agree the basics and go from there. We can have one lawyer to sort it out, no point in having two. Unless you want to. But I choose the lawyer.'

'OK, Annie. You choose the lawyer. Agreed.'

'I'll have to find a space one evening. My schedule's in the office, you'll have to wait till later.'

'Whenever suits you. I'm not in a hurry.'

'Oh? Hasn't she found a little nest for you both? Or is Daddy refusing to cough up for the mortgage?'

'Lucinda? I'd rather not talk about her,' said Trevor, briskly. 'You know she's leaving Intertel?'

'I don't care what she's doing. What are you up to over Christmas? Will you be with Rick and Bryonie?'

'Part of the time. How about you?'

'I'm going down to Wales.'

'I'll be in Nottingham.'

'How's your dad?'

'Doddery but well.'

'We'll get together soon. To sort out the house.'

Annie tried to make herself immune to Christmas. This year, those at work would receive the Intertel card, solid traditional executive version with Caravaggio angels and a copy of *Rough Trade*, the illustrated Book of the Series. Everyone else would receive a gift-wrapped bottle of champagne. And something for Dally. The event into which Kate and Dally and Luke poured their effort and imagination was an inconvenient hiatus. On Christmas Eve, Kate was giving a little party for the children, and then Annie would have to show up at three others in town, no idea how she would get to them all. Next day, it would be Cardiff, taking Mum and the relatives off to a posh hotel. Then she could say – what could she say? She would have to start rehearsing the family lies. You couldn't tell them, not at Christmas. 'We're going through a difficult time, Trevor and me. You know.' They would know. 'We've decided to be apart for a while. I'm sure we'll sort something out.'

It wasn't until June that Trevor came round to Langton Villas. Spring had turned to summer, and Annie had barely noticed it. Although only a few months had passed, it seemed so long since they had been face to face and they were both sitting as though one was about to interview the other. Annie imagined Trevor would have changed but he had only cut his hair short again. It made him look youthful, his face was no more lined than she remembered. He seemed contented and calm, as though he relished being on his own, newly shaven, carefully dressed. Annie was in her jeans, her face bare. She didn't want him to think she had made a special effort.

She handed him a sheet of paper, walking across the rug and returning to the wicker chair, watching while he read it.

'This is very efficient,' he said, with a slight smile.

'A list of everything in the house, apart from the things I bought after I . . . after you went. Isn't that how you wanted it? It won't take long, if we do it room by room. There's nothing in here. Oh yes, a couple of lamps.'

'And the watercolour.'

'You can have that. It doesn't really belong in here. You can tick those off.'

'Have you a pen, Annie?'

She opened her bag, and extracted her fountain pen.

'I thought you'd have lost that by now,' he said, taking off the cap. 'I spent ages choosing it, I'm glad you still have it.'

'I don't lose things I like.'

Trevor got up and examined the picture, hanging insignificantly amongst others at the side of the fireplace.

'Where did we get that? Bath, was it?'

'No, that old junk shop near us in Bristol. It's not particularly well painted, you don't have to take it if you don't want to.'

'I think I will. And the lamps? Mind if I take those?'

'Tick those off, then. How's Rick?'

'Getting on very well. And Kate? Is she still living here?'

'Yes, she's out with Dally and Luke. They're going to move away, Luke's got some job in Sussex, gardening.'

'You'll miss her.'

'I'm hardly around. Trev, I was sorry to hear about you and Lucinda. I actually do feel sympathy for you. I didn't want it to work out, and now it hasn't, I'm sorry. I really am. Now you'll say, typical Annie. Bloody perverse. But it'll be easier for us to be friends, won't it?'

'Yes, yes. You know she's announced her engagement to Jeremy?'

'How unlikely. She always said he bored her to tears.'

'Marriage was the last thing she wanted, I don't think she'll be happy.'

'Does it make you feel better, to think every woman you leave is unhappy?'

'We were talking of Lucinda.'

'So we were. Sorry, Trev. Now, what about the rug over there, which was in the bedroom?'

'It looks different.'

'I had it cleaned.'

'I'm not sure about that. Why don't I put a question mark?'

395

'Oh, for God's sake, take it. Where are you going to put all the stuff?'

'In Rick's garage, for the time being. Until I find somewhere.'

'Don't move to Soho. That's where I've decided to go. I can't go bumping into you in some late-night shop, can I? Anything else?'

'I'd better look through the books.'

'Are you going to make lots of awful gaps?'

'They're mostly history books. Not things which would interest you.'

'How do you know? I might need some background.'

'Let's get the main things out of the way, we can sort out the books when we've done that.'

'We'll go upstairs then. The other room is full of Kate's stuff. Her workroom.'

'I can go up on my own, if you prefer.'

'No. My lawyer said we both had to be present.'

'Our lawyer.'

'Oh, all right. Our lawyer, then.'

'Did you trust her?'

'She's on our side.'

'What does that mean, Annie?'

'She wants it all to be civilized. She said there are bound to be small details we can't agree, but we can go round to her office and talk them out on neutral ground.'

Trevor went upstairs and opened the door of what used to be his office, now knocked through to make a roomy space for Dally. His shelves were stacked with children's books and videos, toys and dolls dressed in the uniforms of what in his day, had been male occupations, a shiny-coated fireman, a doctor with a stethoscope, an engineer with tiny tools stuffed into the belt.

'I'll take the chair, she won't need that, not for a few years. The blind can stay.'

'There's no point in taking a blind. How do you know if it would be the right size?'

'On the other hand, it might fit.'

'Oh, put it down if you want to,' said Annie.

As he walked towards the bedroom, he wrote down: Former Office. One chair.

He was about to suggest that he took the bookshelves, then decided against it. When you'd spent years in a room, you couldn't re-create it or just move it to another place like a castle shipped out to Texas.

'There's nothing in my study,' Annie said. 'I checked. But I suppose you ought to look.'

Trevor surveyed the small stripped-pine desk, the scripts crammed together in the Habitat bookcase with the sliding glass doors, the posters of film festivals framed in black, the small pale green statuette of a Thirties girl holding out her skirt, a shelf of pebbles and fossils they'd gathered on the beach, old postcards she'd sent him from different locations. Hastily, he closed the door. Having briefly surveyed the bathroom, his eye was caught by an aerosol can of shaving cream. Annie knew what he was looking at.

'That belongs to Luke. Kate's taken quite a shine to him, God knows why. He never says much.'

'A good enough reason,' said Trevor, with a wry smile. 'So is Gordon off the scene?'

'Except for lunch.'

They both laughed.

'Come on, the bedroom next.'

Annie looked at her watch and frowned.

'We'll be finished in half an hour, won't we? Then I have to leave.'

'So do I,' replied Trevor.

Their old bedroom was no longer recognizable. Instead of the brass bed, there was a wooden four-poster, with Provençal, printed-cotton drapes dipping down, tied with blue bows, matching curtains and a shiny honey coloured parquet floor. Stretched tight over the bay window, were elaborately figured lace curtains. The built-in wardrobes with Sixties handles had been replaced by others of green-stained oak, stencil-patterned with roses.

'Well, what do you think?' said Annie, although she knew perfectly well what his opinion was. The slight wrinkling of the nose, his hands clasped behind his back, the prof about to give a judgement.

'Pretty. Very pretty.'

'You always say that when you disapprove.'

'Do I? I hadn't noticed. This is not quite you, Annie. Or perhaps it's the new you.'

He went over and casually opened one of the wardrobe doors, as though he was in a shop.

'None of your clothes in there, Trev. Only mine, no-one else's.'

'I'm just looking at the work. Did Martin put these in?'

'Yes. He's retired from the Beeb now, but still does carpentry jobs. One of the old school, we never wanted to take down his sets.'

Annie went to shut the wardrobe door and mistimed her movement, brushing against Trevor's hand. Suddenly they were right up close, she could smell the faint scent of his aftershave, but she quickly left his side and stood against the window.

'This is the only room which Kate left to me to decorate. Big mistake, God knows why I did it like this. Actually I do know. I was trying to conjure up that hotel we stayed in, when we had that weekend in the Loire.'

'La Retraite.'

'You remember? I'd forgotten the name.'

'We had a wonderful weekend there, of course I remember.'

'You promised we wouldn't talk about the past, Trevor.'

'You brought it up.'

'I was describing the room, that's all.'

'Let's go downstairs and have a coffee. Would your lawyer agree to that?'

Annie smiled. 'I don't charge by the hour, we can have coffee.'

He preferred to sit in the kitchen, in his usual place at the end of the pine table, now covered in several carefully applied coats of white paint. Annie leaned against the expanse of gleaming white cupboards, clutching a mug of coffee in her hand.

'What are your students like this year?' she asked.

'They seem a good bunch. Mostly from overseas, of course. I'm supposed to be pushing the study of media in a more vocational direction, more emphasis on financial structures and marketing, that kind of thing.'

'God, Trev, what do you know about that?'

'I did learn something from you!'

They both laughed, leaning towards one another, then they instinctively sat back, retaining the distance between them.

'I still think of vocational in its original sense, something which refers to the voluntary devotion of nuns, priests, doctors and poets.'

'And actors, I hope.'

'Yes, and actors.'

'I'm supposed to sign that piece of paper. Have you finished?'

Annie removed the mug which was standing on the inventory, and left a round stain of coffee.

'I suppose it's still legal with a coffee-mark. Or should I type it out?'

'No, you needn't do that. Do you mind if I add the table?'

'Which table?'

'This one.'

'I'm sorry, Trev. Not this table.'

'Why, it's not valuable, is it? Just an ordinary pine table, which you've painted. Only it would make a really good work table, I could spread everything out. I could do with something like this.'

'Where would you put it? There's no room at Rick and Bryonie's.'

'I'll be moving soon, it can go in the garage till then. And if it's too big, you could always have it back. But you don't really need a table this size, do you?'

'Why assume that? I do, I do need it.'

'What for? You don't entertain in the kitchen, surely? You're always out at restaurants.'

'I chose this table. You said it was too big, if you remember. And I said it would fit in the kitchen.'

'But I paid for it.'

'Did you? I thought we blew the housekeeping money. Have you got a receipt?'

'Of course I haven't got a receipt. It was years ago.'

'If there's a dispute, we have to have a receipt. And then we have to work out the increase in value. I was meant to estimate the cost of everything, but frankly I didn't have the time. Really, Trev. Why on earth are we arguing about a table?'

'I merely said I wanted it.'

'I've given you everything else you asked for and you'll have half of whatever we get for the house. Isn't that fair enough? I happen to like this lump of furniture. It wasn't meant for an office, it was meant for a kitchen. And it's an ugly old thing with that silly round bit on the legs. I'll buy you a decent one, when you've moved and see what space you have.'

'I can't agree to that. I don't want you to buy me anything.'

'In case you owe me?'

399

Trevor laughed.

'All right, Mafia Mamma.'

'Is it so important to you? You're being awkward just for the sake of it. Look, it's not valuable, it's ugly and it's mine.'

'This is stupid, Annie. Calm down. We can sort it out another time.'

'No, we can't. I want everything settled now. Wasn't that the whole idea? So we didn't have to think about stupid things like tables?'

'Get it valued and I'll pay for it.'

'No.'

'You're being obstinate. I really don't understand why.'

'What does it matter?'

'We'll toss for it.'

'Don't be ridiculous, Trev. All right, all right. There's no point in having a row. Rows cost money. Take the bloody table. Take it now, I don't care. I'll call Moves and get them round straight away. Where's the bloody phone? Kate's always putting it somewhere, out of Dally's reach and I can never find it.'

Annie slammed down her mug, and Trevor heard the crash of something hurtling down in the next door room. As he entered, he saw a Greek earthenware pot shattered against the metal fender of the fireplace. Gripping the portable phone, Annie was stabbing at the keys, punching out a number and sweeping the debris away with her foot.

'Annie, put that down.'

'They're engaged. Never mind, I'll try again. Everyone's moving now. I told Luke, you should be in the removal business. At least he'd have a van then.'

'Annie.'

As he stretched out his arm to touch her shoulder, Annie glared up at him.

'Don't, Trevor. There's got to be a difference now, if we're going to be friends. I'm not going to be one of those ex-wives who obliges her husband on the girlfriend's night out. Now you'd better sort out which books you want to take. I'll leave that to you. The buyers of Honeysuckle Cottage are due to exchange any day now. And we can set the price against the total from this house. But they haven't signed yet. Say now, if you want to change your mind.'

'Why should I change my mind? There's no reason for me

to go down there. Are there any books of mine you'd like to keep?'

'The Sylvia Plath poems. I know they were a present from me, but I'd like to keep them. Your books have your name in, mine don't, so it should be easy. There are some here, and the rest are in boxes in my study.'

'I can select the books I want another time. I thought you said you had to be somewhere.'

'I do. But he'll have to wait.'

'A business meeting, is it?'

'Personal. Extremely personal.'

'The new lover?'

'Why do you think there's only one?'

'I don't know how you fit it all in.'

'Amazing, isn't it? I'll have to go upstairs and find something slinky. Now come in the kitchen and put your name on that piece of paper.'

'There isn't by chance a bottle of Rick's whisky still hidden somewhere?'

'No, but I think I can find one.'

This time, Annie sat at the far end of the table, watching as Trevor scrawled his name swiftly across the bottom of the sheet of paper. She had produced a new bottle of single Island malt, an unopened present from one of her Scottish actors. Forgetting that she disliked whisky, she was throwing it back.

'You haven't checked it. I might have forgotten something,' she said.

'This will do.'

Trevor was assessing the tumbler of whisky, as he turned it round and sniffed the aroma. It irritated her. He must have picked up the habit when he was with her, without realizing it, showing off his feigned knowledge of alcohol.

'When shall I make the appointment? Jane Tyler's in Lincoln's Inn, you won't have far to go.'

He didn't amswer, still swirling the liquid in the glass, not until Annie rose from her chair to go and change.

'Anything wrong?' she said, catching his gaze fixed on her.

'You've got thinner. I can see it in your face. Don't get too thin.'

'I'll get how I want.'

'Annie, are you free for dinner?'

'When?'

'I'd like to take you out to dinner tonight.'

'I'll see how I'm fixed, later on.'

'Andy's son has redone his restaurant, you'd like it. Unless you'd rather go into town.'

'I'll see how I feel. Let me get a few things out of the way first.'

All next day, Annie wondered if she had been right in refusing. Why had he asked her to dinner? To remind her of the past? They had promised to speak only of the present. Did he really want only to be a friend? It was a cruel game, trying to be friends, trying to be fair, with love and hate fighting it out second by second. It was shameful that she felt this way, after all the hurt, all the deception but she would never show it. She knew she would never find another man who could provoke, just by a gesture, the rush of excitement, the rush of urgent desire. She would have surrendered, surrendered her anger and pride, just to have him carry her off to bed. Had he recognized this? Was he trying to seduce her, to prove that he would always get his way? She would wait, maybe one month, maybe two. Then she might suggest lunch.

22

ANNIE AND TREVOR

It wasn't until the end of July that Annie saw Trevor again, at the solicitor's meeting. The settlement document was drawn up, and Jane Tyler congratulated them both on their fairness and decency. It only took an hour. The way to an eventual divorce was clear, she said, and then they could both get on with their lives. Annie wondered how many couples had sat at the mahogany table, and heard the same words, as they nervously examined their fingers spread over copies of neatly paragraphed, itemized documents. Afterwards, Trevor stood on the steps of the red-brick building, standing opposite Annie, as though unsure whether to dash off or to embrace her. They didn't notice the warm summer rain spattering the pavement. She was trying to conjure up some significant, memorable lasting phrase, but all she could think of was a scene which had caused her so much grief, forty eight hours in the edit suite trying to make four exchanges work.

The actress was Rosie, her mate Rosie who'd gone from Streetcred *to Shakespeare at the National, leaning against a tree in the New Forest, face sidelit from an imaginary setting sun. Harry, hardbitten Harry, starts walking towards his car. Suddenly he stops in his tracks.*

HARRY: I haven't said everything. [*He throws his scarf tightly round his neck*] We thought life would change but it hasn't. Not for me.
ROSIE: What are you on about?
HARRY: Us. [*Rosie slowly walks towards him. Big close-up kiss. sound of twittering, courting birds in the trees, mix to end title music, roll titles as he looks at her, slips his arm round her*

shoulders. They start to walk away from the car, going into the distance until the bushes and branches obscure them.]

. . . . END . . . .

At first, the writer wanted it to finish with a 'perhaps they'll meet again, perhaps they won't' call in a public phonebox on the moors, track back as he drives off, heading south, in her direction. But Annie changed it, she had an instinct about endings, you could do that in the Eighties, but not in the Nineties. Her audiences wanted happy endings again.

'Is there a pub round here?'

'I don't know, Trev.'

'It's raining and we need a drink. Come on, let's go.'

'Just for half an hour.'

'All right, half an hour.'

Annie was walking silently at Trevor's side, neither of them touching yet still keeping in step, arms by their sides. She was waiting, waiting for the final words.

TREVOR: Annie, I want you to come back. Please come back. Life is so empty without you. I made a mistake. Forgive me. Could you? Will you?

ANNIE: I don't know. Perhaps.

TREVOR: Say yes, Annie. Say yes. You're the only woman I've ever wanted.

He might say these words, or something similar, after they had taken refuge in the pub. She feared the rain on her face might be mistaken for tears, so she groped for her compact, and stabbed on some powder. Trevor was looking past her, trying to ignore her familiar gestures.

'That seemed to go quite well, quite straightforward. Is there anything else to discuss?'

'I don't think so. Do you want a lift anywhere?'

'I'll walk. Do me good. I'm so glad that's over.'

Trevor gave her a quick peck on the cheek.

'Keep in touch. Call me any time you like. I'll let you know when I've found somewhere, when I'm moving to my own place, that is. Bye, Annie.'

404

He moved swiftly away, and Annie could hear the thud of the swing doors.

'Another double,' she said, turning her face away from the barman.

She didn't mean to ring up Trevor when she was drunk, but one night she did. It was the first time in her career that everything had gone so wrong that she could only see herself running round and round in the dripping, cavernous passages of some video game, ending up at the place where she started, unable to reach the upper regions of space and light. She began to feel that her reign had ended, her creative powers had shrivelled to nothing, that some malignant creature had willed the failure of her marriage, now indistinguishable from the impossible chaos of her working life. She had no idea what the time was, you didn't after several gins and two bottles of wine. He said he'd come in the morning, not tonight, he was so tired.

'Tired! This can't wait, love. Come right now.'

'Why now? All of a sudden?'

'Because I want you to. Gavin's taken over. Alan's gone. The whole place is going to be a shithouse. I want to get out. I can't handle it any more, but I'm not allowed to show it. Trev, I'm going nuts, can't see straight, can't talk—'

'Yes, you can, Annie. You knew it was going that way. We all knew. That didn't stop you doing what you wanted. I'm sure it's not as bad as you think.'

Annie gulped.

'I'm asking you to come now and I mean it. I might do something stupid. I might call Gavin and tell him he can go screw himself.'

'Annie, you're over-reacting.'

'Don't I always? Wasn't that the trouble? If only Annie would be reasonable, life would be so much easier. Do you want an easy life, Trev?'

'Not particularly.'

'Then I've got it wrong. I thought you did.'

Trevor came round to Langton Villas. He only had to turn the corner from Langton Crescent, where he was still staying, and let himself in. Annie had forgotten he had the key. He found her lying on the African couch, surrounded by bottles, cigarettes tipping out from a saucer onto the floor.

'Is Kate about?' he asked, as he picked up the bottles. Annie sat up and tried to still the spinning walls.

'She's gone off with Luke. Blissfully happy. Isn't that wonderful? Know what they're going to do? Grow Japanese greens for macrobiotic hippies in a shack in Sussex and Dally's down for some bloody Montessori school. No, no, I'm pleased. She'll be happy. Kate was meant to be happy. Christ, I feel foul.'

'You need some coffee. Stay there. It was much better with the kitchen open, I could keep an eye on you.'

'Fuck that,' shouted Annie.

She knew she was in the kind of mood where she would tell him everything, shout, rave and rage – and then where would she be? Spilling over her fury, her guilt, how production would start on Lucinda's script in the autumn with another's name on the cover, how she leaped into bed with Lance to get her own back, didn't think so at the time but that's how it was. All that bilious throwing up, throwing out her marriage, that's what she had been doing, spattering bits all over everyone else.

'Gavin wants me to do everything on video, small casts, only one film drama a year, chosen to appeal to the American market. And he's lopping off half my budget. He's bringing out a revised line-up for this autumn. Oh, Trevor, it's dreadful. Can't you do something?'

'Like what?'

'You'd be much better than Gavin. Why the hell did the board go for him?'

'You know why. He makes crap look as though it belongs in the Tate. Long words and short ideas. But he's what they want.'

'You're not saying that because he dropped you for *Splash!*?'

'He didn't drop me. I decided there was a conflict of interests.'

'Really? Is that true?'

'Bit of both, I suppose.'

'So you do still believe in what you write? I was beginning to doubt it. I thought you were just out for yourself, that you didn't care any more.'

'That was just how you saw it. I don't blame you, Annie.'

'No, Trevor. I'm giving you an objective opinion. Can you find another bottle of wine somewhere?'

'No, I can't.'

'You telling me what to do?'

'For the moment, yes.'

'You think I've got out of hand. Annie going over the top. Brilliant producer, bad management skills, unpredictable, just-likeawoman. Don't tell me. I know what you're going to say. Leave Intertel, you're too good for them. Hand in your notice and make a big statement in the press. Or at the Edinburgh conference. Make their ears burn, make the bastards suffer. All right, I'll leave. I'll leave.'

'Annie, I wouldn't dream of saying that.'

'Terrible. I thought I knew what you'd say. I'm slipping, Trev.'

'My ideas haven't changed but I think you should stick in there. Irritate the hell out of them and go on producing the goods.'

'*Rough Trade* is no better than what's coming out of Hollywood. I know that. I'm good, but I'm not super super good. *Wild Wind in Montana* might be, if I can get it right.'

'What's that? Your next series?'

'A movie. Just a one-off movie.'

'Want to talk about it?'

'No, no I don't. It's nothing much, something I fancied doing.'

'Not sure about the title.'

'Then I'll change it. Why did you make the coffee so weak? Is that how she liked it?'

'Cut it out, Annie. We said—'

'Yes, we said. I am sorry. Really.'

'Let's talk about what you're going to do.'

'I know what. I'm going to resign.'

'And then, Annie?'

'Sell the house, look around. It takes ages to sell a house. Shame you don't get paid for it.'

'There's no hurry to sell. Sort yourself out first, I would.'

'I think I'll be free for a while. Why are you looking at me like that?'

'Don't make a quick decision, that's all.'

'I've been bred for quick decisions, Trev. You know that.'

Annie was trying to work out why Trevor was keen for her to remain in the company of which he was so critical – what did he know that he hadn't told her? – when her eyes suddenly closed. She vaguely recalled that Trevor had carried her up to bed, taken off her clothes, made her comfortable on the pillow and refused to get in beside her. She had a clear recollection of what happened next, asking him to stay, then telling him to go, she didn't want to know who it was he was going to, they weren't to ask one another questions.

She awoke on her own with an aching head, eyes tightly closed to resist consciousness, and heard a kettle whistling amidst the clatter of pans. Hadn't she known that Kate would be back? Kate in the kitchen, she would always associate the sounds of the kitchen with Kate, always Kate.

'Annie! Come and eat some breakfast!'

Trevor's voice came blaring up the stairs.

'Oh God, he's still here,' Annie said out loud, groping for her dressing-gown, uncertain as to whether she was asleep or awake. She came down clutching her forehead but when he saw her, he made no comment, pushing a mug of coffee into her hand.

'Thanks, Trev. I must look terrible.'

'You ought to, but you don't.'

'Did you stay here? What happened last night?'

'I went back to Rick and Bry's. I didn't want to disturb you.'

'When we were first going out together, I used to leave my make-up on in bed, so you wouldn't see my piggy morning eyes. Do you remember?'

'They never looked piggy to me.'

'Well they wouldn't, not with all that mascara I used to slap on.'

Trevor waited until Annie had demolished the burnt curls of bacon and the cooked-rigid egg, and was gulping down the second cup of coffee.

'I was worried that you might rush out of Intertel without telling me. You won't do that, will you?'

'I think I will, Trev. Why are you trying to stop me?'

'Because if everyone like you at the top walks out, what's going to happen to the others? What about the few who desperately need someone to give them a voice and stand out against the crap? Don't you still want to innovate and challenge the tired old stuff they keep churning out?'

'I don't want to spend my life fighting idiots instead of fighting for what I want to do. And I can't. Not on my own.'

'You won't be on your own.'

'Oh yes, I bloody will. Name one person who'd give up their

408

job and resign for my sake. Isn't that the ultimate test? Name one.'

'Everyone needs you, Annie. They may not say it, but you're the only one they respect.'

'I don't give a damn. I don't want their respect. I want to be free, free of the lot of them.'

'Don't give up fighting. That isn't like you.'

'It is now. Anyway, I might as well be in Hollywood, don't you think?'

'It could work out, I suppose. With the right offer.'

'Should I go? Or not?'

'If you do, why not wait until you've got something definite?'

'Oh Trevor, you're always so bloody cautious.'

'Not always.'

'That's right. How could I forget?'

Annie shrugged and began to clear the table. She was angry at herself for wanting him to beg her, implore her to stay, or even to display some small sign that he would be wretched if she left England.

'It was good to see you again,' she said, when she saw him to the door.

There would be no farewell party when Annie left. The rumours spread down the corridors about how she had had a blockbusting row with Gavin, about how he had always loathed her, woman-hater of the first order, encouraged her husband to pursue that dreadful bitch, Lucinda Sherwood, what a vicious way to behave. No wonder she wanted to get out. Someone had stuck up a picture in the smoking cell, and covered Gavin's face in fake vomit from a joke-shop. He had his arm around his wife Celia who had won some literary prize for her poetry – and there they were again in the Intertel house magazine, posed with awkward smiles and their two children by the photogenic lamppost in Primrose Hill.

Thelma was the first to send a perfumed card of congratulations to Annie when she heard she was starting up an independent production company in Covent Garden, and she also enclosed an invitation to the preview of *Thelma's Thursday*, the new afternoon chat show for the more mature viewer. Trevor helped Annie to find premises for Annie Griffiths Productions, and started reading scripts for her. The first occasion when they went to bed, Annie fell asleep just when he was raring to go for the second time. In the morning they laughed about it. He still burned the bacon. The kitchen was a mess because the cleaning lady was on holiday, but Annie didn't apologize. Trevor was reading the Sunday papers, fuming over some article or other, Annie was scarcely listening.

'Do you think it's a good idea? Because I do.'

Annie put down the *News of the World*.

'What did you say, Trev?'

'To try it out.'

'Try what out?'

'Wake up, Annie Griffiths. I said why don't we get together again? Properly.'

Annie grinned.

'I never thought you'd ask.'

'I thought you might have asked me first.'

'Why the hell should I?'

'You were right all along. Annie, you're the only woman I can live with.'

'Go on, go on, say it. I want to hear.'

'I love you.'

'I suppose I love you, too. Shall we go back to bed?'

Wild Wind in Montana was a great success in America, but for some reason which Annie was unable to understand, it had only one late-night television showing and a limited art-house release in England. Luckily, Trevor was at an academic conference in Mexico at the time it was shown, and Annie didn't mention it to anyone. When it was finally released on video, you could only find it hidden in the Adult section. Hardly a day passed when Annie failed to steel herself, expecting the letter of outrage from Lucinda or her lawyer. But it never came.

Some months later, Annie had just come back from lunch in Covent Garden, when the buzzer sounded in her office. She picked up the phone.

'Someone here who says he knows you,' Anita said. 'I couldn't catch his name. Says he wants to see you. Come through and take a look, see if you recognize him. He looks like a messenger.'

Annie came over to the security screen. A man was standing at the door, dressed in studded black leathers, holding a helmet under his arm. The clean-cut face, with flattened blond hair pushed back, was staring directly into the camera.

'Looks like Morley, the stunt man,' said Annie, trying to place him. 'Tell him to come up.'

A couple of minutes later, Anita leaned round Annie's door.

'Tim Sherwood. Is he some relation? Shall I tell him you're not in?'

Annie hesitated. She had prepared her speech long ago in case she was taken unawares by Lucinda. Yes, I did take your script to America. They were quite interested, but then they changed the idea totally. It was out of my hands. The end result was nothing to do with your original idea. You wouldn't have recognized it. They didn't use your name. If Intertel had sued, it could have cost us half my entire drama budget. And you just don't sue a multi-million-dollar production house. Especially when they're the major providers for the network which has just bought your series. There was nothing I could do. But there's nothing to stop you going ahead and making it here.

'Have you come on Lucinda's behalf?' Annie asked, beckoning Tim to sit down.

'Not really. She's married now.'

'To Jeremy?'

'He's a decent chap. Anyhow, she's got a sprog on the way.'

'Why are you telling me this?'

'I thought it was a lousy business. Lucinda was always a bit wild. Once she'd set her mind on something, or someone, nothing could shift her. Pig-headed, my sister.'

'I don't need to be reminded,' said Annie.

'She heard about the film, *Wild Wind in Montana*, from a friend in Hollywood who'd seen her script.'

'Does she intend to sue, then?' said Annie, calmly.

'Oh no. Absolutely not.'

'Good. I think that's wise. It would be difficult to establish and it would have cost a lot of money. Though I could understand if she wanted to. But it was out of my hands entirely.' She could feel her voice rising. It was only the strange circumstances, she wasn't proud of acting as she did. 'There was nothing I could do. It happens sometimes, and I always prayed it wouldn't happen to me.'

'It wasn't up to her.'

'What do you mean?'

'I wrote *Grains of Evil*.'

Annie stared at him for a moment, trying to hide her shock.

'Can you prove it?' said Annie, quickly.

Tim pulled a furled sheaf of papers from the pocket of his leather jacket.

'Here. Take a look.'

Annie removed the rubber band, flattened the yellowing paper and took out a few pages. It was all there, crossings-out, cuts and additions marked in a bold, masculine hand. She recognized some of the dialogue.

'Why all the pretence? Why did you allow her to say she had written it?' she said.

'Lucy's always had a tough time. Everything she ever did, Father said she was wasting her time. Mother always let her down, hardly there in the school holidays, that kind of thing. Always either depressed or high as a kite, she can't help it. Lucy's creatively manic, Mother is just manic. It's sad, really. I don't expect you to be sympathetic, but Lucinda wanted to prove herself, to show that she was different.'

'With my husband?' Annie burst out.

'It was only because he helped her. Helped her confidence, made her believe in herself.'

'Trevor once said he wondered if she'd written *Grains of Evil*.'

'That was very perceptive. But I knew he had to be somebody special. His comments about what needed to be rewritten were usually bang on, made the script much more powerful, though I didn't like changing Manfred's name to Jaspar. But Lucy insisted.'

Annie didn't answer, but leaned her elbows on the desk, studying his features. He bore an extraordinary resemblance to Lucinda, they could have been twins.

'I still don't understand why you gave away your work. Couldn't she have tried to produce it anyway?'

'No, that wouldn't have been the same. It had to be hers. I was doing well, I knew I'd never do anything with that script. I was always more interested in making money. And I'm very fond of Lucy. I wanted to give her a chance. She always came to me when she was down. Or when she'd been overdoing it. We're very close. She was terrified that people would only do things for her either because of how she looks or because of her father. By giving her my script, she could do something on her own. I didn't see that as particularly terrible. Do you?'

'No,' said Annie. 'In one sense, it was an incredibly generous gesture. It's a remarkable script.'

'A one off,' Tim replied, with a slight smile. 'Everyone has one book, one play inside them. That was mine. Or rather hers.'

'She's an able girl.'

'Able, but not outstanding. Lucy wanted to be outstanding, she always wanted the unattainable.'

'It wasn't difficult to see that.'

'So now she's settled for marriage and motherhood. I think she's reasonably happy. She's working on an idea for a film. One day, perhaps, we'll make something together, just for ourselves. When the kid's older.'

'You're not going to take any action then?'

'Action? Because Hollywood made a balls-up called *Wild Wind in Montana*? No need. It'll be forgotten in a couple of years. Anyway, I don't mind. It isn't important to me. I'd rather make money legitimately. My club's doing rather well, actually.'

'So why did you come?'

'I just thought you might like to know. If you ever see Lucy again, you needn't say I told you.' He stretched out his hand. 'Lucy loved working with you. She still talks about it.'

'I'm glad you came. Thanks, Tim.'

As he began to leave, Tim noticed a pile of Annie's visiting cards on her desk.

'Mind if I take one? I like the design. Are you making a profit?'

'Not bad.'

'I'd never get involved in the film business. It's a mug's game.'

Annie heard him ask Anita for his helmet, waited a few moments until she heard the thud as he closed the outer door. Then she extracted Trevor's timetable from her drawer. His tutorial should be over by now. She pressed the first button on the memory bank of her phone.

'Is Trevor there? It's Annie . . . Could you get him to come to the phone? Yes, it's urgent. I've got something important to tell him . . .'

THE END

ISABEL'S BED
by Elinor Lipman

When Harriet Mahoney first saw it, Isabel Krug's bed was covered in sheared sheep and littered with celebrity biographies. The unpublished, fortyish, and recently jilted Harriet had fled wintry Manhattan for Isabel's dream house atop Cape Cod's dunes. Harriet's job: ghostwrite the story of the *femme fatale*'s scandalous past, all of it tabloid heaven.

Life according to Isabel is a soap opera extravaganza, an experience to be swallowed whole – and the attitude is catching. Soon, memories of Harriet's bagel-baking exboyfriend pale next to the attentions of a gentle man who has the grace to appreciate in Harriet what other men have failed to see. And, after a few New York adventures, Harriet begins her own free fall into happiness . . .

'Elinor Lipman writes witty and smart Cinderella stories. Imagine an American Anita Brookner with younger and more spirited protagonists'
Times Literary Supplement

A Bantam Paperback

0 553 40892 5

IF WISHES WERE HORSES
by Francine Pascal

'*If Wishes Were Horses* is a poignant saga of true love – how it begins and how it ends – spiced with wit, sex, and an insider's look at the good life in the south of France. A book to savour'
Elizabeth Forsythe Hailey

Anna Green bought the villa near Cannes as an escape, a new start after losing Nick. But after five months, she's still caught up in memories of the gloriously impetuous man who had yanked her from the brink of a 'sensible' marriage and helped her become a successful songwriter. Determined to build a new life, she embarks on a series of hilariously heartbreaking adventures: the 'perfect gentleman' who turns out to be a con man, the perfect companion who turns up only in her dreams.

If Wishes Were Horses is the adventure of a love story; a wild, witty and passionate romance that is as un-predictable as life itself.

'**Funny and poignant . . . a long overdue corrective to Peter Mayle's idyllic portraits of Provence . . . Anna in France is a treat**'
Publishers Weekly

A Bantam Paperback

0 553 40816 X

A FINE SELECTION OF CONTEMPORARY FICTION AVAILABLE FROM BANTAM NEW FICTION AND BLACK SWAN

40956 5	TALK BEFORE SLEEP	Elizabeth Berg £5.99
40474 1	THE MUMMY CLUB	Sarah Bird £5.99
40749 X	VIRGIN OF THE RODEO	Sarah Bird £5.99
40484 9	THE PRINCE OF TIDES	Pat Conroy £5.99
40574 8	AND DO REMEMBER ME	Marita Golden £5.99
91681 5	A MAP OF THE WORLD	Jane Hamilton £5.99
99685 8	THE BOOK OF RUTH	Jane Hamilton £5.99
99169 4	GOD KNOWS	Joseph Heller £7.99
99538 X	GOOD AS GOLD	Joseph Heller £6.99
99208 9	THE 158lb MARRIAGE	John Irving £5.99
99204 6	THE CIDER HOUSE RULES	John Irving £6.99
99209 7	THE HOTEL NEW HAMPSHIRE	John Irving £6.99
99369 7	A PRAYER FOR OWEN MEANY	John Irving £6.99
99206 2	SETTING FREE THE BEARS	John Irving £6.99
99207 0	THE WATER-METHOD MAN	John Irving £6.99
99205 4	THE WORLD ACCORDING TO GARP	John Irving £6.99
99573 8	TRYING TO SAVE PIGGY SNEED	John Irving £5.99
40651 5	THE ROSE TREE	Mary Walkin Keane £5.99
50385 5	A DRINK BEFORE THE WAR	Dennis Lehane £5.99
40892 5	ISABEL'S BED	Elinor Lipman £5.99
40235 8	THEN SHE FOUND ME	Elinor Lipman £4.99
40682 5	THE GOOD MOTHER	Sue Miller £5.99
40642 6	FOR LOVE	Sue Miller £5.99
40975 1	A FEATHER ON THE BREATH OF GOD	
		Sigrid Nunez £5.99
40816 X	IF WISHES WERE HORSES	Francine Pascal £5.99
40380 X	SKINNY LEGS AND ALL	Tom Robbins £5.99
40381 8	EVEN COWGIRLS GET THE BLUES	Tom Robbins £5.99
40383 4	JITTERBUG PERFUME	Tom Robbins £5.99
40928 X	HALF ASLEEP IN FROG PAJAMAS	Tom Robbins £5.99
40898 4	STILL LIFE WITH WOODPECKER	Tom Robbins £5.99
40658 2	GOLDMAN'S ANATOMY	Glenn Savan £5.99
40392 3	WHITE PALACE	Glenn Savan £5.99
40646 9	AMERICAN PIE	Julia Watson £5.99
40645 0	RUSSIAN SALAD	Julia Watson £5.99
99592 4	AN IMAGINATIVE EXPERIENCE	Mary Wesley £5.99
99495 2	A DUBIOUS LEGACY	Mary Wesley £6.99
99639 4	THE TENNIS PARTY	Madeleine Wickham £5.99